Torkil Damhaug studied literat................................
Bergen, and then medicine in Oslo, specialising in psychiatry.
Having worked as a psychiatrist for many years, he now writes
full time. In 2011 Torkil's third Oslo Crime Files novel,
FIRERAISER, won the Riverton Prize for Norwegian crime
fiction – an accolade also awarded to Jo Nesbø and Anne Holt
– and his books have been published in fifteen languages. He
lives with his wife and children near Oslo.

There are four deeply dark thrillers to discover in Torkil
Damhaug's Oslo Crime Files series: MEDUSA, DEATH BY
WATER, FIRERAISER and CERTAIN SIGNS THAT YOU
ARE DEAD.

TORKIL
DAMHAUG

DEATH BY WATER

AN OSLO CRIME FILES NOVEL

headline

First published as an ebook in Great Britain in 2015 by
HEADLINE PUBLISHING GROUP

First published in paperback in Great Britain in 2016 by
HEADLINE PUBLISHING GROUP

Published by agreement with Cappelen Damm AS,
Akersgata 47/49, Oslo, Norway

3

Cataloguing in Publication Data is available from the British Library

ISBN 978 1 4722 0687 9

Typeset in Granjon by Palimpsest Book Production Limited,
Falkirk, Stirlingshire

Printed and bound in Great Britain by Clays Ltd, Elcograf S.p.A.

Headline's policy is to use papers that are natural, renewable and recyclable
products and made from wood grown in well-managed forests and other
controlled sources. The logging and manufacturing processes are expected to
conform to the environmental regulations of the country of origin.

MIX
Paper from
responsible sources
FSC® C104740

HEADLINE PUBLISHING GROUP
An Hachette UK Company
Carmelite House
50 Victoria Embankment
London EC4Y 0DZ

www.headline.co.uk
www.hachette.co.uk

To Helen

September 1996

MEDIUM DANGER. THE yellow flag flying. The breakers pound high up the beach though it's only twelve o'clock. He throws his towel on to the sand and runs in, keeping his yellow T-shirt on. Wades out until the water reaches his navel. Starts swimming, diving into the wave that breaks right in front of him, swimming on out towards the buoys, continuing past them. The water starts a tickling and a bubbling inside his chest, as though something nasty is about to happen. But even with the red flag up, he would still have gone swimming. Red flag means hazard.

No other swimmers this far out today. He turns towards the shore. Truls is holding Nini by the hand, the way he's been told to. Out here, past the buoys, it's just possible to hear her shriek each time a giant of a breaker throws itself at her feet.

Further out, the troughs between the waves are deeper. They open up suddenly; he falls down into them, is lifted up and tossed over the next peak, then falls again. Has to use his strength to keep his head up, not to get sucked under. His mouth and nose fill with salty foam. He spits and snorts, gets tossed up again, down again. The waves keep coming, and when he's up on a peak he can see the horizon where the water meets the grey-blue sky, and he knows that the sea continues long past that line, all the way down to Africa. How far would he get if he carried on in the direction of the coast he can't see? With every wave that pulls him down and tosses him up again, he twists his upper body and feels that it is he who is strongest. How far out can he get before he has to give up and let the waves do what they like with him?

Not even when they arrived on the plane that morning, with the sky clear and bright, could he see land on the far side. He had turned to his mother, sitting in the middle seat, to ask her how many hundreds of miles she thought it was over the sea. He could tell from her eyes that she was no longer in a condition to answer a question like that. Had known it before anyway, even before they boarded the plane. They were sitting in the café right next to the gate. They'd got up at three in the morning in order to reach the airport in time. He sat there staring out at the runway. Nini was lying in her pushchair asleep. Truls was out too, curled up in a chair.

– Want something to drink, Jo? Arne asked, winking and acting like a pal, which meant that Jo could have a Coke if he wanted. He knew there was a reason for it. Sure enough, Arne returned with a Coke and some crisps and a doughnut. That was okay. It didn't bother Jo that he'd bought a beer for himself. What he didn't like was the red wine for his mother. It's quarter to six in the morning and there's his mother sitting there drinking wine. No normal grown-up does that. She hadn't touched a drop for several days, and Jo was hoping that this trip, with the sunshine and the swimming and all those things she was always longing for, might mean she didn't need to drink. But before they'd boarded the plane she'd knocked back three glasses and was already at the stage where she wanted to put her arms around him and ruffle his hair. She didn't say 'plane' any more, she said 'pwein', and suddenly Arne's jokes were so funny she was leaning her head back and clucking with laughter.

Once the *pwein* was up in the air and those blue-striped shirts appeared pushing the drinks trolleys along, Arne went right ahead and ordered a cognac for her, even though he knew perfectly well how it would end. Maybe that was why he did it. Jo huddled up by the window and pretended to be asleep. Thought how he should have had a parachute and opened the emergency exit and jumped out over Germany or Poland or wherever they were; landed in some strange town where no one knew who he was nor who his mother and Dickhead Arne were.

A few hours later, they were both sitting on sun loungers by the pool with a drink each, and Mother dropped hers so it smashed on the flagstones. Jo thought he didn't want to be there any more and got up to head down to the beach.

– Take Truls and Nina with you, Arne ordered.

Jo made his way down the stony slope with his younger brother beside him and his baby sister in the pushchair. A little family. He could take Truls and Nina and just leave, go back home again. Not home. Move somewhere else, where he could work and get them food and whatever else they needed. That way they wouldn't have to see Arne again. They wouldn't have to see Mother drinking herself legless and breaking glasses and making a show of herself in front of a crowd of people they didn't know.

But that isn't the worst thing that happens on that first day of the holiday. The worst thing is what happens in the evening. Jo puts Nini to bed after he's given her the allergy medicine and the sleeping draught. Forces it down her, in spite of her protests. Over and over again Mother has repeated that he must remember to give her all four pills before putting her to bed. And then Arne suddenly says that Mother gave them to Nini herself before she went out, only she forgot to mention it to Jo. That means Nini's had twice as many pills as she should have. No wonder she's sleeping so soundly. Lying there without moving.

Jo sits in the room with them for a while. Truls has brought along a pile of *Phantom* comics that Arne gave him. Truls thinks Arne is cool for giving him his old comics. It's like a thing between them. Arne collected these comics when he was a kid. Was a member of the Phantom Club and had the ring with the Sign of Goodness on it. Truls has inherited that too. Jo never accepts anything from Arne any more. Accepts it maybe, but hides it away at the back of a cupboard and never uses it. A Man United shirt, or a football card, whatever it is.

He leans over Nini yet again to hear if she's still breathing. Slowly and deeply, he notes, so it probably wasn't that dangerous with the double dose. All the same, it occurs to him to pop down to the restaurant to ask Mother. Just to be sure. Even though the thought of being near her the way she is now makes him feel sick.

The music pounds towards him from the speakers up by the stage. Some disco stuff. Neither Mother nor Arne will let him play loud music at home, but the rules here are different. That's what being on holiday means. Rules are changed, or dropped.

He sees only strangers when he looks around the restaurant. Hopes that Mother and Arne aren't there. That they've gone for a walk and taken another way home and are back in the apartment . . . Then he sees Mother at a table next to the wall in the far corner. She's sitting with her head on the shoulder of a man Jo has never seen before. Arne's carrying on out on the dance floor. Him and that guy Mother is hanging on to have probably changed partners. Mother for that dark, skinny thing Arne is necking with. Arne likes skinny women and always grins whenever he grabs Mother by the stomach and yanks it over the lining of her trousers.

Jo stands there by the terrace doorway. He can still feel the sea in his body. He could sneak back down there again before the grown-ups catch sight of him. Throw himself into the waves again, not see them rolling up in the darkness, just feel them surging and twisting around him. But if he doesn't stay here in the bar, something will happen to Mother. She might trip on the steps. Get raped, or drown in the pool. Arne doesn't care a shit about things like that.

Suddenly his mother tries to stand up and collapses forwards. The stranger grabs hold of her before she upends the table. Two or three glasses glide over the edge. Everyone turns and stares. The woman dancing with Arne comes hurrying over. She holds Mother up and shouts to her. She and the stranger drag her up the steps towards the bar; they pass right in front of Jo. Mother is deathly pale and doesn't seem to recognise him. Her skirt is hitched up so half her knickers are showing. She staggers on, held up by the skinny woman. When they disappear into the toilet, Jo follows and stands waiting outside the door. Hears funny sounds. Suddenly Mother screams. He's seen her drunk, but never heard her scream like that. As though she's in the process of dying in there. He takes hold of the doorknob. Then he feels a hand on his shoulder.

– Don't go in there.

Jo jerks, trying to free himself, but it's an adult that's holding him, a stranger. At first he thought it was the man his mother was making out with, but it's someone else.

– Someone's in there with your mother. You don't have to look after her.

Something or other makes Jo let go of the handle on the toilet door. Maybe it's because the voice seems familiar. He glances up at the stranger. A man about Arne's age. Unshaven, with sunglasses pushed up on the top of his head, even though it's evening.

– No need for you to care, barks Jo, but he isn't angry.

– No, there isn't, the man replies.

But then he acts exactly as though he does care. – Come with me, he says. – I'll treat you to a Coke.

He heads out towards the terrace without turning round. He's wearing khaki shorts and a short-sleeved black shirt. His hair is quite long and combed straight back and hangs over the collar of his shirt. Jo doesn't hear his mother screaming any more. He stands there, hesitating. Then he slips out after the man.

They sit at a table at the end of the terrace. Far below them the waves are breaking. Louder now, it seems, and Jo still thinks about what it would be like to go down there and throw himself in. The water should still be warm. The night colours it black.

The stranger is drinking a Coke as well. Jo realises why the voice seemed familiar. He's heard it on TV. And not long ago this man was on the front page of *Aftenposten*.

– Seen you in the paper, he says. – And on TV.

– You're probably right there.

– Do lots of people recognise you?

– Quite a few. They stare and seem to find it hard to believe that someone who has been on TV is made of flesh and blood and eats dinner and goes to the toilet. The stranger smiles. – But Norwegians are polite. Once they've finished staring, they'll generally leave you in peace. Actually everyone's shy and scared of making a fool of themselves, same as you and me.

Jo drinks his Coke, glances towards the restaurant. – Not Mother. She makes a fool of herself all the time.

The grown-up leans back. – She is drunk, he agrees. – Everyone changes when they drink.

Jo tries to find something else to talk about. – Don't you drink? He points to the Coke. – I mean, like wine and spirits and stuff?

– Only when I have to. Your name's Jo, isn't it?

– How do you know that?

– Heard your father calling you as we were getting off the plane.

– Arne isn't my father.

– I understand. You don't know my name?

– Heard it lots of times. Don't remember.

The grown-up pats his shirt pockets and takes a squashed cigarette packet out of one of them.

– You can call me Jacket.

– Jacket? That ain't a name.

The grown-up lights his cigarette. – Got it when I was about your age. How old are you? Thirteen? Fourteen?

– Twelve, Jo answers, with a touch of pride.

– Some of my old friends still use that name when we meet up, the grown-up tells him.

– Did you like it? Jo grins. – Being called Jacket?

Jacket runs a hand across his unshaven chin. – Where I come from, everyone had a nickname. Often we got names from the jobs our fathers did. My dad ran a clothes shop, or gents' outfitters as they used to call them back then, and Jacket was an okay name. Actually, I like it even better now. Better anyway than Staples, or Laces, or Scissors. Not to mention Condom.

He laughs, and Jo has to laugh too.

– Jo isn't my name either, only the beginning of it.

– Really?

– But no one dares use the whole of that stupid name. Or I'll kill them.

– Cripes. Then I guess I'd better stick to Jo too.

– I'm not kidding. Some kids at school tried to give me a nickname. They're sorry for it now.

The grown-up takes a drag on his cigarette. – Agree with you there, Jo. You gotta make people respect you.

Arne's up. He's in a foul mood, and that's good, because he doesn't say much when he's like that and Jo gets left in peace. And he won't have to see Mother for a while, maybe not for the whole day. He can hear her whimpering as he sneaks past the bedroom door. There's a bad smell all the way out to the kitchen.

Outside, the sun glows white. The stones burn beneath your feet. Go back and fetch sandals? Then he'd have to knock. He carries on walking, keeping to the narrow strip of shadow along the walls of the houses. It must look stupid. People who see him probably think he's trailing someone. Or that he's a thief. He runs the last bit, past the bar, up the steps to the pool. Most of the sun loungers are already taken. He feels the people staring at him from the beds. Almost as though he can hear them whisper as he approaches: *There's the son of that woman who . . .*

Two girls at the edge of the pool. Jo noticed one of them on board the plane. She was waiting to use the toilet right after him. She has a thin, pointed nose and brown hair hanging wet down her back. Could be older than him. She has tits. Bigger than some of the girls in his class. Her bikini is white with dark red hearts on it. He looks in the other direction as he walks past. Without taking off his yellow T-shirt, he suddenly dives in from the edge even though there's a sign saying it's forbidden. He's a good diver. He once dived in from the top board.

He swims up and down a few lengths. Then he dives and glides underwater past the two girls. He's better at this than any other boy in school, swimming underwater. He can feel their eyes on him, watching him. They're wondering when he's going to surface. Is it possible? He doesn't have to surface, not until his hand touches the wall at the end of the pool.

He pulls himself up on to the edge and sits there dripping some distance away from the two girls. Doesn't look in their direction, looks everywhere else. At least twice he feels certain that one of them turns and sneaks a look at him; not the short, slightly tubby one, but the dark one, the one with the tits. The heat is suffocating. The sun makes a heavy pounding inside his head, and if he goes on sitting there, that pounding is going to get louder and louder and something will happen, though he's not sure what. He jumps to his feet. The soles of his feet hurt, as though they're covered in blisters. He walks on tiptoe past the two girls, who have maybe noticed something's happening to him; quickly round the corner and down the steps. Once out of sight, he starts to run. Doesn't stop until he reaches the little children's playground with the swing and the slide. His breathing tears at his throat, and still there's this heavy thudding inside him, as if someone's standing in the dark and beating away with a sledgehammer. He slumps down on the swing. Cats all around him. Counts them. Six of them, in and out of the bushes. Counts them again. He's never liked cats. They sneak around and pop up without a sound; you never know where you are with them.

One of the smallest, a young one, has lost an eye. He noticed it when they arrived the day before. It was sitting in front of their apartment door and meowing. Grey-brown and skinny as a worm. Where the eye had been, a thin rag of eyelid hangs over the empty space. Now it follows him out of the gate when he opens it and walks after him back to the apartment. Must be because the people who lived there before used to give it food. According to Arne. There must be millions of cats in the world. This skinny creature with just the one eye wouldn't have survived for long unless someone looked after it. Does every kind of creature have a right to live? Jo turns abruptly and makes a sharp whistling noise along the outside of his teeth. The animal gives a start and dives under a bush.

Of course it's Arne that opens the door. He scowls at him and disappears into the crapper. Before Jo has got his sandals on, he sticks his head out and with his face full of shaving foam mumbles:

– When you go out again, take the kids with you.

– They haven't eaten yet, Jo protests. But Truls is already hanging on to his arm. He can't stand the thought of dragging Truls around. Should do, though, so he doesn't have to be around in the apartment when Mother wakes up. Doesn't have to see his mother roll out of bed and creep into the bathroom

to puke up. That's what she's been doing all night, but Truls
has slept like a stone. Nini too, naturally, after her double dose
of sleeping pills.

It's a half-hour before his baby sister has eaten up her
Cheerios and her yoghurt. Mother is still sleeping. Arne's
wandering about the place scowling, but as long as Jo is looking
after the kids, he keeps his mouth shut. Then he squashes
water wings and a beach ball and Truls's diving mask into a
plastic bag and presses it into Jo's hands and bundles them out.

– Boiling, shrieks Nini, hopping up and down as though on
a hotplate, and he has to put her in the pushchair and go back
in again and fetch her sandals.

By the kids' pool he parks them in an empty deckchair.
Wiggles the water wings on to Nini's chalk-white arms. Suntan
lotion, he thinks. Dismisses the thought of going back to the
apartment yet again.

– Now you'll take good care of her, he urges Truls.

– Where are you going?

– Trip down to the beach.

– I'm coming with you.

– No you're bloody well not. You stay here and look after
Nini. You think you're here on holiday or something?

Truls gets that hangdog look that Jo can't stand.

– Hey, pull yourself together, right? Can't you take a joke?
I won't be long. Make sure her water wings are on properly.

He picks up his towel and starts to leave, turns and repeats
what he said about the wings: – Blow them up properly. If she
drowns, it's your fault.

He runs down the steps. The sun is insanely hot. He hates
the heat. Slumps down in the shadow of a stone at the end
of the beach. Even there the sand is baking. Sit there like
that till he boils. Until everything becomes intolerable except
hurling himself into the water. Green flag today. The sea's not
moving.

Some people his own age are playing volleyball. They're pretty good, he can see that, especially the tall lad with the fair curls. He watches them. The tall lad notices and waves. Jo doesn't realise at first that the wave is to him. Gets up from the shade, takes a couple of steps out on to the glowing sand.

– Wanna play, the boy shouts in Norwegian.

Jo isn't sure. He's okay at volleyball. Football's what he's good at.

– Haven't you got anything to wear on your head? the boy asks. – Your brains'll burn up.

– Forgot my cap.

The other boy has a look round.

– Wait a sec.

He sprints up to the first row of straw parasols. Talks to some grown-ups lying there. Comes back with a white headscarf with gold trimming.

– Here, this'll do you.

Jo looks up into the other boy's face. Can't recall having seen him either on the plane or in the restaurant. Of course he must know that Jo's mother was stinking drunk and broke her glass by the pool and was sick in the toilet at the bar. But he doesn't look at him with contempt, or like he pities him. Jo doesn't know which he hates more.

– You play for us. My name's Daniel.

The boy says the names of the others, too. Two Swedish boys, and one that sounds Finnish.

They win three sets. Mostly because Daniel gets the most difficult balls and has such an amazingly hard smash.

– Do you play for a club? Jo asks.

Daniel wrinkles his nose, like volleyball isn't worth talking about. He pulls off his vest and shoes and sprints down to the water's edge, and then on out so the water foams around his knees. The others follow, Jo too. All of them seem to have been there for a while; they're tanned. He hasn't had the sun on his body for months. He keeps his yellow T-shirt on.

– First one out to the buoys, Daniel shouts.

Jo reacts at once and dives in, crawling as fast as he can. Halfway out, he notices a shadow beside him, like a dolphin, or a shark. It glides past and away.

Jo reaches the buoy first and turns to wait for the others.

– You're a good swimmer, says Daniel from behind the buoy, waiting, hanging on by an arm. He doesn't seem even slightly out of breath.

– I'm better underwater, Jo pants, annoyed, gripping the buoy; so close that their faces are almost touching.

– Then let's try that going back, Daniel suggests.

Jo spits. – On out, he says. – Let's keep on going out.

Daniel glances at the horizon, then laughs. – Say when.

Jo listens to his own breathing. Waits until it's slow and deep enough. Takes a few big breaths and makes a sign with his hand. They dive.

He lets Daniel swim in front. It's like gliding through a room of molten glass. The turquoise light gathers in unstable bunches, then disappears down into the darkness. He swims easily. Don't use up all your energy. At school they used a stopwatch to see who could hold their breath the longest. No one got even close to his record. Over two minutes. One of the doubters held a hand in front of his nose and mouth to check if he was cheating. He wasn't cheating. He quite simply stopped breathing. Could stop for ever if necessary . . .

Daniel's some way ahead of him; Jo sees his feet kicking through the columns of light. Keep going between the chilly currents, down even deeper, down towards a stream of tiny black fish, feel the blood begin to pound in his head. You might burst a blood vessel in your brain, his mother shouted once after he surfaced, and now he starts thinking about blood bursting up out of his brain and folding round it like a warm cloth. He feels dizzy. Must have air, his urgent thought, but he carries on, and that willpower comes from something that is not him, something that has started to appear in him, something he might be . . . Far ahead: Daniel's feet. They're pointing straight down, so he has given up. You must surface, your brain will explode, he hears his mother's voice scream, but he doesn't come up. He passes Daniel's feet and keeps going until the pillars of light around him start to dim. Only then does he kick out and his head bursts through the surface of the water.

– You're completely crazy, Daniel shouts over to him. The voice is distant, coming from the far side of a wall. Jo can't answer. A mass of small black fish are still swirling round in the white light, and his stomach is on its way up through his throat. He floats back in towards land, towards Daniel, just about managing to move his arms. Tries to force a grin that says he agrees: *That's right, I'm crazy.*

Mother and Arne have gone out by the time he lets himself back in. They must have taken Truls and Nini, because Jo didn't see them by the kids' pool as he ran past. Not too long since Mother was here, he says to himself, because there's still that rancid smell in the toilet. He finishes quickly, sits down in the living room, which is also where he and Truls and Nini sleep. The sofa hasn't been made up and the mattresses are on the floor. He turns on the air-conditioning, switches the TV on. The news in Greek. A bus accident, people crawling out of a broken window, some of them with blood all over their faces. He pulls back the bedclothes and stretches out on the sofa, his whole body still aching from the beating he gave Daniel at underwater swimming. Drops off for a few moments. Wakes to a sound. A cartoon on TV. He switches off, pads out on to the balcony. It's like walking into a baker's oven. The sun is directly above the roof of the house. He locates the thin grey line that divides sea from sky. If he swims out towards it and keeps going on and on, he'll reach land in Africa. Meet warriors on camels there, robed in white against the sandstorms.

He leans forward and peers on to the neighbouring balcony. Exactly like their own. A plastic table and four chairs. The only thing different is the clothes hanging up to dry. A vest, a green towel, bikini bottoms. White with dark red hearts. Water dripping from it. The girl from the pool is his neighbour.

The balcony door is ajar. Maybe she's alone in the apartment too. If her bikini's hanging out here, what is she wearing? What if she's in the shower . . . He listens out for the sound of running water. No sounds coming from there. Go and knock. Ask to borrow something or other. Matches, for example. Why would he need matches in the middle of the day? Steal one of his mother's cigarettes. The two cartons she bought at the duty-free before boarding the plane are on her bedside table. She won't notice if one packet is missing. Ask the girl next door if she wants one.

A door banging on the other side. He races through the room, opens up, sticks his head out.

It *is* her. Further down the path. On her way to the pools. She's wearing a skirt, and a top. If he'd been just a little bit quicker . . .

The dining room is full. He has to search for the table. They're sitting next to the stage. A bottle of red wine on the table, half full. Arne's drinking beer, so Mother's the one that's been knocking back the wine. She's sitting with her back turned, but he can see that she's already a bit tipsy. Head on one side. The more she drinks, the more of an angle to her head. Nini in the baby chair is asleep. Truls is munching on a sausage. His face lights up when he sees his big brother. At that same moment Jo catches sight of her two tables away, the girl from the next-door apartment. He refuses to be seen with his mother and Arne, the way they show themselves up; stops a few metres away from them. Luckily the girl hasn't seen him.

– Aren't you going to have *shomeshing* to eat then, Jo? Mother says, and she's further gone than he thought.

– Ain't hungry. Just had a hot dog.

It's true. Apart from the bit about the hot dog. His stomach is still churning from having swum halfway to Africa underwater. His head, too. His whole body.

– What rubbish, says Arne.

– Let him decide himself, Mother says, defending him, as if that was any help.

– Off to meet some friends.

– On you go, Mother waves.

– Come back here afterwards and take Truls and Nini with you, Arne commands.

– What are you going to do?

Mother tries to smile. – You look after them this evening, so Arne and I can have some time off. It is our holiday, you know.

– Time off so you can get sloshed, Jo mutters.

– What was that you just said? Arne growls.

Jo glances over towards the girl's table. The fat girl with the fair hair is sitting there too. And two grown-ups. They're busy eating. It's much too hot in the dining room. Jo has never liked the heat. Feels as though something is about to happen. When he closes his eyes, it gets pitch dark. Opening them again, the shadow reappears. It's carrying something that looks like a sledge-hammer . . . He turns and leaves before anyone else notices it.

– He-ey, Joe.

Someone calls to him in English. Jo stops by the edge of the pool and looks round. In a deckchair over by the wall he sees the man he spoke to yesterday evening. The one who wanted Jo to call him Jacket. A candle burns on a table beside him. He's sitting reading a book.

– Hi, says Jo, and feels his breath calming down out here in the dark.

– Busy? asks the man, who obviously wants to talk to him today as well.

Jo takes a step closer. Jacket is still wearing the khaki shorts and short-sleeved black shirt.

– Everything okay now? The business with your mother and all that?

Jo doesn't answer.

– Why not sit down for a few minutes? Jacket waves his hand towards the neighbouring deckchair. Jo perches on the edge of it.

– What are you reading? he asks, just for something to say.

Jacket holds up a little sliver of a book. – A long poem.

– Poem?

– Actually a story. A journey through a dead world. Or a world of the dead.

– Like a ghost story?

– Exactly, Jacket exclaims. – I've read it lots of times. But I still don't know what's going to happen in the end.

Jo wonders what he means by that.

– The part I'm reading now is called 'Death by Water'.

– So maybe it's about drowning, Jo guesses.

– Yes. A young man. A Phoenician.

– Phoenician? Jo interrupts. – You mean the people who lived here thousands of years ago?

Jacket's eyebrows rise and form twin arches. – Well I must say, Jo, you sure do pay attention in school.

Jo does. He's as clever as he can be bothered to be.

– So he drowns, this Phoenician, he affirms, trying to make his voice sound as if it doesn't matter. – A soldier, maybe?

– Actually a travelling salesman, it would seem. He's been floating in the sea for fourteen days already. Not much left of him; skin and muscles have stripped away from the bone. He was probably quite rich, but that's not much use to him now. Lying down there in another world in the depths, can't even hear a seagull cry.

Jo suddenly feels cheered up. Jacket likes to talk to him. He isn't just pretending.

– Pretty good way to die, he says quickly, with a glance across at the grown-up in the flickering candlelight.

Jacket sits there and studies his face. – I've been thinking about the conversation we had last night, he said finally.

This man has been on TV lots of times, and now he's sitting here one metre away, in the flesh, and thinking about things a twelve year old said to him. Suddenly Jo is on the alert.

– Was there all that much to think about?

Jacket lights a smoke.

– How about one for me too?

– What do you think Mother would say if a grown-up stranger started you smoking?

Jo snorts. – It's got nothing to do with her. She'd never find out. If she did find out, she wouldn't give a damn. Anyway, I've smoked lots before.

Jacket hands him the cigarette. – You'll have to make do with one drag. If you squeal, I'll be in trouble. Wouldn't take a lot more than that to get me on the front page of *VG* and *Dagbladet* and *Seen and Heard* and you name it.

Jo grins. – I'd get well paid for it. The thousand-kroner reward.

– Exactly, says Jacket. – *Celebrity on sunshine holiday lures child with cigarettes.*

Jo has to laugh. He takes a deep drag on the cigarette and holds it down, feeling at once that delicious dizziness.

– I always see you alone here, he observes after another puff.

– I *am* alone here.

– You go away on holiday on your own? Don't you have a family and all that?

Again Jacket looks at him for a long time.

– I needed to get away for a while, he answers, leaning back in the deckchair. – Made up my mind the night before, jumped on board a plane, ended up here by chance. Surprisingly good place. Might buy a house here.

Not many grown-ups live like that. Suddenly just up and off on a plane. Buy a house on Crete if they can be bothered to.

– So that business with your mother, it's all okay now?

For some reason or other Jacket returns to the subject Jo least of all wants to talk about. He doesn't answer, and maybe Jacket finally understands; at least he stops going on about it. Instead Jo begins to talk about the girl in the next-door apartment. She's got long legs and tits and she's a real looker. Just the right haughtiness, a bit of a princess like.

– What are you going to do? Jacket wants to know, and offers Jo the cigarette again.

– Do?

– To get talking to her. Don't just sit here having fantasies about her.

Jo doesn't have any plans and is open to advice from someone who probably knows a lot about this kind of stuff.

– What's her name?

Jo shrugs his shoulders.

– You want to find that out, says Jacket. – It's important to know the names of things. It gives you a head start. Which apartment are you in?

– 1206.

– And the girl's, is that further down? Wait here.

Jacket gets up and disappears in the direction of the hotel. It's good to be sitting there after he's gone. On the far side of the wall, way down below the terrace, he hears the breakers. A light blinking out there in the darkness, a ship making its way through the night. And if he leans his head back, he can see constellations he doesn't recognise, with a satellite gliding in and out between them.

Four or five minutes later Jacket comes back. He's carrying two Cokes, gives one to Jo and flops down into the deckchair again.

– Her name is Ylva.

– Who?

Jacket grins. – The girl you were talking about. Her name is Ylva Richter. All I had to do was ask at reception.

Jo's eyes narrow to two slits.

– Thought maybe I could get things started for you, Jacket adds, in a slightly different voice, maybe noticing how uneasy Jo looks. – Girls are a healthy interest. Better than the Boy Scouts and sport and schoolwork.

Jo relaxes again. Jacket's a cool guy. Hard to figure out how he can be bothered to take an interest, to sit and talk like that with a twelve year old. Not pretend conversation, but the real thing. About stuff that matters. Jo doesn't need to think about Mother and Arne making fools of themselves in there in the restaurant. He isn't them. Doesn't give a shit about them.

He's walking in the sand. It's burning, but he doesn't feel it. The white light forces its way in everywhere. Ylva Richter is walking alongside him. She's wearing the bikini with the red hearts on. *I know a place where no one can see us*, she says. *A cave where we can be on our own*. They carry on towards the end of the beach. Around them are flowers growing straight up out of the sand. *How can anything grow in a place like this?* asks Ylva. Jo doesn't know the answer to that, so maybe she doesn't ask that after all, but snuggles up to him as he puts his arm around her naked shoulder.

Just then he hears the chinking of keys outside. He grabs a towel and pulls it over himself.

Mother is standing there. Leaning up against the door post.

– Hey, sweetie, she smiles as she peers into the room at him. She's spilt something red on the strap of her dress. – Sitting in there in the dark, are you?

He makes a face in reply.

— I felt a bit tired, me, she explains as she steps out of her high-heeled sandals.

She gets a bottle of water from the fridge, fills a glass, drinks. It dribbles from the corners of her mouth and down into the red, sunburnt gap between her breasts.

Afterwards she comes into the living room, strokes his hair as she passes, bends over Nini, listens to her breathing, turns again, standing right up close to him.

— Wonderful to have such a smashing big brother.

Her voice is woozy at the edges, and overflowing. But she isn't sloshed. She gives him a hug, kisses him on the cheek. Her breath smells of wine, and the perfume is like lilac. He turns away, but not completely.

She goes to the toilet. Pees for a long time. Flushes, washes her hands. Directly after, she opens the door slightly.

— Are you going to sit here like this in the dark all evening?

He shrugs his shoulders. — There aren't any more rooms.

— Come in here with me for a bit. We need to have a chat now and then.

He follows her. She clears clothes away from the double bed, knickers and tops and a wet bikini, hangs it over the suitcase lid in the corner, lies down on the blanket. Jo leans up against the wall.

— Sit down here, she says, patting the edge of the mattress.

He does as she says. Can't be bothered telling her what he thinks about her drinking and making a fool of herself so that everyone laughs at her.

— You're a nice boy, Jo, she says, and he wants to ask her to shut up. Or explain what she means by that. — You know, things haven't been all that easy recently, she says. He knows all about that. And nothing about it. Doesn't want to know either. He's afraid of what will happen if she starts discussing it. — It's not always easy for me, she says, and he wants to get up again, can hear in her voice that any moment now she's going to start whimpering again. – There's a lot you don't know, Jo. She strokes the back of his head. – I need a proper cuddle, she says. He can't face the thought of bending over her. But he can hear her snivelling, in complete silence. He moves his legs, about to stand up; she probably thinks he's doing it to turn towards her, and she pulls him down on to the bed. One leg remains on the floor, the other is on the covers. – You've always been my best boy, you know. I'll always take care of you. She's lying, he thinks, and the lilac smell is so strong he feels he's going to puke at any moment. And behind it, the smell of her skin, sweat and onions, and something that reminds him of the kitchen cloth when it hasn't been wrung out for several days and he finds it under the dishes in the sink. His leg is aching; he has to pull it up into the bed, lies there with his whole body next to her. She has one arm round him. The other is lying along his thigh. He feels something happening down there, something she mustn't notice, but he can't manage to turn away, and she holds him even tighter. – You're a nice boy, Jo. So nice . . . so nice.

Mother is whimpering in the bedroom. Drowned out by Arne's snoring. Jo has seen something about snoring on TV. They said people who snore don't live as long. They get bad hearts before other people and can die without warning.

– I'm hungry, Nini whines.
– I'll get something for you.
– Mum should do it.
– She's sleeping.
– Mum should do it!
– Then you'd best do it yourself, Jo snarls. – There's a yoghurt in the fridge.

She has tears in her eyes.

– Don't like yoghurt.

He feels like lashing out at her, standing there moaning. Or throwing open the bedroom door and grabbing hold of Mother by the hair and dragging her out of bed. *Nini is hungry, do you hear, you fucked-up cow? She's three years old and hungry.* And if Arne wakes up and starts throwing his weight around, getting a beer can from the shelf in the fridge and smashing it down on his sleepy, bad-tempered face.

– Let's go and eat breakfast, Truls suggests as he pulls on his shorts. – Then afterwards take Nini down to the beach.

Jo spins round, lifts his arm to give him a clout. Truls starts and jumps back. Jo leaves him alone. Kid brother is always having bright ideas about what to do. Irritating, but he means well.

– Okay. Jo's anger slips off him. At least some of it. – Help Nini on to the toilet. I'll go over and save a table for us.

The time is 8.30. As usual, the dining room is packed. He stands in the doorway and looks round. Fortunately everybody's bound up with their own business. Only a few old people near the door stare at him. A woman with a white headband round her grey hair whispers to an old bloke, and Jo is certain it's something about him. About Mother, and Arne. He turns, about to leave. Someone calls his name. Daniel stands up at a table out on the terrace and waves to him. When Jo doesn't respond, he comes over.

– Do you want to sit with us?

Daniel's wearing a Metallica T-shirt and dark-red shorts, and cool sunglasses that look like they cost a lot. – We've got room.

Jo glances across. A woman in a thin dress sitting with her back to them. Her hair is darker than engine oil. Next to her a powerfully built man, and at the end of the table a boy about Nini's age. Family. Having breakfast together. Got an extra place out on that blistering hot terrace. Someone could go over to that table and start smashing at it with a sledgehammer.

– The others'll be here any moment, Jo manages to blurt out. – I need to find places for all of us.

– Wanna play beach footie afterwards?

Daniel doesn't give up, stands there waiting for him to say something. It mustn't happen now, he hears the thought race through him. Not right in front of Daniel and his family and a pack of staring faces. He spots a vacant table and makes his way over to it. It hasn't been cleared after the last guests. Plates with bits of egg, bacon fat, and grape pips in a serviette. Coffee dregs in the cups. Truls arrives with Nini trailing behind. Jo orders him to clear the table. Goes and fetches a huge bowl of cornflakes for Nini.

– I want Honni-Korn, she protests.

– You'll take what you're given, he growls, and for once she realises there's no point in complaining any more. – Look here, four spoonfuls of sugar. That'll taste good.

Truls laughs loudly. He's managed to fix himself up with fried potatoes, bacon and a whole lot of ketchup.

– This place is cool, he says happily.

Jo chews down a slice of bread and jam. He keeps an eye on the table where Daniel's family are sitting. The mother gets up and heads towards the exit. She's slim, and the black dress clings to her. Reminds Jo of a film star whose name he can't recall. The father has finished too, but sits there listening to something Daniel is talking about. He has curls on the back of his neck and looks like he does a lot of training with weights.

The girl he's been waiting for comes in, accompanied by the fat, fair-haired one. They hang their bathing towels up by a table just inside the open sliding doors, not far from Daniel's. They pass by less than two metres away on their way to the buffet. Jo doesn't look at her, but she looks at him, he's certain of it. Jacket advised him not to show too much interest. And then suddenly strike. Jo is massively relieved he's alone there with Truls and Nini. Maybe the girl hasn't seen him with Mother and Arne. Maybe she doesn't have to know about them at all.

Less than three minutes later, she's heading back, carrying a tray. She's just been swimming; her bikini makes a wet patch on her bottom. It's the one with the hearts on, Jo can see that through the thin yellow skirt she's wearing, the one that was hanging to dry on the balcony the day before. Her name is Ylva, Ylva Richter. If Jacket is to be believed. Why shouldn't he believe Jacket? He's funny and he's famous. And for some reason or other, interested in what interests Jo. Jo looks round to see if Jacket is there. But it strikes him that Jacket isn't the type to take an early breakfast. More the type to sit up all night smoking and reading over and over again poems about drowned Phoenicians.

Before Jo has finished his first slice of bread, Ylva stands up. Between the yellow skirt and an even shorter top, her stomach is visible. She has a ring in her navel. Jo has never seen that before. He can't stop himself from staring at it. And beneath the top her breasts jig up and down when she walks. He forces himself to look away. Girls don't like it if you slobber over them, Jacket might have said.

As she disappears around the corner, Jo gets up. – Stay here with Nini.

– Where are you going?

– Toilet. You don't go anywhere, got that?

Truls chews away on a stub of sausage and doesn't look to be in any hurry at all.

– Back in a few minutes, Jo calls over his shoulder.

He leans forward and peers at the neighbouring balcony. The door is closed and the curtain drawn. But she's in there, he doesn't doubt it for a moment. All quiet in the bedroom. Can't even hear Arne snoring. Maybe his heart's stopped; maybe he's lying in bed blue in the face, with his fat tongue poking out of his gob. Maybe he's turned over in his drunken stupor and smothered Mother as well. In that case Jo will have to take Truls and Nini and leave there. Sit next to Ylva on the plane. *You can live with me*, she says. *What about Truls and Nini?* he asks. *I have to take care of them. They've got no one else.* She leans up against him. *My parents can adopt them. They'll be well looked after.*

He does it without any more thought. Sneaks out, over to the neighbouring door. Knocks. No answer. Is he maybe not meant to speak to her? Knocks again. Suddenly shuffling footsteps inside.

– Who is it?

Ylva's voice. He's struck again by something he noticed at the pool the other day. She has a sort of Bergen accent. The thick way she rolls her rs. Bergen or somewhere round there. He feels a desire to say her name, but controls himself.

– It's me . . . I live next door.

She opens up. She's wearing a tank top and shorts. A towel round her head, like a turban.

– Hi, says Jo.

– Hi?

– I live next door, he says again.

– Yeah?

She says it as though she's never seen him before. *I live next door*, he's about to say for the third time. *Can I come in?*

Sit on their sofa. Hold her hand. The look in her eyes doesn't suggest anything like that.

– Can I borrow a tin opener? he says, rescuing himself, relieved at how natural it sounds. Tin openers are things anyone might need, any time. A common thing to borrow from a neighbour.

– Tin opener? She glances towards the kitchen. – Let's see if we have one.

She pushes the door to. Doesn't ask him in. No wonder, considering how surprised she was.

Next moment she's back again, holding out a metal thing, a combination bottle opener and tin opener, with a corkscrew you fold out. Exactly like the one that was in their own kitchen drawer when they arrived and which is now on Mother's bedside table.

Suddenly he feels brave. Looks into her eyes for a long time. They're brown, with black flecks.

– Be right back, he says, and turns away.

– No rush, Ylva says. – You can bring it back later.

He stands there in the half-dark of the kitchen and squeezes the opener in his hand, the little point against his palm. He presses it so far down it goes through the skin and the pain shoots up through his fingers.

Then he hears Mother's voice from the bedroom. Snuffling and full of sleep. Next moment she emerges stark naked on her way to the toilet. He slips back out into the light. Ylva's bathroom window is open. Maybe she's standing in front of the mirror. Combing her long wet hair. He knocks again. This time she opens straight away, without asking who it is.

– Finished already? she says with a little smile.

– Tin of tuna, he explains, couldn't think of anything else. – Nice place, he adds quickly, because he can see she's about to close the door again.

– Very, she says.

– Good beach, he says.

She nods. – I'm going down in a minute. Just need to get ready first.

He feels his face prickle. What she says is nearly *Shall we meet down on the beach?* He raises a hand to touch her, can't bring himself to, rubs his lip.

– See you, he says.

She raises her eyebrows, mostly the right one, he notices.

– Sure . . . yeah, she says, and closes the door.

He stands outside her door and realises he has forgotten to give her the tin opener. She forgot too. Too busy talking to him. But it would be a mistake to knock again. Jacket would advise against, Jo feels certain of that. Instead he puts the opener in his pocket; it gives him the chance to go back later. He jogs away. The cats are still there in the little playground with the swing and the slide. Some slinking round, some climbing the trees. The one-eyed creep is by itself over by the fence. Jo lets himself in. The creep recognises him, slinks across and starts to rub itself against his bare leg. The fur is scruffy but still feels soft. The pitiful little thing looks up at him with its one eye and gives a complaining meow, like maybe it's asking for something. He wants to do something or other with it. Not sure what. Lift it up and feel the fur against his cheek. Feel with his finger inside the empty space below the eyelid. Squeeze this kitten so hard it stops its whining.

He contents himself with kicking at it, so that it won't follow him out through the gate.

Just past the kiosk, he stops and sweeps the beach with his gaze. The parasols are made of straw and make him think of the Hottentot Hoa who bangs away on his drums at night and saves the village from enemy attack. He sidles over to the big tree. She must be somewhere or other on this beach, Ylva, because he's already checked out the other beach, about a hundred metres further away.

Then he sees her. On her way up from the sea in the bikini with the dark red hearts. She takes hold of her hair, twists it round a few times then tosses it like a tail on to her back. The little fair-haired one is waddling along behind her, like a tubby pet. Jo grins and keeps his eyes on Ylva. She walks up to a parasol on the second row down, picks up a towel, dries her face and her thighs, hangs it out, lies down in the sun.

Go over there now, Jo can hear Jacket saying. *Or wait till she goes for another swim. Follow her into the water and get talking to her.* Not difficult to find something to talk about with the breakers washing over them and just about tipping her over.

He chooses the first option, can't be bothered to wait. Makes his way slowly towards the end of the beach where she is. Recognises the grown-ups she was sitting with in the dining room. The man, must be her father, has grey hair. And the mother is completely unlike Ylva, small and with a bigger belly bulge than Mother.

Arne sits two parasols away from them.

Jo freezes. Naturally, Mother is there too. And the couple they were dancing and necking with that first night. Mother is wearing her pink bikini and is lying flat on the sunbed with a straw hat over her face. In the sand next to her are two big green bottles of beer. Arne has his back turned and is talking to the other grown-ups. Hasn't spotted him yet. Jo turns and runs away, reaches the shelter of a tree. Without stopping he carries on up the hill, past the apartments and down on to the other beach.

Fewer people there. In the middle of a crowd of boys he sees Daniel, heads towards him.

– Ready for football?

– Where?

– In the shade, of course. If you don't want your legs to burn up under you.

Daniel always seems to have a crowd of friends around him. He's cool, Jo has to admit it. And good looking. Last night he was sitting by the edge of the swimming pool talking to some girls who looked to be quite a bit older than him.

Others come along and join them as they measure out the pitch and put down towels for goalposts. There are seven of them. The Swedes they hammered at volleyball the other day, and some others whom Daniel speaks to in English.

– Just going to see if Daddy'll play, then we'll be four a side.

It makes Jo smirk to hear Daniel still calling his father *Daddy*, but he keeps the smirk to himself. Daniel sprints across to one of the parasols by the stone staircase. Jo sees the father lay down his newspaper and get up, ambling through the sand. When he arrives, he shakes hands with them all.

– Have to know whom I'm playing with, he says with a broad smile. He's very tall and looks strong, and with his longish hair he reminds Jo of Obi-Wan in *Star Wars*.

One of the Swedes is on their team. His name is Pontus. Short and thin and with very quick feet. Typical winger. Jo prefers playing in the middle. He has a good shot, and the trainer is always praising him for his ability to read the game. It's fine by him that Daniel wants to play up front. His father plays at the back and calls himself a roaming 'keeper.

Daniel of course is good. Frighteningly good. A neat swerve, and fantastic acceleration. Once he takes a shot on the volley. Keeper nowhere near it. Like Marco van Basten. But he's no egomaniac. He centres, runs, plays one-twos.

– Good ball, he shouts to Jo, who's threaded a pass through the sand. And after beating a defender and the keeper, he dribbles the ball over the goal line and then gives him the thumbs-up, as though to say it was the pass that was good, and not what he was able to make out of it.

His father is the same, always encouraging.

– Great work, Jo, he shouts when Jo intercepts a long through ball. – Saved me a lot of trouble there.

After the game Daniel says:

– Come on over with us, we've got a cooler bag with cold drinks. But no Coke. My mother's a health freak. Much worse than Daddy, even though he's a doctor.

Jo hesitates. What does it mean, the way he's always being invited along? There must be something behind it, something that he doesn't know about yet. The whole time he's waiting for Daniel to give some kind of clue. Show that he's laughing at him. But that's not what happens. Is it possible that some people here didn't see Mother legless on the dance floor?

Daniel gives the order: – We need ten litres of juice to put back what we sweated out. Jo ran twice as far as me.

His mother is wearing a white bikini with a big leaf pattern on one of the cheeks. She's lying on her front reading a book and not wearing a top. She glances up at them.

– Hey there, Jo, she says, in a rather deep voice, and then goes on reading.

This is the first time Jo sees Daniel's mum up close. She has hardly any wrinkles and looks years younger than Mother.

– Help yourselves, she yawns. – I'm off duty now.

Daniel's father has wrapped an enormous towel around himself and changed into swimming trunks. Jo can't stop himself from taking a look between his legs. Fortunately the shorts are as big and wide as the ones he and Daniel are wearing.

They swim out breaststroke. Jo keeps his yellow T-shirt on in the water. He realises that he's not going to go bare-chested for the duration of the holiday. Could have taken it off that first day. Now it's too late. But Daniel doesn't mention it.

– Don't try to race him, he warns his father with a nod in Jo's direction. – Especially not underwater.

– Oh really?

– He must have swum fifty metres yesterday. Against the current. *Compleeetely craaazy*. He repeats the phrase from the day before, in a thick accent, joking, but the respect he has for Jo is obvious.

– Is that right, Jo?

– Roughly.

– You must have a fantastic pair of lungs, Daniel's father says. – I noticed that anyway when we were playing earlier. You ran the others into the ground, simple as that.

– Where do you get to if you keep on swimming out? Jo asks, to change the subject.

– Out? Daniel's father peers towards the horizon. – Africa first.

– I mean, whereabouts in Africa?

– Egypt, maybe. Or Libya. If you can keep a steady course, that is. I suggest if we swim out to those buoys that'll do us.

No more than twenty metres out there, thirty at the most. Jo dives, arrowing downwards until he reaches the sandy bottom. Follows it as it slopes into darkness. He feels a prickling in his ears, because he must be three metres below. Follows the depths outwards. Sees the others' legs breaking the delicate surface high above him. There's a throbbing in his head. As if someone's standing there and keeps hitting it. If I don't swim up and join them, he feels the thought race through him, if I just keep going along the bottom here until I disappear, then he'll take over, the one standing in the dark with the sledgehammer.

At that moment he glimpses the buoy up in the light, spins round, cuts the surface and grabs it moments before Daniel and his father arrive.

The sun is half-hidden behind the peak in the west.

– Have you noticed how quickly it gets dark here? Jo observes. He sketches a falling arc in the air. – The sun is directly above you, and then it drops. Like that.

Daniel agrees. – But that's nothing compared to what it's like in Tanzania.

– Have you been to Africa?

– Yup. You have to hurry on home once it gets towards evening. There's never a dusk. It's like somebody suddenly turns off the light. Everything goes dark. Not a single street lamp. It's dead cool.

The flagstones are still hot, but not burning hot, not hot enough to raise blisters under the soles of the feet. They're walking barefoot, towels over their shoulders, shadows in front of them. If Jo stays half a pace ahead, it makes them the same height.

People are already on their way to the restaurant. He's thinking he must get some food inside him. Avoid being seen with Mother and Arne. Have to make do with sweets.

– Just off to the kiosk.

– I'll wait by the pool, says Daniel. – We usually meet there before we go for dinner.

When Jo returns, nibbling on a choc ice, there's a gang sitting around the pool. She's one of them. Half lying on a sunbed, her back turned. The fat fair-haired girl next to her.

– Pudding before dinner? Cool, says Daniel. – We thought we might do something afterwards.

Ylva turns and glances at Jo. He tosses the half-eaten choc ice into a bin.

– Where are you going?

– Up to the miniature golf. Daniel lowers his voice before continuing. – Maybe go to a café that's a bit further up the street. You should come with us.

Ylva looks at the fat little girl, who giggles. They're obviously up for it. Jo stands next to the end of her sunbed and from the corner of his eye, behind the sunglasses, he can see how she lifts her gaze and lets it wander over him. Suddenly he knows that it's Ylva who has decided that they're going to ask him along.

– I'm in, he says to Daniel, and watches to see how she reacts. She smiles and looks pleased . . .

All day the heat has been gathering in him. He hates it being so hot. He could bend down, take her head between his hands, do something or other with it. He takes a quick look at his watch, mutters something about having to get home, heads for the steps with easy strides. Not until he's past the bar and they can't see him any more does he start running. Passes the apartment, on round the last house, down to the beach, not stopping until he reaches the water's edge and the one who stands in the shadows with the sledgehammer raised above his head is drowned out by the breakers that foam in over his feet.

He bumps into Arne in the apartment doorway.

— What have we here? His lordship deigns to put in an appearance.

— I've been with a pal, Jo offers.

— Tell people where you are. What sort of holiday is it going to be for us if we're running round looking for you the whole time?

The question lingers for a few moments.

— Nini's sick, Arne growls, as though there's any need to say that. Nini is always sick. Earache and difficulty breathing. She's always eaten something or other that doesn't agree with her, or it's the heat and the air-conditioning that makes her breathing so heavy. Or the kids' pool hasn't been properly cleaned. All the things Mother complains about without doing a damned shit about it. — You keep an eye on her while we go and get something to eat.

— Okay, says Jo, relieved not to have to sit with them, and the fact that he agrees at once puts Arne in a better mood.

— We'll bring some food back for you. Unless you want to pop out afterwards and get something to eat on your own.

— Okay, Jo says again.

— There's a Coke in the fridge, says Arne, almost friendly now. — But don't touch any of the other bottles, he adds with a guffaw, giving Jo a friendly punch on the shoulder.

He sits Nini up with cushions on the sofa. She is so short of breath it's an effort to say anything at all. But there's a cartoon on one of the TV channels and she's able to follow that. Mother has left the nebuliser ready. And he can run and fetch her at any time if Nini gets worse . . . Does she think he's going to let himself be seen in the dining room with them? Better to go to reception and get hold of a doctor. Or Daniel's father.

Truls returns after half an hour. He's carrying two plastic cartons in a bag. Lasagne, and meatballs in sauce.

– Mother and Father will be back shortly, he announces.

Jo snorts. – And you believe that?

– They're just finishing eating.

Truls is eight and doesn't understand a thing about the world yet. Jo laughs his head off. Is about to tell him what *he* thinks. Checks himself. Let him go on believing in Santa Claus a while longer, he thinks, and it makes him feel like a good big brother. Again that thought of taking Truls and Nini somewhere else. Him and Ylva, because she might well come along, after they've been to that cave she's going to show him. Suddenly he's filled with a furious rage towards Mother and Arne, mostly towards Mother. No one asked him if he would mind sitting the whole evening in the apartment. And he's no intention of doing that either. Get Nini to sleep, maybe wait for Truls to drop off too, because that never takes long. He intends to go out, no matter how bad Nini is. If she stops breathing and they find her early next morning, lifeless and blue in the face, then it's their own fault.

He undresses in the bathroom. Stands a moment in front of the mirror, bends forward and looks down his body, down to the navel. If he closes his eyes, he can see Ylva. She's wearing her bikini, and her bare shoulders are warm. If he wants, he can get her to put her hand on the front of his shorts. *I know a place*, she says very quietly, because no one else is to hear her. They come to the end of the beach and climb over the jagged rock. No, they walk round it, wade out into the warm water and in towards a bay on the other side. *I know a cave*, says Ylva, and she feels what has happened down in his shorts and stops and turns towards him, and then they kiss.

He hears the front door open. He freezes, slips in behind the shower curtain, turns it on. The boiling-hot water makes him groan in pain.

– Jo?

– I'm in the shower, he explains, and twists the tap over down to blue.

– Don't you think it's a *liddle* bit late? Mother snuffles. – I thought you'd gone to bed.

He can hear her sitting down on the toilet seat. Can see her outline through the thin curtain.

– Aren't you going out again? he asks.

– Not while Nini isn't well, of course not.

She finishes and flushes. He can tell from her voice that soon she'll be asleep. He turns towards the wall, lets the cold water cascade down. Hears the curtain being pulled aside.

– I am showering, he repeats, quite angry now.

– I can see that, Jo. It certainly doesn't bother *me* at all. We always used to shower together before. She steps in and stands behind him. He realises she's taken off all her clothes.

– Hey, this is ice cold. Are you trying to *fweeze* to death?

She turns the water back up. It takes a while for it to get warmer.

– There's no need to be shy with me, Jo. I'm your mother after all, aren't I? I've always given you a good soaping and then *rinsened* you off and dried you, haven't I?

She fills her palm with shower oil and begins to rub his shoulders.

– Don't be shy, Jo. Being naked together is quite natural.

She's still standing behind him; she puts her arms around his chest and rubs down towards his stomach. Suddenly she bends forward and kisses his neck.

– Jo, she says, as she goes on rubbing with that slippery oil that smells of lilac. He can't stand lilac. There's someone else standing somewhere in the shadows, beating away with a hammer, someone who appears whenever this happens, who makes him feel like it isn't Jo who's there, but this other boy, who goes along with everything.

– You're a nice boy, Jo. You're so nice . . . so nice.

– I'm not Jo, he murmurs as he lifts his face to the stream of water.

It's approaching 10.30 when he puts on his shoes. Mother's in the bedroom and lies there whimpering in her sleep, naked and still wet, because she wasn't able to dry herself properly. Jo creeps back into the bathroom. Wipes himself clean with a towel yet again. Takes the bottle of aftershave from the shelf. It smells of Arne, and he wrinkles his nose but fills his fist and rubs it over both sides of his neck. He feels it burning, ice cold. He takes a swig of the pale blue liquid. Tastes of soap and flowers. It wants to come back up again. He forces it to stay down. On his way towards the front door, he remembers something, opens the kitchen drawer and finds what he borrowed from Ylva. The combination corkscrew, tin opener and bottle opener. Take it along and give it to her now. Because it's still not too late to find her. She's in a café somewhere up near the main road. Good way to get a conversation going. Joke about the opener. That it was beer he was going to open yesterday morning, or a bottle of wine. At any rate, not tuna. And she'll laugh about the can of tuna, laugh at how he forgot to give it back to her, laugh while she pinches his arm, and then he can wrap himself around her. Pretty much the way Jacket said it would happen.

Daniel and the others aren't at the pool any more. No grown-ups either, but from the terrace comes the sound of shouting and laughter. Jo thinks he can hear Arne's voice, Arne telling jokes, and the skinny old bird laughing. He withdraws into the shadow, over to the steps, runs towards the miniature golf. The course is lit up. He sees the Swedish boy – Pontus – who was on their team when they played football. His hair is almost white and he has a ring in one ear. Pontius Pilate, thinks Jo . . .

She isn't there. Not her friend either, nor Daniel. He ambles over. Two other boys, both Swedes, watch as Pontus concentrates on the ninth hole. They give Jo a quick glance. Doesn't seem like they want to talk to him, and that's not why he's there anyway.

– Where are the others?

Pontus Pilate thinks about it. – A café somewhere.

He nods in the direction of the world outside the hotel area.

Jo hurries along the main road. Suddenly furious with Arne, who made him look after the kids when he should have been out with Ylva. With Mother, who had to come home before he could leave. Two mopeds buzz by. Music from a bar. That kind of strumming on a Greek guitar that gets faster and faster, like a carousel. He curses again, this time because he didn't ask Daniel the name of the café they were going to. Turns and heads back again. Decides to wait at the entrance to the hotel area. Sooner or later they'll have to come this way. Passes a park on the other side of the street. Catches a glimpse of movement between the bushes. *It's them.* Is about to call to them, but the shout never comes out. Daniel is holding her by the hand. There are no others with them. They disappear into the darkness.

He staggers on, round the next corner. He stops behind the building, supports himself against a container. He has to check to see if he's made a mistake. Climbs over a fence, approaches the park from the lower side. Creeps bent double along the hedge.

They're sitting between two bushes. Light from the café on the other side draws the shape of their bodies. They're making out. He creeps even closer, so close he can hear them whispering to each other. Daniel has his hand up under her top. He can't see her hands; they must be out of sight, down his shorts.

It wasn't them he saw. Not Ylva. Not Daniel. It was too dark to see who it was. They weren't whispering together. Go down to her apartment. Knock. If she's home, it must be someone else sitting up there in the bushes, in the darkness. If she isn't home, he can tell her father where she is. Then sneak back up there. Find them lying in the grass, her with the tiny little skirt bunched like a sausage round her stomach and her knickers flopping on one ankle, Daniel on top of her, because not one single sonofabitch in hell could be in any doubt about who that is carrying on up there in that park.

– Ylva, he says aloud. Repeats the name several times, knowing that he'll never, ever say it again.

There's something in his pocket. The tin opener. He digs it out, flips up the corkscrew. It's sharp and makes his fingers prickle when he jabs it around on his underarm. In the kids' playground he finds a tree. Carve on it with that stiletto of a corkscrew. A couple of words he has to get one last time, not *Ylva* but *Fucking Ylva*. Ylva doesn't give a fuck. Not Daniel. Daniel doesn't know anything about Ylva and Jo. Cut around the whole trunk of the tree, peel off the bark in strips so it can't live.

Something soft rubbing against his leg. He jumps. The one-eyed kitten. He bends down and gets hold of it by the skin of its neck. Yes, now you can fucking wail, you moaning bastard, always coming over here and rubbing your arse up against me, you hear me, fucking cat? It wriggles about and tries to scratch him, and that's what makes him really angry. It's small, not much bigger than one of Arne's shoes, and the thought enrages him. With one hand he squashes it hard again the tree; he pulls his belt off with the other, passes a loop around the cat's neck and pulls it as tight as he can. It hangs there, wriggling and squirming about. He fastens the belt around a branch and stares at it. Stares everything evil into that sick little cat face. It's only got one eye, but that's one too fucking many, it seems to him; not him, but the other one, he's the one that's there now, the one who stands in the dark and pounds away with a

sledgehammer shouting *Don't let it see me, no one must see me.*
He holds the little head in an iron grip, pokes away at it with
Ylva's tin opener, holds the animal at arm's length so it can't
reach him with its claws. It's hissing and screeching; he squeezes
harder, and something green spurts out of its tiny mouth. Spit
on me would you, you little fucker. He gets a finger down in
the good eye, holds it open, jabs at it with the corkscrew. The
cat makes a sound like a baby, like Nini when she lies away
screaming all night long. He pushes the coils inwards, twisting
until the eye gives and something wet dribbles out on to the
back of his hand. Twists a few more turns and pulls it out as
hard as he can. The fur in his hand goes limp. He tensions the
belt so much the thin neck closes up and is almost cut right
through. And yet it still isn't dead. He leaves it hanging there
and walks over to the swing and finds a big, sharp stone.
Throws the limp creature onto the ground, bends over and
pounds the stone against the soft head until he hears it splinter
like dry tinder and the tiny ear fills with blood.

Sometime later he loosens the belt and throws the clump of
fur off into the bushes. Hears voices getting closer and hides in
between the slide and the swings. No surprise if someone comes
to see what all the noise was about. But they walk on by, disappear down the steps. He creeps over to the gate, opens it. There's
a cord hanging from it, probably from a sweatshirt. He reaches
down into the bushes and pulls out the slimy fur body. Ties the
cord around its neck and takes it with him. You know exactly
what to do with this, the whisper in his ear says. Whose fucking
door you're going to hang this on.

Calmer now he's done what he was told to do, he walks
back up the steps and back into the playground. Sits on one
of the swings. He's too big and heavy, the whole structure
sways, and this calm can't be trusted, his stomach is still
churning way down low and it won't stop. The yellow flag
was waving on the beach when he and Daniel went up in the

afternoon. Bound to be still up. That's the way it is now, he mutters. Not just medium danger any more.

Soundlessly he lets himself in. The light is on in the room. Truls must have woken up and turned it on. He's sleeping up on the sofa beside Nini. The duvet has slipped off and is lying half on the floor. Jo stands there looking at the sleeping bodies. Truls will miss him. *Truls needs you, Jo.* Mother will be ashamed; she'll start crying. She'll feel so sorry for herself. Nini is too small to understand anything. Only Truls will miss him. He picks up the duvet and wraps it round his brother and sister.

He notices that the whole of his underarm is covered in green slime mixed with bloody goo. Slips into the bathroom and rinses it off. Silent in the bedroom. Mother needs to sleep. Arne isn't back yet. Here's something he can do. Go up to the bar. Find Arne slobbering over that skinny bitch who's with the other bloke. Walk over, grab something from a table, a knife, a corkscrew. Shove it into the side of his neck so it goes all the way through whatever's in there and the blood gushes up out of Dickhead Arne's mouth like a garden hose. Rouse Mother. Shove her and Truls and Nini into the back of a taxi and drive to the airport. *We're finished here, Mother, never come here again, understand?* With Arne lying on the floor of the bar, bleeding to death. On the plane, she doesn't touch a drop, not when they get home either. She'll make their packed lunches and drop off Truls and Nini and then she'll go to work, because her head at the hospital called and said they want her back. She'll never again spend half the day lying in bed, and she'll be there when they come home, and there'll be the smell of roasting meat and freshly baked bread, and she'll stand on the steps and smile at Jo when he comes home from school. *This is how it'll be from now on, Mother. Now Dick head Arne is gone for ever.*

On top of the fridge he finds an envelope, tears off the back of it. Fetches one of Nini's crayons, a light green one. Write something or other. *Hate you* is how he might begin, but that's not what he writes. When he's finished, there are just two words on the paper: *Forget me*.

From the top of the steps, the breakers look like huge kittens licking milk. He takes off his trainers on the bottom step and walks barefoot across the sand. It's cool now. Passes a group of deckchairs at a distance. From the corner of his eye it looks as though someone's sitting there, but he's no intention of checking. He reaches the point at which the foaming water has to give up and go back again. Follows the tideline along. The sand here is firm and hardly sinks underfoot. Keeps going to a point midway along the beach, the place he picked out a few days earlier, without having planned it. Swim out. Past the buoys. Out through the warm black water. Headed for Africa. He'll never get there. He'll grow tired. Afraid, maybe, but mostly tired. Swim till he can't do it any more. The dark warmth will close around him . . . He feels suddenly light. Hardly even angry any more. Just happy. His disappearance will wake Mother up. She'll leave Dickhead Arne. Truls and Nini will have a better life. What is required is that he take this swim. Ylva will never know it has anything to do with her. Or perhaps she'll understand when she comes home and sees what's hanging on her door.

He pulls off his trousers and underpants, keeps the yellow T-shirt on. Behind the tongue of one of his trainers he puts the note he wrote in the kitchen.

He stands just where the breakers turn. They foam around his toes, frothing so the small bubbles burst. They don't come to bring something, he thinks. They come to fetch something. He starts to wade out.

– Hey, Joe.

He stands there without turning round. Tries to tell himself it's his imagination. Realises that it isn't. Realises that Jacket is standing on the sand behind him.

– Bit late for a swim, isn't it?

No one can stop what he has started on now. Postpone it maybe, but not stop it. He has given a promise. Doesn't know who to, if it's not to the one who stands in the dark pounding with the sledgehammer. There is nothing in the world that can make him go back on his word.

He half turns. Jacket is wearing the same dark clothes. His hair looks dirty and uncombed. A cigarette in one hand. Jo's trainer in the other, with the note.

– It's going to be a long night, Joe, says Jacket, and doesn't seem the least bit bothered. – You've got plenty of time.

He takes a drag on the cigarette and offers it to him.

– Come and sit down here with me for a while. I'm not leaving until you tell me how things are working out between you and Ylva Richter.

DEAR LISS,

If you receive this letter, I am no longer. I sit watching how the dust slowly sinks down through the grey light falling from the window, and outside the wind whips up the autumn leaves and lays them down on the snow again. Even now that thought seems so strange. Not to be any more. It's not a last-minute decision; it's been latent for years, and now I've woken it up again. What you do will decide whether I send you this letter I'm writing, or burn it in the fireplace and carry on down my road a while longer. I won't contact you, won't lift a finger to influence you. The closest I can get to a feeling of relief right now is the thought that what is to come lies in your hands, not mine. And related to this relief is another thought: if you receive this letter, then you'll also know what happened that time.

I first saw him on the plane. He passed by on the way to the toilet. I looked up from my book, the only luggage I had with me on that trip. His glance caught mine, but I don't think he noticed me. I still remember the lines of verse I sat reading, over and over again, by the window:

> Who is the third who walks always beside you?
> When I count, there are only you and I together.
> But when I look ahead up the white road
> There is always another one walking beside you
> Gliding wrapt in a brown mantle, hooded
> I do not know whether a man or a woman
> – But who is that on the other side of you?

I could have written a lot about Jo and Jacket. I could have described in detail the first meeting in Makrigialos that *autumn. How I saved him from drowning himself. How he saved me. Not because I need to confess, Liss, but because it matters to me, sitting here, that you understand what you condemn me for . . .*

PART I

1

MAKE-UP OFF. RUBBING, revealing strips of pale red facial skin in the sharp light. The photographer had insisted she cover up with this thick white mask. Something he wanted to bring out. Something stiffened, in contrast to the almost naked body.

She unfastened the clip, let the hair tumble down her back. It looked darker than usual, but still reddish. She sat a moment, considering what she saw in the mirror. The arc of the forehead, the eyebrows she had allowed to grow out wide, the eyes that seemed to be too far apart. It had always looked odd, but a lot of the photographers obviously liked it. Wim, whom she was working with today, maintained with a grin that it made her look elfin. She began drawing a brush through her hair, slowly, following the waves; it got caught in a tug, a quick jerk which she felt at the base of her skull, a reminder that she mustn't linger too long in this distant state. It was past eleven o'clock. Part of her was aware of the need to slip down into a dark hole, sleep there for a day or two, or more. But her pulse was too quick and too hard.

Her mobile phone vibrated on the mirrored shelf. She checked the number – no one she knew – put it down again, carried on brushing. Had never liked this thick, difficult hair, apparently inherited from her grandmother. *Waves of fire*, Zako might say, when he was feeling melodramatic. And against a white wall or a pale sky it shone and attracted the eye, which was then obliged to carry on and see the face with the greenish eyes. She straightened her back so that her breasts became visible in the mirror. They were too small, but Zako was firm about not having them enlarged, at least not yet; they suited her young girl image. Like something out of a Jane Austen novel, he said. Zako had never read Jane Austen. Nor had she, for that matter.

The mobile buzzed again. Message from Rikke. *Liss, we're in the Café Alto. Cool music, Zako's asking about you.*

A flash of anger passed through her. He'd started sending her messages via Rikke. Thought she still didn't know he was sleeping with her. Rikke had let it slip one morning over a week ago. She could read Rikke. Could read most people. The look in Rikke's eyes was different that morning. The laughter a note higher than usual. When Liss asked if she'd seen any more of Zako that night, she'd dropped the breadknife on the floor. Confessed immediately. As though there was anything to confess. *So what*, was Liss's comment once she'd told the whole story. Rikke had been expecting her to flare up and make a scene. When that didn't happen, she declared that Liss was the best friend she'd ever had, and that she was never going to let Zako feel her up any more. But how was she going to resist? Zako had done a thorough job on her. Taken her in such a way that she went around thinking about it for days afterwards, waiting to be taken again in exactly the same way. Walked around dreaming about him in a complete daze. He had her in his pocket. Literally, thought Liss, and noticed a smile in the now make-up-less face in the mirror.

She'd realised immediately once Rikke began doing little favours for him. Got him coke if he'd run out. Rang for a taxi when he was leaving. Rubbed her bulging arse up against his crotch every chance she got. Liss laughed at her on the quiet. To see Rikke as a panting bitch was liberating. Probably because she knew Zako would never get that kind of hold over *her*. Liss didn't need him and wasn't afraid to tell him that. Then he might talk nasty and be threatening. She owed him money, he might say. And didn't he pay for the flat she shared with Rikke? He kept far too much of what she earned on her photo shoots, she might come back at him. Soon she'd have enough good contacts to run the show herself. She didn't need a PhD in economics to make a few phone calls and read through a few contracts. She owed him for coke, he growled. Do you mean to say you're making all this fuss over a few thousand kroner? she might shoot back. Do you want it now? Damn it, Liss, get a grip, he would hiss, but he'd already been driven back, way back inside his own territory.

One morning, this was in the little kitchen in the flat, he'd grabbed both her arms, twisted them behind her and pushed her up against the fridge. It hurt, she had bruises for several days after, but she looked him straight in the eye without showing the slightest sign of pain. He could have hit her, in the course of a few minutes destroyed her physically. But she wasn't afraid of him. His threats aroused nothing but her contempt, and that made her different from all the other girls he had. She didn't need him. He needed her. He'd realised that a long time ago, but he still laboured under the delusion that *she* hadn't realised. He'd made a few connections for her. A lot of them were useless, because she had no intention of going into pornography. Only a handful of the photographers he knew had other ambitions. She'd try them. Not commit herself. Not be tempted by empty promises. Zako wanted her to stop taking the design classes, thought it took up too much time. She had no plans to stop. Had enough talent to get some use from it. The modelling jobs were just a series of tests: what sort of effect did her picture have on others, and why? What else could be done with that picture? How far could she get from what she was, or had once been?

She was finished with Zako. Had started looking for a new apartment. Wouldn't have any problem paying back what she owed him. If the worst came to the worst, ask at home. Not Mother, obviously, but Mailin, who would send money immediately, no questions asked ... The thought of her sister brought a stop to the long, flowing movements of the hairbrush. She sat there squeezing it in her hand. The eyes in the mirror held her. Something had happened. Three days ago. Yet again Zako had insisted that she escort some businessmen for an evening on the town. He had three or four girls who earned money for him that way. He provided the service, it brought in a lot of money, and he let them keep quite a bit for themselves. They didn't have to sleep with anyone, just hang around at receptions and go to nightclubs. *With unlimited access to champagne, coke and the best restaurants in town*, in Zako's tempting description. Rikke was just about hooked. *Easy money*, he promised. He sounded like a used-car salesman, and it started Liss off laughing. He asked what the big joke was. And that was when she dropped the hint, the thing she'd now made up her mind about, that she was going to break with him. His eyes darkened. *Maybe you don't give a damn about what happens to you*, he hissed, *but you've got someone you do give a damn about, just like everyone does*. What do you mean? she had to ask, suddenly struggling to hide her uncertainty. *Don't you have a sister?* Then something happened that hadn't happened for a long time. The light in the room changed. It got brighter, and at the same time seemed to sort of withdraw. *Aren't I here?* She felt the thought race through her, and a pounding began in her chest, so hard she had to take a hold of herself just to go on breathing. And at the same time, that other thought: *he mustn't see what's happening to me*. She held on tight to the edge of the table. He smirked. Didn't say anything, just that smirk, as though to show her that he knew he had her now.

She put down the hairbrush, pulled on her jersey and trousers. Zako had no idea how idiotic it was of him to try to bring her sister into it. The final straw. She would make that blindingly clear to him next time they met.

She put her mascara on, a thin layer, took out her eyeshadow. Suddenly she saw Mailin in her mind's eye. Standing in front of a bed. She's wearing pyjamas, and even though the room is in darkness, Liss knows that they're pale blue. Her sister's hair is gathered in two long braids, the way she used to have it when she was a child. She's standing there saying something or other.

Liss tossed her make-up into her bag, took her leather jacket down from its peg, let herself out of the dressing room. From the kitchen she could hear Wim talking to one of the other photographers he shared the studio with. She stole out so quietly they didn't hear her.

Close on midnight. Packed at the Café Alto. The quartet on the stage in the innermost recess of the cramped premises began playing a tune announced by the pianist as 'Before I Met You'. Liss knew him. He was American and had been out with a couple of the girls from her design class. Now he sat hunched over in the half-dark, staring in what looked like surprise at his own hands as they ran up and down the keyboard.

Rikke waved from a table over by the stairs, shuffled up the bench to make room. Zako had his back turned and was talking to a guy at the next table. Once Liss had wriggled her way in, Rikke leaned over to her. – Zako thinks you're starting to avoid him, she said with her mouth pressed to Liss's ear.

Liss had to laugh. Was Rikke doing his talking for him now? Only then did Zako turn round. His eyes were shining, and it might have looked as though he was having fun, but she knew him by now. He leaned across the table, put a hand on her arm, and looked very closely at her. – Been working right up till now? she made out through the music.

Zako was always on the alert, even when he was high. Always asking questions about what she'd been doing and who she'd been with.

She was hungry. Hadn't eaten since the early afternoon. She picked up a Marlboro packet, lit a cigarette and leaned against the wall. Zako still sat there studying her face as though he were seeing her for the first time. Up on stage, the bass player, whom Liss also knew through the school, was taking a solo. His head was in constant motion; he was playing with it. It looked as though he had a fishing line between his teeth with which he was pulling and drawing out notes from the massive instrument.

A clumpy, damp-smelling joint was passed across to their table. Liss passed it on to Rikke, who was resting her head on her shoulder, girlfriend-like.

– Need something completely different from camel shit.

– Agreed. Come with me.

Rikke went up the stairs first. Liss could feel Zako's gaze on her back, at a point just below the neck.

They let themselves into the toilet. Rikke fished an envelope out of her handbag, a mirror and a straw. Handed it to Liss.

– Might as well have a pee while you do the honours, she said. She lifted her short skirt, yanked down her tights and slipped down on to the toilet seat.

Liss made a line ready. Kept her hair back out of the way with one hand. Rikke held it for her. Liss bent forward, inhaled as deeply as she could along the mirror, ended up with her mouth almost down in her cleavage. Another line in the other nostril.

– What would I have done without you? she snuffled once they had changed places.

Rikke took her two lines, leaned up against the toilet door and watched as she peed.

– Christ, Liss, have you any idea how pretty you are?

Liss enjoyed hearing her say this, even though she knew she would never actually be *pretty*. She stood up, kissed Rikke on the mouth. Just long enough, before pulling up her trousers.

Zako was standing there when they came out. – What's happening?

He was looking straight at Liss as he said this. Rikke put a finger over her mouth and disappeared down the stairs.

– Why didn't you come yesterday? he wanted to know.

– Did I say I would come?

He took her by the arm, not hard. – I know you're pissed off about this thing with Rikke.

She raised her eyebrows. – Why should I be pissed off? You can fuck each other as much as you like for all I care. Be my guest.

Now he grinned. – You *are* pissed off. I know you.

– Wrong on both counts, she said, smiling back at him, pulling free from his grip.

He pressed her up against the wall, looked down into her face. His pupils were like pins, and still the eyes looked black. She wondered what he was on.

– I'm dumping her.

– Who?

– I'm dropping Rikke.

Liss couldn't help laughing. – I thought there was nothing going on between you. And now suddenly you're going to drop her?

He made a face that was perhaps intended to convey the comedy in the contradiction.

– Sorry, he said.

– For what?

– I haven't treated you very well. I'll try to improve.

She was surprised. Had never heard anything resembling an admission from Zako before. That pride had attracted her, the way he never needed to make himself small. And now here he was asking to be forgiven. Not that he meant it. But as a tactic it was doomed either way.

– It has nothing to do with Rikke, she said. – Or with any other girls. I don't need you, Zako.

As she said it, a jolt went up from her chest, passed through her throat. Her head was filled with bubbling gas. Anything could happen. And she was stronger than anything.

– We have an agreement, he said calmly, but now there was an undertone of suppressed anger in his voice. She wasn't the least bit afraid of it.

– Agreement?

– Listen here, Liss. He paused briefly, obviously so that what he was about to say would carry more weight. – All the photo shoots you've had, I got those for you. If you want any more of that, you need to know the right people. When it comes to *fashion*, Amsterdam is fucking nowhere. I know a whole heap of other people in other places. People who matter. You're not going to end up with Wim and Ferdinand and all the other wannabes.

– I'm hugely grateful to you, she said, stressing the *hugely*. – But you don't need to worry about the future. Not mine, at least. No more sleepless nights on my account.

His eyes grew harder. – The flat, he said. – You're living in my flat.

That wasn't true. He'd helped to get it, but he didn't own it.

– I'm moving out next week, she said. – Found somewhere else.

Maybe he realised that not even that was true. But nothing could hurt her in the place where she was. She started walking down the stairs.

– Wait, he said hoarsely behind her. She stopped and turned; it cost nothing to hear what he had to say. He had one hand in his inside jacket pocket. For an instant she thought he had a weapon, a knife, a gun. Not even that thought frightened her.

It wasn't a weapon he was holding. She saw it was a photo-graph. And knew instantly that there was a new twist to the game. He remained standing at the top of the stairs, but she wouldn't climb back up to him, instead waited for him to come down the four steps.

– Recognise her? he asked, holding the photo at an angle so the light from the wall lamp fell on it.

Three days had passed since Zako had mentioned Liss having a sister. Afterwards she'd thought he'd just been taking a chance. Still, she couldn't shake the thought of what he was hinting at.

The photo was taken at a bus stop. Mailin was leaning against a wall, looking at something just outside the frame of the picture. It was taken from the side, some distance away. She had clearly no idea she was being photographed.

Liss held on to the banister. The light changed, pulled away but became more intense. As though it wasn't her who was standing there. And when it wasn't her, anything at all might happen. Maybe she was holding her breath, because there was a pain low down in her lungs, and black dots began to appear through the bright, distant light. Mustn't react now. This was what Zako was like. Went on and on and never realised when he'd gone too far . . . She knew about most of what he was capable of. It didn't frighten her. She'd taken everything into account. But not that he would get someone to go and check on Mailin. Suddenly she felt nauseous. Hadn't eaten all day. Must eat. Must come down. Get away.

– Where did you get that picture from?

He wasn't smiling any more.

– Why are you showing it to me? she continued, her voice as controlled as she could make it.

Again he scrutinised her face. If she carried on standing there, for the very first time he would manage to strip it, layer by layer, until it was quite naked, and the slightest twitch would reveal what was going on in her thoughts.

She turned round, went down the stairs and sat close to Rikke, put an arm around her shoulder, as though to protect her.

She dreamed she was holding an electric drill. It wouldn't work. She squeezed the trigger as hard as she could. Suddenly it roared into life with an explosive banging that made her hands jump. She released the trigger, but the machine wouldn't stop.

When she woke up, the room was still vibrating, the bed she was lying in, the walls. Then it subsided. It was a tram passing. She remembered where she was. She'd left the Café Alto late last night. Couldn't bear the thought of going back to the flat. Maybe Zako would tag along, or appear after she and Rikke had gone to bed. It was the sort of thing he could do if he felt like it. She'd left the place without a word and booked in for the night at a hotel in Leidsestraat.

Light seeped in through the gap below the curtains. She lay there studying the pattern on the wallpaper. Small apple blossoms moving upwards, a film that rolled and rolled up towards the ceiling. And somewhere between them the image of Mailin again. Standing by her bed in the blue pyjamas.

Liss sits up.

What is it?

Mailin puts a finger to her mouth. Then she turns and locks the door.

Tell me what it is, Mailin.

Her sister stands in the dark, listening. Then she creeps into bed, puts an arm around Liss.

I'll look after you, Liss. Nothing bad will ever, ever happen to you.

She got up and went to the bathroom. Put her finger down her throat and emptied out the small amount that was in her stomach. Went back to bed. Wrapped the duvet around herself. The photo of Mailin at the bus stop. Must be Oslo. Looked to be quite recent. Who had taken it? She couldn't ask Zako about it. He knew already that this was the weak spot he had been looking for. Did he realise just how weak it was? If she revealed that, she would lose control. If she gave in to fear, she would start to fear everything. She sat up suddenly, found the mobile in the bag that was hanging over the chair, slid down by the wall under the window, punched in the number. It rang three times before she got an answer.

– Liss? Mailin's voice was full of sleep. – Has something happened?

Liss breathed deeply. – No, no . . . She glanced at the clock on the TV. It showed 6.20. – Sorry, I didn't realise how early it was. I'll call again later.

– Stop it, you've already woken me. Was going to get up early anyway. Looks like good skiing conditions out today.

Liss could imagine it. The ski trail emerging on to the marsh between the pine trees. The wind in the treetops. Otherwise still.

– Wish I could go with you.

Mailin yawned. – Coming home for Christmas after all?

– Don't think so . . .

– Couldn't you use a little break, Liss?

It was scary how often what Mailin said was exactly right.

– Break? That's not exactly what I need.

She did need a break. But she had nowhere to go. At least not in Norway. That wasn't home any more. Would never be again.

– Don't try to change my mind, Mailin.

She heard a grunt in the background, a man. – Is he with you, your friend?

Mailin gave a quick laugh.

– Angling, are we? Trying to get me to admit there's someone other than him here? A lover? A new man in my life?

– Is there?

– You know how boring I am. The man lying beside me is still called Viljam. Just as he has been these last two years . . .

– He's been lying beside you for two years?

– Ha ha. Liss, you don't call me at six thirty on a Saturday morning to make feeble jokes. Now please, tell me what's the matter.

She'd lain awake half the night unable to shake off the thought that someone was threatening her sister. Something to do with Zako and that photo . . . Going to bed, exhausted and agitated, still wired like a high-tension cable, she had been certain something terrible had happened to Mailin. She'd wanted to ring immediately, but forced herself to wait.

– Just wanted to hear how things are. Hear your voice, she thought, but didn't say. – That you're okay.

– Any reason I shouldn't be?

– Well, no . . . But maybe you're taking on too much work. All those people you're taking care of.

– Liss, there is something. Tell me what it is.

Before she could change her mind, Liss said:

– Why don't I remember anything from when I was a child? Mailin didn't answer.

– Something crops up every now and then, she went on. – Pictures of some kind. Just now, for example, I saw you coming into my room. You lock the door and get into bed beside me and hold me. But I don't know if that happened or if it's something I imagined or dreamt.

– It did happen, said Mailin. – At home in Lørenskog.

– You never said anything about that, Liss exclaimed.

A few moments passed before Mailin answered.

– Maybe I was waiting till you asked. There's no need to remember everything.

Liss felt nauseous. Had to go out and vomit again.

– Call you later, she managed to say before ending the call.

2

LISS PADDED NAKED around the flat. Checked to see if the ivy on the windowsill needed water. Brewed herself another cup of espresso. Sat by the kitchen window and looked out. The Christmas decorations in Haarlemmerdijk were pine-bedecked bows with lights hanging beneath them. Like suckling nipples on a bitch's belly, it struck her. A large six-pointed star hung across the middle of the street. Inside it was a heart with red light bulbs glowing.

She had the flat to herself. A girl in her class, someone she hardly knew, had said without a moment's hesitation that she could stay with her till she found somewhere permanent. Now the girl had gone to Venlo to spend the weekend with her family. They had to be pretty well off if they could afford to pay for their daughter's three-bedroomed flat in trendy Jordaan, a part of the old town where Huguenot refugees had once lived. Here the facades had been tastefully refurbished and there were no trams or heavy lorries thundering through at all hours of the day and night.

Liss took her coffee into the bathroom. Stood in front of the mirror. She didn't need make-up. Her skin was soft and smooth, without blemishes. But it felt good to smear a mask on. If the whole of her naked body could be coated in thin film, something she could wrap around herself when she went out, pull off when she returned home, that would leave her skin untouched . . . If she could do the same thing with her eyes. Put something not just on the brows and the lashes but on the pupils themselves. Cover everything that could betray her. Buy contact lenses, though there was nothing wrong with her sight. In another colour, black or brown.

Two thin flutings from her mobile. Message from Mailin: *Didn't hear back from you. Something's just happened that has to do with what you asked me about that morning.*

Her sister had called the previous evening. Liss was in the middle of a photo shoot and said she would call back but didn't. Regretted revealing to her sister that this memory had surfaced. Actually there was nothing wrong with her memory; on a daily and weekly basis she could remember things perfectly well. It was what lay far back that was gone. Other people, like Rikke, seemed to have a detailed overview of their entire lives, starting with the day they got their very first pair of shoes ever. Rikke could rewind; her memory was obviously a film that could be viewed over and over again. Liss's didn't work like that. She could remember a few things from the holiday cabin, but not from before she was ten or twelve. Every summer and winter they had lived in the forest cabin just outside Oslo for several weeks. Weekends and holidays. They drove to Bysetermosan and then hauled a fully loaded sledge along the path to Vangen and then on to Morr Water. Or went on skis from Losby. When they got to be old enough, she and Mailin used to go there on their own, without the grown-ups. Sometimes in the evenings. By the light of the moon over Geitsjø and Røiri Waters. Up through the dark forest with their rucksacks, laughing and reverent in the great silence.

She didn't need to remember more than she did. Mailin perhaps thought that she mentioned that vague memory from the bedroom in Lørenskog because it bothered her. If so, she was wrong, and Liss decided to tell her next time she rang.

It was six months since she had last seen her sister. Mailin had visited her in Amsterdam in the early summer. She'd been attending a conference. Something about child abuse. Something she was researching and she delivered a paper on. She stayed on for a few days afterwards. Liss had shown her the town. Taken her along to the school and to one of the photographic studios where she'd done a few jobs. But most things she kept from her big sister. Nothing about the parties and the coke. And she'd been careful to keep Zako out of the way. Didn't want him to meet Mailin. Two worlds that had to be kept separated. They didn't belong together, couldn't exist simultaneously. And yet still the question from Mailin as Liss was driving her to the airport.

What's to become of you, Liss?

It hit her so hard she couldn't even get angry. *Nothing's going to become of me*, she could have answered. That was her victory over everything she'd run away from. Over the life she would never live.

Mailin didn't give up.

Remember what I said to you last time I fetched you from Central Police Station?

Liss had been picked up several times in the last years before she left. Mailin agreed that the war in Iraq was repellent, and had shuffled about dutifully in a few of these lawful demonstrations where everything was very decorous and proper. That wasn't enough for Liss. She was part of a group of activists that marched on the American embassy and objected to being headed off by the police. In their anger they threw bottles and stones. Several in the group were willing to go even further and give their attackers a taste of their own dirty medicine. *D'you think it does any more good than peaceful protesting?* Mailin wanted to know. The way she looked at it, she was working from the inside. It was one of the rare things that made Liss angry with her. If you were on the inside, you were on the side of power, or at the very best a useful idiot. Mailin wouldn't budge: *This business of fighting with the police is all about finding a superior power that is strong enough, then challenging it in order to get beaten up, which simply confirms how evil everything is.* Time and again Liss demanded that she stop interferring and mind her own business. And yet, no matter what she got up to, she knew Mailin would never let her go.

In the car on the way out to Schiphol she said:

I worry that you're still doing the same thing as when you sat down in the middle of the road and waited for the police to come charging at you. You find someone who is sufficiently brutal and ruthless, so you can fight and get beaten up.

You've never met him, Liss protested.

She'd managed to keep Zako away, but her sister had had a long talk with Rikke. And Mailin didn't need much to form a picture.

Rikke'll say just about anything at all, Liss insisted. *She'll do anything for the chance to go to bed with him.*

Mailin didn't say any more. Every week through the autumn they spoke on the phone, but she never asked about Zako or the life Liss was leading in Amsterdam. Probably waiting for Liss to bring it up. Mailin had always waited for her.

What's to become of you, Liss?

It was quarter past four by the time Liss was finished in the bathroom. She went out without eating. Not that she had any food there anyway. Unlocked the bicycle in a corner behind the basement steps, carried it up and out on to the street. There was a smell of fresh bread from the bakery on the corner. The window was full of cheesecakes, doughnuts and pretzels. For a moment she stopped to inhale the smell, pleased that she didn't feel tempted to buy something, give in to the need to fill her mouth with something soft and crumbly.

She followed Haarlemmerdijk, turned into Prinsengraacht. After days of rain whipping in from the sea in the north, the

December afternoon was still raw, but colder, with light piercing through rifts in the clouds, making the fissures glow with a piercing blueness. The sky changed the whole time, still clearing, and smoke rose from the chimneys of the houseboats along the canal. Suddenly she was filled with a strange exhilaration. She pedalled harder. Could have stopped here, stopped time, frozen this picture of the withered flowers in their pots along the banks of the canal, the bright clouds overhead and the silhouette of Westerkerk forcing its way up into them. One day she might look back on this bike ride, this glimpse of something she was in the middle of yet which was also out of reach for her. But it was hard to see herself ever getting old enough to look back. She had long ago decided that she was made for a short life. Liked to joke about it. Rikke would say she was a melancholic, but that wasn't true: she never remained in a mood long enough to warrant any particular description. All the same, she had a clear image of her own death. She goes out to the cabin. The only place in Norway she misses. Out in the forest, close to Morr Water. It's winter. The snow is quite dry; it crackles under her boots. She passes the rock where they used to dive in the summer. Carries on round the bank of the frozen winter water. Turns away, heading down towards the moor. Finds the place where she is to lie down. The sky between the treetops is clear and dark like coloured glass as she lets go and drifts slowly down into the embracing cold . . . The thought comforted her when she needed it. She had made arrangements with herself about how the end would be. Felt a faint pang of grief at the thought of it. That was where her strength came from.

At Saloon, she dismounted, leaned the bike up against the wall and sat at the table closest to the canal. Several of the letters in the café sign had gone out since the last time she had been there.

Tobi appeared, carrying an empty tray. He bent and allowed himself to be kissed once on each cheek.

– Time for a coffee, he announced.

She could have used a drink, something to bring her down, but she ordered a double espresso and took out her mobile and a packet of Marlboros.

– Saw you on a poster at Nieuwe Zijde, he winked. – Gorgeous.

Rikke arrived in a taxi.

– Can't sit out here, she shivered. – I'm no fairy snow queen like you.

They found a table inside.

– He doesn't want me to see you, Rikke confided.

Liss raised her eyebrows. – And what are you going to do about that?

Rikke pulled a menu over. – No way I'm letting myself be controlled like that. There are limits.

– Have you been doing his escort stuff?

Rikke's mobile gave off a long-drawn-out sigh, downloaded from a site offering tropical animal noises. She read the message and punched in an answer.

– Tried it at the weekend, she said once she was finished. – Arranged a party for these fantastically wealthy businessmen. Quite okay if it hadn't been for the Russians.

Liss lit up a cigarette and clouded the space between them with smoke.

– Do they expect you to have sex with them?

Rikke thought about it. – No one makes you.

Liss leaned across to her. – I've known Zako over a year, she said. – First off he tried to persuade me it was about love and relationships and all that. Nothing was too much trouble for him. It took a while for me to realise what his real game is.

– You're exaggerating, said Rikke. – He lets you have the choice.

Liss laughed mirthlessly. – As long as it's the same as his.

– You're saying that because you're angry with him.

– Get a grip, Rikke. He's got you where he wants you. Soon you won't be able to break out any more. Do you owe him money?

– Not a lot.

– More than a thousand?

Rikke looked round. – Less than ten. I think.

– Christ, you're so naïve, Liss sighed.

Rikke twisted the remains of her cigarette in the bottom of the ashtray. The sound was like footsteps through wet snow.

– He still talks about you, she said. – Wants you back. Seems completely obsessed.

Two things were obvious to Liss. One was that Rikke was there on behalf of Zako. The other was that every bloody word would be reported back to him. That was why she replied: – I'm sure you're right about that. Types like Zako get like rabid dogs when someone denies them something they think is rightfully theirs. I had to tell him that I don't give a shit about his whole act.

Without hesitation she added: – That's the only language he understands.

3

IT WAS COLD in the studio. She'd mentioned it as soon as she arrived, but Wim said it was supposed to be like that. So that her nipples would be stiff under the soft material of the bra. He was well wrapped up in a padded combat jacket.

Liss crossed her legs and leant in towards the camera.

– Not like that, Wim groaned. – It looks like you need a piss.

– That's exactly what I need, she answered without changing her expression.

– Hold that. Right there, the hip out to the side. Let the bra strap slip down your shoulder . . . *shit*, that's it . . . nearly.

Her trousers were tossed away over by the wall, but for the third time since arriving she heard the phone vibrating in her pocket. Wim had insisted she turn off the ringtone before they started. A *real* artist, she thought meanly.

– Hello, Wim yelled. – Planet earth calling Miss Liss. You look totally vacant. Get that hip out to the side, let's see the elastic of your knickers. Yes, that's exactly what I told you, not your hip bone, the edge of your knickers, that's what I want, come over here, yes, arms by your sides, follow me, imagine you're going to stamp on me, like that, yes. Piss, you said; imagine you're trampling on me and pissing on me, yes, there's the look I've been waiting for all day. Follow me now, hate me, imagine you've got me on the ground, do what you want with me.

She shuddered at the thought of having Wim lying on the floor beneath her. Of him wriggling out of his leather trousers and lying there with his dick in the air. And she was supposed to try to look as if this was an image that would make her feel horny. The only thing she felt was how badly she needed a piss.

– I really just have to have one minute on the toilet, she said, and straightened up.

– Can't you hold on? You must have a bladder the size of a mouse's.

He sniggered; he liked to talk about her body, mostly what was inside it. But he was the best she'd worked with. And he wouldn't start groping her. Even if she never met Zako again, Wim knew he'd get his liver punched up into his throat if he ever tried it on.

She grabbed her jeans, slipped into the toilet and groaned with relief when she was able to open up and let it flow freely. At least three litres.

Afterwards she took the phone out of her pocket. She was startled when it vibrated again, like a little animal that woke at her touch. For the third time that day the unknown number showed up in her display. It started with the Norwegian prefix: 0047. She gave in and answered.

– Liss? This is Viljam.

– Viljam? she said, almost dismissively, even though she knew who he was.

– I've never met you, he explained. – But I'm sure Mailin has talked about us.

Of course Mailin had talked about him. They'd been a couple for more than two years. Liss had heard his name mentioned many times but had never taken the trouble to remember it. For some reason or other she didn't like the thought of her sister living with someone.

– Are you in Amsterdam?

He was well spoken. Liss knew he'd studied law and was about the same age as her.

– Why do you ask? She didn't want to continue the conversation, but understood there had to be a reason why the guy was calling. Why he'd called three times. The first time at six in the morning. Suddenly she felt a damp chill across her whole body. She looked in the mirror; her pupils were distended. You are not afraid, she thought. You are never afraid, Liss Bjerke.

– Did you call early this morning? Is it about Mailin?

Viljam didn't answer at first, and that cold chill fastened itself tighter around her. She slumped down on to the toilet seat. She'd had a message from her sister the previous afternoon, one she didn't understand, or didn't want to understand. She had deliberately not called back.

– I don't know, he said finally. – She talked about getting in touch with you yesterday. There was something she wanted to ask about.

– What do you mean?

Liss could hear the anger in her voice. She started to shiver. She didn't want to hear what was about to be said. Anything else she could stand. Just not this.

– She hasn't come home, he said. He was still hesitant. – She's been gone since yesterday evening.

So she's probably broken up with you, Liss might have said, but Mailin wasn't like that. Liss could do it, suddenly do a runner if she got fed up with someone, and say nothing. But not Mailin.

– We didn't quarrel, Viljam said, perhaps guessing the direction of her thoughts. She could hear that he was struggling to keep his voice calm. – We've been getting on better than ever.

Liss clicked to the message from her sister the day before. *On my way from the cabin. Always think of you when I'm out there.* And then, rather cryptically: *Keep Midsummer's Day free next year. Call you tomorrow.*

– She was out at the cabin, she said. – She may well have gone back out there.

Liss could see her sister sitting on the cabin steps and looking down towards Morr Water. It was their place, they owned it jointly. Their father had wanted the two of them to have it, and no one else. It was all they had to remind them of him.

– We went out there and looked for her, Viljam answered. – She wasn't there. She was supposed to be on a TV programme yesterday but never showed up, and no one's seen her . . .

Zako is a shit; it flashed through Liss. He can't have done something like this. I'll kill him.

– What can I do? she managed to say. – I'm over a thousand miles away.

She fumbled at the keys to cut off the call; she had to find somewhere she could be on her own.

At the other end, her sister's partner was breathing heavily. – We called the police last night. They asked me to come in and make a statement. I wanted to talk to you first. Find out if she called you. She said she was going to.

The light in the tiny space around Liss changed, began to force its way into things, the mirror, the basin, pulling away from her. – If Mailin disappears, then I disappear too, she murmured.

Wim was using his mobile when she returned. He pointed to a spot below the skylight where he obviously wanted her to pose. She remained standing outside the toilet door, fiddling with her own phone. No calls from Mailin. Just three from her mother she hadn't answered. She slid down the wall, the rough surface scraping her naked back. Sat there chewing on a cigarette. There were two messages from her mother. She called voicemail. The first: *Hi, Liss, it's Mum. It's Thursday evening, twenty-three forty-three. Can you ring me as soon as you get this message. It's important.* To the point, as always. But the voice sounded frail. Liss could hardly face listening to the next message, but she had to. It was from this morning. *Liss, it's Mum again. You must call me. It's about Mailin.*

She had bitten straight through the filter. Wim was standing over her, talking. Something about time passing, something about a meter; he wasn't cheap, and here she sat helping herself to his time as though he was a nigger eunuch. She got dressed and muttered something about an accident. Obviously he believed her, because suddenly he stopped talking and contented himself with a shake of the head.

– Tomorrow you be here clean and focused, he called after her as she disappeared out the door.

The December day was filled to the brim with a cold damp that gusted along Lijnbaansgracht and froze around her, layer upon layer of floating ice. The roads were slippery, but she cycled alongside the canal as fast as she could. A woman wearing a coat and a broad-brimmed hat who stood smoking by the railing of one of the houseboats turned and waved as she rode by. She pedalled harder. Two old men were fishing from a canal bridge. One was wearing a flat hat; he spat in the water. Suddenly she stopped. Leaned the cycle up against the railings and pulled out her phone.

– It's me. Liss.

A sound at the other end. At first she didn't understand what it was.

Her mother was crying. Liss had never heard her crying before. She could disconnect now. Knew all she needed to know. That something had happened to Mailin. That something had changed, that things would never be the same again. And deep down, inside all the haziness she didn't dare to touch, something like relief.

– How long has she been missing? she heard herself ask.

From the disjointed answer she gathered that it was almost

twenty-four hours. That fitted with what Mailin's partner had said.

– What are we going to do, Liss?

Her mother never asked questions like that. At least she never asked her. She was the one who answered them. Told people what was to be done. Always clear headed. Always a step ahead, prepared down to the last detail. Now here she was not even able to speak properly, just repeating the same words over and over again, *what are we going to do? what are we going to do?*

– I'll call you later, Liss said, and ended the conversation. It hadn't been a conversation, but a hole opening up in broad daylight.

She came back to her senses at the sound of a car horn tooting. She cycled along Marnixstraat, the traffic denser now. It was colder; her breath billowed out in a frosty cloud in front of her. She dived into it, out again.

Passing a Jamin shop, she stopped and went in. Avoid speaking to anyone, just get what she needed. No thoughts, following a pattern she had worked out but not used for a while. Bought ice cream. A litre and a half. Pure vanilla. No bits of nut or chocolate. Grabbed a Pepsi Max and a plastic spoon. It was getting dark. She'd been riding round. Been to Vondelpark. Didn't know what had become of the day. Knew only that it was the end of something. And the start of something else. She bowled along Marnixkade with the Pepsi and the ice cream in a bag. Suddenly she found herself by the flat she had shared with Rikke. An obscure notion to go up and see her, get her to find Zako and trick him into saying what had happened. Find out if he knew anything about Mailin going missing. But Rikke wouldn't be able to manage a job like that.

She passed the asphalt playground where some boys were playing basketball in the dark. They shouted out to her. How about a ride, then? She carried on out to the point, to the little park with the bench, sank down beneath the pale light of the lamp. She'd sat there many times before. The bench was coated with a layer of ice. The cold seeped up from the ground and into her back. It helped, to be freezing. The frost slowed down her thoughts. She could focus on the metallic jangling that reached her ears every time a car rattled across the joint on the bridge on the far side of the canal. She could let her gaze follow the distant trains that passed on their way to and from Centraal Station.

The picture came again. Mailin in the pale blue pyjamas. She turns and locks the door. Creeping into bed, putting her arms around her. There's a sound too, it's part of the picture. Footsteps stopping outside. The latch on the door moving. Knocking that gets louder and louder, becomes beating, and Mailin holding her close and tight. *Nothing bad will ever, ever happen to you, Liss.*

Abruptly she pulled the box out of the bag, broke open the lid. The ice cream was so hard the spoon snapped. She hacked away at it with the handle, gobbled down the pieces that she worked loose. The cold spread to her stomach too. She got out her lighter and moved it back and forth under the base. Soon she was able to dig out larger chunks of the vanilla-sweet mass. Hungry even as she was eating. It only took a few minutes to get the whole lot down. She squeezed the sides of the empty carton and squashed it into a rubbish bin on the other side of the gravel path. Ducked into the bushes and emptied herself. The taste of vanilla as it ran out of her was still just as strong. She couldn't vacate herself completely; the remains of something were still down in her stomach somewhere, something she was unable to get up. She rested a while with her forehead against a tree. Maybe it was an oak; the bark was full of sharp ridges she could press herself against.

Her thoughts no longer whirled around in disarray. They began to gather. Separable, one from the next. Mailin gone.

Find Mailin, before it's too late. Zako got someone to take that photo of her . . . Liss stood up again. Knew what she had to do. She was still freezing. The cold streaming from her stomach kept her thinking calm. She cycled back along Lijnbaansgracht. It had to be past midnight. Houseboat windows all in darkness. A few swans drifting on the black canal.

Dark in his kitchen window too, the one facing Bloemstraat. She could ring him, or send a text message. Decided to wait. Positioned herself in a doorway on the other side. Even colder now. She needed this cold. The thought of Mailin being missing kept slipping away from her. Only the imprint of it remained. Her mother's voice breaking up. She, Liss, was the one who should have gone missing. Anything could happen to her. The ground beneath her feet was always on the point of giving way. She lived in places where people disappeared. They ran off, or they gave up. If someone had called Mother and told her that her daughter Liss had disappeared it would have grieved her, but the grief would not have been unexpected. She was already half mourned. If something happened to Mailin, it would tear her apart.

An hour, perhaps more, had passed when she heard a motorcycle turn up from the bridge at Prinsengracht. A few seconds later he pulled up outside the entrance. He was alone. She resisted the impulse to race across the street and grab hold of his jacket. Waited till he'd gone in. Waited till the kitchen light went on. Waited a while longer, and then called him.

– What do you want? he asked, not even offering a greeting.

– Was just in the neighbourhood. On my way home. Thought I'd call in.

Zako grunted and ended the call. Two and a half minutes later, she rang the bell. He let her in. The fourth-floor door was ajar. The hallway smelt as though it had been freshly washed. He always got girls to come and clean up for him and never paid them a cent.

She stopped in the middle of the room. He was sitting on the sofa with a can of Amstel in his hand, looked up from the screen where a bunch of footballers were running round yelling at each other. Without waiting to be asked, she sat down. He didn't bother asking what she was doing in his place. Had obviously taken it for granted that she would show up again.

– I've come here because there's something I need you to tell me. Two weeks ago you showed me that picture, at the Café Alto. Of my sister.

He leaned back in the sofa, put his feet on the table. Finally he turned his gaze to her. The small lips twitched, as though suppressing a smile.

– Your sister, he repeated up into the air.

She might have run out to the kitchen, grabbed a breadknife, held it to his throat, threatened it out of him. She forced herself back to her calmness, the calmness that came from the cold still occupying her empty stomach. Don't let him get the upper hand now. If Zako gets the upper hand, he'll never let you go again.

– Have you . . . any more pictures of her?

– Sure have, he grinned.

– Who took them?

He whistled between his teeth.

– You don't want to know that, Liss. You want to know as little as possible.

– You're bluffing me, Zako. You've always been like that. Want people to believe you know everything.

He jerked slightly. – I can hear you haven't had it for a while. Is that why you're here?

– Could be. She acted as though she was thinking it over. – But first you've got to tell me about those pictures.

He sat up and dug a packet out of his jacket pocket. – A line each. And we'll make things good again.

She forced a smile. A line and a fuck. How simple the world

could be. She took off her jacket and pullover. Let the skirt drop, stood there in black tights and a thin blouse, knew he liked to see her like that.

– You're as stubborn as a goat, he growled.

– Didn't know you had anything against goats.

Now he laughed.

– Who took that picture? she tried again.

– Someone I know. He sprinkled the white power on to the glass table. – Someone who owed me a favour.

– Does he live in Oslo?

He made three lines with a Visa card. – Nope.

A word he usually used when he was lying.

– Why do you send people to Oslo to take pictures of my sister?

He glanced up at her. – Is this an interrogation?

– I don't believe you, Mr Bluff.

He took a note from his cardholder, rolled it into a cylinder. – It's up to you what you believe.

– Give me some proof that you got someone to take those pictures and I'll never doubt you again.

He looked at her for a long time. She could have screamed it out now, that Mailin had gone missing, that he had to tell her what he knew, otherwise she'd report him. Instead she closed her eyes, shook her head, acting exasperated.

– You always have these big plans, Zako. Why should I believe you'll ever amount to anything?

He stood up suddenly, took out his phone. Punched a key and held it up for her.

– The pictures were sent to me from Oslo. Understand? I mean what I say.

Liss turned towards the window, bit her lip. I know him well, she told herself again. He could go to great lengths to make her feel insecure. But abduct Mailin? . . . What did she actually know about him? Did she in fact understand

anything of what went on around her? Had she ever understood anything of this world she was living in? This picture:
go out into the forest, it's night, lie down in the snow, look
up at the sky between the tops of the fir trees, glide into the
grey-black, give up and sleep for ever.

– Why did you do it? she asked without turning round.

She heard Zako put his beer bottle down on the glass table.
– You need me, Liss, he said, almost friendly. – Fuck, think
what we could do together, the two of us.

He snorted. Twice.

– The third one is yours.

She sat down beside him. Picked up the note and breathed
in, saw how the last grains got sucked in, felt the burning high
up in her nostrils. Clear your thoughts, she told herself. Stay
calm a little longer.

Zako took hold of her hand and pushed it down towards
his flies. She could feel the movement beneath the smooth
material of the trousers. Like pastry swelling, she thought.

– I need to go to the toilet.

– Be quick, he growled. – And bring me an Amstel from
the fridge.

She dried herself and flushed, let the cold tap run, put both
hands there and held them under. – Liss, she murmured to
herself. It sounded sad. Same sound as in *missing*. Occasionally
the kids at school would call after her: *Liss, Liss, piss, piss*.

She opened the cupboard above the basin. In an envelope she
found dozens of small light blue pills. She tore off a sheet of
toilet paper, wrapped six of them inside, picked up the tumbler
with the toothbrush and toothpaste in and pressed the base of
it against the pills, ground them into a fine powder against the
basin, packed it inside the paper. In the kitchen she took a beer
and opened it. Emptied the powder into it, cleaned off the grains
that clung to the neck of the bottle. Shook it carefully.

– What's keeping you?

She slipped back into the living room, put the bottle down on the table in front of him.

– This game is shit. He scowled at the screen.

– Feel like one too, she said and fetched another Amstel from the kitchen, sat down close to him. He opened his flies and showed her what he had to offer.

– Cheers, she said, and pressed the ice-cold bottle against the strutting penis.

– Think doing that'll make it collapse, he grinned as he picked up his own bottle and half emptied it in one swig. Within a few minutes his head began to droop. He pulled at the top of her tights, tried to get them down past her thighs.

– Let me help you, she said and slowly peeled them off. Then she unbuttoned her blouse. Stood in front of him wearing nothing but her G-string. He lifted his arm to take it off.

– What's going on? he mumbled, and had to give up, sank back down into the sofa, eyes closed.

She picked up his phone, unlocked it, navigated to the photos of Mailin. In the first one she was on her way out of a gate. There was someone with her, a guy she presumed was Viljam. He was tall and well built, fair haired and with slightly slanted eyes. Then a series of eleven other pictures, including the one Zako had shown her at the Café Alto. The same fair-haired guy was in a couple of these two. The photos had been sent from a number that began with 0047. Funny that Zako didn't delete the message, she thought. If he really had put someone on Mailin's trail, he probably wouldn't leave their number on his phone. Zako was a shit, but he wasn't an idiot. She noted the number down on a newspaper lying on the table, ripped off the strip, put it in her jacket pocket, pulled it out again, wrote down the date the message was sent. Quickly searched the drawers in his desk. In the bottom one she found what she was looking for: the photo of Mailin. She stuffed this into her jacket pocket too, didn't find any more that had been printed out.

She pulled her clothes on as fast as she could. Zako was lying with his head against the arm of the sofa. She grabbed him under the arms and pulled him into a position that looked a bit safer. She took the almost empty bottle out to the kitchen, poured away the remains and rinsed it thoroughly. No need for him to wake up and find out what had happened. She rinsed her own out too and then dried it. Why? she asked herself without bothering to look for an answer.

Zako was still slumped like a sack on the sofa, snoring. Before leaving, she lifted his head backwards, put his tackle back inside his trousers and zipped up his flies.

Back in the flat in Haarlemmerdijk. Still high. It would soon pass. She had some coke in an envelope in her bedside table. Take it now, hang on to this feeling of being invulnerable, make it last. She was alone. It was night. Silent in the street below. Mailin was missing. You must come down, Liss.

She sat down at her computer. Googled the Norwegian telephone directory and ran a search for the number she'd noted down on the strip of newspaper. *Judith van Ravens* was the name that came up. An address in Ekeberg Way in Oslo. It was now 2.30. She decided not to call until morning. Pulled her clothes off in two movements, dropped them to the floor and curled up in the bed.

She's at the cabin. Mailin is there too. They walk down to the water. It's summer; they've both got bathing towels with them. Liss runs up on to the rock she usually dives off. The water's very deep there. As she's about to dive in, she notices the water is covered in ice.

She woke up cold. A grey, muted light crept in through the window facing the back yard. She picked up her phone. Had slept for twelve hours. Sat upright with a jerk. Thirsty. Staggered out to the bathroom, put her mouth under the tap, took a long drink. Sank down on to the toilet, let it all run out again. Sat there looking at her face in the mirror. – Mailin, she murmured. *I'll look after you, Liss.*

Afterwards, she rang Viljam. Certain for a moment that everything was as it should be, that her sister had come back.

She had not come back.

– She's been missing for almost forty-eight hours.

– What is everyone doing? Liss wailed. – The police?

– They've put out a missing persons report. They've been here a couple of times. And I've been down to talk to the crime response unit. They keep on and on asking if we had a quarrel and all that kind of stuff. If she was depressed and had talked about killing herself.

– Mailin kill herself?

– None of us believe anything like that.

– But somebody has to do something!

– It doesn't look as if they have any leads to go on. Tage and I went to the cabin at Morr Water. The police have been out there too. That's all I know.

Liss stood looking down on Haarlemmerdijk. The café owner on the other side was hanging a Christmas decoration above the entrance. – Someone has to do something, she repeated. Said it aloud. Stood there without moving. Remembered just then about the telephone number.

She reached an answering service, a woman's voice speaking in Dutch and then English: *This is Judith van Raven's telephone, please leave a message . . .*

She showered. Dressed. Put on her make-up. Everything she normally did. Ran down the stairs and let herself out, cut across the street and into the café. From the top of a rickety stepladder the owner beamed at her. He looked to be somewhere in his fifties, with a pink dome framed by a pretzel-shaped rim of grey curls. The steps were up on a table, and a ghostly blonde wearing black was holding them while he hung gold and silver balls from the ceiling. There was music coming from behind the bar. *It's gonna be a cold, cold Christmas.*

She ordered a double espresso and sat by the window. By the time it was finished, she had made up her mind. Ring Zako. Meet him one last time. Ask him straight out if he knew that Mailin was missing. She'd be able to tell if he was lying to her.

She called his number. It rang four times, five times. A deep male voice answered.

– Is Zako there?

– Who's calling? the voice asked.

She hesitated before saying: – A friend.

– A friend? What is your business with him?

– I asked to speak to Zako, she exclaimed. – Is he there?

– Zako is dead.

She almost dropped her phone. – Don't mess me about. Who the hell are you?

– Detective Inspector Wouters. Will you please answer the question I asked you?

She couldn't remember what he had asked her. Out in Haarlemmerdijk the lights were being turned on. The six-pointed star with the red heart inside. A cyclist went by. A man with a child on a seat in front of him.

The voice on the phone: – When was the last time you saw Zako?

From very far away she heard her own answer: – A few days ago. Maybe a week.

There were more questions. About her relationship to him. About the drugs he used. If they had taken drugs together. She had to provide her full name and address. Tell him what she did in Amsterdam.

– We may need you to come in for a further talk with us.

– Of course, she muttered. – I'll come in.

Afterwards she sat and stared at her phone. The skin around her mouth prickled. The sensation spread up into her cheeks.

The proprietor of the café had hung up all his balls and surrounded them with green garlands. He tottered down the rickety stepladder, gave her a smile. – There now. Now Christmas can come.

From the bar came the sound of John Lennon's voice: *War is over, if you want it*. She felt her nose running. Fumbled out a handkerchief. When she took it away, it was full of blood. She pressed it to her nose again, hurried to the toilet.

– Everything all right? the proprietor asked as she passed him.

She locked the door. Held the handkerchief under the ice-cold water, used it to press her nostrils together. The diluted blood ran down over her chin and dripped on to the white porcelain.

Back at her table, she called Rikke. Rikke answered, but couldn't get a word out.

– It's not true, is it? Liss wailed. – Please tell me it isn't true.

Rikke ended the call.

A few minutes later she called back.

– They found him this morning . . . two of his cousins . . . On the sofa . . . choked on his own vomit.

Then she was gone again. Liss pushed a note under her coffee cup and struggled out into the street.

The picture appeared again as she hurried along through the streets of Jordaan: disappear into the forest, down to the spot by the marsh, between the pines, a place only she, not even Mailin, knew about. For as long as she could remember she had thought of it as *the last place*, and it always used to calm her down to think of it. Nothing could calm her down now.

At Haarlemmerplein she hailed a taxi. Huddled up in the back seat. The driver was shaven headed and wearing a grey suit, reeked of a type of aftershave Zako sometimes used. She grabbed the door handle to get out again.

– Where does the young lady want taking to?

She slumped back. Thought she'd told him where she was going.

– Schiphol, she murmured, and pulled the thin leather jacket around herself.

The taxi driver turned again, winked at her in the mirror.

– Travelling light, he observed as he offered her a cigarette.

As I WRITE *this, I think of all the things I would have said to you, dear Liss, if only you had let me tell you. Everything that happened that spring. And how I got through that summer, how I found myself on Crete in the autumn, under a different sun, but with the same black light shining inside me. Among people gorging themselves, drinking, coupling. They argued and vomited and left the kids to look after themselves. That's where I got to know Jo. In the evening I sat and read on the terrace outside the restaurant, the same poem over and over again, by the light of a candle. It's about the end time, I think, or at least it felt to me as though it was about my end time; roaming through a waste land, no water, no meaning, blindness, emptiness, death. What are you reading? Jo asked when he came up to me. He was suspicious, as he no doubt was of everyone he met; what he needed more than anyone else was someone he could trust. I told him about the poem, recited the section called 'Death by Water', told him about the image of the dead Phoenician at the bottom of the sea.*

Jo was twelve years old and left completely on his own. He knew what I felt like.

PART II

PART II

1

As THE PLANE began its descent and the captain announced that they were approaching Oslo airport, Liss woke in the midst of an avalanche of thoughts. Two of them remained with her. *Mailin is missing. I must find Mailin.*

Sunday afternoon. Just after four. She'd spent the night on a bench at Schiphol, hadn't managed to find a seat on a plane until morning. Almost twenty-four hours had passed since she'd sat in the café in Haarlemmerdijk. Wouters was the name of the policeman who'd answered when she called Zako's number. Could one ever forget such a name? *It isn't true that I last saw Zako a week ago. I was there that night. Just before he died . . .* Enclose those thoughts in a room. Lock it. The name *Wouters* on a sign on the door. Not to be opened. Will it ever be possible to forget that there is something inside that room? Start with the name, Wouters, forget the policeman's name. Forget his voice, and what he told her. Then it might also be possible to forget where she was on Saturday night. *I must find Mailin. I don't care a damn about anything else.*

The woman sitting next to her had finished reading *VG*. She handed it to Liss, even though Liss hadn't asked for it.

She flipped through without reading. A few pages in, she stopped and just stared at the headline above a big story: *Missing woman (29) due to appear on* Taboo. It was about Mailin. Her partner had mentioned this TV programme. *VG* called it 'a scandal show'. A talk show hosted by Berger, she read, a name she associated with obsolete rock music. Now he was attracting huge audiences with this series on the subject of taboos. Yesterday's show was apparently about sexuality. It had caught fire when Berger defended the idea that child sex might be okay. Liss struggled to put this into context. What could Mailin, always so careful about the views she sponsored, be doing on a TV show with someone like that? *The 29-year-old psychologist never turned up at Channel Six's studio in Nydalen. She had not been heard from since earlier that evening. Several times in the course of the show Berger claimed that she must have got cold feet. He now refuses to make any further comment.*

The woman beside her sat with eyes closed and held on tightly to the armrests. Liss wedged the paper down into her seat pocket, pressed her head against the window. The layer of cloud beneath them was thinning out. She could just see the fjord below and the fortress at the top of it. Leaving four years earlier, she had thought she would never be back.

What's to become of you, Liss?

She had told the taxi driver Ekeberg Way, but not the number. As they got close, she asked him to stop. Paid with her credit card and got out.

Up here on the hilltop above Oslo, it was biting cold. Liss was dressed for a mild day in Amsterdam; she'd fled to the airport without even thinking about going home and packing some clothes. The temperature on the dashboard read minus twelve. She buttoned the thin leather jacket all the way up to the neck, not that it helped, tried to stuff her hands down into the tiny pockets.

She found the number, a large, bright yellow functionalist villa. The name on the letter box was right. The driveway was paved in red flagstones, so slippery that she had to tiptoe up with tiny steps, like an old woman. She rang the doorbell. Rang again, a bit too quickly because already she could hear sounds inside. A woman put her head out. Dark hair, bunched at the neck, nicely made up. She might be in her mid-thirties, some ten years older than Liss.

– Judith van Ravens?

The woman gave a little smile in response, as if she'd been sitting in the house waiting for a floral delivery. Liss noticed that she had a bundle in her arm, something wrapped in a crocheted blanket.

– I must talk to you, she continued in Dutch, pointing to the hallway.

A hostile look showed in the woman's eyes. – What's this about?

Liss struggled to control herself. She was freezing from her toes and up through her back to the roots of her hair. She hadn't slept in over twenty-four hours. She had killed someone. All she could hold on to were the two thoughts: *Mailin is missing. I must find Mailin.*

– Let me come inside for a moment and I'll explain.

The woman shook her head firmly and tucked at the bundle she was holding next to her body. She was on the point of closing the door. Liss put her foot across the threshold. She pulled the photo of her sister from her bag and held it up in front of the woman's face. The woman blinked in confusion and released her hold on the door. Liss shoved it open and pushed her way past her and inside.

The large room seemed almost empty. A suite of chairs that might have come from IKEA, a dining table in one corner, a large, pallid painting on the biggest wall.

– We're only living here temporarily, the woman excused herself. – My husband is working for Statoil. He spends most of the time in Stavanger, but I couldn't live there.

Her uncertainty evidently made her talkative. Unless this

information about Statoil was offered up as a way of showing the intruder the powers that stood behind her. She held the bundle up to her shoulder. There was a pushchair bag on the sofa; perhaps she didn't dare lay the sleeping child down.

Liss remained standing in the middle of the room. The woman didn't offer her a seat.

– What is this about the photo?

– You took it, Liss stated, as calmly as she could.

– Did I?

– It was sent from your phone to a recipient in Amsterdam.

The woman drew a breath, and Liss readied herself. At any moment some great brute of a husband might turn up and throw her out. Maybe they'd call the police. But she was determined to stay put until she found out why these pictures of Mailin had been taken. A sudden vision of grabbing that bundled baby, threatening to beat its dark little head against the wall unless the woman told her what she knew.

It was as though this threat from some dark and closed place deep down inside her materialised itself, moved through the room and touched something in Judith van Ravens. She picked up the pushchair bag and headed for the door.

– Just going to put her down. Be right back.

Liss imagined her ringing her husband, if he wasn't at home, or the neighbours, or the emergency number. It didn't bother her at all. She knew she had come to the right house.

A few moments later, Judith van Ravens was back again.

– You're right, she blurted out before Liss had a chance to say anything. – I did take that picture, but I don't see why that gives you any reason at all to come barging in here. My daughter needs changing and feeding very soon, I've got hundreds of things to do, I'm expecting guests . . .

– The woman you took that picture of has gone missing.

Judith van Ravens stared at her. – What do you mean?

Liss took out the *VG* she had pocketed on the way out of

the plane, opened it to the page and spread it on the table. Judith van Ravens read, looked at her, read again.

– How do you know that . . .?

– My sister, Liss answered dully. – It's my sister that's gone missing. And before I leave here, you're going to tell me everything about these pictures. After that I'm going to the police.

– The police? Is that necessary?

– That's for me to decide, Liss said firmly.

Judith van Ravens stood over by the window. – I haven't done anything wrong, she said, suddenly sounding like a child who's been dragged in to see the headmaster. – It's just that I don't want my husband to know anything about this.

She glanced across at Liss. – It's true. I sent some pictures of that woman to Amsterdam, to someone I know.

– Zako.

– You know who he is?

Liss shrugged her shoulders. – Why did you do it?

Judith van Ravens rubbed her hands along her cheeks, pulling her entire face backwards.

– I've . . . known Zako some years. We're friends.

Liss almost interrupted, but stopped herself. *Zako doesn't have women* friends, she was going to say, and at the same instant saw him in her mind's eye, lying on the sofa with vomit round his mouth. She could hear the voice of the policeman named Wouters, the one who was waiting for her to come and tell him what had happened that night.

– Sometimes we speak on the phone, Judith van Ravens continued, – and sometimes when I'm in Amsterdam we meet.

She was slender, a little below medium height, round hips and breasts not too big, even though she was probably breastfeeding. Not a typical Zako woman, Liss thought.

– And your husband's not supposed to know about this, she noted with a touch of contempt.

– Actually nothing happens when Zako and I meet, Judith

van Ravens assured her. – Not much, anyway, she corrected herself, – but my husband doesn't have to know everything I do. He's the suspicious type.

– What about the photo?

Judith van Ravens again stroked her cheeks, the movement continuing on up through her lustrous hair. – Zako called a few weeks ago. Asked for a favour. He wanted to surprise someone he knew, just for fun. I suppose that was probably you?

– Keep going.

– I was to take some pictures of a woman without her knowing it. I was given the name and address of an office. Waited outside in the car until she showed up. Followed her to a tram stop. She was with a man . . . It was a joke!

– When was this?

Judith van Ravens looked to be thinking about it. – Maybe three weeks ago. The end of last month. We flew to Houston the week after.

Three weeks fitted with the date Liss had noted in Zako's flat.

– How long were you in the USA?

– We came back on Friday evening. I'm still a bit jet-lagged. Judith van Ravens closed her eyes. – I owed him a favour. The disappearance of this woman, your sister, can't have anything at all to do with those pictures. Zako and I went to the film academy together. He's strange, and he gets up to some weird things, but he isn't involved in kidnapping or anything like that.

– Zako is dead.

The woman at the window stiffened. The colour drained from the already pale cheeks.

– It was an accident, Liss went on. It felt comforting, saying it like that. Something she might end up believing herself, if she repeated it often enough.

– How . . . ?

Liss sat in one of the chairs by the coffee table.

– Overdose. A mixture of things. He fell asleep, vomited and choked.

Judith van Ravens slumped down into the sofa. – That's not possible. Zako isn't like that. He always has control.

Liss didn't respond. For a few moments they sat in silence. In another room, a mobile phone began to ring. Judith van Ravens didn't react. Sat hunched forward, legs crossed, staring at the tabletop. Suddenly she said:

– We have to go to the police. It'll be a nightmare for me, but we have to.

– Why?

She didn't raise her eyes. – It can't be coincidental, this business with the pictures. If Zako has got himself mixed up in something or other, and someone has made this look like an accident . . .

Liss interrupted: – I'm sure you were right when you said it was only meant as a joke.

Judith van Ravens looked up. – Are you?

Liss nodded firmly. – Having spoken to you, it figures.

– Did you two . . . have a relationship?

Liss ignored the question. – It's like you say. Zako wanted to surprise me. He didn't mean any harm. It's just a coincidence that my sister went missing directly after you took those pictures.

A moment's relief: regardless of what had happened to Mailin, it wasn't because of anything she, Liss, had done. It lasted for a few seconds, and then the doubt returned.

– Do you still have those pictures?

Judith van Ravens stood up, went into the next room, came back with a mobile phone.

– I didn't delete them, she said, and showed Liss the screen. – Had forgotten all about the whole business.

94 TORKIL DAMHAUG

Just then the baby began screaming in the next room.

– So you don't think there's any need for me to go to the police?

Liss waited a few seconds before answering. – As far as I know, no one believes Zako's death was anything but accidental.

2

SHE NEEDED TO walk. Followed Kongs Way down towards town. It had snowed quite a lot, and the pavements hadn't been cleared. Her thin boots were stiff with cold, and she slipped on icy bumps. Her phone began to ring. She thought of the detective inspector, Wouters. *Sooner or later they're going to find out, Liss. That someone else was there that night. That it was a woman in her mid-twenties, above average height, much too thin, with long reddish hair. No need to send out an alert. Anyone who knew Zako could point her out . . .*

It was Rikke who'd called. Shortly afterwards, a text: *Where are you? Have to talk to you.*

It took almost an hour to reach Harald Hardrådes Square. She popped into a kiosk, bought a pack of Marlboros and a bottle of water, lit up the moment she was outside. Further up on Schweigaards Street was the commune where she'd been living just before she left. It probably still existed. Others would have moved in. Catrine still sent her messages at intervals; she'd even been out to Amsterdam to visit a couple of times. Maybe the closest thing to a best friend Liss had had.

She got her phone out to call her. At the moment Catrine was living in student accommodation. She'd also stopped throwing stones and bottles at walls of policemen with helmets and shields. Two years ago she'd started studying political science at Blindern and claimed to have found a better way to display her opposition. For Liss, it hadn't been enough to move to the other side of town. She'd had to get far away.

When her call wasn't picked up at once, she put the phone back in her bag, carried on towards Grønlandsleiret, and down to the church. There she stopped. Turned and looked up at the concrete block of the Oslo police headquarters. At the back were the security cells where she'd spent quite a few hours. No feeling worse than the sound of the door closing behind you. Being shut in. No knowing how long for . . . To the right of the station, the driveway leading up to the prison. What was the sentence for murder? Manslaughter, if they chose to believe her? She would be extradited to appear in court in Holland. Were the sentences longer there? Five years? Ten or fifteen? She might be over forty by the time she got out again . . . Locked up. Not for a few hours or a night, but for months, years. The only thing that scared her. Not to be able to go out the door when she felt she needed to. Pacing restlessly around in a tiny locked room. Shaking the bars, scratching at the walls. Waiting for the steps in the corridor, the rattling of keys. The appointed hour for exercise. Knowing that this is what it will be like until you're old. This isn't about you, Liss, she tried to tell herself. All that matters is to find Mailin. Nothing else is important.

She trudged up to the entrance to the police headquarters. What would you have said, Mailin? She tried to conjure up her sister's voice. *No one can make your choices for you, Liss.* That wasn't much help. She tried again. *I don't want you to get hurt, Liss. There is nothing in the world I care about more than you.*

She pulled at the heavy door. Didn't budge. It's a sign, she thought, they won't let you in. But the one beside it slid open and she stepped into the large hallway.

A girl about her own age in a Securitas uniform in the security booth. Two thin, pale braids hanging over the collar of her shirt. She looked as if she'd learnt to put make-up on in a children's theatre.

– Can I help you? she said sullenly.

Liss peered up at the galleries around the hall. Different departments looked to be colour coded in red, blue and yellow.

– I'm here because of my sister. She's gone missing.

– Okay, said the blonde without altering her facial expression. – You want to report a missing person?

Liss shook her head. – You've been looking for her for four days.

She didn't want to tell any more to this creature slouched there chewing gum. – The detectives in charge of the case probably want to talk to me.

– What is your sister's name?

– Mailin. Mailin Synnøve Bjerke.

– Sit down over there and wait.

A couple of minutes later, Liss was summoned back to the counter.

– None of the detectives can talk to you at the moment. Write your name and telephone number on this piece of paper and they'll get in touch with you.

3

THE TAXI DRIVER handed Liss's credit card back to her. She'd been living on it for a while now. Wasn't sure how much more she could squeeze out of it; didn't want to find out. She stepped out into the slushy snow. The weather had turned milder during the night. She'd spent most of it in the hotel room in Parkveien looking out the window at the rain.

She stepped experimentally through the puddles in the driveway. It was something like four years since she'd last been there.

Almost as soon as she rang, the door was cautiously opened. Tage's head appeared.

– Liss, he exclaimed, and put his hand to his forehead. He had grown a beard since she last saw him, short and grey. There was hardly a wisp of hair left on his head. And the eyes seemed smaller behind the round spectacles. She felt almost relieved to see him. Perhaps because it wasn't her mother who had opened the door.

For a moment it looked as though he was going to embrace her, but fortunately he decided against it.

– What in the world? But come in, come in. He shouted back into the house: – Ragnhild!

Tage still pronounced her name in that strange Swedish way. They had never got used to it. She remembered what she thought that day fifteen years ago, the first time he came to their house: a person who says Mother's name in such a weird way is definitely not going to be allowed to move into our house. But thinking that hadn't helped.

Tage got no answer and called out again, adding this time:
– It's Liss.

Liss heard a sound from the living room. The next moment her mother was standing in the doorway, her face drawn and without make-up. She gasped, but her eyes looked far away.

– Liss, she murmured, and stayed where she was.

Liss kicked off her boots, crossed the threshold, into the hallway. Had decided in advance to give Mother a hug, but that didn't happen.

– You're here. Mother took hold of her arm, as though to reassure herself her eyes were not deceiving her. – There, you see, Tage, she came.

– I never said she wouldn't, Tage protested as he looked around. – Where are your things?

– What things?

– Suitcase, or bag.

– I just left.

– Okay then, Tage noted. He was an assistant professor in sociology, unless he'd finally got the chair he'd applied for hundreds of times. He always noted things before he permitted himself to have an opinion on them.

They sat in the living room. Not much was said. Liss reeled off something about not being able to sit calmly and wait in Amsterdam. Her mother contented herself with a nod, but was hardly listening. Seemed even more remote now than when Liss had arrived. She must have taken some tranquillisers. It wasn't like her; she never touched medicines. But now her eyelids were heavy and her pupils small.

Tage withdrew to the kitchen to heat up some leftovers, though Liss had at first said no thanks. He wanted to bring the food into the living room, but she preferred to eat at the kitchen table. He sat with her. Her mother stayed where she was on the sofa. Leafing through a newspaper, Liss could hear.

– How long can you stay? Tage wanted to know.

As though she could give an answer to that. – It all depends.

He nodded, seeming to understand what she meant.

– Tell me what you know about Mailin, she said.

It was the first time since entering the house that she had been able to say the name. In this kitchen where they had sat together since they were small children. Liss wasn't sure what she actually remembered and what she had seen in old photographs, but in her mind's eye she saw them sitting at this pine table eating breakfast and supper, scissoring and gluing, rolling dice.

– She went missing on Thursday, is that right?

Tage rubbed the tip of his nose. – She hasn't been seen since Wednesday. Not that we know of.

– What do you mean by that?

He shook his head. – I don't know what I mean, Liss. I daren't have any opinion at all.

– I have to know everything.

Her voice sounded hard. Tage removed his glasses, wiped them with a handkerchief. The fat, probably spitting up from the frying pan, didn't disappear but spread out in a film across the lenses. He blew on them, misting them, wiped again, still no effect.

– She went out to the cabin, he said once he'd abandoned the cleaning and got his glasses on again. – That was Wednesday night. She always goes out there when she's working on difficult projects. She spent the night out there, left there the next afternoon, it looks like. People heading for that café in the forest . . .

– Vangen, said Liss.

– Exactly, Vangen, people saw her car parked in the parking space down by . . .

– Bysetermosan.

– They saw it there Wednesday evening and the following morning. In the afternoon it was gone.

– She hasn't come off the road somewhere?

An image of Mailin, trapped in her wrecked car in a deep ditch. Or at the foot of some cliff. Liss ran over the familiar roads in her mind.

– We found her car, Tage told her. – It was parked in Welhavens Street, close by her office. She must have driven there Thursday, in the afternoon. She was supposed to be taking part in that talk show.

– I saw that in the paper. That old rock-preacher Berger.

Tage cleared his throat. – None of us have any idea why she agreed to do that. The man is a complete arsehole, pardon my French.

Liss shrugged her shoulders. – He wants to break down a few taboos. Is that such a bad thing?

– My dear Liss, Berger and his disciples are parasites on the conception of free thinking, Tage announced. – But pretty soon no one's going to be allowed to say so out loud any more. The fear of being called politically correct is a more efficient way of censoring people than any dictatorship could come up with.

It was clear that she'd got him going on one of his hobby horses. He walked over to the fridge, took out a beer, fetched two glasses and filled them both.

– On the pretext of freeing us from old prejudices, they create new ones that are a great deal worse.

Tage seemed irritated, which was unlike him. He could be grumpy and peevish, but he'd always found it difficult to display anger.

– The worst thing is, young people have started turning him into a cult figure. Even my most serious students regard him as a revolutionary. And now you think of me as some old codger who doesn't understand the changing times, or worse still, has no sense of humour.

She had probably always thought of him as an old codger. But she could see that he had his own special sense of dry, intellectual humour. He could even make her laugh with his puns and his word games. All in all he was a decent, well-intentioned person. It was just that she'd never liked him.

– Berger flirts with heroin abuse, with paedophilia, with Satanism; he turns all accepted ideas of what's right and wrong upside down. But what I say to my students is this: that with views expressed in the public arena comes responsibility; these are public acts, something quite different from choosing which suit you think you look best in.

– Mailin wanted to take part in his programme, Liss pointed out.

Tage sighed deeply. – I'm sure her intentions were good. But I doubt she would have achieved anything beyond confirming that the right to be a bastard takes precedence over everything else, as long as people find it entertaining.

It looked as if he were getting rid of a long-pent-up frustration by abusing some clapped-out old rock star who'd been allowed to let it all hang out on TV. You had to be pretty naïve to allow yourself to be provoked by something like that, thought Liss. Norwegian, at the very least – or Swedish. In Holland, that stuff didn't attract much attention any more.

She let him carry on while she ate a few mouthfuls. Then she interrupted: – You say her car was parked outside her office?

Tage tugged at his beard. – She probably called in there on her way to the TV studio. We were sitting down and all ready to watch, but when the programme started, she wasn't there. And that arsehole was cracking jokes at her expense. That she didn't have the guts to turn up and other disgraceful comments like that.

– And she hasn't been seen since?

Liss heard her mother getting up from the sofa in the living room. She joined them in the kitchen.

– You've had a bite to eat, I see, she said listlessly, resting a hand on Liss's shoulder. – I'm just going for a little lie-down.

She disappeared again and went up the stairs.

Tage watched her. – I don't know if she'll be able to take it if something really has happened.

Really has happened, Liss almost interrupted. Four days had passed since anyone had seen Mailin. She controlled herself, poked at her spaghetti, chewed at a half-mouthful of the meat sauce. It tasted of nothing. Had to be at least twenty-four hours since she'd last eaten, but she didn't feel even remotely hungry. Emptied the glass of beer.

– The police?

Tage refilled her glass. – They've questioned us about everything under the sun. If she was depressed, if she's ever gone missing before, all that. About her relationship with Viljam.

– What do you think about that?

He scratched his liver-spotted crown with a finger. – What can one say? Anything might have happened . . . Dear Liss, we're terrified. I'm sure you are too.

Terrified? Was that what she was? She went in and out of mental states. Mostly she felt remote. Now and then as though she was being torn to pieces. Then suddenly relieved: everything would come to an end. And then again the suffocating blackness that paralysed her. She'd killed someone. In her jacket pocket was a photo of Mailin. She could throw it down on the table in front of Tage: take me to the police station. Lock me up. But I can't face the thought of talking about it.

He patted her gently on the arm. – Of course the police are investigating everything that might possibly be significant. It wouldn't be the first time it's happened. People who live together quarrel and . . . He replaced the rest of the sentence with a cough. – Incidentally, have you met Viljam?

She shook her head. – Spoke to him on the phone three days ago, that's all.

Mailin had never said much about this Viljam, but then she never did when it came to boyfriends, and Liss hadn't particularly wanted to hear about him anyway. She remembered the message she'd received: *Keep Midsummer's Day free next year.*

– He's a law student, isn't he?

– Correct. They've been a couple for over two years now. He seems a likeable young man to me. As far as Ragnhild is concerned, he isn't right for Mailin, but then you know . . .

He inclined his head towards the door his wife had just left through.

– Ragnhild implies that she gets these odd *vibrations* from him. She can't quite make him out.

Liss could feel the old irritation beginning to stir. In her mother's eyes, none of Mailin's boyfriends had ever been good enough for her. She always gave the impression that her daughters should feel free to choose whoever they liked, and at the same time she left them in no doubt as to what they *ought* to do. Usually she didn't give up until things went her way.

– Do the police think this guy Viljam might have . . . done something?

Tage thought it over. – They interviewed him twice. But he was at work with a group of other students the whole of the afternoon when Mailin disappeared. I picked him up there, he came out here to watch the broadcast with us. The plan was for Mailin to join us afterwards. Viljam and I were out looking for her all night. In the morning we went out to the cabin to have a look there too. He seems as crushed as we are.

– Why did you go out to the cabin? Didn't you say her car was in town?

– We didn't know what to do. Just knew we had to try everything.

– Might she have gone off somewhere?

She could hear herself how thin it sounded, but she had to ask in order to endure being there at all, to keep a grip on the conversation, not get sucked down and dragged away . . . Of course Mailin hadn't gone off anywhere without leaving a message. She wasn't the type to let people worry on her account. Liss might have just taken off. But Mailin always wanted people to know exactly where they were with her.

– We've asked ourselves every imaginable sort of question, Tage said in that slow way of his that perhaps expressed a kind of calm. – But where could she have gone, and why? Ragnhild even called Canada, to ask your father if Mailin had turned up there. An absurd notion, but as long as there was a theoretical possibility . . .

Ragnhild had called her father. Liss knew that they hadn't spoken for years. Fifteen, maybe, nearer twenty.

– What did he say? she wanted to know.

– She couldn't get hold of him. He's probably off travelling somewhere. Tage said this in a voice devoid of hidden insinuations. He had always been smart enough never to say anything implicitly critical of their father.

Suddenly Liss felt herself drained of energy.

She lay down in the room that had once been Mailin's, in her bed. Too exhausted to sleep, her pulse hammering in her throat. She hadn't spent the night in this house since leaving secondary school. Had to get up and walk, pacing over and over again the few steps between the door and the window. Switched on the light, sat down at the desk and froze. The photos were still up on the shelf above the table. One of Mailin in her graduation party outfit. The fair hair, the bright eyes that were so like her mother's, but seemed happier. Another picture of Mailin and herself. She was probably about eight, which would make Mailin twelve. They're standing on the rock outside the cabin, the one they used to dive into Morr Water from, Liss flailing her arms. It looks as if she's about to fall. Mailin is holding on to her.

She took the photo down, studied every detail. The spruce next to the rock. The way the light created an ellipse in the water far behind them. And Mailin's anxious face. *What's to become of you, Liss?*

She couldn't remember the picture being taken, but she could feel what it was like to stand teetering there, falling, and being held. – I'll never be closer to anyone than you, she murmured. – Must find you, Mailin.

4

SHE TOOK THE metro from Jernbanetorget. A copy of *Dagbladet* was wedged down the inside of her seat. It was a couple of days old. A story low down on page eight: *Woman (29) missing in Oslo.* Not been seen since last Thursday, she read. The police do not yet know whether there are any suspicious circumstances. Seven lines, no name, no picture.

She flipped through it. Six months ago, she had been written up in *Dagbladet*'s magazine. She had been in an advert that was shown in cinemas in Holland. No idea how *Dagbladet* had managed to get hold of her. A journalist and a photographer turned up outside the flat in Marnixkaade. Zako claimed that he was the one who had tipped them off. They wanted to do a story. Young Norwegian girl on the verge of a career in modelling. They twisted things around, blew things up, created a picture of a non-existent her. *Isn't it a tough life for a girl in this business, with all the focus on your appearance?* And then the standard question. *What do you think about all the anorexia, the drugs, the instant disposability?* The journalist wanted to combine a touch of glamour with a frisson of politically correct scepticism. You have to know what you yourself want, Liss had answered. You have to take control and make sure you don't hand it over to anyone. *What are your views on women as objects of the male gaze?* She started to tire of the interview. I've got nothing against being an object, she said, and realised that she meant it. She could have expanded on her answer, refined it, made it acceptable, but couldn't be bothered. On the contrary, she allowed herself to be lured into making pithy remarks that made her seem interesting. The result was presented as an example of the way the new generation of women thought. They skimmed the cream off what their mothers had fought to achieve, used it when it suited them. Enjoyed life, and themselves. Mailin called and congratulated her on the interview, even though she was sceptical about the message. Liss never heard a word from her mother.

She looked up and saw that they were at Carl Berners Place and just managed to get out before the carriage doors closed. Jogged up the steps, into the daylight. Her boots were dry again, both of them with an uneven grey rim round the outside of the ankle. A few days ago she would have hated to have them looking like that. In the life she lived, every imperfection acquired a significance. But not now. Not here in this misty winter city.

She was on her way to meet Mailin's partner. Passed a post office. *Wouters*, she thought when she saw it. Saw in her mind's eye the name of the detective inspector on an office door. She's standing outside it with a letter in her hand. She's written down exactly what happened that night in Zako's flat. How she tricked him into taking all that Rohypnol and sat there watching as he became more and more helpless. How she left him there to collapse and drown in his own vomit. Mailin is missing, she protested. I can't do anything for her if I write that letter.

She carried on down towards Rodeløkka. There had always been something about Mailin's boyfriends. When she was younger, Liss had been obsessed with the need to find out about them. As if there was a code to them, something that told her what she should be looking out for herself. Once, perhaps in an attempt to crack this code, she'd allowed herself to be carried away. After that, she wanted to know as little as possible about her sister's love life.

The house was away down at the end of Lang Street. She rang, waited, rang again. The front door wasn't locked. She opened it and looked in. Light in the hallway and a staircase on the right.

– Hello?

She heard a door opening upstairs. He appeared at the top of the stairs. Then began descending towards her.

– Sorry, I was in the bathroom.

He stopped before he was all the way down. The eyes were quite large, the cheekbones high. His dark hair was longish and combed back. He gave a quick smile, came all the way down and held out his hand.

– Viljam.

He was quite a bit taller than her, but not particularly well built. She was surprised; she had imagined he would be like the person in the picture on Zako's phone. But this wasn't the man on his way out through the gate with Mailin.

He squeezed her hand, not hard, released it at once. He was unshaven, but his sideburns curved in a delicate bow towards the angles of his jaw and were symmetrically trimmed. It struck her that he was better looking than any of Mailin's former boyfriends. He seemed calm, and was perhaps deliberately striving to maintain that calm. She never trusted her first impression of people she met. It was always accompanied by uncertainty, and often deceptive. She picked up a host of signals, full of contradictions and hidden significances. Being prepared was no help, she thought as Viljam walked in front of her down the hall. Most of what she picked up on she couldn't think about until the encounter was over, and often not even then.

Liss looked round at the room. The ceiling was high, the room going halfway up into the next floor. The painting on the wall appeared to be of a winter landscape, snow through dark trees beneath a grey sky. Muted but full of light.

– Do you and Mailin own this house? she asked, though she knew the circumstances of how they came to be living there.

– Rent it cheaply, Viljam told her. – A friend of Linne's working in the US on an open-ended contract. Not even certain he'll come back. If he doesn't, then it's possible we'll buy it.

He called her Linne. Liss had done the same when she was younger.

He took her upstairs and showed her around. The bedroom was in bright colours, with a solid double bed made of oak. There was a spare bed in an office. Liss tried to work out what was Mailin in the house. The bed and the dark brown leather furniture, the orchids on the windowsill in the living room, the painting, the piano.

Afterwards they sat in the kitchen, at a surface that stuck out from the wall and divided the room in two.

Viljam poured coffee from a cafetière.

– Keep expecting every moment that she'll come in the front door, he said. – Kick the snow off on the threshold.

He sipped at his cup, looked away. Liss studied his hands. The fingers were long and thin. She glanced up at his profiled face against the afternoon light from the window. Thought of what Tage had said about Ragnhild's reaction; that there was something about Viljam that gave her mother a funny feeling . . . These funny feelings of hers always filled the room with something floating and invisible; back home they used to swim in them all the time. Liss recalled why it was she had left, and would never come back.

– Mailin says you're studying law. And that you also work.

He nodded. – The Justice Bus. Free legal aid for people who can't afford to pay.

Was he trying to hide something? According to Tage, Viljam had been at work with some other students when Mailin disappeared. And the rest of that evening and night and the following day at the house in Lørenskog.

She swallowed some coffee. It was black and strong, just the way she liked it. – On the phone that day, you said that Mailin was going to call me.

Even in the light from the window his eyes were dark blue. She still didn't know what she thought of him. Other than that he was good looking in an almost feminine way. As was usually the case with Mailin's men.

– She said there was something she wanted to talk to you about. Don't know what it was. Then she went out to the cabin.

– Just for one day? Liss could hear the scepticism in her own voice.

– She's been spending a lot of time there recently. Working on a very demanding project. Part of her PhD. Says she thinks better out there. Nothing to disturb her. And on Thursday of course she was supposed to take part in *Taboo*.

Lisa could see her, sitting by the large French windows in the room at the cabin. View of a stretch of Morr Water between the trees.

– So that old rock-preacher Berger has turned himself into a talk show host, she remarked.

– You've never seen *Taboo*? Everybody's talking about it.

– It's years since I saw a Norwegian TV programme. I gather I'm missing something.

Viljam drained his coffee cup, poured them both refills.

– Read about it in a newspaper on the plane, she added. – Every week he discusses a new taboo which he claims we should get rid of. Smart guy.

Viljam took the bait. – Berger is an unscrupulous bastard who has discovered how much attention he can get just by digging in the dirt.

Liss wasn't sure whether he sounded irritated or not.

– In the beginning he was untouchable, ostracised. Now he's cool. Everyone who's famous for being famous turns up on his show and yaps away with him.

– You mean Mailin?

He shook his head. – I was extremely surprised when she accepted the invitation. Then I realised it was for a reason. She wrote a piece for the newspapers about his show.

He pulled down a cutting from the cork noticeboard, *Berger – a hero for our times*. From *Aftenposten*, 1 December. – She discusses his project and shows what a narrow-minded idiot he really is.

Liss read the opening paragraph. Mailin could be absolutely ruthless when it came to something she disapproved of.

– She's been working on incest and abuse and so on for years, Viljam continued. – You know that's what her doctoral thesis is about? In Thursday's programme Berger revealed that as a child he had had a relationship with an older man. It didn't harm him in the slightest. Far from it: a relationship like that could actually be good for a child.

– I saw that in *VG*. A lot of very angry responses.

– He got in touch with Mailin a few weeks ago. She's had several meetings with him. He claims that the taboo on paedophilia is against one of life's natural expressions. He tries to promote himself as a kind of saviour. Everyone knows that he's making a fortune out of the fact that people can never get enough of scandal. The more outraged viewers and Christians who threaten to boycott the channel – and best of all, the death threats – the better it is for his image and for the viewing figures.

Viljam got up and took a packet out of the freezer in the top of the fridge. – I'll heat some rolls for us.

– Mailin would never let herself be used by a guy like that, said Liss. – She's much too savvy.

Viljam opened the bag with a thin, curved knife. – Agreed. *She* was the one who was going to use *him*.

He put the rolls into the microwave. – She's very careful about the oath of confidentiality and all that. But the day before she was due to go on *Taboo*, she mentioned something . . . something she'd found out. Something she was going to reveal in the programme. I'm not quite sure what.

He didn't say any more.

– And Berger didn't know about this? asked Liss.

– She told me she would give him a fair chance. She was going to arrange another meeting with him. Talk to him just before the broadcast. Give him the choice of whether to cancel it or not.

– But he didn't cancel.

– On the contrary. He made fun of the fact that she'd withdrawn. Got a lot of bullshit off his chest. Not a word of explanation for why she wasn't there.

– Presumably because he didn't know that before the programme went out?

Viljam shrugged.

– At first I thought she'd changed her mind. That she'd decided after all not to give Berger cred by appearing on his show. But anyone who knows Mailin knows she's not the type to drop out like that.

The rolls were thawed and ready; he took them out of the microwave, put them on a plate. Put out cheese and jam.

– After *Taboo* was over, I was certain she'd show up in Lørenskog. We sat there and waited, Tage, Ragnhild and I. Then we started ringing round. Later on that night we called the police. There was nothing they could do. Not until I called again the next day. They asked me to come in and give a statement.

Liss leaned forward across the table. – Did you tell them this about Berger and the meeting she was supposed to have with him?

Viljam sat back down in his chair. – Naturally. But they

were more interested in hearing what *I* had been up to over the last twenty-four hours.

What she saw in his eyes then was fear. The partner is always the first to be suspected, she thought. Was Viljam the type of guy who could do something like that? What was *like that*? Suddenly she realised she was staring back at him with the same look of fear in her eyes. She excused herself, pushed aside the plate with the fresh warm roll, went out into the hallway and up the stairs.

As she bent double over the toilet bowl, she saw an image of Mailin's naked body in the dark.

– She's dead, she murmured. – Mailin is dead.

5

SHE FOLLOWED SANNER Street in towards the city centre. The traffic approaching from the opposite direction created a film of dust and noise around her. She turned away by the bridge, took the path that ran alongside the river. Stopped and sat down on a bench. Light snow was falling, and in the dead grass two boys were chasing around after a ball. A woman in a turquoise outfit with her head covered in a shawl shouted something to them, something sharp and high pitched in a language Liss didn't understand. The boys ignored her and raced off in the direction of the riverbank.

What was it about Viljam that gave Ragnhild her funny feeling? Was it anything other than jealousy because Mailin had chosen him? Viljam is more than just despairing, she thought. More than just afraid. Or was she imagining that? At times she was certain she could tell when people were lying to her. Wasn't that just her imagination too?

As she walked on, it stopped snowing. Columns of light passed swiftly between the clouds, as though the sun were hurrying away. She carried on up to Our Saviour's cemetery. She felt her phone vibrating. She saw it was Rikke and took the call.

– Liss, where are you? I've been trying to get hold of you for days.

– I'm in Oslo.

Before Rikke could ask, she told her about Mailin. Just a few words. Silence at the other end.

– I had to come home.

– First Zako and now your sister. It's crazy.

– Have they got a cause of death for him yet?

– I was called in for an interview. Zako was at my flat directly before he went home that night.

She was probably afraid Liss was going to ask what they had been doing there.

– It's okay, Rikke, you don't have to tell me everything.

A wail from the other end. – I've been a real bitch, Liss. I understand if you're mad at me.

– I'm not mad at you. What did the police say?

– They questioned me about everything. When he left, what we'd taken. If we'd had sex. If I went back to his place with him afterwards. It was pretty creepy. Is it my fault if he took too much? They asked about you too.

– What did you say?

– What could I say? I mean, you hadn't seen him for over a week. That's right, isn't it?

– Yes.

– When are you coming back?

– Don't know.

– I understand.

– What?

– How terrible it must be.

The main street entrance was locked. She looked down the list of names on the doorbells, found Mailin's. Beneath it, another name she recognised. As the connection dawned on her, she turned, about to walk away. Waited a few seconds and then changed her mind and rang one of the other bells, marked *T. Gabrielsen*. A woman's voice over the intercom asked who it was. Liss told her; there was a buzzing from the lock.

The stairwell smelt mouldy. The woodwork was worn and

the paint flaking. A woman appeared from a door on the first floor.

– So you're Liss. Mailin has told me about you. I'm Torunn. This is so awful. Not you coming here, of course. You know what I mean.

Liss didn't answer. This Torunn, presumably surnamed Gabrielsen, was in her thirties. She came up to Liss's chin. She was quite chubby. Her hair was shoulder length and pitch black, but in the roots its true grey was visible.

– Mailin's office is on the second floor. Have you got a key? I'm expecting a client. Just say if there's anything I can do to help.

As Liss was halfway up the stairs she continued: – Are you looking for anything in particular? The police have already been here. She shuddered, took off her glasses and rubbed her eyes.

– No, nothing special, said Liss. – Just want to see her office.

Just want to look for her, she might have said. The woman nodded as though she understood.

On the second floor, Liss let herself into a room furnished as a waiting room. A sofa, some chairs, a radio on a table in the corner, poster art on the walls. Two doors leading out of it. *Pål Øvreby – Psychologist*, it said on one of them. Again she felt an urge to leave the place. A vague pain in the stomach, spreading down into her groin. Pål Øvreby isn't going to decide what I do or don't do, she thought, and turned away from his door.

On the other door, Mailin's name was printed on a brass plate. Liss looked through the spare bunch of keys Viljam had given her, selected the largest one and let herself in. The office wasn't big, but the ceiling was high, as was probably the case with all the rooms in an old city-centre building like this. Here too the paint had begun to flake off, but the run-down effect was partly relieved by a woven rug on one of the walls, two children reaching out towards the sun. And the thick reddish carpet was soft to walk on. Liss recognised the desk, something inherited from their grandmother. It was in heavy, dark wood and was much too big and distinguished for the office. Behind the desk were three shelves housing books and folders.

She sat in the swivel chair and leaned across the desk. A glimpse of the street down below, the tram wires, the traffic lights. She remained sitting for a long time. Mailin's voice was somewhere inside that empty office. If she closed her eyes and tried hard, she could hear it.

What's to become of you, Liss?

Mailin had decided to help those who needed help the most. She took care of people who had known the worst they could know. Abuse. Violence. Incest. People with real reasons for their suffering, thought Liss. Not like me, who had chances but wasted them. She let her gaze wander over the folders on the shelves, Mailin had noted on the spines what the contents were. On the backs of the books she saw a few familiar names. Freud, Jung, Reich. Others who she'd never heard of: Igra, Bion, Ferenczi, Kohout. Now and then Liss had felt the same kind of curiosity as her sister. To understand how the world adds up. How language shapes us. How we collect memories and dispose of them. But she had never had Mailin's patience. Could never sit for hours with a book. Had to interrupt herself, every time. Fill her thoughts with something other than letters. Sounds and pictures, something that moved.

There was a cork noticeboard next to the shelves. Two newspaper cuttings pinned to the top of it, one of them an interview with Berger. Liss switched on the desktop lamp, read something Mailin had underlined: *Nothing bores me more than watching the way a shoal of cunts move.* There was also a postcard hanging there. It was from Amsterdam, Bloemenmarket. Liss recognised it. She'd sent it a long time ago, at least a year, and Mailin still kept it up on her noticeboard. Below the card she discovered a Post-it note with something scribbled on it. Liss angled the lamp so that she could make the writing out. One of the few things she was better at than her sister was writing neatly. *Ask him about death by water*, she read in Mailin's untidy scrawl.

She turned back towards the desk. It had been tidied. A few documents in a file. She opened the top drawer, found a stapler, some pens and a packet of paperclips. The drawer below it was locked. She managed to open it with the smallest key in the bunch. Inside was a small bound book with a wine-red cover in some kind of soft, plush material. She ran her fingers across it. *Mailin S. Bjerke* was written inside. Apart from that the pages were empty. What were you going to fill them with, Mailin? Write about your patients? Or your own thoughts? Liss shoved the book into her shoulder bag.

Further back in the drawer, she found a diary. The daily planners were covered in initials and appointment times, obviously patients her sister was treating. Six or seven every day, sometimes eight. They all came to her with their stories. Everything she had to listen to, take care of, cure them of. Dense with initials; on the hour, every hour someone crossing her threshold to unburden themselves, and Mailin was supposed to sit there and take it all in, swallow it until she felt she was going dizzy . . . Liss flipped through the diary, toward the end of the year. Thursday 11 December was blank, but below the listing of hours she had written: *17.00 JH*. And at the bottom of the page *BERGER – Channel Six, Nydalen, 8 o'clock*, and something about a jacket.

She had to pee, went out into the corridor. At the end of it she found a tiny loo with a washbasin. After she'd locked herself in and sat down, she heard a door go, and then footsteps. They disappeared, obviously into the waiting room. In an instant, this thought: Pål Øvreby comes striding down the corridor, tears open the door and finds her sitting on the toilet . . . She finished, hurried back to the office. The door was ajar. A man was leaning over Mailin's desk, turned round on hearing her.

– I'm looking for someone, he said, and glanced round in confusion. – Mailin still works here, right?

Liss stayed in the doorway. – She isn't here.

The guy couldn't have been much older than her. He was thin and bony, wearing a dark blue reefer jacket with the collar turned up and a motif on the breast pocket, an anchor.

– I can see that, he said. – That she's not here. Who are you?

Liss didn't think that was any of his business. She closed the door behind her.

– Do you have an appointment? she countered.

The man peered out the window. The black curly hair was gelled up and hung in a thick wave down one side of his forehead.

– Not actually today. I've been here before, some time ago. I dropped out. Been trying to get in touch with Mailin to make an appointment, but she doesn't answer. Thought I might as well just call in. Will she be along later today?

Liss studied him. The eyes were dark and restless. He was rubbing his hands together and obviously trying to keep them still. Abstinent, she thought.

– I don't know when she'll be back, she answered. *If* she'll be back, she should have said. Mailin won't be coming any more. – I'll make a note that you were here. What's your name?

The man's gaze flickered around her, over to the rug on the wall, out the window again. He had so much gel in his hair, it put her in mind of the feathers on a seabird mired in oil.

– Doesn't matter, he mumbled. – I'll try again later.

He squeezed past her on his way out.

– I'm looking for Mailin too, said Liss.

He stopped. Stood there, rocked a moment on the threshold.
– Are you here waiting for her?

She closed her eyes. *That's what I'm doing*.

– Gotta go, the young man mumbled.

Liss slumped down into the office chair again. Noticed in the same instant that the appointment book, which she had left lying on the desk, was now back in the drawer. She picked it up, flipped back through. The page for Thursday 11 December had been torn out. She jumped up and ran out into the corridor. Heard the street door closing down below.

6

LARGE FLAKES OF wet snow were falling in her hair. She was already drenched and on the point of giving up when Viljam opened the door. The heavy eyes and the creases on the pale cheeks showed what he had been doing since she left some hours earlier.

– You're home, she said as she held up the office keys. – Sorry if I woke you. Just wanted to hand these back.

He blinked in the afternoon light. – Doesn't matter. Come in. More coffee?

She pulled off the soaking wet boots.

– Don't you have lectures or something to go to?

He shrugged. In the kitchen he added: – Can't take anything in anyway. Not getting much sleep these nights.

Liss put the keys on the table. Decided to tell him about the patient who had appeared and then disappeared again.

– He tore a page out of the diary? Viljam exclaimed.

– The one with the appointments for the day Mailin went missing.

– Have you told the police?

She had called them. Still no one there who had anything to do with the case. She had left another message.

– They're doing nothing, she groaned. – Absolutely fuck all.

He didn't respond, but once he had produced the rolls from earlier on he asked: – What did this guy look like?

She described him. Black curly hair, unkempt. Acne scars on

his cheeks, shifty eyes. – I had the feeling he was on something or other.

Viljam poured coffee from a little grey bag into the cafetière. – Quite a lot of Mailin's patients are. I've asked her if it's safe to have an office without any kind of alarm system. She just shrugs it off.

As he chewed at half a roll with nothing on it, Liss unobtrusively watched his dark blue eyes. He had a heavy growth of beard and still hadn't shaved. On the other hand, the narrow nose and full lips accentuated the feminine prettiness of the face. Not hard to see why Mailin was attracted to him. Although her sister was more concerned about what lay behind an appearance; she dived down to investigate what was not immediately apparent to the naked eye. Liss, by way of contrast, had always been fascinated by the surface of things, what the masks looked like, not what was hidden behind them. Even so, she too tried to follow her intuition in deciding whether to trust someone or not. As regards Viljam, she still hadn't made up her mind.

– Did you find what you were looking for in her office?

She didn't know what she had been looking for. If she told him she'd been looking for Mailin, he might stop asking.

– I spent an evening with my mother, she said instead. – She sits there completely paralysed, can hardly get a word out. She's wilting in front of our very eyes.

She dragged her fingers through her hair; they stopped at a knot, which she began to twist at.

– I must do something. Anything at all. Go over every single thing Mailin did recently. Go where she went. Just not carry on sitting here waiting.

He didn't answer, sat there staring at the table.

– What about the thesis she was working on? she asked. – Is it lying around here somewhere?

He drank from his coffee cup. – Her computer is missing.

It wasn't in the car. Not at her office either, nor at the cabin. Doesn't make sense.

Liss mulled this over.

– What else does she use it for?

– Journals. Everyone who came to her for treatment.

– Presumably she backs it all up?

– Think so. We can see up in her study.

He went ahead of her up the stairs and into the little room with the desk and the couch. A model of a seagull hung from the ceiling, and the draught from the opening door was enough to set the wings in motion.

– She's very good at organising her work systematically, Viljam remarked. – So the journals aren't just lying around all over the place. I helped her buy a fireproof safe for her office. She shares it with the other people who work there.

They looked through the drawers without finding anything of interest.

– What are you looking for? Viljam wanted to know.

– Don't know. I need to see what kind of things she was doing.

As they were about to head back downstairs again, she said: – I just leapt on the plane last Sunday, didn't have time to pack anything. Can I take a look and see if Mailin has any clothes I could borrow?

Viljam glanced at her. Clearly he now saw for the first time the wet hair and the jacket with its large dark patchy stains from the shoulders and down over the chest. He opened the bedroom door. – The furthest cupboard is hers.

He popped into the bathroom, came back with a towel.

– Sorry for not thinking of it before, he said, and disappeared out.

In the cupboard, Liss found what she was looking for. Put on a clean pair of tights, but the bras were two sizes too large and she gave up on them. Borrowed a couple of pullovers, underwear and a bottle-green cashmere cardigan. Mailin's trousers were too short in the leg for her, so she pulled her own on again.

– I've heard a lot about you, Viljam said when she came down again. – Mailin liked to talk about you.

– Really. So you know the worst?

– Quite the contrary. But the fact that you arrive in Norway without a change of clothes and use her wardrobe as though it was your own fits the picture.

Briefly his face lightened. She was relieved that he took it like that.

– Does she still have the same supervisor? she asked as she forced her feet down into the wet boots. – Is it still Dahlstrøm?

– Dahlstrøm? Do you know him? Viljam asked, and looked surprised.

– I met him when he was at that conference in Amsterdam this summer, with Mailin. I'd like to talk to him. She glanced at her watch. – Actually, I met one of Mailin's colleague's at the office. It was her who let me in. Torunn Gabrielsen, do you know her?

– Slightly.

Really it was her other colleague she wanted to ask about. How could Mailin bring herself to share an office with him? She wondered whether Viljam knew that Pål Øvreby and Mailin had once been a couple. The thought filled her with unease, and she couldn't face asking any more questions.

The sleet had stopped. The streets looked as though they were soaked in oil. She walked aimlessly. Crossed a park. Down a narrow street. There was a café at the end of it. She looked in. Only two customers there, sitting at the back in the half-dark, an elderly couple each with a glass of beer. She picked a table by the window. The view out was on to a factory gate and a roundabout. On the pavement outside, a bush decked with garish Christmas lights. Her phone rang. She jumped. *Wouters*; the name pounded in her head. They've found out. Soon they'd be there to fetch her.

– Liss Bjerke? This is Judith van Ravens.

– How did you get my number?

– My call list. You called me several times before you got here.

Everything connected with Zako had been shoved behind a door. Liss had worked to keep it there. Now that door swung open again and it all came tumbling out. Suddenly she was angry. *Why didn't you delete me from the list?* she nearly shouted.

– I've been thinking so much, said the voice at the other end.

– And now you've got something to tell me?

Judith van Ravens sighed. – I had to find out about it.

– About what?

– This business with the photo of your sister, what Zako was going to do with it . . . I haven't been able to sleep since you were here. I called some friends in Amsterdam. The police think Zako's death was accidental.

– I told you that.

– All the same, perhaps I should tell them about these photos. Don't you think?

Liss said nothing for a moment. Inside her head, everything was still spinning. The image of Zako on the sofa. Hands washing bottles beneath a tap. Her own hands.

– I don't think so.

– Why not?

Judith van Ravens' voice was sharper, as though at any moment the doubt could turn into suspicion.

– I want the police to find my sister. That's all that matters. If they start getting a lot of confusing information, it'll take them longer, and by then it might be too late. Surely you can understand that.

* * *

She drank the rest of the coffee that had been brought to her table. Had no reason to be sitting there. Had nowhere else to go. Put her hand down into her bag for her cigarettes and touched something else. She lifted out the notebook she'd taken from Mailin's office. Sat there studying how her sister had written her name inside the cover. Then she wrote her own name, imitating the calligraphy. Mailin had always been able to use her head better than her. Mailin was stronger, had more endurance, but somehow her hands seemed to live in a different world.

Liss.

She sat for a long time and looked at the four letters.

Liss is Mailin's sister, she wrote. *Liss Bjerke.*

Liss Bjerke contacts the police. She hasn't heard from them. Does she know something that might help them find Mailin?

The appointment on 11 December, the afternoon she went missing: JH.

The image of Zako lying on the sofa paled as she sat there writing. Didn't disappear, but detached itself from her other thoughts.

Thinking about you helps, Mailin.

What was it you were going to tell Berger before the TV broadcast?

Viljam knows. Get him to tell you.

Had no idea where she got that from. She ordered another espresso. The waiter was from the Middle East, probably, or maybe Pakistan. The way he was looking at her was easy to interpret. He wanted her body without knowing anything else about who she was. It was uncomplicated. Awakened something in her, something she had control over. She held his gaze so long that in the end he was the one who had to look away. He returned, put her coffee on the table, remained standing there as though waiting for something.

– Do you want me to pay now?

– Pay when you leave.

He leaned slightly towards her. He had a dense growth of hair and thick eyebrows. He smelt strongly of something fatty and salty, disgusting in a way that for a few seconds allowed her to stop thinking.

As he walked back to the counter, she followed him with her eyes. So intensely did she scrutinise the broad back and the narrow hips that he must have noticed it.

She took the notebook out again.

Tell Mailin everything. About what happened in Bloemstraat. Zako was choked. Someone put sleeping tablets in his beer. What would you have said, Mailin?

You would have told me to talk to someone or other about it. Ring Dahlstrøm.

She sat for a few moments, pressing the pen against a point on her forehead.

You mustn't go away, Mailin. I need you.

7

TORMOD DAHLSTRØM TOOK her hand and held it tightly, obviously to express his sympathy. She knew he was somewhere in his mid-fifties, but there was something about him that made him seem younger. It wasn't the jutting chin or the outline of the almost bald head beneath the thin crest of fair hair. Maybe the deep-set pale blue eyes. She had met him for the first time four years previously. The second time was six months ago, when he attended the conference in Amsterdam with Mailin. He was one of the keynote speakers, said Mailin proudly, and insisted that Liss take them to a really good restaurant. Liss had her suspicions about why her sister was so keen, but went along with it anyway. For some years Dahlstrøm had had a regular column in *Dagbladet* where people could write in about their problems. He advised them on their marital difficulties, gambling and drug addictions, infidelities, lack of libido, and eating disorders. On this latter topic he had written several books, Mailin pointed out to her.

His office was in a daylight basement room in his villa, with a view of the garden and some spruce trees in a copse along Frognerseter Way.

– Does she still come to you for mentoring? Liss asked after sitting down in the soft leather chair.

– Did you know that? He seemed surprised. – Mailin doesn't usually reveal whom she's going to for mentoring, does she?

– She tells me lots of things. She trusts me.

– I didn't mean it like that, Dahlstrøm reassured her.

She hadn't taken it that way either, but she had an idea that Mailin had talked to him about her, and now she sat there with an uncomfortable feeling that he knew what was going on in her head.

He poured coffee from a thermos, tasted it, made a face, offered to brew a fresh pot. She said no. There was a girl of about her own age sitting in the waiting room. – I won't take up much of your time, I know you're busy.

– I'm glad you want to talk to me, he said.

Liss had always felt a need to be on the alert when she was with her sister's colleagues. When she was younger and Mailin introduced her to her fellow students, she had had the idea that psychologists could see through people, and that the slightest thing she said or did, or even thought, might give her away. In time her belief in such magical powers faded, and instead she had to guard against her own irritation, control that urge to provoke that all therapists aroused in her. Twice she had started in treatment and both times terminated after a few sessions. She had sworn never again to see a psychologist, and definitely not a psychiatrist.

Dahlstrøm was a psychiatrist.

– I'm having trouble functioning normally, he added. – At the moment it's hard to think of anything apart from Mailin.

It sounded as though he meant it. He began by asking how things were at home in Lørenskog, and she had no problem talking about her mother's reaction, or about Tage's well-meaning but hopeless attempts to comfort her. But Dahlstrøm also wanted to know how she was coping.

– What's your opinion on that TV show Mailin was supposed to be on? she interrupted.

He ran a finger over the depression in the bridge of his nose; it was crooked and looked to have been broken. Sitting in the

Vermeer restaurant in Amsterdam, he had joked about how he used to box when he was younger.

– I mentor Mailin on the treatment of patients, he answered. – Anything else she does is none of my business. But if she had asked, I would have advised against having anything to do with Berger and what he's up to.

– So you don't like him either, Liss pressed.

Dahlstrøm appeared to be thinking this over.

– Any bully with a minimum of talent who is sufficiently ruthless is doomed to succeed, he said.

– There's no harm in laughing at ourselves, is there?

– On the contrary, Liss, it's good for us. But for those of us who work with the victims of cynicism, the world looks a little different.

He put one leg over the other and leaned back. – There is nothing we aren't prepared to joke about. No matter what you say about sex or death or God, you won't be breaking any taboos. Not as long as you do it ironically. Seriousness is the only taboo of our age. Taboo has migrated from content to form.

Liss said suddenly: – Mailin found out something about him. Something Berger's supposed to have done. She was going to expose it on TV that evening. She was due to meet him directly before the show to give him a chance to cancel the broadcast.

– How do you know this?

– Viljam, her partner.

But I don't know if I can trust him, she was on the point of adding.

Dahlstrøm sat up straight. – Have the police been informed of this?

– Viljam has tried to tell them. But they don't seem interested. At least according to him.

– They have to work through a great many possibilities.

– I don't think they're doing anything at all.

– That isn't correct, Dahlstrøm said firmly. – But I'll make a call. I know someone at police headquarters you can talk to.

Liss prepared to bring the conversation to a close. She noticed how good it felt to sit with this man whom Mailin admired and trusted. If she went on sitting there much longer, she might end up telling him things she didn't want him to know.

– It's impossible to imagine someone hurting Mailin.

Dahlstrøm nodded. – Mailin is what I would call a fundamentally decent human being. But she's also courageous, which means she makes enemies. On top of that, she's spent a long time working in a landscape that is basically a minefield.

He sat there, brow wrinkled, looking out of the window.

– I know you can't tell me anything about Mailin's patients, said Liss. – But I know she's working on a doctoral thesis about incest and that kind of thing. That's no secret?

– Of course not. It's going to be published . . . She's studying a group of young men who have been the subject of serious abuse.

– Is it possible one of them might have harmed her?

Dahlstrøm hesitated before answering: – When Mailin started this study a couple of years ago, she chose seven men who she was going to follow over a period of time. She was very careful to find victims who had not themselves become perpetrators.

He raised his coffee cup, changed his mind, put it down again. – What is it that enables a vicious circle of sexual violence and abuse to be broken? What makes some people choose to endure the pain inflicted on them without taking it out on other innocents? That is what she wants to study.

Liss thought this through.

– You can't know for certain whether one of the seven she ended up with hasn't abused someone else, she objected. – Even though they might deny it when asked.

– That is correct. Mailin can only relate to what they tell

her about themselves, and to the fact that they have no criminal record. But we've reached the limit of what I can discuss with you, Liss. I hope you understand that.

– But you will go to the police with what you know, if any of her patients have threatened her?

– You can rest assured that I will do everything I can to prevent anything happening to Mailin . . .

– But she's been missing for six days, Liss protested. – We can't just sit calmly and wait.

– I'm not doing that, he assured her. – I've already spoken to the police, and I'll speak to them again.

– I'll have to do that too, she mumbled.

Dahlstrøm looked quizzically at her. Now you can say it; she heard the thought race through her. You have killed a person, Liss Bjerke.

– I am her sister, after all, she added quickly. – No one knows her better than me.

Dahlstrøm's gaze was on her the whole time and took in everything. He wouldn't have been in a moment's doubt about what she ought to do . . . She had to get out of this chair now, before she started talking and was unable to stop.

8

In the evening, she took the bus out to Lørenskog. Had no other place to go. Tage had given her a spare key. He didn't say anything, just put it into her hand as she was going out the door the day before.

She let herself in.

– Is that you, Tage? She heard her mother's voice from the living room

Liss shuffled in. Her mother was sitting on the sofa, in exactly the same place as she had been a day and a half earlier. She had lit a candle; there was a pile of newspapers on the table in front of her, and she had a book in her hands.

– Are you hungry, Liss? I can heat something up for you.

Liss wasn't hungry. She'd forced down half a kebab before heading for the bus. Didn't want to do anything else but get up to her room and curl up in bed.

She sat in the chair at the end of the table.

– I am sorry, her mother said.

– For what?

Her mother put the book down. – I'm glad you're here, Liss. Liss gave a quick nod.

– But right at the moment it's impossible to be happy about anything, her mother continued.

– I know.

– There are so many things I'd like to ask you about. About Amsterdam. About what you're up to these days.

Liss got up, went out into the kitchen, put some coffee on. Returned with cups, glasses and a jug of water.

– Are those new clothes? Isn't that something Mailin usually wears?

– Had to borrow some of hers. Didn't have time to pack a change of clothing.

Her mother raised her hand and stroked the bottle-green cashmere cardigan. Maybe that was a smile moving in her face.

– How long can you stay? she asked.

Liss poured them both a glass of water. It was colder than ice. She emptied a whole glass, a thin string of pain flashed through her throat and down into her shoulder.

– I'm not leaving until we know.

Not until Mailin has been found, she added silently.

To stave off the silence, she said: – What are you reading?

Her mother picked up the book. – *The Charterhouse of Parma*.

She held it up in the air, as though to prove to Liss that a book with that title really did exist.

– Stendhal, she continued. – Always read Stendhal when I need to find a place to get away from it all.

Liss sat in Tage's office, switched on the computer. He'd given her the password for the guest log-in.

She opened Google. In the search field she typed: *manslaughter + range of sentence*. Deleted it. Typed instead: *death by water*, the words Mailin had scribbled on the Post-it note pinned to the noticeboard in her office. 46,700 hits. Articles about poisoned water, Silicon Valley, and Shakespeare's Ophelia. She was too restless to start sorting through the chaos and instead ran a search for *Berger + Taboo*. Over twelve thousand hits. Clicked into Wikipedia. Before calling himself Berger, the talk show host's name was Elijah Bergersen, or Elijah Frelsøi. Studied theology. Formed the rock band Baalzebub in 1976; a career as a solo artist followed. A couple of hits in the mid-nineties.

Later best known as a stand-up comedian, and most recently on television with a number of controversial productions.

She found a lot of comments on the talk show *Taboo*. An article in *Vårt Land* under the headline *Time to set a limit* claimed that Berger was a member of an international network whose aim was to destroy Christianity and replace it with Satanism. Something called *The Magazine* urged all Christians to boycott the companies that sponsored his TV shows. *Morgenbladet* had an article entitled 'Berger – a child of his times', which almost read like a tribute to the man behind *Taboo*:

> *A lot of players are still splashing around in the backwater following developments over the last decade which have opened up new doors in the field of comedy and driven out political correctness, but Berger is in a class of his own. Free of all inhibition, he uses himself and others, and in doing so breaks the boundaries that define the place of entertainment, the space between entertainer and audience. He curses his way out into the realities of everyday Norwegian life and grabs the sleepy consumers of culture by the balls. Hello – is there anyone out there?*

She heard the car going into the garage, and shortly afterwards Tage out in the hallway. It was close to midnight. She switched off the computer, wandered out into the kitchen. He popped his head in.

– Hi, Liss. Has Ragnhild gone to bed?

She offered him a cup of coffee. As though she were the one who lived there.

– I can't take caffeine any more, he said. – Especially not this late.

He got them both a beer and sat down at the table. – I'm worried about her.

– Mailin? said Liss, wilfully misunderstanding him.

– Yes, of course, naturally. But about Ragnhild too. I don't know if she'll be able to deal with it. If something really has happened. There's always been something special between Ragnhild and Mailin.

He took off his glasses, rubbed fiercely at his eyes and peered across at her, near sighted as an old mole.

– Neither you nor I could ever occupy that sort of place.

He got his glasses back on to his nose again and glanced at the door before continuing: – Now and then, in the privacy of my own mind, it has occurred to me that it might have been too close. At least on Ragnhild's part. But Mailin has done well. She seems more comfortable with herself than anyone else I know.

He drank straight from the bottle. Downed most of it in two deep swallows. – But, my dear Liss, if there is anything at all I can do for you . . .

He patted her on the arm. She glanced up at him, on the alert as always when someone touched her. Registered that it did not irritate her. Not even that sloppy 'dear Liss', which he always reeled off and which she had always hated, seemed to bother her this time. From the very beginning Tage had wanted to get to know them both, Mailin and her. During all the years they had lived together under the same roof, he had put up with being ridiculed and rejected. It was more or less to be expected, he seemed to think, when you appeared as a replacement for an absent father. After the wedding, he had taken their family name, and his devotion to Ragnhild was so great that he put up with everything. Like a well-trained dog, thought Liss, but then for a moment had to abandon the contempt with which she had always treated him, and was suddenly grateful to this man who had found his place in a home with women who didn't love him, not any of them.

* * *

She let herself into the room that had once been hers. It was tidy and clean. No posters on the walls, but they were still crimson red and the doors and frames black. At the age of sixteen Liss had finally got her mother to give in and allow her to paint the room in these colours, and for some reason or other she had let it stay like that, even seven years after Liss had moved out.

She switched off the light and lay naked under the duvet, rubbing her feet against one another for warmth. Still freezing, she drifted into a state that was halfway between waking and sleeping. She sees someone there, a man in a long coat climbing some steps. His name is Wouters, Liss. You will never be able to forget it. She runs into the dark room. Bends over Zako and listens to his breathing. It is deep and irregular.

There is a knock on the door.

Don't open it, Liss. You mustn't open it.

Mailin is standing there, in the middle of the room. She isn't wearing the blue pyjamas, but yellow ones that glow in the dark. And she has cut her hair.

Liss leapt out of bed, stood there listening out in the dark, certain that someone had just knocked.

Her back felt clammy; she opened the window and turned on the light. Found the notebook in her handbag and took it back to bed with her. Sat for a long time stroking the plush cover before opening it and starting to write:

Did it happen several times, Mailin, that you came here and locked us in? Got into bed and put your arms around me. Held your hands over my ears so that I wouldn't hear the hammering on the door. So I wouldn't hear the voice out there, what it was shouting in to us.

9

Liss let herself into Mailin's office and switched on the light. She didn't know exactly what she was looking for this time either, but she had an idea where to start. She walked over to the shelves and took down the three folders marked *PhD*. Two of them were full of articles, many printed from the internet. She put them to one side and opened the third. This contained documents that appeared to have been written by Mailin herself, systematically arranged with numbered dividing sheets. There was a list of books at the front. Then a title page: *Victim and perpetrator. A study of eight young men who were subjected to sexual abuse.* She flipped through several pages of notes, some handwritten. On the back of the next divider she came across what looked like the draft of a more extensive text:

> *Starting from Ferenczi's thesis (cf. 'Confusions of tongues between adult and child', 1933), two points will be illustrated in the introduction. (1) The child's search for tenderness can contain infantile erotic elements, but these will be pitched in the direction of play, security and contentment. The adult's passionate sexuality on the other hand exists in the tension between love and hate; it is the urge to transgression, which also includes destructive elements. (2) Abuse occurs when the child in search of tenderness and care encounters the*

passion of the adult. Passion can take the form of sexual desire, but can also be aggressive/punitive, and involve the child being compelled to bear the adult's feeling of guilt.

She flipped forward to the third divider:

In this chapter I will describe eight male patients all of whom have been subjected to sexual abuse. As far as possible it has been ascertained that they have not themselves subjected others to abuse. The eight will be interviewed before the treatment begins, and thereafter every six months over a period of three years. Evaluation criteria for aggressive behaviour, depression, anxiety and general quality of life will be employed . . .

This was followed by several pages describing methods, but in these papers Mailin had obviously not included any information on the eight patients. Maybe the rest of the thesis was in the archive safe she shared with the others who had offices there.

Liss looked out at the wet snow melting against the grey wall on the other side of Welhavens Street. Outside of town, in the surrounding forest, it would definitely be cold enough for the snow to lie. She could take the bus to Lørenskog and fetch the skis from her mother's garage, take a ski trip out in the forest. Until the silence wrapped itself around her. She decided that she would go out to the cabin the next day.

Again she looked at the postcard from Bloemenmarkt, the one she had sent to Mailin. Resisted the temptation to take it down. Always embarrassing to read something she had written herself. Instead she tugged at the Post-it note hanging below it. *Ask him about death by water*, Mailin had scribbled on it. In haste, by the look of it, a thought that had struck her while working on something else, and which for some reason or other she wanted to remember. She stuck it into the notebook she'd taken the last time she was there.

As she let herself out of the office again, the door at the other end of the room opened. The man who emerged was of medium height and narrow shouldered, wearing a suit jacket and blue jeans.

– Well if it isn't you, he exclaimed, and stood there looking at her. Then he approached until he was suddenly much too close. She took a step back, towards Mailin's door.

Older now, Pål Øvreby had grown a thin beard, but he smelled the same. Tobacco and something vaguely rubbery, mixed with Calvin Klein deodorant.

– I heard you were here a couple of days ago, he said quietly.

– Wanted to see her office, Liss managed to say.

Pål Øvreby shook his head. – This business with Mailin is of course . . . It looked as though he were searching for the right word to use. – Actually just beyond comprehension.

She didn't reply. It struck her that talking about Mailin was merely an excuse for him to intrude. But she couldn't bring herself to raise her hands and push him away.

At that moment the door to the waiting room opened. Pål Øvreby stepped back, startled. Liss recognised the woman who put her head round the door: Torunn Gabrielsen, whose office was on the floor below.

– I'm waiting, she said impatiently, and from the way she said it, Liss knew that Pål Øvreby was her property. – Oh, it's you, she added to Liss, and then sniffed, as though to find out what had been happening in the room.

Only now did Liss realise how irritated she was. – I was looking for something I forgot last time, she said brusquely.

– It's terrible, Torunn Gabrielsen said, and suddenly the suspicious note was gone from her voice. – To carry on like this and not know. I'm hardly getting any sleep at night.

She didn't look as if she was suffering from lack of sleep.

– Sit down, Liss. We ought to take the time to have a little chat.

– Weren't we going to . . .? Pål Øvreby interjected.

– It's worse for Liss than for us, Pål. The least we can do is find out how she's coping.

– It isn't necessary, said Liss, but she sat down in one of the chairs. – I can manage.

Pål Øvreby remained standing, diagonally behind her. She twisted round, wanted to know where he was.

– I know you and Mailin are very close, said Torunn, and slumped down into the sofa.

Liss could hear how she sort of folded her voice to sound sympathetic. – Maybe, she said, and turned the conversation in another direction. – Did the three of you work together?

The two psychologists exchanged glances. Pål Øvreby said: – We share a break room, we often have lunch together.

He still had that ridiculous American accent when he spoke. To Liss it had always seemed fake.

– Mailin was here on Thursday afternoon. Did you see her?

Again the pair looked at each other, Liss had the feeling they were deciding which of them should answer.

– We've spoken to the police about this, Liss, said Torunn Gabrielsen in a motherly fashion. – Her car was parked up the street here, but neither of us were here when she came.

She peered through the lenses of her glasses; maybe they weren't strong enough, and the frames didn't look as though they'd been renewed since the eighties.

– How much do you know about what Mailin was working on? Liss wanted to know.

– We sometimes discuss difficult cases over lunch, Pål Øvreby answered. – You have to in this business, back each other up.

He and Mailin had once been a couple. Almost ten years ago now. Liss couldn't imagine her sister needing backing from someone like him.

– Mailin and I cooperated quite a bit in the past, said Torunn Gabrielsen. – We wrote a number of articles together.

– About what?

– Abuse of women. Threats, psychological violence, rape. We want to live in a city that is safe for everyone, regardless of gender.

– But you don't work together now?

– Not so much.

Torunn Gabrielsen buttoned up her jacket.

– They can't agree with each other, Pål Øvreby chuckled. – So they have to argue instead.

She looked coldly at him. – This is something you don't understand, Pål, and there's no need to bother Liss with it. She's got other things to think about.

Liss interjected: – On that Thursday, Mailin was supposed to be seeing a patient here at five in the afternoon. His initials are J. H. Do either of you have any idea who that might be?

She could feel their gazes pressing in on her from both sides.

– Sounds as if you're investigating the case, Pål Øvreby remarked. He stood there, smiling in a way that suggested he believed Liss had come there in order to see him.

– Stop it, Pål, Torunn Gabrielsen hissed. – Even you can understand why she wants to know what's happened.

She turned towards Liss again. – I don't know who Mailin had an appointment with that day. We don't know each other's patients.

It seemed as though she was making an effort to control herself and speak calmly, and Liss had her suspicions about what it was that was making her so angry.

– But you all use the same archive safe?

Torunn Gabrielsen stood up. – We don't have access to Mailin's notes. She has her own lockable drawers.

10

Torunn Gabrielsen finished with her last patient and showed him out. All afternoon she had been in a bit of a state and it had affected her work, but she had managed to keep her mask up. Over and over again her thoughts returned to what had happened earlier in the day. Walking into the waiting room and finding Pål there pawing away at Liss Bjerke.

Torunn had seen pictures of her in *Dagbladet*'s magazine a few months earlier. Liss was completely unlike her sister, beautiful in a curious way, and not even the idiotic things she had to say on the subject of being a young woman could diminish that impression. In the flesh, her face had an even stronger radiance than in the photographs. A combination of naivety and self-assurance that had a confusing effect. Mailin often talked about her sister. The impression Torunn had was that Liss was a sort of pilgrim who had embarked on a dangerous journey through the world. The stories about this vulnerable and sensitive sister didn't interest her much. Not until she found out about this business involving Pål and Liss.

She stuck her hand down into the bag she had shoved under the desk, fished out her phone. She needed to talk to someone. It was almost a year now since she had last spoken to Tormod Dahlstrøm. The mentoring had come to an end at her suggestion. For a long time she continued to hope that he would protest, persuade her to carry on, give some explanation of why she wanted to terminate the process. He hadn't done any of those things. He had accepted the reason she gave, though he no doubt had his own opinions on the matter, and that had added fuel to the anger she felt.

Rather than call him, she finished a note in the patients' journal, put a few documents away in the drawer, locked it and headed up the stairs. The door to Pål's office was ajar, as usual when he wasn't seeing patients. She knocked once, pushed it wide open and stood in the entrance. He was punching away at his computer keyboard, feigning indifference. She banged the door shut behind her.

– What did she want with you? she asked without any preamble.

He wrinkled his brow and gave her a look that suggested he had no idea what she was talking about.

– Liss, you mean? Liss Bjerke?

She didn't bother to confirm it. She knew when he was lying, when he was bluffing, and when he was about to lie, because she knew every twitch on that face and could read it like a children's primer. Almost before he had got started, he abandoned the hopeless task.

– Well you heard her yourself. She's trying to find out what's happened to Mailin. Not everyone just keeps breezing along as though nothing has happened when someone they know goes missing.

If that was supposed to be a dig at her, it missed badly. She took a few paces into the room.

– I want you to stay away from her, she said firmly. – Well away.

Again he wrinkled his brow, and this time he managed to look genuinely astonished.

– Well I'll be damned. Someone lets themselves into Mailin's office, I go to see who it is that's poking around in there. Had no idea it was her baby sister.

Torunn hated to hear him use that phrase. – All I'm saying is, stay away from her.

She could see his anger forming. A way of tensing the neck, until it manifested itself in his eyes.

– Even if it was me that asked her to come, that has absolutely nothing to do with you, Gabrielsen. He pointed at her. – Not one fucking bit.

She took another step in his direction. – I've lied for your sake, she said between gritted teeth. – Lied to the police. I hope you haven't forgotten that. Given false evidence. That is a punishable offence. I might change that statement, little Påly. I might tell them what actually happened, that you weren't home at six o'clock on the day Mailin went missing, that you didn't show up until after nine, and that you were in an absolute state. And that it certainly didn't have anything to do with one of your patients, as you tried to get me to believe in the first place.

– I said that to spare your feelings.

– So now it's me you're protecting. Poor Torunn, I'll take good care of her. Spare me the hypocrisy, you're making me sick.

He gave up. Always did. He might toss off something in a flash of anger, take the occasional jab at her, but then he couldn't keep it up. Couldn't commit to anything, whether it be a quarrel or the opposite of a quarrel.

– I've got a few things to do, he said wearily. – Got to get this finished. He circled his forefinger over some documents lying on his desk, but she didn't believe for a moment that he was going to do any paperwork. He loathed it, could hardly even bring himself to make journal notes, and the disability allowance application forms never got filled. – Or will you pick up Oda?

She had been waiting for that. For him to end up there. With something about their daughter.

– You pick her up, she said as coldly as she could. – I don't remember making any alternative arrangement.

He shrugged his shoulders. – Then left me finish up here.

His arrogance made her anger flare up again. – She found out about you and Liss that time.

– Who found out what?

She could hear that he was taken aback. Without her needing to say any more, it was clear that he understood what she was talking about.

– So what? he said tentatively. But she knew how his neck dipped, whether he was going to lose his temper, or lie down and whimper. She had him under control, and now she gave an extra twist:

– I told Mailin.

– Get out of here, he hissed, and continued to tap away at the keyboard.

Back in her office, she again dug her phone out and opened the contacts. She was the one who had suggested that Mailin approach Tormod Dahlstrøm three years ago, when she was looking for a mentor. And it was she who had recommended her friend to Dahlstrøm, called her conscientious, talented, thorough. Had she thought that Mailin would take over such a large part of him, even to the extent of persuading him to mentor the research project, she would never have brought them together. Dahlstrøm never had much time – among other things, he had declined to mentor Torunn's own project when she asked him the year before. She had analysed her anger a long time ago, acknowledged that it stemmed from jealousy, not that it did anything to dampen her anger. Nor did it make matters any better that whenever a professional disagreement arose, Dahlstrøm always seemed to side with Mailin. But after what had happened now, it might be possible to put all this behind her and move forward.

She sat there looking at her computer screen, wondering what Oda was doing. It was Thursday, when the children in the nursery were served hot food; they'd probably eaten by now and were outside playing . . . She must have it out with Pål. Get him to tell her what he was doing on that evening Mailin went missing. She couldn't live with the uncertainty. She stood up and headed for the door, then stopped with her hand on the knob. Better to wait until he had calmed down, she realised. Stroke him the right way. When he was in a bad mood, he could be self-destructive. He'd been drinking a lot recently. He'd started reminding her again of how he and Mailin had been a couple for almost three years. Using it against her. Everything Mailin was which she could never be. Torunn ignored things like that, refused to appear weak. During one quarrel a couple of weeks ago, he had started going on about Mailin. Said something about Liss. Torunn pretended she wasn't interested. But she was almost nauseous with rage when she put together the different threads of his ravings. She made certain the whole story came out. Afterwards he said it was all supposed to be a joke. Drunken babbling, he called it. True enough, he could say the most unbelievable things when he'd been drinking. But never anything like this business with Liss.

Just over a week earlier, Torunn and Mailin had shared a lunch break. It wasn't something that happened often these days. After all the arguments about Mailin's articles, it was a strain for them to sit and eat together. Again Mailin had remarked how worried she was about her little sister, who was clearly adrift in some very murky waters indeed. Maybe it was something she chose to talk about because it was far removed from the professional disputes they were involved in. Torunn used the occasion to ask about Liss, and Mailin appeared relieved at this show of concern. Cautiously Torunn approached the time some nine or ten years earlier when Mailin and Pål were a couple. She received then confirmation of the very thing she didn't want to know.

11

LISS SAT IN the café outside the factory gates with the news-papers in front of her on the table. A week had passed since Mailin's disappearance, and now her sister had reached the front pages in both *Dagbladet* and *VG*. The police had contacted her mother the day before. They wanted to extend the search, with a name and a photo, hoping members of the public might come forward with something new. Her mother asked for Liss's view, though it was clear she had already decided to give her permission.

Liss had put off reading the newspapers for as long as possible. But in every kiosk and general store she passed, there was Mailin's face staring out at her. It didn't help simply to look away. *VG* had a long article about Berger, with the headline *No regrets*. The talk show host made it clear that he didn't see anything wrong in making fun of his guest when she didn't show up. One of his comments was quoted: *It looks as though the young feminist psychologist is not going to honour us with her presence. No doubt she was called to order by the rest of the cunt shoal.*

In *Dagbladet*, there was a backstory feature on Mailin. About her work with victims of abuse, quotes from former patients who had been helped by her. On the next page, an inter-view with Tormod Dahlstrøm in which he praised her research work. Beneath that the headline *Colleagues in shock*. Pictures of Torunn Gabrielsen and of *him*, Pål Øvreby. It looked to have been taken in the waiting room where Liss had spoken to them a few hours earlier.

She sat there looking out at the little Christmas tree with its brightly coloured lights. People walked by, their hands full of bags of shopping. They hurried about buying Christmas presents as though nothing had happened, as though Mailin's face on the front pages didn't have anything to do with them . . . Both *Dagbladet* and *VG* used a picture of her Liss had never seen before, obviously quite a recent one. Somewhere behind that calm gaze Liss could see that she was calling for help. She folded up the newspapers and threw them on to the floor.

The waiter was standing by her table. Clearly he remembered her from the last visit.

– Espresso? he asked.

– Double.

– Anything else?

There was something else. She had an impulse. Ask him to sit down at her table and place his huge hands over hers. The backs of them were completely covered in short black hair. Reminded her of Zako's hands.

Moments later, he was back with her coffee. On the saucer was a little chocolate in a gold wrapping.

– Soon be Christmas, he said, with something that might have been a smile in his eyes.

She took out the red notebook. Studied Mailin's lettering. It was uneven and forward-leaning, an almost childlike hand, it struck her. There was something childlike about Mailin herself too. The one who always knew what to do.

She wrote: *Mailin taught me almost everything I know. But not how to use it.*

Passion is both hatred and love.

The child who looks for love and is met with lust.

Was Mailin at her office that evening?

Torunn Gabrielsen. Jealousy.

Ask Dahlstrøm what happened between her and Mailin.

Pål's hands are always cold and clammy.

*Mailin: to the cabin on Wednesday afternoon. Called Viljam.
Call anybody else? Sent me text message Thursday. Contacted
Berger. Did she meet Berger?*

Taboos. We need taboos.

The patient she had an appointment with: JH. Did she meet him?

*Death by water. Title of something. A film? Possible to die from
drinking too much water? Ophelia.*

What is it about Viljam? Has Mailin noticed who he looks like?

She sat and looked at that last sentence. Hadn't noticed the
resemblance herself until she wrote it.

The way he talks. Something about his facial expressions.

When was the last time any of us heard from Father?

Dad.

She put the notebook back in her bag. It felt good having
it with her. Mailin's notebook. Now it was hers. Maybe Mailin
wanted her to write in it. The thought made her take it out
again.

Why do I remember almost nothing from when I was a child?

*I remember the way to school, a couple of the teachers, the names
of some of the others who were in my class. I remember Tage
coming to our house and that we hated him being there. I remember
we sat on the sofa and watched Dad on TV and Mum went out
and wouldn't sit and watch with us. But I should have asked you
about all the rest, Mailin. I have no memories of Dad from before
the time he left. And yet I can picture him so clearly.*

*What happened to the memories? Are they gone, or just hidden
away in boxes that can no longer be opened?*

*There is a policeman named Wouters in Amsterdam. I have tried
to forget his name. If I manage that, maybe I can forget what
happened there too. If I tell myself another story of what happened
that night in Bloemstraat. Tell it over and over again. So many
times that it turns into a memory and drives away what I see in
front of me now.*

*   *   *

She took the metro to Jernbanetorget, ran up the steps to Oslo Central. Another half-hour before the bus to Lørenskog. She slightly dreaded going out there. Her mother had made some attempt at putting up decorations. Hung the star up in the living-room window. Dug out the stable and crib she always put on the bookshelf at Advent. When they were children, Mailin and Liss were allowed to take turns each day putting a new figure into the display. Joseph and the asses, the wise men, the shepherds, the angels, Mary. The baby Jesus was saved until Christmas Eve morning. Her mother had carried on with the ritual after they moved out. Not for one moment had she ever believed what was supposed to have happened in that stable, yet the figures had to be displayed there, same ritual, year in and year out. And now it was as though she was putting them there to get Mailin to come home for Christmas, as she always did after the crib with the infant was finally in place.

Liss slowly crossed the pedestrian bridge to the bus terminal. Half turned. Couldn't face the thought of spending the night at the house in Lørenskog. Headed back towards the railway station. Suddenly she caught sight of a figure over by a newspaper kiosk. He was thin and bony, with untidy black hair. She recognised him at once as the man who had turned up at Mailin's office the first time she went there. He was wearing the same reefer jacket, with the anchor badge on the breast pocket. He was standing talking to a girl in a quilted jacket and dirty jeans.

Liss went straight up to him. – Do you recognise me?

The man glanced at her. There was a swollen scar on his forehead, beneath his fringe.

– Should I? he said, uninterested.

– I met you two days ago, at Mailin Bjerke's office.

This time there was no sign of his previous unease.

– Dunno what you're talking about.

But Liss had always had a better memory for faces than anything else.

– It was you. You stole something when you were there. What's your name?

He turned his back and hurried away, the girl in the quilted jacket following. Liss ran after them.

– Why did you tear a page out of her appointments book?

– What the fuck are you talking about?

– I've told the police. They're looking for you.

He stopped, took a step towards her. – If you say one more word to me, I will knock your teeth out.

He grabbed the girl by the hand and disappeared in the direction of the exit.

12

SHE CALLED VILJAM. Someone shouted something in the background when he answered. He didn't hear what she said and she had to repeat it.

– I'm at a seminar, he said apologetically. – I've only got a minute before the break's over. What is this about Mailin's car?

– I need to borrow it.

– Borrow the car? Is that all right?

– Why wouldn't it be?

– I don't know. It might be evidence . . . Sorry, Liss, I'm just not quite with it. I'm sure it'll be all right. I've got a spare key. When do you need it?

She had no deadline.

– I'm going out to the cabin this afternoon. I can come down and pick up the key. There's something else I've got to do first.

The man who opened the door looked to be in his forties, slightly built and thin on top, with a widow's peak. Though it was still quite early in the day, he was wearing a suit and a white shirt, although it wasn't buttoned at the collar.

– Liss Bjerke, I presume? he said with the hint of a lisp. When she confirmed her name, he let her in.

– I am Odd. His butler, he added with a little bow before heading down the carpeted corridor and opening a door. – Berger, your visitor has arrived.

Liss heard a rumbling response. The man who called himself Odd beckoned to her.

– Berger will see you in the living room.

She almost burst out laughing at the absurd formality of his speech, but managed to hold it in.

The room was large and well lit, with wide windows and a balcony looking out on to Løvenskiolds Street. A man she recognised from pictures in the newspapers and on TV sat behind a desk by the window, tapping with two fingers on a computer keyboard. In the flesh he looked older, the face yellowish and sunken.

– Sit down, he said without looking up.

She remained standing. Never liked being ordered to do something, especially not by elderly men.

Finally Berger gave her his attention. – Quite all right that you remain standing. He smiled as he let his gaze roam across her. – A woman like you should never sit down until she has been seen.

He pointed to a sofa against the other wall. – You don't look like your sister, he announced. – Not in the least. Coffee?

He stood up, dominating the room. There was a brass bell on the desk; he picked it up, rang it. Almost immediately, Odd appeared in the doorway.

– Bring us some coffee, would you, said Berger.

Odd addressed himself to Liss.

– Latte? Espresso? Americano?

His lisp seemed more pronounced than when she had arrived, and she suspected it might be an affectation.

– Espresso, she answered. – Preferably double.

Again the little bow before he disappeared. It seemed even more ridiculous this time, and Liss began wondering what sort of performance she was witness to.

– He introduced himself as your butler, she said as she reluctantly took a seat.

– That is precisely what he is, Berger replied. – As a matter of fact, a graduate of the best training school for butlers in London. I don't know how I would manage without the man.

– Must be good for your image, Liss remarked.

Berger limped across to a chair on the other side of his desk. – Of course. That is what I live off. A butler's salary is not *so* large and the returns are very quick.

He fished out a packet of cigarettes, French Gauloises, offered her one and a light from a gold lighter with the initials EB engraved on it.

– A present from my sponsors, he smiled as he noticed her studying it. – The closest I come to grace in this life is the way my sponsors treat me. I live on grace. By grace.

The door opened soundlessly and Odd appeared again, carrying a tray on which stood a silver pot, cups, saucers, sugar and a small jug of milk. He had pulled on a pair of thin white gloves, and this time Liss couldn't contain her slight outburst of laughter. No one asked what she was laughing at, and after pouring their coffees Odd withdrew once more, as silently as he had entered.

– I have, as you know, met your sister, said Berger. – But not on the evening when she was due to have come to the studio.

Liss had the feeling he said this to pre-empt her question.

He sat there, still observing her. – And now you want to know what has happened to Mailin. That is very natural. I gather you've just returned home from Amsterdam.

He exposed what looked like tiny and very white milk teeth. It gave his smile a childlike mischief that was in contrast to the worn face and large body.

– And *I* gather you defend child abuse, she responded as she dragged on the strong tobacco.

– Do I? he yawned. – My job is to provoke people, talk out loud about everything that outrages and fascinates them. I'm sure you've seen the sales figures for my show. No? The last show had a viewing audience of over nine hundred thousand. We're full speed ahead for the magic one million. We have to close down our phone lines after every show, can't handle the volume of calls. The Oslo papers alone had more than twenty-five pages on the last *Taboo*. But do we really need to talk about this? I so seldom receive visitors, and especially not strange women.

– What else is there to talk about?

– You, Liss Bjerke. That is much more interesting. A young woman travels to Amsterdam to study design but ends up spending much more of her time on assignments as a fashion model. Of a rather dubious nature, some of them, no doubt, at least by ordinary petit bourgeois standards. Let us speak of your party habits and your choice of lover boys.

She put the cup down so hard that the coffee splashed over into the saucer. *Who the hell told you that?* she wanted to ask, but managed to contain herself. Drove off the thought that even at that very moment someone was wandering around Oslo asking people how to find her. *Wouters,* the name flashed through her.

– Tell me about yourself, Liss, Berger encouraged her. – I love a good story.

She blinked several times, regained her self-possession. Had Mailin spoken to this guy about her? Mailin wasn't like that. She looked over at him. The dyed black fringe hanging over his forehead emphasised rather than disguised how ravaged his face really was. But in the middle of what looked like a battlefield, the eyes behind the small square spectacles were mild and bright. She'd seen a few extracts from *Taboo* on the internet. Berger talked about children, about how, in a market-driven society like ours, it was inevitable that child sexuality would become a commodity too, like everything else. He talked about performance-enhancing drugs, how they were necessary if sport were to go on meeting our need to cultivate the

superhuman. About the legalisation of heroin, a more interesting and cleaner stimulant than alcohol. Remarkably few
people were killed by heroin. What killed people was its
criminalisation and everything that led to it. Dirty needles.
Dangerous sex. Murders as a result of unpaid debts.

– I love a good story, he repeated. – And I love them
especially when they're told by someone like you, even if my
interest in young women is becoming increasingly academic.
He sketched a gesture of frustration from his groin up
towards his head. – More and more of it disappears up here,
he sighed. – But that's enough about that; tell me about
yourself. In return, I give you my word you will get answers
to all the questions you came here to ask.

This was not what she had come prepared for. For a
moment she was so confused that she might even have sat in
his lap like a little girl if he'd suggested it. Stay sharp, she
warned herself, and spoke briefly about wanting to be a
designer. This made him smile behind his cloud of Gauloises
smoke, which in turn caused her to reel off something about
trying out the modelling business: it meant nothing to her,
but some people, she had no idea why, urged her to make a
career out of it.

– Don't pretend you don't understand why, Berger admon-
ished her. – You've known for a long time how your presence
affects people. You've probably always known it.

– Not always, she blurted out. – I'm the typical ugly duckling
that ended up in the wrong nest. At primary school no one
wanted to have anything to do with me. Not at secondary
school either.

– Yes, I can imagine that, he nodded.

She wanted to stop there, but ended up telling him more.
About life in Amsterdam. The photo shoots. The parties. Was
even about to mention Zako. At the last moment she managed
to turn the conversation back.

– You were going to tell me about Mailin. How you met her.

Again the corners of the mouth lifted and the little white mouse's teeth showed. He had noticed how obviously she changed the subject.

– I like Mailin, he said. – I like you both, as different as you are from each other.

– Why did you want to have her on *Taboo*?

He sat upright with a little grimace, as though he suffered from back pain.

– What I do, Liss, is something completely different from those endless reality shows, which people got sick to death of long ago. Something happens when I show up on the screen. My shows contain something uncontrollable, something that's definitely not 'nice' and is even potentially dangerous. First and foremost I use myself, my life. My own history of abuse. Violence, sex, breakdowns. Then I invite a bunch of clowns along, people who will do anything at all to be seen on TV. In the beginning I was an untouchable; now it's becoming acceptable for politicians and media parasites to be seen with me. It gives them cred. I can make fools of these guests, dress them down, say what I like. Doesn't matter what I come up with, they'll keep on smiling, happy to be cool, longing to be cool.

He gave a hollow laugh and started coughing.

– Other guests are invited because I want opposition, he continued once he had got his breath back. – I had read some of Mailin's articles in the papers and got in touch with her. She's every bit as intelligent as I thought she was. But different. No feminist preaching. It's the world that concerns her, not ideologies.

– You've met her several times?

– Three times. She was here at my house a few weeks ago. We sat and talked about the show.

– I don't believe you. Mailin would never allow herself to be used in support of the sort of things that you get up to.

Again he laughed.

– Well we never got the chance to find out. She wanted to turn the show into something other than I had planned. That's fine. There would have been an edge. I like people to speak their minds. But then she never turned up.

– She got in touch with you.

– She called me the day before, he confirmed. – Said there was something she wanted to talk to me about. Practical things she wanted to get sorted out before the broadcast. She is irritatingly thorough. We arranged for me to call in at her office on the way to the studio. And I did.

– So you did meet her that evening?

– I got a text message that she'd been delayed. She sent me the code to the street door, asked me to wait in the waiting room. But as I say, she never arrived.

– And you just sat there?

– Hey, Liss, I've already explained all this to the police. If you ask me any more, I'll begin to suspect that you're working for them.

Beneath the teasing tone she sensed another that was sharper, like a warning. She stubbed out her cigarette, decided on a different approach.

– Do you believe we can manage without taboos?

He took a deep drag, held the smoke for a few moments before letting it drift out between his teeth with a whistling sound.

– We get rid of some, but then new ones appear. I try to destroy them a little quicker than they crop up again.

– Why?

– Because I am a revolutionary, a visionary, someone who wants to uncover something that is truer and purer than this culture of bullshit that is gradually choking us to death . . .

He looked at her seriously. Then he beamed.

– Don't let me fool you. Naturally this has bugger-all to do with politics. I do what I've always enjoyed doing, provoking people. Do you see why I could no longer be a priest? When you give toys to children, most of them start playing with them. But some immediately want to take them apart, to see what's inside. Afterwards they throw them away. That is the kind of child I am. I'll never be any different. Luckily for me, I earn a helluva lot of money from this kind of stuff.

He laughed his hollow laugh.

– But now I'm thinking about quitting.

– Quitting TV?

– Everything, actually . . . The New Year broadcast will be the final show. Know what it's going to be about?

She didn't know.

– Death! Death is the ultimate taboo. It defies everything. It won't even let you scratch it.

– A talk show about death? You wouldn't be the first to come up with something like that.

– My approach will be different. He didn't expand.

– Now you're making me curious, said Liss.

– It will not be without a certain irony, he smiled and looked proud. – And yet it will be deadly serious. That's all I'm going to say. You've already got me to say too much as it is.

13

SHE JUMPED ON board a tram on Frogner Way. Sat in the
rear carriage without paying. Sent a text message to Viljam.
He was still at his seminar, but she got an answer: *Per På
Hjørnet at one okay?*

She was there at quarter to. Had an espresso. Went outside
in the cold for a smoke, bought a newspaper and went back
into the bar again. It was twenty past by the time he arrived,
it irritated her.

– Don't you get tired of sitting there swotting up on points
of law? she contented herself with saying.

– Don't even talk about it.

He ordered a latte. She had another espresso. Suddenly felt
the urge for something that would pep her up more than coffee.

– It's so dark in this town. The light just keeps disappearing.

– It must be almost as dark in Amsterdam in the winter,
Viljam protested.

Liss didn't want to talk about Amsterdam. – I was at
Berger's today.

– Berger, he exclaimed. – What were you doing there?

She didn't answer. An elderly woman scurried past on the
pavement outside. Walked along holding on to her tiny hat.

– There's no wind at all out there.

Viljam sipped his coffee. – Did you go there because there's
no wind?

She looked at him. He had dark rings under his eyes.

– What you said about Mailin having found something out

about Berger. That she was going to put pressure on him before the show.

– Did you ask him about that?

– I called on him because I wanted to form some impression of him. Maybe next time I'll ask him straight out.

Viljam shook his head. – And what do you think that will achieve? That he'll fall on his knees and confess to something or other? He seemed exasperated. – Leave that kind of thing to the police, Liss. If you keep on like that, you might be making it more difficult for them to find out what's happened.

He brushed his long fringe back. – I'm not too happy either about the way they're working, he said quietly. – They don't seem to understand that with each passing day our chances are less. If something doesn't happen soon . . .

Liss waited. The implication of what he almost said hung somewhere in the air between them. She took two big gulps, shivered and put the cup down.

– I feel sure you know what it was Mailin found out about Berger.

– You're right, he answered.

He said no more; she grew impatient.

– I want you to tell me what it was.

She could see the muscles of his jaw working. Then he breathed out heavily.

– Mailin spoke to someone about him, he said. – Someone who was initiated into the world of grown-up secrets by Berger a long time ago. That was what she was going to reveal during the broadcast. Look directly into the camera and come out with it.

Liss opened her eyes wide. – Expose Berger live and on air as a fucking paedo?

Viljam began picking at his serviette. – She wanted to force him to cancel the broadcast, as a way of demonstrating that there are in fact certain limits. I asked if she knew what sort

of reaction she would get. She claimed she did. I'm afraid she
was wrong about that.

Liss thought about this for a few moments and then said:
– According to Berger, she never showed up for their meeting.

The serviette was in pieces. Viljam dropped it on the floor.
– Could be he's telling the truth.

To Liss it seemed as if things had gone very quiet around
them. As though people sitting at the other tables had stopped
talking. He's suffering, she thought. *You're* suffering, Liss.

She laid a hand on his arm. – Let's go for a walk. Have
you got time?

They crossed the square in front of the Town Hall, continued
along the quays. Nativity stars glowed in all the windows.

– You were supposed to be getting married in the summer,
she said out of nowhere.

Viljam glanced at her. – How did you know that?

– Mailin sent me a text. Asked me to keep next Midsummer's
Day free.

– And there we were planning to keep it to ourselves for
the time being, not say anything until Christmas Eve. He stared
straight ahead. – She admires you, he said suddenly.

Liss looked startled. – Who?

– Mailin says you've always been braver than her. Not scared
of anything. Climbing steep hillsides. Always the first one in.
Diving from the top of big rocks.

Liss scoffed.

– You broke away and went to Amsterdam, he continued.
– Mailin feels such a strong sense of being tied up in everything
here at home.

What's to become of you, Liss?

– What about you? she asked, to change the subject. – Are
you brave?

– When necessary.

They were standing by the torch of peace, at the end of the quays. A few boats bobbed up and down in their berths. The wind had got up. Thin flakes of snow wafted around, unable to land.

– When are you going out to the cabin?

– This afternoon.

He dug out a bunch of keys, opened it and slipped a car key out.

– Think you'll find out anything else about Mailin there?

She shook her head. – You and Tage have already been there. And the police.

She turned to the flame burning in its leaf-shaped container, reached out her hand. Found out how close she could hold it without getting burned.

14

LISS PARKED MAILIN'S car at Bysetermosan. Continued on foot up the forest track, into the silence. Not silence, but all the sounds of the forest: the winter birds, the wind in the treetops, her own footsteps.

She reached the place where she had to turn off the track. The snow had melted and frozen again. She could walk on it without using snowshoes. First a fairly steep upward incline. Almost four years since she'd been there, but she remembered every tree and every rocky outcrop. Wherever she went, this landscape always went with her.

She climbed over a rise and could just make out the roof of the cabin ahead through the trees. Stood a moment looking out across Morr Water and the ridge on the far side. Not until it had begun to turn dark did she carry on down.

There was a strong smell of brown creosote. She remembered that back in the autumn, Mailin had mentioned that she and Viljam were going out there to do some painting. She'd asked if Liss would come home and help them. Liss ran her hand over the rough planks of the outer wall. The sensation conjured up images of Mailin. It felt as though she were there, and for a moment Liss wondered whether she would be able to go in.

She lit the paraffin lamp in the kitchen, took it into the living room. Noticed the burnt-out logs at the back of the fireplace. Mailin must have been in a hurry. Neither of them ever left the cabin without tidying it up. The place should be clean, the ash removed and fresh logs brought in, so that all the next one to visit had to do was put a match to them. Now Liss had to sweep out the fireplace and then go out to the wood shed for more logs. Viljam and Tage had taken a quick look in there, as had someone from the police. Had they perhaps made a fire? It wasn't like Mailin to ignore the strict rules they had made themselves.

Later she turned on the radio, tuned in to some piano music. Even that was too much and she switched off again, needed to empty the room of sound. She stood by the window and looked down towards Morr Water through the dim evening. Many years since she had stood there like this, Mailin by her side; that had been a winter day too, the sun about to disappear behind the hills, the trees full of twinkling needles. *We'll never give up this place, Liss. It's ours, yours and mine.*

Liss wept. Didn't understand what was happening, had to touch her cheeks to feel. Mailin, if this is my fault . . . she murmured. *It is not your fault. You couldn't do anything about what happened.* I must turn myself in. I killed him.

She pulled on the head lamp, picked up the two buckets and walked down through the trees. Followed the little stream down to the rock. It was as steep as a cliff. Deep below it. In the summer they could dive in from it. Had to dive far enough out to clear the shelf. Below the rock there was a channel in the ice. If it was glazed over, the ice was thinner than cut glass. The current from the stream kept the water open, no matter how cold it got. Old trees decomposing in the depths of the water released gases that also hindered the formation of ice. She threw one of the zinc buckets in, kept a tight hold on the rope, it fell almost three metres before it hit down below. She hauled it up, eased it over the outcrop, then did the same thing with the second bucket.

Further away on the left, there was a little bay. Our beach, they called it, because it was covered in rough sand. It was just big enough for both of them to lie there and sunbathe. Naked, if they were alone out there. Above it, between the trees, an old boathouse that contained a rowing boat and a canoe.

She returned via the beach. Put one foot on the ice, tested her weight on it; it would hold if she walked straight ahead. If she headed right, towards the rock and the stream, it would break, she would go through, sink down into the icy water. *Death by water*, she thought. If Mailin had gone this way . . . She hadn't. The car was found in Oslo. Could someone have driven it there?

She got the wood stove going, boiled water. Went out on to the steps and lit a cigarette. Mailin didn't allow smoking indoors. The stink lingers for years, she said, and Liss would never break the rule.

After a bowl of minestrone soup, she had a thorough look through the living room, the kitchen and the two bedrooms. She examined the cupboards, used her head lamp to look under the beds. Lifted up the mattress on the upper bunk bed, where Mailin used to sleep. Apart from the ashes in the fire, everything appeared to be as it should be.

She put on two more logs, curled her legs up under her in the corner of the sofa. Let her gaze wander. The antlers on the wall, next to the barometer. They were absolutely huge and must have belonged to a giant of an elk. She was the one who had found them. Down by Feren Lake. In summer they used to take the canoe out and carry it between the waters. Searched for beavers' dams. Spent the nights out under the open sky. Woke at dawn and crept over to the place where the grouse fought each other in mating duels. All this she could remember; she was twelve and Mailin sixteen. But from the time when she was younger, there were just stray memories and diffuse recollections. When Mailin spoke of things that had happened when they were children, she was always surprised at how little Liss remembered of it. *Don't you remember how you nearly drowned in Morr Water?* Liss didn't. *You were in your first year at school and thought you knew how to swim. I had to jump in with my clothes on and rescue you.*

Her gaze stopped at the photo albums on the shelf. They were Father's. At home, there was nothing that had belonged to him, but because it had been his cabin before he gave it to the two of them, he had left the albums here. She took one of them down. Hadn't flipped through any of them since she was eleven or twelve. There was a certain thrill about it, almost forbidden. Father's past. There had always been something about that side of the family. Something that was never talked about. Liss could just about remember her grandfather, huge and white bearded. Mailin said he always wore a suit and could imitate all sorts of bird calls. Cuckoos and crows and tits, of course, because you heard them there all the time. But, strangely enough, vultures too, and condors and flamingos. Not easy to say where he'd picked these up from, because he never travelled anywhere and hardly ever watched television.

Her father looked seriously out at her in one of the photos. Tall and pale and long haired, he was standing outside his parents' house on the edge of the forest. It was pulled down years ago. Now there was an institution for difficult children there. In another photo her father was skiing somewhere in the mountains, wearing an anorak with the hood up. Liss turned to the picture she liked best. She was sitting on his shoulders, holding on to his long brown hair as though she were riding a horse. She felt a prickling in her stomach as she looked at the photo, and suddenly she remembered: he stumbles, and she shrieks as she falls towards the ground, but he recovers just in time. And then he does it again. She sobs for him to stop, put her down, but he realises she wants him to do it again, and then again.

The brown photo album was older. From Father's childhood. He was helping out on one of the neighbouring farms; Mailin had pointed it out to her once. Father helped to round up the cows in the evening. Or to hang the hay out for drying. His body was thin and angular, like hers. *She* was standing in the doorway. His mother. *You look exactly like her, Liss. Can you see that?* Her father's voice saying this. She could recall the timbre of it. Maybe they had been sitting here in the cabin, on this sofa. They're flipping through this album together when he says this about how alike they are, as though it were a secret that she mustn't tell anyone . . . The photo of Grandmother was black and white, but Liss was certain that even their colouring was the same. That tall, skinny woman in the blouse and the long skirt, pale and with a strange look in her eyes, half there, half dreaming. The hair pinned up in an old-fashioned way. In one of the other pictures she was standing out on the steps, smiling and looking even more like certain pictures Liss had seen of herself. Everything she knew about her came from Ragnhild. Grandmother had had her own studio where she spent the days painting, although nothing ever came of it apparently. She had left the family when Father was ten years old, but Liss didn't know where she'd gone. Maybe Father had never known either. According to Ragnhild, she was ill in some way and ended her days in the mental hospital at Gaustad.

Liss took out the notebook. Mailin's book.

Why do you remember everything, Mailin, and I've forgotten?

She sat for a while, considering the question, before she continued writing.

All the things I want to ask you about when you come back.

There is something in Viljam's eyes that reminds me of these pictures of Dad, have you noticed? Something around the forehead too. And something about the way he talks. But the mouth is different.

Mailin, I miss you.

I miss you too, Liss.

Why didn't you clear out the fireplace before you left?

I can't tell you that.

There are only five more days to Christmas. I want you to come home.

She wrote down in detail what Mailin might have done at the cabin on that last visit: cooked some food, sat with a glass of wine and stared into the fireplace, or worked on her computer by the light of the paraffin lamp. She wrote down what her sister might have been thinking before she fell asleep. How she packed the next day, suddenly in a rush because she had to meet someone and didn't have time to clean the fireplace. She hurried through the trees and down to the car. Drove out of the parking space.

Liss couldn't imagine what happened after that.

15

THE COMMUNAL KITCHEN was sparsely equipped. A fridge, a table and five chairs, a small cooker, a microwave. On one wall hung a poster of Salvador Dali's melting wristwatch.

A guy in a hoodie came in, gave Liss a quick look, took something out of the fridge, it looked like liver pâté. He cut himself a slice of bread, buttered it and hurried out again with the bread in his hand.

Just then Catrine returned from the toilet.

– Promise me you'll never move into a student village, she warned her. – The moment I can afford something else, I'm out of here. She scowled in the direction of the kitchen surface, which was covered in dirty dishes and leftovers. – You've no idea how tired I am of people not tidying up after themselves. The guy that was just in here is one of the messiest pigs I've ever shared a kitchen with, and that's saying something.

When they were living together in the commune in Schweigaards Street, Catrine had often been annoyed by the same things: pigs, usually of the male variety, who never cleaned up. Liss refreshed her friend's memory, and Catrine had to concede that there had been a couple there who were almost as bad.

– If I ever move in with a guy, it'll be a male nurse, she said now. – At least they know how to keep things tidy.

– I can't actually see you with a male nurse, Liss observed.

– Don't say that. I don't mind if he's a bit of a wimp. Maybe even gay. As long as he tidies up after himself.

It had been more than three years since Liss had last seen her. Catrine had let her hair grow, and dyed it black. She'd changed her way of dressing, too. From baggy pullovers to tight-fitting tops with low necklines trimmed with lace from the push-up bra beneath. From wide unisex jeans to skinny jeans that gave her a better-shaped bum than she'd ever had before. When Liss asked, she had to confess that she'd starting going to the gym as well. She was still into politics, but it was a long time since she'd last squatted in a house or fought in a street battle. She was studying political science now and sat on the board of some student body.

– How are things at home?

Liss didn't think of the house in Lørenskog as home, but she let it pass.

– I'm sure you can imagine what it's like.

Catrine nodded. – It seems so unreal to me. For you it must be completely . . .

She couldn't finish the sentence, and Liss didn't respond. She had visited Catrine for a break. Not to have to talk about all the things that were troubling her. Catrine obviously understood this. She stood up, fetched coffee, apple juice and biscuits.

– I see you're still on a negative calorie budget, said Liss when she saw the packet.

– Yep.

– You don't eat meat either?

– Now and then. But not wolf or bear.

Liss had to smile, a moment's light relief, and then the thoughts began again.

– What does *death by water* mean to you? she said as she tipped three rounded spoonfuls of instant coffee into a cup.
– Got thousands of hits when I googled it. I think it must be the title of a film. Or a novel.

Catrine was better read than she was and went to see a lot of weird movies.

– Has a familiar ring to it, she agreed. – How about the name of a rock band?

She popped out to her room, returned with a computer, got online. Almost immediately she exclaimed:

– Of course. *The Waste Land* by T. S. Eliot. I did actually once read it.

Liss peered over her shoulder.

– I like that. A drowned Phoenician.

– Why the sudden interest in poetry? Catrine wondered. – You've never been much of a reader.

– It might have something to do with Mailin, she said. – She wrote *Ask him about death by water* on a note and pinned it to her noticeboard.

Catrine clicked forward to a commentary and read aloud:

– *The Waste Land* is a journey through a kaleidoscopic world labouring beneath a curse of sterility. Few who appear in that desolate landscape see any hope, almost all are blind.

She turned to Liss. – Do you think this has something to do with Mailin's disappearance?

– Very unlikely. But every trace of her I come across seems to have some kind of significance for me. Everything that might tell me something about what she was thinking, what she was doing.

After the coffee, Catrine brought out a bottle of Southern Comfort. She'd always liked sweet-tasting things. After a couple of drinks she suggested that she and Liss take a trip into town. Liss didn't know what to say. She didn't know whether Catrine really wanted to spend the whole evening with her. Felt herself surrounded by a membrane that protected her but also certainly made her inaccessible.

– I'm not exactly a bundle of laughs right now, she said.

– Get a grip, Liss Bjerke. Catrine sounded offended. – If you really think I'm out for a bundle of laughs, then . . .

– Well I could certainly do with having something completely different to occupy my mind, Liss said, interrupting her as she emptied her glass. She couldn't face the thought of going back to Lørenskog and spending the night before Christmas Eve with her mother and Tage.

Despite having a pretty limited wardrobe of clothes, Catrine took almost an hour to decide what to wear. Liss was given the job of stylist, for which Catrine asserted she was extremely well qualified, adding, with appropriate irony, that she had read in *Dagbladet*'s magazine article that she was on the brink of a career as a top model. Liss didn't mention that she herself had spent less than ten minutes getting ready to go out. She had chosen one of the pullovers she found in Mailin's dresser. Her leather jacket was finally dry, but it had some disfiguring stains on the lapel. Catrine ended up with a short, clinging satin dress. She lay down on the floor and struggled into a pair of sheer tights without knickers. She had arranged to meet a friend from her political science course. Her name was Therese, and she had something going with a footballer. – He plays in the First Division, Catrine revealed as they sat on the metro heading into town. – A premium quality piece of beef, I believe.

Therese was standing outside Club Mono doing something with her phone. She was short and dark, with intense black eyes. An unlit cigarette dangled from her narrow lips.

– Where's the fillet steak? Catrine enquired.

– On his way.

Liss was only mildly interested in the codes they spoke in, but Catrine had clearly decided that her friend wasn't going to feel left out of things this evening.

– Therese and I have developed a system of classification for our dates, she explained.

– Simplicity itself, Therese added. – The same as they use at the meat counter. That's to say, shoulder and rump are *ziemlich schlecht*.

– Offal is worst, Catrine said with a grimace. – I can't stand liver.

– OK, liver and offal are worst, Therese conceded. – Next comes shoulder and rump and so on. Cutlets and ham aren't bad.

– And your date tonight is fillet steak, Liss interjected, to show that she understood. – What about sell-by dates?

– Of course, Catrine exclaimed. We'll start using that. Best-before dates.

– Use-by, Therese added.

They found seats on an old-fashioned sofa in the back room of the café. Catrine leaned towards Liss and shouted above the music that flooded from the speakers in the ceiling.

– I'll tell Therese, just as well she knows . . . Liss is Mailin Bjerke's sister.

Therese stared at her. Liss liked her dark eyes.

– The woman who . . . oh shit. Sorry about that.

Liss gave her a quick squeeze on the arm. – It's quite all right. Catrine invited me out so I'd have something else to think about. But tell me about your footballer.

Therese recovered quickly. – Hello, Catrine, thought I could tell you things without the whole town having to know about it.

– Only told Liss, cross my heart. You can trust her.

The first beer was gone and another round ordered. Liss had hardly eaten and guessed she was going to be drunk before the evening was over.

– No one'll hear it from me, she swore and crossed herself. The atmosphere of secrecy had a calming influence on her.

– He's so sexy I might even end up going to watch a football match, Therese shouted. – It's about the most brain-dead thing I can imagine, but if he's gonna be rushing about in skimpy little shorts, then . . .

– Footballers wear enormous shorts, Catrine corrected her. – They probably need all that space for their family jewels. Handball players are the ones with the tight little shorts.

Liss had to smile. Catrine had always been interested in the male anatomy and ever since primary school had conducted her own studies in the field.

– What did you say his name was, the fillet steak?

– Jomar.

Catrine gaped. – Are you going out with a guy named Jomar?

– That's exactly what I'm doing.

– You could always call him something else, Liss suggested. – Jay, for example.

– And you better start reading up on football too, Catrine teased her. – Study the sports pages, all the league tables from Germany and Belgium.

Therese put down her glass. – He's not like that. He can talk about other things. He studies.

– At the sports academy, Catrine added with a meaningful look over at Liss.

Therese scoffed. – Well, would *you* go out with one of those political science wimps?

– *Pas du tout*, Catrine confirmed. – Not if I was looking for sex.

– Which you are.

– I don't go home with somebody on a Saturday night to talk about the Norwegian welfare state with him, if that's what you mean.

– Bad guys are for fun, said Therese, – good guys for . . .

– Study groups, Catrine interrupted.

Liss burst out laughing. The membrane around her was

invisble, and maybe the others hadn't noticed it. She thought she would be getting in touch with Catrine again. And she felt she wanted to put her arms around Therese with the dark eyes and squeeze her tight.

It was past 11.30 by the time he arrived. For some reason or other Liss knew straight away that the guy standing in the doorway of the room they were sitting in was the footballer. He was tall, so she could see his head above the others hanging around him. He had tangled fair hair that looked bleached. Therese caught sight of him and waved. He came across with another guy, who was black and wore his hair in dreadlocks.

Therese introduced everybody. – Catrine, this is Jomar Vindheim.

He was wearing a suit beneath his leather jacket, a white scarf with gold threads running through it tied around his neck. Catrine gave him a sort of sour smile, probably reacting to his name.

– Jomar, this is Catrine, and this is . . .

He turned towards Liss. Took her hand. Surprised, she tried to withdraw it, but he kept hold. His eyes were quite slanted and in the light from the lamps on the wall looked greyish.

– Jomar, he said.

– Liss, she said as she managed to free her hand.

His friend's name was Didier and it turned out that he had just been bought from Cameroon. Suddenly they were aglow with an interest in football, Catrine and Therese. Both of them were suspiciously knowledgeable.

– Lyn play with a flat four, Catrine volunteered.

– A flat eleven, Jomar corrected her, translating for Didier, who burst out laughing.

– Bright girl, he said, and patted her arm.

– *Bien sure, comme une vache*, she answered with her most brilliant smile.

Catrine's grandmother was Belgian, and when her friend started speaking French it always sounded fluent to Liss. Didier was visibly impressed too and looked like being a pushover. On the other side of the table Therese had attached herself firmly to her fillet steak, describing an invisible but distinct chalk circle around him, territory she was prepared to defend with any and all means necessary. Liss was in the corner of the sofa, on the outside. That was where she wanted to be, partly present, mostly somewhere else.

16

JOMAR VINDHEIM's BMW was parked right outside. He said he would drive; had hardly drunk anything, he assured them. Therese squeezed in beside him. Didier wedged himself into the middle of the back. Every so often he broke off from his conversation in French with Catrine to say something to Liss in Afro-English. He put an arm around each of them and smelled of a perfume Liss had never come across before. She liked the weight of his fist on her shoulder.

They sped up Trondheims Way, across Carl Berners Place. Jomar was looking for an address in Sinsen. By the time they clambered out of the car, it had started to snow again. Heavy, ragged flakes that hit the ground and melted instantly. They could hear music from an open window. Liss still felt only slightly affected by the drinking.

They ended up in a large flat on the fifth floor. The music was so loud she didn't have to talk to anyone, could just glide from one room to the next, note the looks, some indifferent, some interested. Found a seat on a sofa in the darkest of the rooms. Sat and watched people dancing. Someone had a joint. It appeared between her fingers, sweet-smelling, and she took two deep drags before passing it on. It was stronger than usual, she realised at once that it would make her distant. Just then someone put on some rai music, at any rate the kind of stuff Zako used to listen to. His name flashed through her mind. Looking for a way into the locked room. The door behind which he still lay on his back on the sofa.

But she didn't open it, and was pulled on into the music, as thick as cannabis oil. She glanced at Catrine, who had manoeuvred Didier into a corner of the room. Her evening is saved, she thought, closing her eyes and drifting deeper into the music. Shook her head when someone asked her to dance.

– I won't take no for an answer, he said.

Liss opened her eyes. Jomar Vindheim squatted down beside her.

– I want to dance. With you.

Again she shook her head. But when he took her by the arm and pulled her up, she didn't protest. Looked round for Therese but didn't see her.

He wasn't all over her. Led a touch unrhythmically, but she couldn't be bothered to make things more difficult for him. The room was filled with the voice of the Arabic rai singer; it was slow and heavy with scents. She was in a garden with hanging flowers, a place where no one could reach her.

– Therese sent me a text before I met you at Mono. Said you were the sister of that . . .

She half turned, signalling to him that she didn't want to talk about it. He laid his hand on her bare shoulder, one finger gliding along her hairline.

– I must see you again, he said.

– I like Therese, she replied.

– Me too. But I must see you again.

And then Therese was there, Liss pulled herself free and swayed back towards the sofa. There she sank back into the garden she had made. Through avenues of jasmine and poppies she peered out at the dancers. Catrine was now wearing a red Santa hat with a flashing light on the tassel. She was draped round Didier's neck. His hands had a firm hold around her trim buttocks. A little further away, Therese stood on tiptoes and kissed her fillet steak on the cheek. He looked away. Liss met his gaze and again shook her head.

After leaving the toilet, she wandered into the inner bedroom. Had an idea what was going on in there. All the traffic traipsing in and out. A guy in a denim jacket, without a hair on his head, sat over a glass table and scattered snow across it.

– First round is on the house, he yawned.

He made three lines. A boy who had been sitting beside Liss on the sofa and had given up trying to pick her up took out a brass pipe, snorted a line and handed it to her; he didn't look a day over seventeen. She bent forward, sniffed it up. She felt it burn from the bridge of her nose all the way to the top of her head. An instant of intense pleasure. An image of the cabin appeared. Lie in the snow among the trees on the marsh, looking up into the black sky.

– I'll go back there tomorrow, she said aloud.

The boy leaned towards her. He was wearing tight-fitting yellow trousers that made her think of portraits of Renaissance princes. But he has no codpiece, she thought, and it made her laugh.

– Back where? he wanted to know.

– Never mind, she said.

– Neverland?

She nodded.

– You're cool. I like you. He put his arm around her, ran a finger down into her neckline. She twisted away, smacked him across the head with a bright smile, glided out into the corridor, headed for the living room, stopped in the doorway.

The guy who had laid the lines out on the glass table emerged into the hallway behind her. Opened the front door. A man with curly black hair stood there wearing a reefer jacket. She recognised him at once. He had been at Mailin's office that day, torn a page out of her appointments book. Just then Jomar appeared and said something to him.

– That's none of your fucking business, the guy in the reefer jacket growled, and pushed a bag into the dealer's hand. In return he received an envelope, checked the contents and disappeared again.

Liss slipped out of the front door, the guy in the reefer jacket was already on the next landing down.

– Hey, she shouted.

He didn't answer, carried on down. She ran after him, caught up with him just by the street door.

– I'm talking to you, she said, feeling stronger than ever.

The guy turned towards her with that same evasive look she had seen in the office.

– What's the idea, following me about?

– You know exactly what I mean, she hissed.

He tried to get out the door, she grabbed hold of his arm.

– You were at Mailin's office that day.

– Oh yeah?

– You knew she wasn't there, but still you went there poking about in her stuff.

He glared at her. – You've had too much, bitch.

– Why did you tear that page out of her appointments book?

She felt an enormous rage, wanted to lay into him, hit him, bite his throat.

– What's your problem, he shouted, and pushed her against the wall. – Stay away from me, you fucking psycho.

He took hold of her by the throat. She felt faint, the dizziness rising to her head; it could end here, like this . . . Far away, footsteps on the stairs, running down.

She collapsed. Someone slapped her on the cheek. Repeated her name, over and over.

She looked up into Jomar Vindheim's face. His eyes were filled with anger.

– Who the hell did this?

– Never mind, she coughed. – It was my fault.

She awoke to the smell of sweet water. Aftershave. She was in a man's house. Looked round. Alone in a large bed. Felt down. Clothes still on. The room was in darkness, but she could see a strip of light below the drawn blind.

It wouldn't be much fun trying to piece together what had happened before she ended up in this bed. She must try to keep to the main details. Not get sidetracked by all the fragmentary flashes of memory that came whirling by: in town with Catrine. Meeting Therese. Fillet steak and the African. The party at Sinsen. The guy who had been at Mailin's office. She'd gone for him. The fillet steak, whose name was of all things Jomar, had carried her out to his car and put her in the back seat. When he pulled up outside Casualty, she sat up. Refused to go in. So instead he'd taken her back to his place. She hadn't the strength to protest, but seemed to remember talking away as she lay in his car. About Mailin. About the cabin at Morr Water. About Amsterdam too, probably. Had she mentioned Zako? . . . She'd passed out as soon as they got into his flat. A recipe for idiocy. Three highs. End up at the home of some unknown male and in no condition to take care of herself . . . He hadn't touched her, she could feel it. He had put her in this bed and gone off to sleep somewhere else.

She got up quietly and came into a room. The TV clock said quarter to eight. One door led to the kitchen, another to a hallway. A third door was ajar. She could hear his deep, even breathing from inside.

The cold hit her as she opened the front door. She was wearing only Mailin's thinnest pullover, had left her jacket behind at the place where the party was. She backed inside again. Some outdoor clothing hanging on a stand. Leather

Marlboro jacket like this guy Jomar had been strutting about in the night before, two heavy-weather jackets, some suit jackets and a snowsuit. She put on what looked like the older of the heavy-weather jackets. Checked the pockets, emptied out some chewing gum, a few receipts and a packet of condoms, put them on the table by the entrance. Opened the door again and slipped away down the steps.

17

TORMOD DAHLSTRØM WAS still seeing a patient when she arrived. A woman, judging by the fur coat hanging just inside the door to the waiting room. Liss slumped down in the leather chair and began flipping through *Vogue*, couldn't face reading it, not even looking at the pictures. The distant hum of voices could be heard from the office, broken by a long pause. Then a few sentences, then another pause. She picked up *Dagbladet*'s magazine section. Berger with his mouse's teeth grinning out at her from the front page. She turned to the interview. He talked about his childhood. A father who was a pastor in the Pentecostal church. How glad he was to have grown up with this clear distinction of black and white, between what was Christ's and what was the Devil's.

The office door opened, and a woman in a dark green outfit emerged. She was quite a bit older than Liss. She held a handkerchief to her nose and took no notice of her, so it was a few seconds before Liss realised that this was a woman who had featured on the front pages of the weeklies for years, even in Amsterdam. The woman unhooked her fur and trudged out without putting it on.

Dahlstrøm appeared in the doorway.

– I'd no idea you had patients on Christmas Eve. Sorry if I . . . .

– It's fine, he assured her. – I've had a cancellation today. He added: – I'm glad to see you.

To judge by his look, he was sincere, his tone of voice too. Liss looked for a chink in it, something that would reveal the false bottom, but didn't spot one.

– As for the woman you just saw leaving here . . . Dahlstrøm put a finger to his thin lips. – I'm counting on your discretion.

– Of course, said Liss. – I won't give another thought to all those thousands I could have got from *Seen and Heard*.

– A thick wad, I've no doubt, he agreed as he held out a hand towards the even softer leather chair inside his office.

– Are any more of your patients famous across the whole of Europe?

– No comment.

He smiled, and the deep-set eyes seemed to come a little closer. – Because I've written books and my ugly mug's been on TV for years, a lot of celebrities think I'm in a particularly good position to understand their problems.

His face grew serious again, and the eyes returned to the deep holes from which they looked out on to the world and didn't miss a thing.

– How is your mum bearing up?

Liss shrugged her shoulders. – I haven't been there for a few days.

– You're living with friends?

– Sort of round and about.

She was still high after last night's adventures in town, he must have noticed, but he said nothing. She had a reason for coming here, something she wanted to talk to him about, but suddenly she couldn't think of anything to say.

– With each passing day we have to give up another fragment of the hope we're clinging to, he said suddenly. – Not an hour passes without my thinking about Mailin. I feel sick, Liss, both mentally and physically. It is impossible to imagine that she won't be back here again, knocking on the door . . . I always know when it's her.

Liss's energy returned. – If Mailin disappears, then I disappear too, she said.

Dahlstrøm sat up in his chair. – Disappear?

She looked at the table, feeling the weight of his gaze.

– Not literally. I didn't mean it like that. But without her, I'll become a different person.

He seemed to be thinking this over. Then he said: – I think something is bothering you. Not just Mailin's disappearance.

She shrank. He noticed everything about her. Suddenly she felt naked. Yet it was still possible to talk to him. Start just where she was sitting. Continue to the party at Sinsen, the guy in the reefer jacket . . . There was something she had to remember, something she'd seen up in that flat. It slipped away and was gone in a welter of thoughts, everything that had happened since she came back, and before that, Bloemstraat, Zako dead on the sofa, the photo of Mailin . . . That time in Amsterdam was four years on the run, and before that, running from home, the commune in Schweigaards Street; before that again, living with Mother and Tage, and then the time before Mailin moved out, Mailin the good, Mailin whom Mother was so proud of, the bearer of all hopes, the one who was going to make something of herself. And before that, on the other side, where the memories refused to let her in . . . *Liss, where do you come from?*

She pulled herself together, forced away the need to tell him all this.

– I just have this feeling that I must look for Mailin, she said.
– But there are no places to look . . . I've started writing things down.

He looked at her with interest. – Like what?

She hooked a lock of hair and twisted it round her finger.
– Thoughts. And questions. What might have happened to her. Where she was when, who she met. Stuff like that.

– What the police do, he commented.

– Actually I've made notes of something I wanted to ask

you about, she said. – About the people she works with down in Welhavens Street. Do you know them?

– I know Torunn Gabrielsen.

– Not Pål Øvreby?

Dahlstrøm ran a hand across the light, downy hair still showing on his head. – I've met him a few times. A psychologist who uses unorthodox methods in treating his patients. Why do you ask?

Liss didn't know why. Probably because she wanted to hear something that would confirm what she herself thought about him.

– Torunn Gabrielsen and he live together, don't they? She seems jealous of the fact that Pål and Mailin were once a couple.

– I wouldn't know anything about that, said Dahlstrøm. – But I think Torunn Gabrielsen feels bitter towards Mailin for a quite different reason.

He seemed to ponder this. – There's a lot of gossip here, Liss. I don't usually sit here chattering away about my colleagues, though this is a special situation . . . I mean, I'm refusing to accept that anyone might have harmed Mailin. That's the very last possibility we want to entertain, isn't it? When every other possibility has been ruled out.

Liss knew exactly what he meant.

– Mailin and Torunn Gabrielsen sat on the editorial board of *The Shoal*. You've heard of that magazine?

She'd looked through a few editions Mailin had sent her.

– I'm sure you know that they also published a book together, he went on. – But at some point things went wrong. Mailin has been working with victims of abuse ever since she was a student. Her work is unusually good, it's attracting a lot of attention.

– About the child's need for tenderness and the adult's passion?

Dahlstrøm leaned back in his chair on the other side of the low glass table.

– Mailin is fascinated by a Hungarian psychoanalyst named Ferenczi. One of Freud's closest associates, and yet still a controversial figure.

Liss had seen several books by him in her sister's office.

– Ferenczi was convinced that the abuse of children took place on a large scale, and at all levels of society. Freud of course came to believe that most accounts of this were the result of the child's subconscious and imagination.

– But what is it about Mailin's work that provokes the others at *The Shoal*? Liss interrupted.

– Mailin is interested in the fact that victims who present in a particular way expose themselves to risk, Dahlstrøm replied. – She wants to show people, women and men, how to look after themselves better, given the world we actually live in. And she has written a lot about how some repeatedly end up in situations that result in them being subjected to abuse. The hidden damage done to them traps them in a recurring pattern of behaviour. Torunn and the others on the board seem to believe that an account like this takes the focus off the perpetrators of the abuse, even to the extent of accusing Mailin of legitimising attacks on women.

He rubbed his finger over the slight hollow in the bridge of his nose. – A few months ago, Mailin wrote a response in *Dagbladet*. She criticised the others on the staff of *The Shoal* for avoiding any consideration of the behaviour of female victims, and in doing so denying them the chance of moving on. She was very crude, very direct, the way Mailin can be if she's provoked.

Dahlstrøm stood up, crossed to the coffee percolator, lifted the jug and sniffed at it.

– Torunn Gabrielsen's working method involves the patients meticulously describing the assaults they have been subjected to. She wants them to relive them, so to speak. The idea is that they will remember and in that way neutralise the damage inflicted on their psyche. Mailin has become increasingly sceptical about this way of doing things. She believes that it often makes things worse if the traumatic event is relived in detail. It can easily seem like another assault. Torunn is interested in Ferenczi too, but Mailin's interpretation is different. She wrote an article about his theories in which she maintained that it can be just as important to learn to forget as to remember. This is among the things she's looking at in the treatment of the seven young men as part of her PhD.

– Seven? Liss exclaimed. – Eight, isn't it? I had a peek at one of the folders in Mailin's office. I'm certain it said there that there were eight men in the study.

Dahlstrøm looked surprised.

– I must say, you're going about this very thoroughly, Liss. Yes, originally there were eight subjects. One was dropped, or withdrew. That was in the early stages, over two years ago.

He poured out two cups of coffee, handed one to Liss. – I think we'll take a chance that this is okay today as well.

– Has it been there since last time?

– Can't remember, he winked. – I'm really quite an absent-minded person.

He didn't seem the least bit absent-minded; on the contrary, Liss felt sure he was taking in every last thing about her.

– What's it like, living in Amsterdam? It's a wonderful city.

Liss didn't answer.

– Mailin said you had a boyfriend down there.

Had Mailin spoken to Dahlstrøm about her? And about Zako?

– Then she's misunderstood, or you have. I don't have a boyfriend.

Zako was never your boyfriend. He used you. You let him use you. Zako is dead. You killed him, Liss Bjerke.

– There's something wrong with me, she said.

Through the window the sky had turned dark grey. Suddenly she felt like a sack that was about to split open. I shouldn't have come here, she heard herself think.

– Sorry. I come here and start to talk about myself. You aren't my shrink.

– That's not something that should worry you, Liss.

– I've never been like other people, she muttered.

– A lot of people feel that way. Most of us perhaps.

– I'm from another place, far away. No idea how I ended up here. Just know the whole thing is a misunderstanding. I don't know anyone who . . .

There was a knock on the door. Dahlstrøm stood up and opened it slightly.

– Two minutes, he said, and turned towards her again. – Liss, I'm glad we can talk together. I hope you'll come back and see me again.

He added: – And I don't mean as your therapist.

18

It was still snowing as she walked down Slemdals Way. It was colder now, and the wind came in sharp gusts that blew the snow into tiny drifts on the pavement in front of her. She pulled the heavy-weather jacket tightly around her. It was extra large and could have fitted two of her. The question of how she was going to return it struck her. Avoid meeting the owner. Images from the night before appeared again, but they were less distinct and no longer gave rise to so many emotions. Maybe this was the effect of the conversation with Dahlstrøm. The mere thought that there was somebody she could talk to made her feel calmer.

Approaching Ris Church, a man in a Father Christmas suit and thin shoes crossed the road. He had trouble keeping his feet on the slippery surface. He had a burlap Christmas sack over one shoulder. He padded along the pavement, picking his way tentatively between the frozen patches, slipped, fell and swore. The episode reminded her that it was Christmas Eve. She dreaded going out to Lørenskog, but she had hardly slept at all, and she needed a shower, even something to eat . . . Sit there and watch as Ragnhild slowly went to pieces. Tage's futile attempts to keep her from falling apart.

A quick throb from her mobile. She took it out. *Bitch!* it said on the display; that was all. She didn't know Therese's number but realised who the message was from. It was a pretty accurate description of how she felt about herself as she headed on through the snow.

* * *

Viljam looked as though he'd just come out of the shower. The longish dark hair was wet and combed straight back. There had been no need for her to call in to wish him a merry Christmas. A text message would have done just as well.

– I'll pay you ten kroner for a shower, clean clothes and a cup of coffee, she offered.

For the first time she saw a flash of something like humour in the dark blue eyes.

– Salvation Army closed already? he asked.

– I'll go there if I need a roll and some soup as well.

He took her at her word. When she came down, freshly showered with sweet-smelling hair and clean underwear from Mailin's wardrobe, he was standing there stirring something in a saucepan. She sniffed.

– Mexican tomato soup, he informed her. – Pretty good considering it comes from a packet.

He heated rolls, put some cheese and a bowl of apples on the table.

– Good of you to help out an old wretch like me, she said in the quavering voice of an old beggar woman.

He smiled dutifully. – And someone's given you a new jacket, I see, he remarked. – Obviously you bring out the best in people.

She slurped at the soup, had no wish to tell him anything about yesterday's events.

– What are you doing this evening? she asked, changing the subject.

He hesitated a moment. – Mailin and I had planned to have Christmas dinner with Ragnhild and Tage. Now I don't know.

– Can't you come along anyway, she asked, – so I don't have to sit there with them on my own.

– Maybe . . . Actually, what is this with you and your mother?

– Is there something between me and her? she said guardedly.

He put his head very slightly on one side. – Nothing, apart from the fact that it seems as though you can't stand her.

– That isn't right. I don't have a relationship with her, either a good one or a bad one.

– With your own mother? Sounds strange. But Mailin and Ragnhild are very close.

She couldn't ignore this. – So now you suppose I'm the jealous little sister?

– I don't suppose anything specific at all. Far as I'm concerned, the subject is closed.

– There is no subject, she insisted. – Ragnhild is the way she is. Impossible to live with, unless you're made of rubber, like Tage. She has her idea of the world, and if yours is any different then you must be pretty stupid. She made it impossible for our father to live there. She froze him out.

Viljam looked at her for a few moments.

– Mailin's idea of what happened is slightly different.

Liss pushed her soup bowl away. – Mailin is a compromiser. I'm not.

She looked out into the street. The snow was coming down heavily. A man hurried by with two children wearing their Sunday best in tow. A post office van stopped outside.

– Need a smoke, she said and got up.

She stood outside on the steps. The cigarette tasted like sheep's wool, but she needed it. She needed something else too, something to keep her going, help her make it through the day . . . A week and a half since she'd returned to Oslo. She had no plans to stay. No plans to go back. Limbo. Something must happen. She flicked the half-smoked cigarette between two parked cars, opened the letter box and pulled out the letters and brochures, *Aftenposten*, and a package in a thick brown envelope.

She laid the mail on the kitchen table. – Your Christmas post has arrived, she called to Viljam, who had disappeared down into the living room.

– Great, he called back without notable enthusiasm.

She sat down and carried on eating her soup. It was luke-warm by this time but still tasted incredibly good. She looked at the pile of mail. Suddenly she had a thought. The brown package was addressed to Mailin, the name written with a black felt-tip pen. No sender's address.

– Viljam?

He came up from the living room.

– We should open that, she said and pointed at the package.

– Perhaps.

It didn't look as if he wanted to. She carefully felt the padded envelope. Inside was something hard. At once she thought she knew what it was.

– It's not possible . . . She prised open the flap, put a hand inside and pulled out a mobile phone.

Viljam stared at it.

– Hers? she asked.

– Put it back. Don't fiddle with it. The police need to see it without us messing with it . . .

– It's already got my fingerprints all over it. She turned it on – Do you know the PIN code?

– Liss, this isn't very smart . . .

– I want to see, she interrupted.

He sat at the table. – She often used her birthday as a code. Liss tried; it didn't work. – What about yours?

He gave her the four digits. No luck there either.

– I give up, we better go down to the police station.

She gave it one last try, using her own birthday. The display flickered into life.

– Shit, she called out, and held it up to show him. The phone was looking for a signal. The battery icon showed it was almost discharged. She opened the menu.

– Liss, let the police do this.

She ignored him, navigated to the call list. Last call was outgoing: 11 December, at 19.03. She grabbed the pen that was hanging on the noticeboard and a piece of paper.

– What are you doing? He sounded as nervous as she was.

– I need this call list.

She opened the messages. Kept on taking notes. Found the one Mailin had sent to her: *Keep Midsummer's Day free next year. Call you tomorrow.* By the time she was finished, she had covered two whole pages.

– Don't you trust the police?

– Are *you* impressed by what they've done so far? she said as she navigated to the images file.

– She didn't use the phone much for pictures, Viljam volunteered. – She bought herself a good-quality digital camera in the summer. Carried it with her almost everywhere.

It looked as though he was right. The last photo had been taken fourteen days earlier, obviously at a restaurant. Viljam's face in golden-brown light.

He gave a quick smile. – Annen Etage. The evening we got engaged. I surprised her.

Liss opened the folder with video clips, sat there with her mouth open.

– What is it? Viljam stood up and walked round the table.

She pointed to the display. The last recording had been made on 12 December at 05.35.

– The day after she disappeared . . .

– Listen, Liss, I said we should let them have this straight away.

She didn't answer. Pressed play.

Indoors, in darkness, difficult to make out detail. A torch is switched on, must be the person doing the filming who is holding it. A floor is illuminated. A few newspapers strewn about, some bottles. A figure lying there, tied to something.

– Mailin, Liss screamed, bit her lip without even noticing it.

The camera zoomed in, the torch was shone into the face. Suddenly Mailin's voice: *Are you there, is that light there?*

– What's the matter with her eyes? Liss whispered.

There was blood around her sister's eyes, and they stared blindly into the light without blinking. *What are you doing? Are you filming me?*

Panning round the room, some crates stacked against a wall, a wheel next to two barrels. The camera turned back to Mailin's face.

Sand . . .

She said something else, indistinctly. Then she shouted: *Liss!*

There was a cut. Then a glimpse of a building.

THAT EVENING AS *I sat in darkness down by the beach listening to the sound of the breakers, I had almost made up my mind. Go down there and disappear into the darkness, let myself be swallowed up and consumed by the water, along with the Phoenician and all the other drowned bodies.*

Then a figure appeared over by the stone steps. I had a feeling it was Jo. He passed by in the darkness without spotting me, wandered on through the sand. I could see he was taking his clothes off. That scrawny white boy's body in the cold moonlight. I waited until he was undressed before getting up and sort of casually strolling up behind him. He was standing staring out to sea, still hadn't noticed me. I saw there was a note in one of his shoes. There was something written on it, like Forget me, in big, scrawled handwriting. He was going to drown himself. I saved him, Liss. He saved me. On the beach that night, with the breakers washing in over our feet, we made a promise to each other, without a word being said.

PART III

PART III

1

JENNIFER PLÅTERUD STRUGGLED across the grass. The hill was coated with a layer of fresh snow some fifteen or twenty centimetres thick. It was Christmas Eve, approaching two o'clock, and still it hadn't been cleared away. Trym, the elder of the boys, was on shovelling duty that day. The last thing she did before going out to shop was call up to his room and remind him of the fact. Now she was furious as she went over in her mind how she would confront him, firmly, but short and effective, so as not to ruin the Christmas mood. Trym was the phlegmatic type. It wasn't something he got from her; on the contrary, he was exactly like his father. Only a touch worse. A characteristic like that was probably more strongly reinforced through the succeeding generations, she shuddered. The phlegm had accumulated in her husband's family over the centuries, she had long ago realised. Now and then with an undercurrent of melancholy. As a pathologist Jennifer demanded the highest standards of scientific accuracy, and she was always dismissive of facile conclusions in the field of genetics, neurobiology and anything else that had to do with it. But when it came to psychology, to which she had a contemptuous attitude, she was oddly enough a sworn upholder of the ancient teaching about the four bodily fluids: depending which of these we have in the greatest abundance, one of four characteristics will be predominant.

She herself was decidedly sanguine, but with a touch of the choleric, she had to admit. The fact that she had fallen for a man with quite the opposite characteristics – a brooding and silent bear from the other side of the world – and allowed herself to be transported to his much too cold and much too dark homeland only showed that opposites attract, another idea she sometimes advanced, with as little scientific basis as when applying it to the psychology of human beings.

In the hallway she put down her bags of shopping and pulled off her boots, which were made of antelope hide and had stiletto heels, and then called out to her oldest boy. She got no answer, not surprisingly, since the bass notes from his amplifier were making the ceiling above her shake. She was about to run upstairs to deliver the necessary rebuke when her mobile rang. She pulled it out of her jacket pocket.

– Flatland here.

The moment she heard that grey voice, she knew she had to be off. At the institute they had discussed who should be on duty over the Christmas weekend, and she had volunteered. As a rule, things were quiet on days like this; the odd call maybe, questions that could be dealt with over the phone. But Flatland was an experienced technician who never called about trivial matters.

Passing the crossing at Skedsmo on the slushy motorway, she took a quick look at her watch and assessed her chances of getting back in time for Christmas dinner at six o'clock. Missing the tidying up and the decorating was nothing to get upset about. And Ivar was cooking the rib of pork, the sausages and the sauerkraut. He was a keen and competent cook, and she would never get the hang of that Norwegian Christmas food anyway. She had introduced a few Australian traditions to the family. Stockings filled with small presents hung on the boys' beds on Christmas morning. And in the afternoon, they would eat turkey and Yorkshire pudding, followed by mince pies with brandy butter.

She would even miss the traditional lighting of candles on her father-in-law's grave, and the rice pudding at her mother-in-law's that the boys, a few hours before their own Christmas meal, had to gorge themselves on in order to find the hidden almond. And then there was all the mulled wine, and as many ginger biscuits as they could get down while subjected to Grandma's alternating cries of encouragement and admonishment. Ivar's brothers and sisters and their children would also be there, and sitting there in the car Jennifer felt a relief that she would be getting out of it all.

Karihaugen appeared through the haze. She turned on the radio. Located a station she didn't have to listen to. Eight days earlier, she had been unfaithful. It had happened so unexpectedly that she had to shut her eyes tightly every time she thought of it. Not from shame, but surprise. A man whom she had not remotely suspected she was attracted to. And maybe she wasn't either, neither before nor after it happened. But he had turned her on in a way no one else had in years. Not since Sean. But *that* was different. She had been in love with Sean. More than that: unhappily and incurably obsessed from the moment he placed a hand on her shoulder in the lab. When he went back to Dublin, she would have gone with him unhesitatingly if he had suggested it. Of course she would have hesitated. But it might have ended with her leaving the boys and the farm and this wintry land . . . Sean was a scar that evoked a delicious pain when touched, and what had happened eight days earlier was fortunately nothing like that. Just frantically and crudely exciting. It began and ended there. Possible it might happen again, though not necessarily with *him*, but it might well force itself to the surface once again. That reminder of the part of herself that kept everything else going.

* * *

She parked in the drive outside Oslo police station and called Flatland. A few minutes later his silver-grey Audi emerged from the gates. She sat beside him in a front seat that was draped in thick plastic. The man seemed to worry more about dirtying his car than anything else.

– Good job it's you that's on duty, he said, and she didn't doubt that he meant it. He was in his fifties, hardly more than ten years older than her, but greying and as scrawny as an old dingo.

– What's the news? she asked as he swung down Grønlandsleiret.

– We may have found the woman who's been missing for over a week.

– The psychologist?

– We're pretty sure it is.

– And since you want me along, I assume she's in no condition to give an account of herself.

He glanced across at her without answering.

– Where are we going?

– Down to Hurum. A disused factory.

Jennifer sighed.

– Not more than an hour's drive, Flatland added in his usual monotone.

– Who found her?

– A patrol from the sheriff's office down there.

– And what were they doing in a disused factory on Christmas Eve?

The technician looked over his shoulder before gliding on to the E18.

– We got a tip-off. The woman's partner and her sister turned up at the crime response unit with her mobile phone. Claimed it arrived in the post. There was a video on it.

He changed lanes and accelerated down into Festning Tunnel. – Someone videoed the missing woman. A factory tower was shown in the film. From the postmark on the package, we were able to locate the place within an hour.

– Videoed her and sent it to her partner? Jennifer exclaimed.
– So we're talking about premeditated murder?

– I'm not prepared to commit myself on that.

Jennifer had worked with Flatland many times before. He was the type who never said more than was strictly necessary. She glanced round the inside of the car. It wasn't just her seat; the others were covered in the same thick protective plastic. The man is more than a touch compulsive, she thought. Definitely an advantage in a job like his.

On the roof of the factory there was still a large sign bearing the name *Icosand*. At the gate was another: *Stop at red signal*. It had to be years since that broken light had given any signal at all. A tall woman in uniform waved them in.

Two quick-response vehicles and an unmarked car were parked by the factory tower. The policewoman approached them when they stopped. Clearly she knew who they were and identified herself by name, rank and where she was stationed.

– We've cordoned off the whole area, she told them. – And we're using the lower entrance. She pointed to the largest of the buildings, a concrete block four storeys tall. – That's the one least likely to have been used by the perpetrators.

Each carrying their own case, they headed off towards the furthest end of the building, a rusty door that was stuck open and refused to be closed behind them. Inside, it was dark. Flatland took a long-handled torch out of his case. They found a staircase, followed it up to the second floor, as the constable had told them, and turned into a corridor. Several of the windows were broken, the glass lay in piles along one of the walls.

They emerged on to a gallery in a hall illuminated by two powerful lights. In the middle of the pool of light lay a naked body, propped against a concrete pillar. Two figures in white moved about down there, and a third was bent over a camera pointed at the floor.

Flatland pulled out protective overalls, hoods and shoe covers. Jennifer was still wearing her high-heeled antelope leather boots, and the shoe covers didn't fit very well. She found a couple of unused hair bands in her pocket, and that helped them stay on.

They clambered down a rusting metal conduit, Flatland went first, making sure it was safe for her.

– We've made our entry point there, the technician with the camera said, pointing.

Jennifer stood a couple of metres away from the unclothed body. The head was held up by a strap around the neck, fastened to a hook in the concrete pillar. A line of blood ran from the hairline and down over one cheek, but otherwise she looked unharmed. The eyes were half open.

– When was she found?

– According to the sheriff, they entered the building at about one thirty; that's to say almost two hours ago.

The technician's breath misted as he spoke. The temperature inside the hall was no higher than it was outside.

– Has a local doctor been here to verify death? Jennifer asked.

– The people who found her didn't think it was necessary. There's no doubt that what we have here is a death.

Jennifer frowned. The body lying there was probably suffering from severe exposure; great care must be taken to ensure that death really had occurred. She approached the body directly. Only then did she notice the pool of dried blood the woman was partially lying in. It was mixed with something of a lighter consistency. She leaned forward and shone her torch on the back of the head. Beneath the caked and bloody hair there was a gaping half-moon-shaped hole. A greyish substance had seeped out of it and down the neck.

– Agreed, she commented between gritted teeth. – Not much room for doubt there.

All the same, she pulled her stethoscope out of her case.

Listened to the heart and lungs, careful not to touch the strands of hair that lay between two accretions of blood around the navel and obviously did not come from the woman herself. Having ascertained that there was no sign of a pulse or respiratory sounds, she dug out a penlight to take a closer look at the pupils. Squatted there for a long time studying the woman's eyes. They were badly damaged, the membranes covered in blood, as though jabbed with a pointed object. One eye was almost completely ripped to pieces.

Having completed her examination, she withdrew to a corner of the hall to dictate her notes. Flatland came ambling over. Stood waiting until she was finished.

– Well? he said, offering her a liquorice pastille.

– The woman is dead, Jennifer confirmed.

Flatland grinned mirthlessly. – You're usually a little more forthcoming than that.

– I know. She grinned back at him. – And since this is Christmas Eve, I'll give you everything I have, and a bit more too.

The edge of a pouch of snuff appeared under his lip. She realised that what she had said might be open to misinterpretation and hoped he wouldn't immediately make a certain kind of joke. Under different circumstances she would have had no objection. Fortunately, Flatland wasn't the type to get carried away.

– Not much marbling, she hurriedly added, – nor blistering of the skin. As you know, those are early signs of decay, but at low temperatures the appearance is delayed.

– What you're saying is that she's been here for some time.

Here or somewhere else equally cold for several days. Maybe as long as a week. The temperature in the rectum and the vagina is two degrees, and the lividity on the stomach and in the groin is lighter than usual.

– Cause of death?

– You want a provisional answer? The markings on the neck show that the strap has been pulled tight.

– Choked?

– Yes, but not necessarily to death. She may have been alive when the skull was crushed.

Flatland pushed the snuff bag back into place with the tip of his tongue.

– On the floor at the back by the wall there's an area with a lot of bloodstaining.

Jennifer peered over at the dark corner he was pointing to.
– In other words, she was dragged from over there and hung from this pillar by the neck. In addition, her eyes are, as you can see, covered in marks from being jabbed by some sharp object. Didn't you say they looked to be damaged in the video on her mobile?

Flatland gave a quick nod of assent.

– Before she was choked and had her skull crushed, Jennifer concluded, – she could have been sitting here in the freezing cold staring blindly out in front of her.

2

Thursday 25 December

THE SKY ABOVE Oslo was filled with orange and gold-grey wrinkles, but over the hills in the north it was still almost black. Jennifer Plåterud glanced at her wristwatch as she let herself in to the Pathological Institute. The time was 8.15. Even before the finding of the body, the case had attracted a lot of media attention, and now things were about to get a hundred times worse. She couldn't bear lagging behind, had to deliver her results before people began asking for them. And yet there was another reason why she had chosen to go to work even before the Devil had put his boots on.

She hung her coat up in the cloakroom, found a clean outfit and pulled on the trousers, shirt, coat, hat and mask. Three minutes later, she was opening the door to the autopsy room. Going through that door was a signal: take off one way of thinking and feeling about the world, and put on another.

But on that particular morning she remained standing in the darkness inside. Images from the factory the afternoon before had pursued her all through Christmas Eve, forcing their way in through the light sleep she fell into now and then. Christmas dinner had been postponed for almost two hours, but no one expressed any annoyance when she took her place at the table without the slightest indication of what she had just been doing, and she didn't think it showed on her either. For twenty-five years, more than half her life, she had practised medicine, the last fifteen of them mainly on dead bodies; it had become routine a long time ago. But arriving at that crime scene, stopping in the gallery of that factory and seeing the naked young woman lying there in the sharp light . . .

At the table, she had managed to look as if she ate with a hearty appetite, and afterwards things took their usual course. The boys pretended that they no longer looked forward to opening their presents, hid their expectations behind slow yawns, punching away on their mobile phones and generally giving the impression that there were a thousand other things more important. As for Ivar, he was a picture of pride as he served out the rib and sausages, and enjoyed himself even more afterwards as he sat down with a glass of cognac and starting handing out the packages arranged under the tree, reading out the tos and froms, usually with some comment about what could possibly be hidden inside that lovely wrapping paper – *maybe a collapsible bike*, or *I'm guessing this is a fire engine* – and astonished delight when he unwrapped her present to him, a pullover he had himself tried on in H&M few days earlier. She didn't begrudge him his childlike joy in Christmas.

With an almost inaudible sigh, she closed off the stream of thoughts, switched on the light in the autopsy room and went to work.

After a quick lunch, she hurried over to her office and wrote a preliminary post-mortem report. Reading through it afterwards, she found herself mentally searching for something that was not to be found in the succession of strictly descriptive terminological sentences. She couldn't shake off the thought that there was something she ought to have seen. Twenty-nine-year-old woman, she summarised. Fair-haired, regular features. She didn't know much about the dead woman, no more than what she had already read in the newspapers. A psychologist, almost completed her PhD despite her young age. Jennifer struggled to abstract something that wasn't connected to her appearance or what she already knew about her. Choked, she repeated to herself, and beaten to death; the eyes . . .

Suddenly she knew what it was. She picked up her phone and opened the call list.

To begin with, Jennifer's characterisation of human types on the Hippocratic model was not seriously meant. Naturally she had never believed that it really was the four bodily fluids that determined a person's temperament and character, but it amused her to assert that this theory, with its origins several centuries before the birth of Christ, was every bit as scientific as the Freudian waffle that certain psychiatrists continued to promote twenty centuries *after* that same birth. In time, however, she had come to believe that Hippocrates' categorisation, as developed by Galen and by doctors of the Renaissance period, accorded strikingly well with the people she had come across in her life. Almost unnoticed, the irony that had accompanied her interest in the theory had faded away, until a time came when she had to confess to herself that she believed in it almost without reservation. People's inner worlds could be arranged in such a way as to give her the illusion of comprehending the incomprehensible. And over the years, her categorisations grew more and more sophisticated. She came to believe that a person's temperament and character did not necessarily derive from one of these four categories alone. For example, she regarded herself as first and foremost sanguine, a *bon vivant* who didn't easily let things get her down; but she had to admit that she was also much under the sway of the choleric. Mercurial anger could at any moment descend on her like a sly dog, even on days when she couldn't explain it away as a result of hormonal fluctuations. It was reassuring then to think of it as the accumulation of bile, no matter how metaphorically meant.

Detective Chief Inspector Hans Magnus Viken from the Department of Violent Crimes was another choleric, she had soon realised. She didn't yet know whether this was combined with the melancholic, which would be typically Norwegian, or with the phlegmatic, which would actually be equally typically Norwegian. When he telephoned her at about two o'clock, she knew at once what he wanted.

Viken was not the kind of detective to rely on reports. He had to carry out the investigation himself. In and of itself this was a good quality, but she wasn't altogether sure she liked him looking over her shoulder in the autopsy room. She had to admit he had a certain talent, even if the so-called 'bear murders' the year before had done fairly serious damage to his reputation. But he wasn't the only one to have to give an account of himself in the wake of that investigation. The section head involved had to find something else to do, and several others had handed in their resignations. Viken, however, wasn't the type to let something like that get to him. He'd hung on and survived, and would probably stay with the department until they had to carry him out, thought Jennifer. He even had the guts to apply for the post of section leader that fell vacant as a result of that infamous case. She liked that kind of obstinacy, every bit as much as she disliked his know-all attitude.

He arrived at 3.10, opened wide the door of the room and strode in, a disposable cap balanced on his head. He probably wants it to look like a mitre, she had time to think before she noticed who he had brought along with him. She swore silently. Viken was one thing. She knew more or less where she had him. And for a choleric he kept his temper under good control. On top of that he was susceptible to flattery, which made it easy to disarm him. As for the man who appeared in the doorway behind him, she did not want him there under any circumstances. He was much younger than the detective chief inspector. Younger than her, too. Much too young. Not much past thirty-five. She felt herself blushing. She hadn't seen him since the Christmas party. Not since the night after the Christmas party, to be more precise. He'd sent her a couple of text messages, even including one on Christmas Eve. Mostly she wanted to forget the whole thing. And not forget the whole thing. But she had to avoid letting Roar Horvath get too close to her. At least at work.

– I saw your preliminary report, Jenny, said Viken jovially.

When in the world did he start calling me that? she wondered as she returned his smile, and gave Roar Horvath a quick nod. He responded with a wink. That was okay; it showed that he wasn't the least bit embarrassed. Evidently he wanted to carry on in the same vein that she had found so charming at the Christmas do. *Concentration*, she said to herself, and then repeated it a couple of times.

– Cause of death confirmed? Viken wanted to know.

– We've got three, possibly four causes, each of which individually would have been fatal, she began, pointing with her scalpel at the throat, which was open in two places. – The belt that was tied around her throat has occluded both the arteries and veins, since the face is pale and not swollen. What's more, the groove made by the belt is horizontal, which indicates that she was strangled before she was hung up in the position in which she was found. She lifted a flap of the skin on the neck to one side. – Here you can see fractures in both the thyroid cartilage and the lingual bone. That shows how much force was used to tighten the belt.

The two officers bent to examine the gaping throat. Jennifer picked up a pair of tweezers and indicated the damaged areas she had described.

– Beneath the skin there are three linear accumulations of blood, which appear to come from the belt, and then this deeper groove.

– Which means?

– It might indicate that she was strangled several times. The perpetrator appears to have loosened the belt and then tightened it again, a little harder each time.

– A macabre form of entertainment, Viken observed. – And yet you say that strangulation was not necessarily the cause of death?

Jennifer lifted up the dead woman's head. – She was hit four or five times, laterally, from above.

– These look like injuries I've seen from being hit with a hammer, Roar Horvath volunteered.

Jennifer shook her head. – This was done with something bigger and heavier.

– A stone? Viken suggested.

– Possibly, but in that case one with a flat and finely chiselled surface. Possibly attached to a handle. Jennifer pointed. – Note these linked, rather circular fracture lines in the occipital bone. A fairly large and evenly bowed fragment has been impressed into the surface of the brain, causing severe contusion and massive loss of blood. It means we can say with some degree of certainty that she was alive when these blows were delivered. We'll be opening the skull later today. What we expect to see then is that the power of these blows has shaken the whole brain backwards and forwards. The victim was obviously lying on the floor with the right temple facing downwards. We can see the scrape marks here on the base of the scalp.

– So that's why you presume that something with a handle was used. Viken lowered his head slightly, a habit when drawing a conclusion that Jennifer had previously noticed. – And the third possible cause of death?

She took two steps to the side. – Numerous punctiform haemorrhages in the bowel mucosa, she said, pointing with her scalpel into the open belly. – Something similar here. She moved her scalpel to the thoracic cavity and scraped at a membrane surrounding the lung. – The blood is also unusually

pale red, which we often find in cases of death from hypo-
thermia. The question is whether the other wounds killed her,
or whether she managed to freeze to death. The temperature
in that factory was obviously well below freezing.

She straightened up and fastened her gaze on Viken.

– Additionally you can see these two marks in the neck,
which must be from a hypodermic. She had heroin in her
blood, but it was not given intravenously, and there are no
other needle marks on her body.

– Ergo the heroin was used to sedate her or keep her passive,
said Viken.

Jennifer raised one of the body's hands. – There is superficial
scratching here, which might indicate that she was handcuffed
before she was found. She described a circle round each wrist.
– Note also the tips of the right thumb and forefinger.

– Oil? Horvath asked.

– It turns out to be soot. But nothing was found in the
vicinity that was either burnt or sooted. She laid the dead arm
back on the table. – And then of course there are the eyes, as
you can see from the report.

She raised both eyelids. The exposed eyeballs were almost
black from the coagulated blood that had gathered there. Viken
bent forward, and she handed him a magnifying glass and a
torch. While he was standing there examining the punctured
eyes, she glanced over at Roar Horvath. He was wearing a
suitably serious expression for the occasion, and she was glad
to see this sign that he was adult enough not to start flirting
there and then. He didn't look particularly stylish, in his green
lab coat and with the paper hat pulled down over his ears. It
made his face seem rounder, the nose stick out more. But he
had that dimple in his chin – it was, as she had noticed before
he put on the face mask, even more prominent in the light from
the ceiling – and he was so entertaining, had made her laugh
out loud more than once at the Christmas party, and even more

afterwards. And he was by no means the worst lover she had ever gone to bed with; far from it. She hadn't taken him for an Adonis that evening either, since she had been stone-cold sober from the moment she arrived to the moment she left, as she had to confess to herself with both pride and shame. That was why she had offered to drive him home, since he lived on the same side of town. Or at least, not in the completely opposite direction, as it turned out. *Concentration, Jennifer*, she warned herself again. You're at work now.

– To sum up, I conclude that Mailin Bjerke died from such extensive trauma to the brain that the medulla oblongata was severed, which led to the cessation of the respiratory and circulatory functions. Prior to this she had been repeatedly choked, but the evidence indicates that she did not die of this. As you know, in cases involving this kind of asphyxiation, it can take up to five minutes for death to occur. At the time of her death she was almost certainly severely hypothermic, but this in itself is not the likely cause of death. As for the presence of heroin in the blood, the concentration was so low that the effect of it must have worn off several hours before she died.

Viken handed the torch and the magnifying glass to Roar Horvath. – Stabbed with a pointed object, he observed as his younger colleague leaned over to examine the damage to the eyes. – Repeatedly. But with something rather less sharp than the needle of a hypodermic. To what purpose?

– Prevent the victim from seeing, Horvath offered.

– Much easier, surely, simply to blindfold her.

Jennifer said: – I have some information that might be worth taking a closer look at.

As ever, Viken had that openly scrutinising look in his eyes, which he made no attempt to disguise. Probably something that's bound to happen when you've worked as a detective for decades, she thought. Roar Horvath straightened up and looked at her as well. It didn't bother her. She had long since accepted that she didn't have the figure of a twenty year old. She consoled herself with the thought that there were a surprising number of advantages to having passed forty, and felt the heat begin to prickle in her cheeks. Which was not one of them. Not even when she was a little girl had she blushed as much as she had started doing recently.

– Five years ago, a nineteen-year-old girl was killed in Bergen, she began. – She was found in the woods about twenty kilometres south of the town. The case was never solved.

– Everybody remembers that, Viken said, immediately impatient. – We live, thank God, in a country in which murders aren't forgotten in three days.

She wasn't sure what he was referring to, but chose to ignore the interruption.

– The girl was found tied to a tree. She was handcuffed, and had frozen to death.

– That much we gathered, grunted Viken. – Even if they gave an exemplary demonstration on that occasion of how not to share the details of the case with others.

– What struck me as I examined Mailin Bjerke, Jennifer went on, – was the damage inflicted on the eyes. The girl in Bergen had something similar.

– And how on earth did you find that out?

She explained. The seminar she had attended at Gades Pathological Institute in Bergen a few months after the girl was found. A colleague whom she knew well had spoken about the case over a drink in the hotel bar one evening. Confidentially, naturally.

– I took the liberty of calling my colleague earlier today.

She paused. Could feel Viken's irritation rising.

– He was struck by the similarities with what I described, she continued. – The eyelids in both cases were not damaged. The person who did this must have forced them open and stabbed the eyeballs directly with a nail or some other sharp object. But one of the wounds is bigger. I examined it, and it appears to have been done by something like a screw with a fairly large distance between the threads. It was screwed directly through the cornea. She let that sink in. – In addition, both victims were found in remote places.

Initially Viken said nothing. Then he said, rather irritably: – You're divulging important information to someone who is not directly involved in our case.

Jennifer's anger flared up. – I can assure you that it will go no further, she said as calmly as she could. She realised she had been expecting some recognition of the value of what she had done. – Well, I've spent enough time on this, she concluded. – If you think it is interesting enough, you can get in touch.

– Of course, said Viken tartly. – Everything is of interest.

– It looks as if Mailin Bjerke was drugged, Roar Horvath interposed in a conciliatory tone. – What about the girl in Bergen?

Jennifer permitted herself a small smile as she met his gaze. – There I am afraid I must disappoint you. She was totally clean.

He nodded thoughtfully, as though to demonstrate that at least *he* thought her information was interesting.

3

THEY SAT IN the vestibule. The middle-aged man was the first to catch sight of Jennifer and get to his feet. He wore a cord jacket under his overcoat, had round glasses and a grey beard. The other visitor, a woman with reddish hair, sat with her back turned.

The grey-bearded man held out his hand and introduced himself. – Tage Turén Bjerke.

She heard at once that he was Swedish. His palm was moist and his lips trembled.

– Are you the deceased's father?

He shook his head. – I'm married to her mother. She was in no condition to come here today.

Jennifer turned to the other visitor, who had now also got to her feet. The young woman was tall and unusually slim, but her eyes were what attracted the attention. They were large and green, or perhaps hazel, and there was something about the gaze that made it hard to look away. Beautiful women had always fascinated Jennifer. She subscribed to three or four fashion magazines, partly to keep herself up to date on matters of clothing and make-up, mostly to browse through the pictures of stylised feminine beauty. She had been prepared for something else that morning. She'd worked out what she was going to say, how she would accompany the bereaved to the chapel, even how she would draw aside the sheet covering the dead woman's body, and how much of it she should expose. But the sight of the young woman's face momentarily disorientated her. Not only the eyes, but the bow of the mouth and the curve of the forehead under the auburn hair.

– Liss Bjerke. I'm Mailin Bjerke's sister.

The hand the woman held out was cold and dry, the skin like marble. Jennifer explained who she was and recovered the thread of the ritual she had prepared. She walked ahead of them, stopping when she reached the door to the chapel.

– I know what a strain it must be to come here.

The young woman nodded almost imperceptibly. The grey-bearded man was shaking even more.

Jennifer opened the door. The bier with the dead body on it stood in the middle of the room, beneath the light from the ceiling lamp. She stood beside it, waved them over. The grey-bearded man remained in the doorway as though frozen, apparently unable to move. But the young woman crossed the floor. When she stopped by the bier, Jennifer waited a few seconds before lifting the sheet and drawing it slowly down to the chest. At that moment she felt relieved that it had been possible to hide the worst injuries to the body lying there. The mortuary assistant had wrapped a towel around the head, hiding all the crushed areas, and washed the hair; it had been matted with dried blood and matter that had oozed out from inside the skull. Jennifer was able to show the sister a face that the brutal death had not rendered physically repulsive; nothing crushed, no skin cut into pieces or melted. Scant comfort, she thought, but a comfort to me at least.

Suddenly the young woman bent down, took hold of her dead sister's hands, pressed her cheek against her own. A tremor passed through her back, two or three times, as she murmured her sister's name. She said something else, something whispered that Jennifer didn't catch as she had withdrawn a few paces and half turned away. For a long time the young woman stood there with her cheek pressed to the dead woman's. So long that Jennifer began to think she might have to give some kind of sign. Before that happened, however, the visitor straightened up. Still looking at the body, she asked:

– What's the matter with her eyes?

The voice was unexpectedly firm and clear. Jennifer looked down at the dead woman's face. It had not been possible to close the eyelids completely; beneath them, the rim of the destroyed membranes was still visible.

She said: – There are signs of damage to both the deceased's eyes.

The woman turned towards her. The gaze was veiled, the effect now even stronger.

– What kind of damage?

– From a pointed object.

– Was she blind when she died?

– It's hard to tell. It's possible she could still see, at least light.

Suddenly the young woman lifted the hand she was holding.

– Where is her ring? Did you take it off?

Jennifer had noticed the marks of a ring on the fourth finger of the left hand.

– She wasn't wearing one when we found her. What did it look like?

– A wedding ring, the dead woman's sister answered. – From our grandmother. She bit her lower lip. – What did she die of?

– We still can't say with absolute certainty, replied Jennifer. – Probably head wounds. But it looks as if she was already in a hypothermic state when death occurred. It may have made the pain less.

The grounds for making the claim were not convincing, but it felt good to say it.

– Could still see light, Liss Bjerke repeated to herself. She had not let go of her dead sister's hand. – You were freezing, Mailin.

4

ROAR HORVATH CLIMBED the three icy steps gingerly and rang on the doorbell. They hadn't arranged anything in advance. There was a chance the trip would be wasted, but Detective Chief Inspector Viken insisted that it was worth a try. In cases that were particularly special, he made a point of popping up unexpectedly and surprising the person they wanted to interview. Sometimes they learnt something that would not otherwise have emerged in the interview.

There was the sound of footsteps from within and the door glided open, not suddenly, not slowly. The man standing there was above average height, dark, with longish hair and carefully trimmed sideburns. The face had a wintry pallor; the features were regular. The good-looking young-guy type, thought Roar Horvath. He introduced himself and showed his ID. The young man glanced at it and his immediate response appeared to be one of relief rather than suspicion.

– I'm Viljam Vogt-Nielsen. I'm sure you already know that.

– We made a presumption, said Roar Horvath, and introduced Viken.

The two investigators followed him along a hallway and down a flight of stairs into a room with large windows facing out on to a patch of garden in which an Argentinian barbecue and a tool shed could be seen. A few bushes were partially covered in snow. The room wasn't large, but the ceiling was unusually high. There was an open fireplace in one corner. On the wall behind the sofa hung an enormous painting that looked very dull to Roar Horvath, though he had never thought of himself as a connoisseur of modern art.

– Nice place, he observed.

– The people who own it are architects, Viljam Vogt-Nielsen informed him. – We're renting it for a year.

Roar Horvath sat down in the sofa. – You've already made a statement to the crime response unit, he said. – But then it was about a missing person. We're investigating a murder now.

Viljam Vogt-Nielsen did not respond. He slipped into the chair nearest the stairs and gazed out of the window. It gave Roar Horvath a chance to get a closer look at him. He had interrogated a number of people who had later been found guilty of murder. He'd seen bad liars and good actors. Many people were capable of manufacturing a carefully crafted first impression, but if they were playing a part, then sooner or later something would always emerge that didn't quite fit. He glanced over at Viken, who was sitting in the easy chair at the end of the table. They had arranged beforehand that Roar Horvath would lead the interview and Viken would observe. From the start, Viken had made it clear that he was perfectly happy to be working with Roar. It seemed as though, for some reason or other, he had decided he wanted to guide this newcomer to the department through his first period with them. And over the last year, Roar had learnt things about investigating cases of serious violence that he would never have learnt had he stayed in his old job at Romerike police station.

– As you will appreciate, we have to go through the sequence of events all over again, he said. – Not just with you, but with everyone involved.

He added this in the hope of getting Viljam Vogt-Nielsen to relax: someone who felt he was the object of suspicion would be careful about what he said, whereas someone who felt he was being looked after was more liable to slip up.

– Of course, Viljam Vogt-Nielsen answered. – We can go over it as many times as you feel is necessary.

There was no sign of tension in his voice, no discontinuity between what he said and the way he said it. Despair? Grief? Any trace of shock? Again Roar Horvath let his gaze wander over the pale face. If this young man was acting, he certainly wasn't overdoing it.

– Let's take it from the point at which you saw Mailin Bjerke for the last time.

An idea seemed to strike Viljam Vogt-Nielsen. – Coffee? he asked.

Roar Horvath said no thanks, Viken remained silent, and the young man sank back into his chair. – I saw her on the day before she disappeared, that's to say, Wednesday the tenth. It was nearly five o'clock . . . quarter to five, he corrected himself. – She was standing outside on the steps, rucksack on her back. We hugged each other. Then I closed the door. That was the last . . . A tiny break in the voice, a few seconds' silence and then he carried on. – She was going to the cabin. Often used to go out there to work. It's such a lovely place. Quiet and peaceful. No stress, can't even get a signal on your mobile.

– What were you talking about just before she left? Roar Horvath wanted to know.

Viljam Vogt-Nielsen thought about it; it was evident the crime response unit hadn't asked him this.

– What was going to happen the next day. The programme she was due to appear on, *Taboo*. I'm sure you've heard of it.

The detective sergeant nodded briefly, not wishing to interrupt.

– We'd talked about it a lot over the preceding few days. Mailin is not exactly a fan of Berger's. I asked whether she was worried that her appearing on it might give him some kind of academic respectability, but she had a very particular reason for wanting to go on the show.

Roar had noticed a similar assertion in the statement made to the crime response unit.

– Can you be any more precise about what that reason might have been?

– She had been told something about Berger. I think it was a former patient who approached her. Mailin was quite excited about it. It sounded as if Berger had once at some point sexually assaulted a child.

– Can you give us a name?

Viljam Vogt-Nielsen shook his head. – She is very strict about observing confidentiality, and that even applied to me, obviously.

– But you think she intended to reveal this on his live TV show?

– Mailin wasn't specific about exactly what she intended to do. But she was determined to strip away that absurd clown's mask of his. Berger was in for a shock.

– Clown's mask, was that the phrase she used?

– *That absurd clown's mask*. She'd already met Berger a couple of times, before the information about his past emerged. She said she was going to get in touch with him before the broadcast and give him a chance to cancel it.

Roar Horvath wasn't taking any notes. He trusted his memory, which he thought was very precise.

– And that was the last thing you talked about?

Viljam rubbed a finger back and forth over his forehead, as though struggling to remember something.

– She said she had to call in at the post office. Put some cash into her account.

– Cash?

– Some of her patients paid her by the hour. She put it aside and deposited it once a week.

The nearest post office was the one up by Carl Berners Place. Roar glanced at his watch. They should make it before closing time.

– What did you do after she left on that Wednesday?

– Sat here and read for a lot of the afternoon. Went down to the gym just before eight thirty. I play indoor bandy with a few mates. I was back home by about eleven. Just caught the evening news broadcast.

– And the next day?

– Lecture in the morning. Sat in the library afterwards. I called in here at about three, before I left for work.

– Work?

– Justice Bus, he explained. – I try to help out there as much as I can.

Roar made a mental note. Well-spoken young man with a social conscience.

– Had Mailin been here when you called in on Thursday?

– Don't think so. She would have left her rucksack, or her computer. But I got a couple of text messages from her.

He showed him his mobile. Only now did Roar take out his notebook and write down the exact times.

– We'd arranged to meet at her parents'. I was going to watch *Taboo* there, and Mailin was going to come back there later.

– In other words, you were at work the whole evening on Thursday the eleventh?

– From three thirty to eight thirty. Then Tage picked me up, her stepfather. He works at the university.

– And you were on the Justice Bus with other students the whole time?

– Popped out to Deli de Luca on Karl Johan to get something to eat. Ten minutes, maybe quarter of an hour, ask the others. Aside from that, I was there until Tage arrived. We drove out to Lørenskog, called in at Menu on the way and did some shopping. He slumped a little in his chair. – I called at once, as soon as she didn't show up on the programme. Her phone was switched off. It looked as if he was reluctant to say any more.

– And then what happened?

Viljam Vogt-Nielsen pushed his hair back with both hands. – We drove into town, Tage and I. Checked to see if she'd gone home. We went up to the TV studio. Tried to get a word with that Berger guy, but he'd apparently already left. I called round, everyone I could think of. No one knew anything. I even tried to get in touch with Mailin's sister, in Amsterdam . . . Tage persuaded me to go back home with him. Ragnhild went into a panic, and he had to look after her while I carried on ringing round. Early next morning Tage and I went out to the cabin by Morr Water. Searched all around there. Of course, we knew that she'd left there, but we had to do something. At about twelve, we reported it to the police, and then drove back out to Lørenskog again. Only then did it begin to really dawn on me . . .

Roar Horvath didn't offer any expressions of comfort; sat observing him, waiting. For the first time, Viken spoke: – How did you know that she had left the cabin?

Viljam turned to him, momentarily surprised; perhaps he'd forgotten that the chief inspector was there too.

– You said you knew she wasn't there any more, Viken repeated. – How could you know that?

Viljam blinked several times. – Her car . . . it wasn't in the parking space. Tage found it in town later, a block down from where she rents the office.

Roar Horvath started the engine as Viken got in.

– Nothing particularly striking at first glance, he remarked.

Viken said nothing.

– At least it should be easy to check if what he says is true,

Roar claimed. – We'd best have a word with the other people on the Justice Bus. And the staff at Deli de Luca.

– When did she disappear? Viken suddenly asked.

Roar inched the car out of its narrow parking space. – The parking ticket shows that the car was parked in Welhavens Street at four minutes past five on that Thursday.

– That's the car, but when did the woman who owns it disappear?

It didn't look as if the snowploughs had been down the narrow street for the past week. – It's not improbable that she went to her office after she left the cabin, Roar insisted as he manoeuvred past the rear of a badly parked taxi. – We'll have to see what the people she shares the office with say.

As he swung down into the much broader Gøteborg Street he added: – At least it looks as if the partner can account for all his movements.

Viken said: – In principle there isn't an alibi in the world that can't be torn apart. Not a single one. Even if someone can prove they were at an audience with the king at the time in question, that doesn't necessarily let them off the hook in a case like this.

5

Sunday 28 December

JUST AS THE elk stew appeared on the table, the three-note alert sounded on Jennifer's phone announcing an incoming message. Twice more the cheery notes sang out from her handbag, which she had hung over the arm of her chair.

Ivar nudged her. – And you're the one who isn't on duty this evening, he growled, but after living together for twenty years, he was used to the fact that she was more or less never completely free.

Jennifer excused herself to her hostess, her sister-in-law, and went out into the next room. The fire was on in there; the Christmas tree had been pulled out into the middle of the floor. Outside, the snow had hung on despite the mild weather and lay across the garden and the field beyond in a soggy carpet. It smelled good in Ivar's sister's house. Always freshly washed, always tidy. Just so, as she used to say herself. Important to have everything just so.

Jennifer had been hoping that Roar Horvath wouldn't send any more messages, but when she saw it was from him, she had to admit that she'd also hoped the opposite. She listened to the talk in the dining room, how she always had to be ready at a moment's notice, how vital her work was. Soon they would get on to the case they knew she was working on, the woman found dead in a disused factory in Hurum. *Fancy a cup of coffee?* she read on the display.

A roll after the office Christmas party was one thing. The statistics were on her side there. Most people could manage that. Bump up against each other by the buffet, like the random collision of two billiards balls, then a dance, then a quick kiss good night in the car, and the kiss so to speak trips and loses its footing, and ends up in a bed that was fortunately very solidly constructed. After something like that, it was still possible to be around each other almost as though nothing had happened. But to meet again, outside the office, that was taking it too far. Another meeting wouldn't just happen, it would have to be arranged, and with that a completely new set of rules would come into play. Accommodations and transgressions would follow. Judgements concerning the right degree of involvement, plausible excuses for being away from home, dealing with guilt, and all the rest of it. Above all the pattern of everyday life would be disturbed, the ground beneath her feet less secure. It had taken her six months to regain her self-composure after Sean left. Roar Horvath was hardly the type she could fall in love with, and from that perspective he made a better choice as a lover. Moreover, he was ten years her junior, divorced less than a year previously, and had a daughter to look after every other weekend.

She felt like a coffee. She felt like meeting him. The night she drove him home after the Christmas party he had lifted her up almost before she was through the front door and carried her into the bedroom while continuing their conversation, and that spontaneous lifting seemed like the most natural thing in the world. He went on making her laugh as he removed her clothing piece by piece before undressing himself in two quick movements that left him standing naked and proud in front of her, enjoying the way she looked at him . . . and this time too, he kissed her in the hall, even before she had taken off her coat, and she was just as unprepared for it, noticing that he had already drunk the coffee he had invited her to join him in, and eaten something salty, possibly smoked, drunk beer too, but his kiss was so passionate that the thought of smoked salmon, the most curious of all Norwegian dishes, disappeared as quickly as it had appeared; he put his hand up her skirt, pulled down her panties, lifted her up, opened his flies and removed his trousers smoothly, entered her with a jolt, she tried to suppress the scream but screamed anyway, not that she noticed it, and when she came and was hanging from his neck like a dishcloth, he didn't let her go, but turned one of her legs around and carried her into the bedroom as he had done before. She had already got used to it.

By the time the promised cup of coffee finally appeared on the table, over an hour had passed since her arrival. With her legs still trembling, and a throbbing tenderness between them, she sank on to one of the chairs by the kitchen table. It obviously hadn't occurred to him to sit in the living room, from which there was a view of the block next door, and that was fine by her; she'd had a quick look and established that the furnishing had been done by a recently divorced man in his thirties. She preferred the kitchen.

— And there I was thinking that coffee was just an excuse to have sex, she sighed as she inhaled from the steaming cup.

— Other way round, he said with that teasing smile she had to admit she liked a lot. — I knew you would never come here and drink coffee with me unless there was a chance of sex.

She tasted it, controlled the urge to turn up her nose.

— You surely didn't get a woman to leave a family gathering at Christmas and drive over twenty miles for coffee like this.

— I wanted to talk to you too, he said and put his hand over hers, and for a moment it seemed to her that he really meant it. It made her happy as much as it bothered her. She didn't want to have to spoil the good atmosphere between them with a lot of rules and regulations. But he was thirty-four and old enough to take it on the chin, despite that air of boyishness.

Fortunately he went on: – A chat over a cup of coffee is fine, but when I saw you standing there in the hall, I just got carried away.

– Do you often get whims like that? she asked, and tried to put on a concerned face.

– It's been a while since last time.

– Yes, I noticed.

– Ditto.

He opened a bottle of beer. – I wondered what it would be like to talk to you without having a dead body next to us.

She took a few swigs and handed the bottle back. – Are you talking about Viken? she wondered, not wanting to get into any joking about the young woman they'd had lying between them on the autopsy table two days previously.

He laughed, but left it at that.

– Lot of action up at your place right now, she said after a while.

Roar glanced out of the window. – Never known anything like it since the Orderud murders.

Then you should have been there last autumn, said Jennifer, – when all that business with the bear murders was going on. Funny that Viken didn't go in the general clear-out after that.

Abruptly Roar looked uncomfortable.

– There's a shortage of people with his experience, he objected. – He's probably the best investigator I've worked with.

Jennifer had heard this from others too, despite what had happened the year before.

– Some people thought they might go for him as the new section head, Roar said.

– That would have been impossible, she asserted.

– Maybe so. But the appointment they did make . . . Roar blew air between his compressed lips. – I've got nothing against

Sigge Helgarsson. I know him from before, we worked together in Romerike. He got a boss's job there too and it went okay. But head of Violent Crimes in Oslo is something different. The guy's not much older than me. He isn't Norwegian. And he and Viken aren't exactly the best of friends, and that's putting it mildly.

– Well they can hardly confer with Viken every time they make an appointment, said Jennifer. When Roar didn't respond, she realised he didn't want to talk about the detective chief inspector any more. – How far have you got with this latest case? she asked, moving the conversation on to another track.

– We're fumbling away out there in the mist, Roar yawned. – Gradually the visibility will improve, I expect. We need another tactician or two. At the moment there's still only the four of us. And you can imagine the amount of material there is to go through.

– Then it's about priorities, she said, thinking about something quite specific.

Roar emptied the bottle of beer and fetched another from the fridge. – Of course we have to start with the ones who are closest. The man she lived with has been interviewed three times.

– Have you got anything on him?

– He seems to have a fairly good alibi.

– No better than fairly good?

– In cases of murder there is not a single alibi that cannot be torn to shreds, declared Roar. – That's the rule we have to go by. Even if someone can prove they were at an audience with the king at the time, that doesn't necessarily let them off the hook in a case like this.

– And definitely not if it's the king who's been murdered, Jennifer observed.

Roar gave a quick smile. – In the great majority of cases of this kind, what lies behind is usually something involving lovers, people who live together or are married, close family.

– Statistics aren't much help in individual cases, Jennifer objected.

– Of course not. But topping the list of suspects is always going to be the husband or partner. The way the investigation proceeds determines whether or not they drop down the list, or even out of it entirely.

– Can't say I'm surprised to hear that Viken thinks that way, she said acidly.

– It doesn't mean we're fixated, Roar assured her. – Everyone close to her is being interviewed as a potential perpetrator, that goes without saying. The stepfather, her mother, and the father, who apparently lives in Canada. Then after that we look at her colleagues at work and her patients . . .

Suddenly he fell silent.

– You're not sure how much you can tell me, Jennifer volunteered.

He thought about it. – Well, you are part of the investigation, in a way.

– In a way? How far do you think you'll get if we don't do our job down at the path lab?

He conceded that she had a point.

– It appears that Mailin Bjerke had a meeting arranged at her office with Berger a few hours before they were due in the *Taboo* studio that Thursday, he told her. – Apparently he turned up, but she wasn't there. We know from her phone that she sent him a text at about five thirty. She called him but got no answer just after seven, and then sent him another message.

– Wasn't that around the time when she went missing?

Roar went over it in his mind. – Actually the last sighting of her was the day before, after she left home. She called in at the post office on Carl Berners Place.

– And you are sure about that?

– The man who was working there was quite certain about it. He remembered in detail what she did when she was there. She used a computer, printed out a few things from the internet, put a small deposit in her account and left. Directly afterwards she came back in again, bought a padded envelope and sent a package. According to the person serving, she suddenly seemed frightened. He's absolutely certain of all this, but where the package was addressed to he has no idea.

– She was afraid because of this package?

– We don't know anything about that. It's quite common for witnesses to dramatise things, especially once they know a murder is involved.

Jennifer said, out of the blue: – I mentioned a case to you. The girl who was killed five years ago in Bergen.

– We talked about it at our morning briefing yesterday, Roar said with a nod.

– And?

– And what?

Jennifer furrowed her brows. – What are you going to do about it?

Roar seemed surprised by her harsh tone of voice. Maybe it dawned on him that this was what she had been heading the conversation towards.

– Obviously we'll take a look at that case. But we can't do everything at once.

Jennifer became agitated. – The girl in Bergen was found naked in a remote part of the woods. She had been tied up, but there were no signs of sexual assault. It was in November, and she froze to death. She had been repeatedly stabbed through the eyes with a pointed object. Think about the circumstances in our case and tell me why our top priority isn't to look for a connection here.

Roar raised both hands. – Don't hit me, he said in a weedy voice.

Jennifer felt her irritation drain away. – That's exactly what you need, she said severely. – A right good spanking. On your barest arse.

– Okay, said Roar as he got to his feet, – but it will have to be in the bedroom. I don't want the neighbours involved in this.

6

Monday 29 December

EMPTY STREETS. IT'S night. He hasn't eaten. Not since early this morning. It's getting colder. He should've put a jacket on. Didn't find it in the rush. He sprints down Wergelandsveien. Runs himself warm. A clock strikes down in the city. He counts three strokes. Empty streets. He's started running again. Every night for the last couple of weeks. He heads round the corner, down Pilestredet, towards the mouth of the Ibsen Tunnel. Tunnels set their own deadlines; he has to get out of them again before a car passes him from behind. Try Festning Tunnel too, that's longer. And Ekeberg Tunnel. Formerly he ran on fast tracks. Lots of people watching. He had an acceleration down the final straight no one else could match. Could stay well at the back and wait. Coming out of the final bend, he changed gear and left them standing. They didn't know where he'd come from. Another planet, he called out to them. Not Mars or Venus, but a planet in another galaxy.

He'd always run. Felt calmer when he was running than when he was standing or sitting down. Still not too late to start putting his name down for races. Comeback man. He'd come back before. They didn't believe in him any more. He'd had so many chances, they said. First of all that stuff they called care. The world of athletics was big hearted about anyone who came off the rails. Don't push kids out into the cold when what they need is warmth. But then he got caught a couple more times. Coke and pepper. They were even prepared to overlook that. He was done with it, he said, but didn't mean it. He signed a new contract. Got another chance on condition he went for treatment. No wonder they cared about him. No one had his acceleration, not even Vebjørn Rodal when he was at his peak. I could've taken him, he grinned as he ran. I would've beaten Rodal in Atlanta, he shouted. If it had been twelve years later. Or sixteen. Rodal was too slow. Too much dead Trøndelag meat there. As for him, he was born with that acceleration. Had it in his blood, in his fibres, in the atoms of his blood.

As he was approaching the exit to the tunnel, a car approached, a taxi. He gave it what he had left, the taxi sounded its horn, he gave it the finger and went up a gear, left it for dead and skipped up on to the narrow pavement. He ran straight across the roundabout and carried on up Schweigaards Street. A long, flat open stretch there. The road was slippery, but he had perfect balance and could adjust in a fraction of a second. His breath was warm and tasted of iron. He owed too much. Thirty grand, according to Karam. It couldn't be that much. But no point in arguing with Karam. The guy said he hadn't been selling enough. Taking too much off the top himself. This is business. Thirty grand before Wednesday or you won't be able to run any more, not even crawl. Karam knows him well enough to know what the worst thing is. It's not to be floating out somewhere in the fjord with the mackerel stripping the flesh off you until there's only bone left. Worst of all is to be chained to a wheelchair for the rest of your life. Never run again. Not even crawl. Karam had sketched it out for him. It's not the fucking mackerel that eat at you as you're sitting there, but what's crawling around inside you.

Mailin Bjerke was the first who had never demanded anything. That was why he couldn't face going to see her. Just a couple of times and then he dropped out. Because of that look in her eye and the way she sat there listening to him and demanding nothing. It made him desperate. Had nothing to say. Could have stood up and taken that computer of hers and chucked it at the wall. Or lifted her up out of her chair and put her down on the desk and watched her eyes turn black. Scared of me at last, finally seeing a part of what you don't know the first thing about. How could you control anything of what goes chasing around inside of me. But she didn't give up. Wanted him to come back. Comeback man.

At times he believed in her. That she really might be able to help him. That it would help to talk. He should keep coming, she insisted, and she did all she could to make new appointments for him. If he didn't turn up anyway, all he had to do was send a text. They could make another appointment, at a time that suited him better. For her, any time was all right, even at short notice. He made appointments and missed them, never sent a message, but she didn't give up. She was naïve. Believed that all her talk could stop what it was that ravaged him inside. The same thing that made him run, that made him do drugs. She claimed to understand the connections between things. To understand why all he ever thought about was the next snort or the next pill. That those were the thoughts that enabled him to keep going. And the running. She suggested medication. No monkey dope and stuff that turns people into fat, slobbering idiots, but something new that would reduce the craving. But even if she had understood, it wouldn't help him much now. Mailin is dead, he shouted as he accelerated past the last block before Galgeberg.

Mailin was dead, and someone else he'd never seen before had turned up at her office, tall and thin with a strange look in her eyes. Another patient, definitely, he could always tell; someone strung out like him. But then she started following him, showed up at the station in Oslo, and then again up at Sinsen, wanting to ask him questions. Went for him and tried to choke him.

He would have to find out who she was. Knew the right person to ask. The only person he could trust now.

7

JENNIFER HAD BEEN working with Professor Olav Korn for over ten years now. And yet still she hadn't managed to locate him in her system of Hippocratic categorisations. Korn radiated a calm that was infectious. She might have been inclined to call him a phlegmatic, but he was a highly efficient worker who dispensed with tasks quickly, from pathologists' reports to budget proposals. He had done research on sudden and unexplained infant deaths, on the effects of alcohol and drug abuse during pregnancy, as well as in a number of other fields. He published articles in the most important Norwegian and international scientific journals, and was an active voice in public debates on matters like biotechnology and ethics. And even though he spoke at seminars and conferences all over the world, to the staff at the Pathological Institute he remained their very present and involved leader. Had it not been for Korn, Jennifer would not have remained at the institute as long as she had; indeed, she might never even have become an expert on forensic medicine. She was glad that his retirement was still some years in the future, in spite of the fact that on several occasions he had hinted that she would be a very suitable candidate to succeed him as head of the department.

Korn was on the phone when she entered his office, but he gestured for her to sit down. She observed him surreptitiously as he brought the conversation to a close. He was sixty-two, and in terms of his individual features probably looked it, but there was something about his eyes, his repertoire of facial gestures and the way he moved that suggested a younger man. He had a rich head of iron-grey hair, was clean shaven, his eyebrows weren't bushy and there were no balls of hair emerging from his nostrils and ears, as had begun to be the case with Ivar. All in all Korn took good care of his appearance without seeming the least bit vain about it. Jennifer had always been attracted to men older than herself.

He replaced the receiver and turned towards her.

– It's about the woman who was found down in Hurum, she said.

– I hear Viken has been given the case, he nodded, perhaps hinting at a couple of earlier occasions on which she had come to him for advice on how best to handle cooperation with the detective chief inspector.

– That's fine by me, said Jennifer. – I don't have any trouble with him now. But of course he doesn't like me getting involved in the investigation.

Korn raised his eyebrows. – And do you?

She sighed. – He appeared in the middle of the autopsy, and I tried to pass along a piece of information that might be very important.

She told him her thoughts on the similarity with the case in Bergen.

– Those people down in Grønland should be very thankful it was you who volunteered for work over Christmas, Korn observed. – Not everyone would have spent Christmas morning in our basement unless they had to. And as for what you've just told me, they ought to be pulling out all the stops to find out whether or not there might be a connection.

She took the compliment with a smile. He was one of the few people who could praise her and not have her looking for some ulterior motive.

– I've asked myself if there's anything more I can do. I've talked it over on the telephone with a colleague at the Gades

Institute, and he thinks it's interesting too. But of course he can't send over any of their material.

– Of course not.

She said what she had come to say to him: – What if I were to go there? Take the pictures from here. Do a comparison of the forensic evidence. Get something more to show to Viken and his people.

Korn didn't look in the least surprised. He mulled the suggestion over for a few moments before replying.

– I've always appreciated the fact that you show so much initiative, Jennifer. And that you are not the least bit afraid of trespassing on someone else's territory.

She could feel herself blushing. With only Korn present, it didn't matter that much.

– I remember the case in Bergen very well, he said, his gaze moving to follow something or other through the window, probably to spare her even more embarrassment. – You say the eyes were mutilated? In the same way?

He had spent fifteen years more than her working as a forensic expert, yet it seemed as though all that proximity with death actually made him more and more solicitous of the well-being of the living.

He leaned over the desk. – I don't think it's a good idea to go to Bergen. But I'll call the department of Violent Crimes and have a word with the head down there. This has to be about priorities.

Jennifer had a mental picture of Viken being carpeted by Sigge Helgarsson, the section head who just a short while ago had been his junior and whom Viken, by all accounts, had regularly used as a whipping boy. She felt a malicious pleasure bubbling up in her and was unable to resist indulging it.

– What was her name again, the girl in Bergen? Korn asked, the telephone already in his hand.

– Richter, she answered. Ylva Richter.

8

Tuesday 30 December

ROAR HORVATH RANG on one of the bells down in the yard, the one with *T. Gabrielsen* written next to it. She didn't answer immediately, and he had time to start feeling annoyed. He was on time, but people in her line of business were not renowned for their concern for other people's ideas of punctuality.

Finally there was a buzzing from the lock. The staircase inside was musty and twisted, the whole building looking ripe for renovation. As he reached the landing on the first floor, a woman with a round face poked her head out.

– Wait just a moment in there, she said, pointing to a door. – I'll be finished in about half a minute.

Roar let himself into a kitchen that perhaps also functioned as a common room. On a table directly behind the door was a hotplate, with a coffee machine next to it. A tiny fridge was slotted in below the window facing the back yard, a stand with a flipover leaning up against it. The cupboard on the wall contained a packet of coffee filters, a few cups and glasses, a large bag of salt and a curious little plastic container with a long spout. In the corner, between the fridge and the wall, stood a grey-lacquered filing cabinet. It had three drawers, all of which were locked. On the flipover, arrows had been drawn in blue felt tip between words written in black: *dilemma*, *self-development*, *defence*. He flipped back through it. From the handwriting, it was clear that more than one person had used it as an aid to explanations.

Over ten minutes went by before Torunn Gabrielsen appeared again. She started making coffee without offering any apology for the delay, and left it up to her visitor to decide whether he wanted to stand or sit.

She could be about his own age, thought Roar, although she seemed older. He couldn't decide if her hair was longish, or shortish. She was neither tall nor short, neither fair nor dark. The face was pale and rather lumpy, and the eyes a touch red around the rims. She wasn't wearing glasses, but he saw the traces of them across the bridge of her nose, and she squinted when she looked up at him. If he had to assess her as a woman, he would, if he was feeling diplomatic about it, have said that she wasn't his type. Not exactly vivacious, either, he thought, or maybe she was just tired. *Alert now, Roar*, he warned himself as he felt his dislike beginning to get the upper hand.

– It's very convenient for us to meet here, he said. – It gives me the chance to see Mailin Bjerke's office at the same time.

– Is this the last place where she was before she went missing?

– That we don't know yet, said Roar.

– But I gather she had an appointment here, that she called in after she'd been to her cabin. And her car was parked outside, further up the street.

He realised she was a woman who would rather ask questions than answer them.

– Did you see the car when you left here?

She shook her head firmly. – I walked the other way, down towards Holbergs Place.

– And the time then was?

– Around half three. My tram goes at twenty to. I explained this when I was down talking to the crime response unit.

– You'll have to forgive us if you get asked the same questions more than once, he said evenly, glancing over at the coffee machine, which had started to bubble. – So you didn't see her that day at all?

– The day before was the last time I saw Mailin. She popped in to leave a message. That was at three o'clock. She was on her way out to the cabin.

This concurred with what Viljam Vogt-Nielsen had told them. Roar sat down. The back of the rickety wooden chair slid out of its joints and it felt as if the whole thing would collapse if he so much as moved a finger.

– What was the message about?

Torunn Gabrielsen sat down too.

– A patient, she said, appearing to study the content of her coffee cup. – There's a limit to the information I can give you about that.

Roar could see the way things were heading. Countless cases dragged on or were never even solved on account of this damned professional secrecy, which in reality was just an excuse for doing nothing and had precious little to do with the protection of individual rights. So it was a surprise when Torunn Gabrielsen continued:

– It was about a patient who used to come and go. He could appear suddenly without any warning and usually didn't turn up when he had an appointment. Mailin asked me to let her know if he'd been there.

– Even though your office is on the floor below?

– I take breaks, or when I'm doing paperwork I leave the corridor door open.

She stood up and fetched the coffee jug and two cups. There was an inscription on Roar's: *Today is your day*. It had no handle and the rim was chipped.

– Do you know of anyone who might want to harm Mailin Bjerke?

Torunn Gabrielsen took a mouthful of coffee and held it for a long time before swallowing. Funny way to drink coffee, thought Roar. He didn't expect a reply to his question. Again he was taken by surprise.

– Are we talking about someone who might *want* to, or someone who was actually capable of it?

– Both, he said hopefully.

Another swig of coffee, more pondering as she swilled her mouth with it.

– Mailin was someone it was easy to like. But she was also very upfront and never afraid to say exactly what she thought.

– Meaning?

– That she could be really quite . . . direct. Sometimes people felt hurt. A lot of people can't take it when things are said straight out, without a lot of padding and packaging.

Roar waited for more and didn't interrupt.

– But mostly this is about patients. As I'm sure you know, Mailin worked with people who had been the victims of abuse. Several of them turned into abusers themselves.

– Anyone in particular you have in mind? he asked, fishing.

– Actually, yes.

She poured herself more coffee. – A couple of years ago Mailin had a patient who . . . I'm not quite sure what happened. I think he threatened her.

– You say *he*.

– It was a man. Mailin didn't say much about it. But she had to terminate the treatment. It wasn't her way to give up, quite the contrary, she could be amazingly stubborn with hopeless cases.

– But this time she was threatened.

– I don't *know* that's what he did, but that was my impression. It must have been serious, because Mailin seemed very upset.

– When was this?

Torunn Gabrielsen looked to be thinking it over. – Autumn two years ago. Directly after Pål got his office here.

– Did you meet this patient?

He took the fact that she didn't reply as an encouragement and went on. – Since he wasn't your patient, I'm guessing you're at liberty to say who it was.

She let out a sigh. – I never met him. I think he came in the evenings. And Mailin never said what his name was. He was here just a few times, before she terminated. After that, I heard nothing more about it.

Roar persisted. – Autumn two years ago. August? September?

– Pål came here in September. It was straight after that.

– All the patients are presumably registered with social security?

– Not many. Mailin wasn't part of the reimbursement scheme. Most of her patients were people who'd fallen outside the net completely.

Roar took a note. At that moment, the door slid open. The man standing there was wearing a T-shirt and cord trousers; he was unshaven and his hair was unkempt. For an instant, Roar assumed he was a patient.

– Sorry, said the new arrival on seeing the officer. – Didn't know you were still at it.

– Quite all right, Roar assured him as soon as he realised who this was. – You are Pål Øvreby?

– Correct, said the other and held out his hand.

Roar noticed that he spoke with an accent; it sounded American, despite the very Norwegian name.

– You've already given us a statement about Thursday the eleventh of December, he said. – But just to avoid any misunderstandings I'd like to ask you a few of the questions again.

– Sure, he replied in English.

– You were working here most of the afternoon?

– I am definitely not a morning person. Late but strong.

– How long were you here on that particular day?

– Left here at about five, Pål Øvreby replied without thinking.

– Can you be more exact? Two minutes to, or two minutes past?

– Why have we never installed a time clock here? he chuckled to Torunn Gabrielsen.

– And you didn't see any sign of Mailin Bjerke either before you left? Roar went on, ignoring the psychologist's slightly flippant tone.

– Neither saw nor heard.

– Would you have done? Heard her?

Øvreby chewed it over for a moment. – Depends on what she was doing in there. He chuckled again. – But her car was just up the road. I passed it on my way.

– That's what you told the crime response unit. And you are still quite sure it was hers?

– White, Japanese, a little dent on the passenger-side door. If you ask me enough times, I'll probably start to doubt it.

– The parking ticket on Mailin's car was stamped four minutes past five, Roar informed him. – Pretty much the exact time you passed. Would you have seen her if she was sitting in the car?

– From a distance of one metre? I should imagine so.

Roar quickly considered the possibilities that opened up if Øvreby was telling the truth.

– The ticket is from the machine on Hegdehaugs Way, he observed. – Less than fifty metres from Welhavens Street. Might she have been standing there paying as you walked by?

Pål Øvreby looked to be thinking this over. There was still the faint trace of a smile around his mouth.

– As far as I recall, I didn't look that way. Besides, it was quite dark. In other words, yes, it is possible.

– Where did you go?

He wrinkled his nose. – Does that have any bearing on the case?

Roar nodded his head, back and forth, twice. – Everything has a bearing on the case.

– Everything and nothing, Øvreby remarked, whatever he meant by that. – Well, I took a little drive. I do that sometimes after a stressful day at the office.

– Was that day particularly stressful?

– Not more so than most of the others. I took the car and drove out to Høvikodden. Usually go walking there, with Lara.

Roar looked at him quizzically.

– My dog. What did you think?

Roar didn't feel like telling him what he might have thought. – When did you get home?

– About nine, wasn't it?

Øvreby glanced over at Torunn Gabrielsen. She didn't answer.

– Actually, there was a lot of noise just as I was about to leave the office.

– Noise?

– Sounded like someone hammering like crazy on the street door. When I got down, there was no one there. I guess I forgot about that when I last spoke to you.

Roar picked up his notebook and wrote something. Not because he wouldn't remember it, but because it often made a distinct impression on witnesses if what they were saying was written down.

– You've spent some time abroad? he asked without looking up.

– Correct. Chicago, between the ages of fifteen and twenty-two.

Roar wondered in passing why some people just soaked up new dialects and accents while others stubbornly held on to what they grew up with. A good question for a psychologist.

– I hear you offer a very special type of treatment, he said.

– Who told you that?

– Sorry, professional confidentiality, Roar said as he struggled vainly to hide a grin. – Vegetarian therapy, is that it?

– Vegetotherapy, Øvreby grinned back at him.

– Tell me about that.

– It's a little hard to explain in simple terms. It's body-orientated, you might say. Freeing up the armour we surround ourselves with. If you can free the energy tied up in the tension in the muscles, you can free up your psychological tensions too.

– Are we talking about massage here?

Øvreby yawned. – Much more powerful than that. I can send you a link with more about it.

– Thank you, said Roar, with a distinct lack of enthusiasm. He stood up. – I'd like to see Mailin Bjerke's office. Do either of you have the keys?

9

TORUNN WAS SITTING with her mobile in her hand and was about to call Dahlstrøm when Pål came bursting into the office without knocking.

– Well that went pretty well, he said as he slumped down into a chair. – No dogs buried and none dug up either.

He often tossed off some phrase like that in an effort to seem interesting. Suddenly, and for no special reason, she was furious with him. No special reason other than the thousand she already had, that she had been living with for years.

– I'm working, she said quietly, and carried on making entries in the journal she was updating.

Pål ignored her. – They don't exactly send us the brightest bulb on the Christmas tree, he went on, taking out a toothpick, which he prodded between two of his teeth and left there. – Or is that exactly what they do? Imagine if the guy that was just here is the best they can come up with. Pretty soon I'll be joining the choir that's always calling out for more resources for the police.

She gave up the attempt to work and turned towards him. – If you only knew how tired people are of your attempt to control the whole world with your pathetic arrogance, I think the shame just might kill you.

He sat bolt upright. Ended up chuckling. – Well I'll be, my precious. That time of the month, is it? Or even later? I don't keep up with it any more.

His response made her anger slip away. She felt sorry for him.

– Pål, I know things aren't easy for you at the moment.

It didn't sound good, she could hear that herself, even before he flared up.

– Then maybe you should make an appointment for me, he growled. – Most of your patients drop out anyway, so there ought to be room for me.

She shook her head wearily. – I don't think it's any good.

He calmed down. – Not even with the sort of treatment *you* offer? he said, trying to make a joke.

– I mean us, she said.

She hadn't intended to bring it up now. Not in the middle of all this business with Mailin.

– What about us?

He forced her to say it. – I want you to move out.

He pulled out the toothpick, looked at it, began pushing it in and out between the teeth of his upper jaw.

– At last something other than gibberish, he said. – I've been thinking about it for so bloody long I'd almost forgotten.

– We can talk about it once we've got some distance to this business with Mailin.

– I want to talk about it now, he hissed. – This very moment. You don't just toss out something like that and then leave.

– All right, then, she said, a little more feebly.

– For starters, where will Oda live?

– Oda? I don't even want to discuss that.

Again that chuckle.

– Because you think it's all a done deal, he said without raising his voice. – If it comes to a court case, there's a thing or two I'll have to tell them, you do know that?

Looking at him, she could see that he thought he was already beginning to get the upper hand. – No, I don't know that. Certainly not.

He leaned well back in his chair. – Twice I've driven Oda to Casualty. Once with a broken arm. Once with burns on her chest. Do you think they're complete morons down there? Don't you think someone might have started putting two and two together?

She sat there, her mouth half open, waiting for him to start laughing. Yet another of his nasty, macabre jokes. And when that didn't happen, she had to hit back.

– You'll never get me to say that you were out with Lara when Mailin disappeared, understand? It was *me* who took Lara for a walk that evening. You didn't come home until after eleven. If you're not careful, you'll find yourself hauled up to the police station and charged with giving false information, and while you're there, you can submit your application for custody of Oda at the same time.

That hurt. He pulled out the toothpick, broke it into small pieces and showered them on to the tabletop.

– You don't think I have anything to do with what happened to Mailin.

– You have no idea what I think, Pål. First you tell me exactly what you were doing that evening, and then I'll tell you what I do and don't think.

He pulled out his wry smile. She knew he felt he was charming when he smiled like that, sheepish and self-confident at the same time. Once upon a time she'd felt the same way about it; now it just looked like an empty pout. He practised a therapy that was supposed to help people who had wrapped their own bodies in armour, while he himself was progressively disappearing behind a shell. She had struggled to get inside it. Now the thought of what was in there disgusted her.

– You don't want to know, he said. – You don't want to know where I was.

She played her final card, the one she had been saving for last.

– Mailin found out what you were doing here in the evenings.
– Oh yeah, he said stiffly.

– She asked me if I knew about it.

– Really? And what did you say?

– I told her I knew all about what went on inside your office. That was the day before she went missing. That was the last thing I heard her say, that she was going to call in at your office to talk to you about it.

Torunn presumed that Tormod Dahlstrøm still had her number on his call list. So he would see that it was her who was ringing. He could answer, or at least call back. If he didn't, it would confirm that she meant nothing to him.

Then his voice was there. – Tormod, he said, and she couldn't go on sitting in the chair, she had to get up and pace the room. The thought of having him as her supervisor again now that Mailin was no longer there would have been too grotesque, and she didn't think it.

– Hi, Tormod, she said weakly. – It's Torunn.

She let the two names float together for a moment.

– I saw it was you, he said, and seemed relieved. – I've been meaning to call you.

She realised that he meant it. But also why he had been thinking of her.

– It's just too awful, she said. – It's unreal, I can't get myself to believe it.

It was true. And yet it sounded hollow. She had many reasons for calling. This was the only one she could talk about. – I've been wondering about something Mailin said to me. I need to hear what you think.

She paused, and he didn't interrupt. She had never had a better supervisor, and was only too aware of how stupid she had been to give him up. She'd let anger rule her, pretended to herself that she could hurt him like that. And maybe, in spite of it all, he had been hurt.

– A couple of years ago, Mailin had a patient she didn't want to continue with. She terminated the treatment abruptly. She wasn't the type to give up when the going got rough. But back then she seemed really afraid.

– Did she go into any detail about what happened? Dahlstrøm asked.

– She had just taken him on. It was in the early days of her PhD, and she was considering making him a part of it. I'm pretty sure he threatened her.

– Any idea who this patient might have been?

– I never met him. And Mailin never mentioned a name. I've no idea if he was recommended by a doctor. Social services might know, I'm sure I can find out roughly when he was here. Maybe she talked to you about it.

She knew that it would take a lot for him to reveal anything of what was said in his sessions as Mailin's supervisor.

– I think I know what you're referring to, he said. – It was something that happened several years ago, and Mailin didn't think she needed supervision to talk about it. That might mean she didn't think the episode was quite as serious as the impression you got of it. Quite a number of the people she was treating are unstable and quick tempered.

– The police were here today. They want access to her filing cabinet. I don't think they'll find anything there. It's almost empty. Things connected with her thesis, but no names. I don't know where she kept that kind of thing.

Dahlstrøm was silent for a few moments. Then he said: – I have a list of the patients who were involved in her study. I'll get in touch and urge each one of them to contact the police.

Torunn felt that she could hardly trust her voice any more. – I should have said something about this before, she managed to say.

– You did what you could, Torunn. It's easy to reproach yourself. We just have to help each other the best we can.

His comforting words were too much for her. She let him hear that she was crying before closing the conversation, without mentioning any of the things that she most needed to talk to him about.

10

ROAR HORVATH SPENT an hour preparing himself. He scrolled through hundreds of documents on the internet, printed out a few articles, including one from an obscure website calling itself baalzebub.com. Elijah Frelsøi – Berger's real name – grew up in Oslo. A pupil at Kampen school, and then on to Hersleb. After secondary school he studied theology. His family were members of the Pentecostal church. Frelsøi broke with them at the age of eighteen and took his mother's name, Bergersen. Active in the circles around the anarchist publication *Street Paper*. At the same time a member of several punk rock bands, and started one of his own, Hell's Razors, later Baalzebub, who kept going until the end of the eighties. After that, he worked as a solo artist under the name Berger. Had several hits in the nineties. Lyrics dealing with desire and faith, low key and often acoustic. At the same time wrote several shows, appeared in them himself, and over time developed a format in which he sang his own songs interspersed with a pure stand-up comedy routine. Typically this involved sharp attacks on the powerful in Norwegian society and, in due course, the powerless as well. Early in the 2000s, Berger was given his own show on NRK, but it was taken off air after just three broadcasts, officially because of poor viewing figures. He did a season as a stand-up-rock satirist on TV2. Contract not renewed despite the fact that it was the show people talked about. Early this autumn, he suddenly reappeared again, brought in from the cold by the newly established Channel Six. In the course of a few months, well before Mailin Bjerke went missing, Berger's TV show *Taboo* made the front pages of the tabloids more than ten times: *Berger defends drug use in athletes . . . Berger attacks 'feminist fannies' . . . Berger eats marzipan pig in shape of Muhammad . . . Berger a heroin user . . . Berger a paedophile?*

Roar recalled that one of his best friends, a journalist on Romerikes Blad, had interviewed the infamous TV talk-show host. He left a message on his voicemail before heading down into the garage and taking out a service car.

He was passing Slotts Park when his friend called back.

– Dan-Levi here, you called me.

Roar fiddled with the hands-free and almost didn't see the tram that turned down Henrik Ibsen's Street.

– I'm guessing you didn't call me to say that you're still into swearing and various other forms of sinful behaviour, he heard from the other end.

Dan-Levi Jakobsen had been Roar's best friend from primary school onwards. As the oldest son of a pastor in the Pentecostal church, he was condemned to an outsider's existence, especially during the secondary school years. Roar probably exaggerated his own sense of being different that came from the fact that he was half Hungarian. Later he came to realise that every single pupil at Kjellervolla school felt like an outsider in those days. Most of them managed to hide it, but the pastor's son Dan-Levi never had a chance, and nor did Roar, with his surname. To make up for it, they cultivated a fellowship based on their own version of 'I'm black and I'm proud'. Deep down, the fear of being like everyone else was probably greater than the fear of being rejected.

– Dan-Levi, I called you for two reasons. In the first place, it's getting on for three years since we last went out for a drink.

In actual fact it had been something like three months. Roar was using irony to try to put his old friend on the defensive. Dan-Levi was a father of four and still unassailably married to his teenage sweetheart, Sara. That she had originally been Roar's girlfriend, and the first with whom he went further than a bit of necking in the back row of the cinema, was one of the few things they never joked about.

– I'm ready when you are, *señor*, his friend parried. – You're the one who's let himself get stuck in that swamp of a so-called capital city.

– You're right. I get homesick just thinking about the smell of the river Nitelva.

After moving from Lillestrøm eighteen months ago, leaving behind the wreck of a marriage and a heap of friends all wondering which of the two exes they should stay in touch with, Roar took every opportunity to trash the place. It had conned its way into being called a town. The town centre was a cross between a dump and a permanent building site. The football team was nothing but a gang of grouchy old peasants, *und so weiter*. None of it was particularly seriously meant, but it felt liberating to say it.

– That was the first thing, said Dan-Levi after they'd agreed to meet at Klimt on New Year's Day. – What was the other thing?

– I'm wondering about an interview you did a few years back. But you must promise that this is strictly between us.

Dan-Levi swore. Roar couldn't actually see him cross his heart and hope to die, but his old journalist buddy was someone he trusted, and he'd been very helpful to Roar during his years at Romerike police station. In return, Roar had given Dan-Levi tip-offs that brought the local paper a number of scoops.

– I'm on my way to interview Berger, said Roar. – Give me a bit of gen on the guy.

– Are you suggesting there might be some connection between Berger and this woman they found down in Hurum? Dan-Levi exclaimed.

– No comment, said Roar in English. – I'm the one asking the questions here. I want everything you know about him.

Weak points, what to look out for, *und so weiter*. I'm asking because you interviewed the guy. And because Berger has deep roots in the Pentecostal movement. Once a Pentacostalist, always a Pentacostalist. I'm sure you know people who can talk about his childhood among the speakers in tongues.

– You want to get hold of someone who can tell you whether the guy had psychopathic tendencies even as a child? What's in it for me?

– A beer. Maybe two.

A few moments' silence.

– I'll try and dig up something by Thursday, said Dan-Levi finally. – But here's a tip to be going on with: don't reveal anything about yourself when you talk to him. When I turned up for the interview, I'd hardly finished introducing myself before he started asking me about the Pentecostal movement. He claimed that my name was the giveaway. After that, he was the one grilling me, not the other way around, not for a moment.

11

BERGER LIVED AN apartment in Løvenskiolds Street. The registered owner was someone called Odd Løkkemo, Roar had discovered, and when the door was opened by a man with a reddish-grey rim of hair around his head, he showed his ID and said: – Might you be Odd Løkkemo.

– Might be, the man responded testily. His eyes were red rimmed, as though he had just been crying.

Roar informed him that he had an appointment to see Berger. The man who might have been Løkkemo turned his head. – Elijah, he shouted. – Visitor for you.

The feminine voice and the way he sashayed down the hallway and into a room were enough to persuade Roar that he shared more than just a kitchen with the TV celebrity.

No one emerged to greet him, and rather than just stand there pathetically waiting in the entrance, Roar stepped inside and opened the first door he came to. It led to a bathroom. It looked to have been newly decorated, with tiled walls in the style of the old Roman baths and a large jacuzzi in one corner. Still no sign of life out in the hallway. Roar opened one of the cupboards. Towels and face cloths on shelves. In the next one he found tubes and bottles of pills, most of them prescribed for E. Berger. Co-codamol, he noted. Temgesic. A few morphine tablets. He made a note of the name of the prescribing doctor. Not that he thought he might get something out of him, but it might be interesting to find out if this was someone who was casual about prescribing opiates.

He opened several doors in the corridor, found the kitchen and what looked like a library. The fourth door opened on to an enormous room. A man sat at a desk with his back to the door, bending motionless over a computer keyboard. He didn't react, not even when Roar tried to attract his attention by a noisy clearing of the throat. Not until he closed the door heavily behind him did the man turn round, as though suddenly waking up. His eyes slid up towards his visitor. The long hair was obviously dyed and looked anything but natural against the wrinkled pale yellow skin of the face. Roar noticed that the man's pupils were the size of pinpoints, though the light in the room was not particularly bright.

– The police? Was that today? Berger exclaimed on seeing his ID.

His surprise seemed genuine, despite the fact that it was less than two hours since they had spoken on the phone. Roar had asked him to come down to his office for an interview, and Berger had replied that he had no intention of setting foot inside Oslo police station.

– What did you say your name was? Horvath, yes, that was it. You rang. Hungarian?

Roar remembered what Dan-Levi had said about how Berger took control as soon as he saw an opening. He contented himself with a non-committal nod and said:

– As you know, there are certain questions we'd like to have answers to.

– But of course, said Berger in a slurred, nasal voice. – Of course, of course. He indicated a straight-backed chair by the wall. – So sorry I can't offer you anything, Horvath, but you see my butler has the afternoon off today.

Roar smiled briefly at this silly joke.

– What was all this about again? Berger snuffled. – Help me out here. Was it something to do with my last show?

On the phone Roar had explained exactly what the interview

was about, but he would not let himself be irritated by the game the television clown was trying to play. Though the snuffling and the pupils might suggest that his memory really was switched off. What the hell is this guy on? he thought. Definitely not any kind of upper. He'd looked at a couple of episodes of *Taboo*, including one that had a piece about heroin. Surely the guy hadn't taken a hit just before he was due to talk to the police?

– Mailin Bjerke, he said evenly.

– Of course, groaned Berger. – Tragic business. Tragic. Tragic. He made a face. – What is my situation here? Am I a suspect, Horvath? Is that why you've come, to get a confession?

– Do you have anything to confess?

Berger moved his head backwards, as though to laugh. All that came out was a thin, whinnying sound. Roar thought about taking him in.

– If I were to confess everything on my conscience, Horvath, I'm telling you, you'd have a real party. He gestured with his hand, his elbow slipped off the rest and his body slumped to one side.

– You are being interviewed as a witness, Roar explained. – You had an appointment with Mailin Bjerke on Thursday the eleventh of December, in the evening. She sent you a message. The last one she sent.

Berger leaned forward, rubbed his doughy cheeks briskly with both hands.

– Message, did I get a message? He put a hand into the pocket of his worn jacket, pulled out a mobile phone. – Message on Thursday the eleventh of December? He searched for a while. – Correct, Horvath. What you guys know. *Delayed a few minutes. Entry code is 1982. Door to waiting room on first floor is open. Important we talk. M. Bjerke.*

– Did you wait in the waiting room?

– What else do you do in a waiting room? Berger sniggered.

– Yes, Mister Constable. I was there. But it didn't please the lady to turn up. I had to be at the studio. Told everyone Miss Bjerke was going to be part of the programme. But she didn't turn up there either.

– Perhaps you understand why, Roar observed. – How long did you wait? Five minutes? Ten?

Berger sat staring up at the high stuccoed ceiling.

– I don't walk around with a stopwatch. But I was up at Nydalen before eight thirty.

– Was there anyone else in that waiting room?

– Not a soul. The lights were off when I got there. Didn't hear anyone, see anyone, smell anyone. Berger straightened up and his voice was a little clearer now. – Had a cigarette, found a urinal down the corridor, used it, carefully, left it as clean as I found it, and absented myself.

– And you met no one?

– You know that better than me, Mr Horvath. I'm assuming you are in complete control of the situation.

– We are, Roar assured him. – No one, as far as we know, saw you coming or going in Welhavens Street. No one but you has any idea where you were before ten past nine. When you arrive, out of breath and almost thirty minutes later than usual, and rush into the make-up department to be readied for the broadcast.

Berger closed his eyes and rested his head in one hand.

– There, you see, he said, sounding as if he was on the verge of sleep. – You know all this, so why are you asking me?

– We want to know how it is you could take two hours to get from Mailin Bjerke's office in Welhavens Street up to Nydalen on an evening when traffic was normal.

Berger slid even lower down in his chair. – I leave that to you to find out, Horvath. Shouldn't be too hard for an averagely well-equipped constable. I'm talking strictly about intelligence here, you understand.

He waved his hand. – Sorry I can't see you to the door. And that my butler is off.

Roar stood up and took a step towards him. – I haven't finished with you, Berger. Next time, be in good enough shape to talk properly. If you aren't, I'll see to it that you spend a day or two in our cells before the interview. Preferably with another junkie for company.

He knew it wasn't particularly smart to say something like that. It felt good.

12

When Odd Løkkemo heard the policeman leaving the apartment, he sat up in bed. His migraine was ebbing away. He knew how to deal with it, knew exactly what he could do and what had to be avoided. On the first day of the attack he was more or less a dead man. First a tingling over one half of his body, double vision, colours dancing against the white wall. Then the sudden lameness. One corner of his mouth drooping, loss of feeling in half the face, unable to move his arm, and his foot dangling and trailing if he tried to lift his leg. And then the pain breaking over him in waves one metre high. Two days in a dark room with the curtains closed. Vomiting in a bucket, crawling along the floor to get to the toilet.

During the days Odd had been lying in the dark feeling like a victim of torture, Elijah had had a visitor. Not a friend of them both, otherwise the person would have popped in to the bedroom to see how things were. Almost certainly an admirer. The music he heard coming from Elijah's study suggested as much. A young man, he imagined, knowing that women no longer roused anything but memories in his partner.

A few hours previously, when Odd could finally face getting up, he'd found Elijah naked on the kitchen table. He noticed at once: Elijah had had sex. Always that same dreamy look on his face, like a lovesick kid. Fucking hell, he'd thought, but managed not to say anything. The slightest sign of a quarrel and his migraine would flare up again . . . It had actually started a couple of weeks earlier, when Odd was in Lillehammer.

On the day he came back, Elijah had that look on his face, that vacant smile, that smell of young lust. He acted secretive, kept dropping hints. He knew how much it hurt; Odd had realised a long time ago that that was the reason he did it. Elijah loved to make him jealous. Not because he needed to show who had the power, but because he never tired of feeling that someone was jealous because of him. In general he liked to arouse feelings in people that they had no control over themselves. It made them more interesting, in his view. *Even a relentless bore like you, Odd, becomes exciting when that delightfully immature anger surfaces.* Or he might say something along the lines of: *I absolutely love you, Odd, when you get in a rage and try to control it, when you show the dangerous and unknown sides of yourself. Apart from that, you are predictable to the point of absurdity.* And yet still Elijah stuck with him. Or perhaps that was precisely why. Even he needed something predictable in his life. He'd be helpless without you, thought Odd. Now more than ever, after what happened . . . For a while Elijah had tried to keep it to himself, but Odd had found out in the end. Come across a letter he should never have seen. He might be predictable, but he had this talent for finding things out about Elijah; he knew more about him than anyone else ever had. He consoled himself with this thought, cultivated it and nurtured it every day.

In the front room, Elijah Berger lay in the wing chair. His head was bent backwards and his mouth was half open. His breathing was heavy and uneven.

Odd put a hand on his forehead. – How are you?

Berger opened one eye. – Would you tidy up, he groaned with a nod in the direction of the desk.

Odd went over and pulled out the top drawer. In it lay a tourniquet and a syringe with a milky residue mixed with a thin trail of blood in the bottom.

– Kindly warn me the next time we have a visit from the police.

– I did, Odd said.

Berger waved him away. He lay there a while longer, staring at the ceiling. Then he sat up straight. – Migraine gone now? he asked in a friendly way.

Odd stood beside him again, stroked his hair. – Thank you for caring, Elijah.

A short grunt emerged from Berger's throat. – Need the place to myself for a while tonight, he said. – Can you go out somewhere?

Odd withdrew his hand and slumped down by the table. He could get angry now. Tell it like it was. That he was the one who owned the flat. That Elijah lived there because he, Odd, allowed him to do so. That Elijah could find himself somewhere else to entertain his fuck-friends. He could have used that very phrase. He could have shouted out that he hated him. But stuff like that had no effect on Elijah. Even less than before, after what had happened. It was no good telling it like it was, because Elijah wasn't living there because he had to. He was living there because Odd wanted him to live there, in his apartment and nowhere else. Because he wanted him there beside him. Because he wanted him to be just exactly as he was.

– How can I help you if you reject me?

Berger looked at him for a long time. His gaze opened and for a moment was devoid of mockery. Then he laid his hand on Odd's, in the way Odd had been longing for.

– The sign of deepest friendship, Odd, is that you help your friend to bury a body in the ground.

– No, Odd protested. He stood up and sat on the armrest next to him. It wasn't the first time over the past few weeks that Elijah had said exactly the same thing, and this time he had his answer prepared. – The sign of friendship is that you help him dig *up* bodies.

Berger sank back into the chair without saying anything else and resumed his staring at the ceiling.

Help him, thought Odd. That was what he ought to do, help him through this. Not think about afterwards. There is no afterwards.

13

IN THE LIFT on the way down from the seventh floor of the Oslo police headquarters, Roar Horvath thought about the interview he was about to conduct. As usual, he had set himself certain goals regarding what it was he wanted clarified. It was, naturally, crucial that his agenda was flexible and didn't get in the way of something else important that might crop up along the way. He had spent the morning going through a pile of transcriptions of the interviews once more. He had looked at the report written by another member of the investigative team about the murdered woman's background, and in a separate addendum made a number of comments of his own. Now he ran through in his head the most important questions he wanted to ask Mailin Bjerke's sister.

As he emerged from the lift, he caught sight of her. She was standing a few metres away from the reception desk, in the middle of the floor. When he held out his hand and introduced himself, he abruptly felt completely unprepared. He had to make an effort to keep eye contact with her. Realised afterwards that he hadn't heard her answer. He had interviewed a lot of young women, some ugly, some beautiful, most of them somewhere in between. He should be professional enough to remain unaffected by such concerns. He took a hold of himself as he turned and walked ahead of her. *Alert, Roar*, he warned himself. *Level five alert.*

– My condolences, he managed to say as they stood in the narrow lift. She was almost as tall as him. The hair somewhere between red and brown. And eyes that looked green in the sharp electric light.

She lowered her eyes without answering.

– This must be a terrible time for the closest relatives.

Roar considered himself above average when it came to speaking to people in difficult situations. Right now he felt like an elephant.

He closed the office door behind her and caught a whiff of perfume. *Alert*, *Roar*, he reminded himself irritably. *Level eight*. Ten was maximum on the scale of how much it was reasonable to expect him to control himself.

She was dressed in ordinary clothing, he noted once he had taken his seat behind the desk. An all-weather jacket that looked much too big. Green woollen pullover underneath it. Black trousers, not especially tight fitting, high-heeled boots. It looked as though she was wearing almost no make-up. Her hands were narrow, the fingers long and thin, the nails well manicured. He repeated the description to himself in silence; it improved his grip of the situation.

– We've been trying to get hold of you for several days, he began. – No one knew exactly where you were.

– Who is *no one*? she asked. The voice was calm and quite deep.

– Your parents. They haven't seen you since Christmas Eve.

He had been surprised that she had not been with her family in the shock and distress of the first few days.

– When did you last see your sister? he asked.

– In the summer, Liss Bjerke answered, looking straight at him. He was used to her look by now.

– Was your relationship perhaps not particularly close?

Liss Bjerke smoothed her suede gloves along her thigh. – What makes you think that?

– Well, I . . . Relationships between sisters probably aren't all the same closeness.

– Have *you* got any brothers or sisters? she asked.

The interview had been going on for just a couple of minutes and already things were headed in a completely different direction to the one he had planned; but instead of brushing her question aside, he answered her:

– One sister and one brother.

– And you're the oldest?

– Good guess, he smiled.

– Mailin is the person in the world who means most to me, she said suddenly. – I didn't see much of her after I moved to Amsterdam, but the relationship between us was as close as always.

– I understand, Roar commented, though he didn't have any particularly good reason to say something like that. – It must have been terribly . . .

– To the best of my knowledge you're neither a priest nor a psychologist, Liss Bjerke interrupted him sharply. – I'm here to answer questions that might help you find out what's happened.

Alert now, Roar, he thought yet again, and turned towards his computer. He opened the list of questions he'd made and took them from the top down. Things went more smoothly now. He got a clear picture of the contact between the sisters over the last few months. They'd spoken on the telephone at least once a week. In addition to a steady stream of text messages. Liss Bjerke showed him some of them, and that deep, calm tone had returned to her voice. Roar knew, however, that he would have to watch his step.

The last message from her sister was sent on the afternoon of Thursday 11 December. *On my way from the cabin. Always think of you when I'm out there. Keep Midsummer's Day free next year. Call you tomorrow.*

– What's this about Midsummer's Day? Roar asked.

Liss Bjerke appeared to think about it for a moment before replying: – She was going to get married.

Roar typed something. – Who to?

– Don't tell me you don't know who her partner is, said Liss Bjerke impatiently. – You've interviewed him at least three times. The irritation was back in her voice.

– Right, so that's Viljam Vogt-Nielsen, nodded Roar.

– Mailin wasn't the type to live with one person and make plans to marry someone else, Liss added, and Roar had to admit that she was right. He was already getting used to these sudden changes of mood in her. She was a bit temperamental, he thought; women who looked like that often were. He started asking her what she was doing in Amsterdam, but it quickly became apparent that she had no wish to talk about herself. At least not with him.

– Did you know Viljam Vogt-Nielsen previously? he asked instead.

She gave him a sceptical look, or maybe it was condescending, as though she was about to ridicule that question too, but she answered:

– I met him for the first time just after I came home. That's more than two weeks ago.

Before he could say anything else, she said: – You want to know what I think of him, right? If I think he could have done this to Mailin.

– And do you think so?

– Even though he was at my parents' when she went missing? Even though he and Mailin got on well together?

Her cheeks had grown slightly flushed. The way she defends her sister's boyfriend, he thought. Check to make sure they never met before.

There was a knock on the door and Viken popped his head in. When he saw Liss Bjerke, he stepped inside. He was well dressed as usual: dark blue blazer and white shirt. He might have passed for some famous old crooner. He stood observing her for a few seconds.

– Viken, Detective Chief Inspector. He squeezed her hand. – My condolences, he added.

– Thank you, she said.

He carried on with a few well-chosen words, the kind of things a priest might have said, thought Roar, although Viken wasn't subject to the same kind of censure as he had been. On the contrary, to judge by Liss Bjerke's face, she accepted the detective chief inspector's expressions of sympathy.

– It's lucky you're here, Viken went on. – I got a reply to this business of the mobile phone just a couple of minutes ago.

She looked up at him enquiringly. – Mailin's mobile phone?

– Exactly. We've had an expert going over the videos. We're very interested in trying to find out what she's actually saying.

– It wasn't very clear, said Liss Bjerke, suddenly keen. – And I couldn't bring myself to play it again.

– I understand that. Viken had at once found the tone Roar had been struggling to find for almost half an hour. – And it's not certain it would have helped you to hear it several times either. Our experts have played it over and over again, but they're still not a hundred per cent sure.

He produced a piece of paper from his jacket pocket, unfolded it, spread it out. – It's particularly important for us to hear what you think it is, since the video ends with Mailin calling out your name. But let me ask you one thing first. It is of crucial importance for the investigation that none of this gets out.

Liss Bjerke leaned forward, began twining a lock of hair around her index finger. – I'll keep it to myself.

– Good. It sounds as if Mailin says four or five words. *Sand*, *oar* – maybe *or* – and then *fare*, *end*, *she*, before she calls out *Liss*. Did you get that?

Liss repeated: – *Sand*, *oar*, maybe *or*, *fare*, *end*, *she*, and then *Liss*.

– Exactly, said Viken. – Does that mean anything to you?

He sat on the edge of the table and waited, not putting any pressure on her.

After about half a minute she said: – Can I have a bit more time?

– Of course, Liss. Take all the time you need.

Roar worked away on the keyboard. He couldn't remember having heard Viken address a witness by their first name before.

The detective chief inspector handed her a card. – I want you to ring me if you come up with anything. Whenever it might be, do you promise me that? Even if it's the dead of night.

She looked at the card, sat there a while fingering it. – Have you found out any more about the guy who was in her office? she asked.

Viken's bushy eyebrows curved together above his nose. – What do you mean?

– I rang you twice and told you about a guy sneaking round in Mailin's office the first time I went there. He ripped a page out of her diary with her appointments for the day she disappeared.

Viken looked at Roar. This visitor had been mentioned in a memorandum from the crime response unit, but nothing about any appointments book. Roar wrinkled his brow to show that this was news to him too.

– I don't think they completely understood what you were getting at, he said tactfully. – Tell me what you saw.

Liss Bjerke gave him an exasperated look, thinking perhaps it was his fault that they'd screwed up at the crime response unit. He pretended not to notice and began to transcribe her account, word for word.

– And the initials were J. H.? he said, double-checking. – And you saw this man at Central Station a few days later?

– And at a party, in a flat in Sinsen.

– What's the name of the person who owns this flat?

Liss Bjerke's fingers were now no longer twining one of the reddish locks of hair but a chain she had hanging around her neck.

– I can find that out.

– Who did you go to this party with? Viken wanted to know.

She gave the names of some girlfriends and a couple of professional footballers. Roar had the strong impression she was sifting through the information before she handed it on to them, and it gave him some idea of the sort of thing that had been going on in the Sinsen apartment.

– So you live in Amsterdam, Viken remarked once they had made a record of what Liss Bjerke had to tell them, or was prepared to tell them. – A lovely city.

She glanced over at him. – Does that have anything to do with the case?

Viken spread his hands wide. – Everything has to do with everything. What do you do over there?

She sat up straight in her chair, crossed one leg over the other. – Study design.

Viken said: – I've also heard it rumoured you're a model.

Roar saw how her eyes widened.

– Is this part of the interview?

– Not exactly. But every witness has more to tell us than they themselves realise.

– What the fuck do you mean by that? She jumped to her feet. – I'm here so that you can find out what happened to my sister, what sort of sick bastard it was who tortured and killed her. What *I* do has no connection with the case at all.

For a few moments she stood there looking at a point somewhere between the two policemen. Then she turned on her heel, let herself out and was gone before they had a chance to say anything. On the floor beside the chair lay Viken's card, squashed into a ball.

* * *

Viken was still there when Roar returned after a vain attempt to get the witness to come back and finish the interview. He was standing by the desk reading through what Roar had typed in.

– That's one genuinely unstable young lady, Roar remarked. – The same thing happened when I asked her about Amsterdam. She clammed up completely.

Viken thought about it. – Don't forget what she's been through, he said forgivingly. – You'll have to get her back in here so she can sign your witness statement. And we need her to help us find out about this guy sneaking around in the office.

Roar sat behind the desk and opened another memo. – One of her psychologist colleagues said that Mailin Bjerke might have been threatened by a patient. We need to find out if this has any connection with what her sister told us.

The detective chief inspector was on his way out, turned in the doorway. – I almost forgot what it was I really came in here to tell you.

He pulled the door closed. – The Boss in his wisdom has decided to break off his Christmas holiday and honour us with his presence, he said with a phoney formality.

Viken enjoyed calling the section's acting head Sigge Helgarsson 'the Boss'. It was no secret that the relationship between them was a trifle strained.

– You remember I'm sure that Plåterud suggested there might be a connection with the Ylva Richter case over in Bergen.

Roar had certainly not forgotten that morning in the autopsy room. He confined himself to a nod.

– Well now the lady has got Professor Korn to get in touch with our own boss. The result of this delightful bit of meddling is that Helgarsson wants us to check out this Bergen business before we do anything else.

– All right then, Roar responded neutrally.

– Oh there'll be some fun here all right when the whole show is run from the Riks Hospital. The Boss obviously thinks it's quite in order, so he's been here and said his bit and now he's gone again, and that means we've got to spread ourselves even thinner. Which means a trip to Bergen for you, Roar, you lucky bastard.

Viken flicked away something or other that had landed on his lapel.

– Cow, he added testily, without making it clear who he was referring to.

14

LISS PUT THE notebook aside and looked around the café. The waiter misunderstood and was there in a flash, undressing her with his eyes. He still smelled bad.

– More coffee?

She'd been drinking coffee all day, but nodded, mostly to get rid of him. His trousers were tight fitting and his bum was small and muscular. She didn't like men to have such narrow hips. Suddenly she recalled the policeman, the older one, the short one with the aquiline nose and the bushy eyebrows. For a moment there in the office she'd been on the point of revealing what had happened in Amsterdam.

She opened the notebook again. Could she manage to tell herself another story, one in which Zako and Rikke had become lovers? He's moved from Bloemstraat and into her place on Marnixkaade.

Still not possible to write that story.

What happened to the ring, Mailin? she scribbled down.

Her grandmother on Mother's side wrote books about women's lives. She was famous and meant a lot to a lot of people. A pioneer, Ragnhild used to call her. When she died, Mailin was the one who inherited her wedding ring. A sign of the legacy to be carried forward.

Did he take it off you before he beat you to death?

Without her noticing, the waiter was there again, touched her shoulder as he put the coffee down.

– This one's free. New Year's present.

She was about to protest. Didn't want to accept anything from this man, even if it was New Year's Eve . . . There were already sounds out in the streets, the odd rocket shooting up in the dark grey afternoon light. She couldn't bear the thought of being around people who were celebrating, toasting each other and shouting. She should be out of town, somewhere far away when the old year came to a close.

If you go any closer to grief it will swallow you up. Is that what you want? Never come out into the light again?

Didn't know where that came from. Didn't know why she was writing stuff down in this book at all. Had never been much interested in words, but now there they were.

Mailin's book. Writing to you, Mailin. Only thing I can do now. What would you have done?

She flipped back to the page on which she had written the words the police had asked her about:

Sand, oar/or, fare, end, she.

Read them slowly, over and over again. *Sand* and *oar* had something to do with the cabin. One summer Mailin had found a rotting oar that drifted ashore on their beach. They had invented a story to go with it. A man rowing out there. The boat capsizes. He drowns but doesn't die. Rows and rows with one oar on Morr Water by night. One day he'll turn up on our beach. He's come to fetch this oar. If he doesn't find it, he'll take us instead. They lay there telling each other this story in the evenings, listening out for the man in the boat.

Can you hear someone rowing out there, Mailin?

Mailin gets out of bed, crosses to the open window. The night is pale grey.

I hear it. He's rowing in the night. He's getting nearer.

Liss hides her head under the pillow. Mailin gets into her bed, puts her arms around her.

If he comes, he can take me. I'll never let him lay a finger on you, Liss.

Fare, end, she. In the car, she continued to think about the words. *Feren*, she suddenly said out loud. The lake they often skied across. Instead of *she*, could Mailin have been saying *ski*? All the ski trips they had taken across the lakes. Feren was one of the biggest, halfway to Flateby. And back through the woods after dark. This whole swathe of forest was theirs. Has Mailin given me a message about a skiing trip we once made? Then it might have something to do with a specific winter holiday. Or an Easter holiday. Up until Mailin finished at secondary school and went to university, they'd spent most of their holidays out there, just the two of them. Mailin had boyfriends, but never took any of them there. Not until she met Pål Øvreby. The first who was allowed to visit the cabin. She'd been a student for six months. Liss didn't like Pål. Straight away he acted as though he owned the place. Bossed them around: who was to fetch the water, who fetch the wood. Before, these things had just taken care of themselves. Liss liked to keep things moving, get up first and make sure there was water in the buckets and wood in the fireplace. Now there were objections, arguments. And Pål Øvreby tried to persuade them that he owned Mailin, too.

That winter holiday was Liss's last year at middle school. There were only the three of them there. She went out to the shed one morning. Sat on the toilet. Hadn't bothered to hook the door closed. Heard footsteps outside. It wasn't Mailin. She dried herself and stood up to pull on her trousers. The door opened wide. Pål didn't say sorry; just stood there, staring at her. She couldn't get the tight trousers up. He didn't retreat, he stepped inside. Stood right up close to her. Put his hand between her legs. *You're so fucking gorgeous.* She was freezing cold and couldn't move. She felt his finger inside her. *Liss*, he murmured, bending down to kiss her. His mouth smelled of tobacco and mouldy cheese, or was the smell coming from the toilet? That was what freed her feet; she whirled round and threw herself against the door.

Why had she never told her sister? If she found out what Pål was like, Mailin would be hurt. That it might hurt her even more if she carried on seeing him was something Liss couldn't even bear to think about. Not long afterwards Mailin finished with him anyway, so there was no longer any need to tell her.

Someone's been here. The thought struck her as she climbed over the hilltop and slid down towards the panel fence. Stood there a few moments thinking about it. The curtain, she decided. She had drawn the living-room curtain on this side wall too, always did that before leaving the cabin. Now it was open. She stalked around the corner, to the veranda, unhooked the key from under the gutter, let herself in. No sign of a break-in. Everything looked untouched. Apart from that curtain. Could she be wrong about that? Or had Tage been here? Viljam? Her mother? That was out of the question – her mother hadn't left the house since Christmas Eve.

Liss inspected all the rooms, didn't find anything out of the ordinary. Took another circuit of the cabin and out to the toilet. Poked her head into that smell of stale dung. Mostly the family's dung, collected and broken down over the decades. The reek of something like chlorine when she raised the toilet seat. Dead flies in the window. Maybe some of them not quite dead. Lying there all through the winter waiting for it to be warm enough outside for them to return to life. If Mailin wasn't dead either . . . if she were deep-frozen and could be thawed out. Slowly moving her lips, opening her eyes. They were destroyed. She would never be able to see with them. Who is out there who doesn't want Mailin to see any more?

She got up, tossed the lid back over the opening, suddenly

furious, the same fury that had frozen her to the floor that
time ten years ago. Now she swung the door open and howled
up into the trees and at the hill behind the cabin.

It was almost dark when she took the water buckets and made
her way down to the rock. The ice was probably safer now than
when she was there before Christmas; the open channel as
always followed the line of the current from the stream and on
outwards, Morr Water's black winter eye staring up at her. She
bent forward, switched on the torch and shone it on to the gap.
The light broke through the clear cold water and disappeared
in the depths.

Sand and *oar*. She cleared her way to the boathouse door.
The boat lay there, belly upwards. It needed tarring. She
smelled it. Water and rot. Hanging up under the roof, fishing
rods and the obsolete remains of the old wooden skis people
once used, long before she was born. Both oars were up there.
She lifted them down, turned them over, shone the torch beam
along the length of them, studied every centimetre of the wood,
every cut, every crack. Nothing different from the way she
remembered it. *Feren* and *ski*.

She lay on the sofa. The smell of fir and winter dust. Silence.
No sound but the sound of her thoughts. Mailin's voice: *Shall
I wax your skis for you, Liss?* Easter weekend, a couple of months
after the winter holidays when Pål came out. Mother's comment:
She always waxes her own skis. But on this morning Liss was
lying on the sofa. A few minutes earlier she'd been bent double
behind the toilet shed, because no one must see her vomiting,
no one must know she felt nauseous the whole time. Mailin
was the only one she told. Not that Mother would have
condemned her; she never condemned people. But she would
have wanted to know how it had happened, why Liss hadn't
taken precautions, and who was responsible. Her skis were
waxed and ready. Mailin stood waiting for her. She didn't get

up to the cabin much any more. Went up into the Nordmarka forest with student friends, or studied for her exams. Maybe it would be the last holiday they had there together, Liss had thought. She felt nauseous. Afraid. She feared this thing inside her body; it would grow, emerge, turn her into something else. And Mailin couldn't be told either who she'd been with. She couldn't understand why Liss wouldn't say, but in the end gave up trying to find out.

It was dark outside. Liss took out the notebook.

Mailin: We'll take the track across Feren today. Shall I wax your skis, Liss?

What if you'd found out what had happened before that Easter, Mailin? You would have hated me.

She hunched up, felt that she would soon fall asleep. Out here she always felt dog tired in the evenings. Slept deeply and soundly, as though her restlessness spread on the wind and was sucked up by the trees, until all that remained in her body was a faint murmuring. She reached out a hand, turned down the paraffin lamp on the table; the two logs in the fireplace could just burn up. She abandoned the thought of washing and brushing her teeth and getting into bed. Sank down into sleep. Could sleep here all winter, was the last thought she was aware of, not emerge until spring. Stand down on the beach and see Mailin come rowing to shore. Her back to the land. Rowing and rowing. *Turn round, Mailin, so I can see that it's you.* She turns. It isn't Mailin. It's Grandma, her father's mother. Wearing a black dress, her red hair like a veil flowing down her back . . .

Liss starts restlessly as she lies there. Someone has entered the room. She tries to wake up. *What's happened to my eyes? I can't see properly.* The old woman doesn't move, stands in front of the fireplace staring at her. She's wearing a sort of uniform, with a long green coat over it. A towel tied around her forehead, drenched in blood.

What do you want? Where is Mailin?

Her own shout awoke her. She saw the outlines of a face outside the living-room window. – You are not afraid, Liss, she murmured. – You're never afraid any more. She got to her feet. The shape outside disappeared. She stumbled out into the kitchen. Had to pee. Put her hands into the bucket and rubbed her face hard with the icy water. Took the lamp out into the darkness. It was still snowing, harder now. On the veranda outside the living-room window she saw footprints. She shone the lamp on them. Boots, bigger than hers, from the door and over to the window, from there to the corner. She went back inside, put on the head lamp, threw on the enormous all-weather jacket she still hadn't returned to its owner. From the corner she tracked the footprints over towards the outside toilet, where they disappeared into the trees beyond.

It snowed for the rest of the night. She didn't sleep. Locked the door. Lay with her eyes open in the dark. Placed an empty wine bottle next to the sofa. Didn't know what she intended to do with it. Smash it, use it to stab with maybe. – I am not afraid, she repeated. – I am not afraid any more. Everything that's happened to Mailin, I could stand it too.

In the end she must have dropped off, because suddenly the grey light of dawn was outside. She got up, went outside to pee. No footprints on the veranda now. Snowed over. Should have taken a photo of them, she thought. But who would she show it to? Wouldn't be talking to the police any more, she had decided.

She made fires in the woodstove and the open fireplace. Boiled water, sprinkled in the coffee powder. Wrapped a blanket around herself, lit a cigarette, sat by the window and watched the day arrive. Nowhere she had to be. At the same time, a feeling that there was something she had to do before it was too late. She took out the notebook.

Footprints in the snow. Winter boots. Several sizes bigger than mine.

Dream: Mailin rowing towards land, turns, it isn't Mailin. Grandma standing in the room. Wants to tell me something.

She sucked the last drags from the cigarette, felt the burning deep down in her chest. Needed to eat. Eat and puke. Nothing suitable for that to eat here. Needed to inhale something that would make her strong, invincible, furious, if only for a half-hour. Didn't have that here either.

I'll never leave here again.

You can't stay here, Liss.

I don't have anywhere else.

You can't hide yourself away. The world is wherever you are.

She glanced over at the sofa where she'd spent the night. One of the cushions had fallen on to the floor. She picked it up, noticed as she did so that the zip fastener on the cover was half open. Inside was a sheet of paper. Scrunched up into a ball. She smoothed it out. A story from *VG*'s online edition dated 21 November 2003, but the printout was from 10 December 2008, the day before Mailin's disappearance.

Missing girl (19) found dead outside Bergen was the headline.

15

Thursday 1 January 2009

IT WAS NOWHERE near crowded at Klimt that evening, but a couple of regulars were nursing beers at the bar, and at one table New Year was still being celebrated. Roar Horvath swapped a few pleasantries with the lads behind the bar; one of them he hadn't seen since they played in the back four together for LSK juniors, but he'd gathered that Roar was working on the murder of the woman who was supposed to be on *Taboo*. Roar could only respond with his most ironic *No comment*, and in return got a pat on the shoulder and a *Cheers* anyway. Almost before he knew what was going on, the first beer had come and gone. Going out in Lillestrøm was a homecoming after all.

Dan-Levi appeared in the doorway that led down to the toilets. At first Roar thought he'd had his dark hair cut, but then realised his old friend had tied it in a ponytail that hung down his back. Not exactly the latest style for men, but then Dan-Levi would never abandon his long tresses; he called them his freak flag, after one of his favourite songs.

They sat in a corner where they could talk undisturbed. As usual Dan-Levi wanted to hear about Roar's bachelor life. Roar admitted he had something going and hoped that would be enough to satisfy his friend's curiosity. No such luck, as it turned out. Dan-Levi looked as though he'd hooked an enormous trout on the end of his fishing rod and started to reel it in.

– Not a policewoman, is it? Then the outlook isn't good.

It was hardly a scientifically based conclusion, but it was smart and aimed at eliciting further hard facts.

– Both yes and no, Roar conceded. – In a sense.

He didn't want to break with the joking way they'd always had with each other, and the openness it allowed them. This openness had been good for them both. Around the time of the divorce, Dan-Levi had always been there for him, inviting him out for an evening in town, or to go fishing up in the Østmarka forest. As well as something they both referred to as their annual hunting trip, though it was a few years now since the last time. Dan-Levi wasn't completely hopeless with a fishing rod, but he would never make any kind of hunter. The best he'd managed that autumn when Roar got divorced was a couple of hares that turned out to be, on closer inspection, pet rabbits that some idiot of a farmer up in Nes had allowed to run about freely. It was a story Roar never tired of reminding his friend about. After a while he contented himself with just holding two slightly bent fingers up in the air to make his point. The gesture seemed to have no effect at all on Dan-Levi's masculine pride. He'd even written a little sidebar about the episode for *Romerikes Blad*, in which he exaggerated his own clumsiness and claimed to have nearly hit one of the farmer's cows into the bargain – but a big one, with horns almost the size of a moose.

– In a sense what? he went on now with a journalist's persistence. – She surely can't both be a policewoman and *not* be a policewoman?

Roar gave him a couple of clues, almost let slip the story about the Christmas party to which some of the forensic people, for reasons that had nothing to do with him, had been invited. He stressed that there was absolutely no question of a relationship. That this lady was too old for him, as well as too smart and too married.

Dan-Levi smacked his lips in satisfaction. – Mother fixation, he suggested, but by now Roar had had enough and headed off to buy another round of beers.

– Now what about Berger? he wanted to know when he returned. – Have you for once put your investigative talents to any useful purpose?

Dan-Levi swigged at his beer, the froth settling on his moustache and his little goatee. – In a sense, as you like to put it. He waited until he saw his friend's weary smile before continuing. – I spoke to a former elder of the Pentecostal church, a friend of my dad's. He knows the Frelsøi family well and has followed Berger's career.

He took another drink of beer, was in no rush.

– And?

– You want to hear what he said, or what he didn't say?

– Let's have it.

– Okay. Berger's father was a pastor in the Pentecostal church.

– As was your father.

Dan-Levi made a face. – We're talking about two very different kinds of father here. One who followed the New Testament on how to bring up children, and one who followed the Old. Whom you love also punish, *und so weiter*. Frelsøi senior was apparently the type who would have dragged his son up the nearest mountain without a moment's hesitation and cut his throat if he thought God demanded such a sacrifice. The elder wouldn't go into detail, but I gathered from him that the Bergersen Frelsøi family had been the subject of considerable concern in the community, and don't forget this is the Pentecostal movement nineteen-fifty-something we're talking about here.

– Violence? Abuse?

Dan-Levi considered the question. – My source won't name

any names, not even of those who are dead. Most of all them. If you approach the community as an investigator, you're going to get the door slammed in your face. But that's what it was like in those days. Everything should be sorted out internally, and nothing got done. It ended in the worst possible way, without anybody at all getting involved. It's incredible what some people can do after a literal reading of the Bible. *And if thy right eye offend thee, pluck it out, and cast it from thee: for it is profitable for thee that one of thy members should perish, and not that thy whole body should be cast into hell. Und so weiter.*

Roar put his glass down on the table with a bang. – What you just said then, about eyes, is that what it says in the Bible?

– Yes indeed. Matthew chapter 5, verses 29 and 30.

Dan-Levi came from a family in which biblical texts weren't followed to the letter. Roar had always liked being at his house; his parents were warm hearted and generous, and Dan-Levi's father was much less strict than his own, who had arrived from Hungary an eighteen-year-old refugee with nothing more than *two bare hands and a will of steel*. But Dan-Levi had been obliged to learn the Bible by heart, and Roar suspected that he was putting the next generation through the same school.

His mobile phone rang. He saw who it was and took the call on the pavement outside.

– Take it easy, I'm not going to invite myself over to your place this evening.

Roar had to laugh, surprised at how happy it made him to hear that voice with its crisp Australian accent. When he'd found himself sitting next to her at the Christmas party, he had at first assumed Jennifer Plåterud was American, but when he hinted as much, she was greatly offended and assured him that she was a good deal less American than he was.

– Pity, I'd've enjoyed a visit, Roar responded now. – That's to say, I've got Emily and I'm staying the night at my mother's. Probably not a brilliant idea to meet there.

Jennifer's laughter was a touch strained, he thought. Maybe being introduced to his family in this way was a bit much, even in jest.

– I'm calling from the office, she said.

– Cripes, do you always work this late?

– Often. There's always plenty to do.

Her capacity for work was dizzying. She was superior to him there as well, not that she made an issue of it.

– I just got a call from Liss Bjerke.

– What? You mean she called *you*?

– It sounds as if she doesn't want to have anything more to do with you, or anyone else from the station. I wasn't able to find out why. She could well be in a state of shock, I imagine.

Roar chose not to say anything about what had happened at the interview the day before.

– What did she want?

Jennifer hesitated. – She has information she'd rather give to me than any of you. She said she had more faith in someone who was a doctor.

– What kind of information?

– I believe it has something to do with a document she's found. She wouldn't say over the phone. We agreed that she would come out here early tomorrow morning. Naturally I did all I could to persuade her to go to you, but she refuses.

Viken was always stressing that those he worked with could call him at any time; he was always available. It had struck Roar how little he knew about him. Viken didn't wear a ring, and never spoke about a family. In fact he never spoke about himself at all.

As he punched in the number to inform him of what Jennifer had told him, Roar felt like a bright young lad rushing home with important news.

The detective chief inspector said: – Why did she call you?

– Who, Plåterud? Roar could hear how stupid his own question sounded.

– Why did she ring you? Viken repeated.

Roar looked around. The main street in Lillestrøm was deserted. – Don't know.

He moved quickly on to what he'd found out about Berger's background, thinking it would appeal to Viken's taste for the psychological.

At the other end the DCI listened in silence. Then he said: – We'd better bring him in. I'll take care of it.

– By the way, I've been in touch with the Montreal Community Police Department this evening, he added.

Roar had offered to handle the job of tracing Mailin Bjerke's father, but Viken was determined to do it himself.

– They still haven't found him?

It sounded as if the inspector was sipping away at something or other. Probably coffee, because as Roar knew, he was a teetotaller.

– It appears that he's away travelling, but no one knows where or for how long. They've been to his home on the outskirts of Montreal several times, talked with neighbours and friends.

– An artist, isn't he? Roar grinned. – Meaning he comes and goes as he pleases.

Viken let the observation pass.

– They've sent out an internal be-on-the-lookout, he said. – It's up to us if they make it public. We'll wait, for the time being.

– Almost worse than being a journalist, Dan-Levi sighed as Roar returned to the table. – Always on the job.

– How do you know it was a work call?

Dan-Levi thought about it. – It could of course have been the *lady*, he suggested. – The doctor lady.

Roar glanced over his shoulder. – If this gets out, Dan, I wouldn't think twice about committing murder. Not for one second.

– Ooops, his friend said teasingly. – And here was me thinking of going home and doing a feature on people who left Lillestrøm and now live *la dolce vita* in the capital. I guess it'll have to be something on the Beckhams instead. Imagine this scenario: David decides to end his career as a right-winger for LSK. He sends wicked Vicky on ahead to check out the night life in the city of Lillestrøm.

Roar declined to be distracted. He repeated his threat, illustrating with a sweep of the finger where the throat would be cut. – Halal.

Dan-Levi raised both arms and bowed his neck.

– Do you watch *Taboo*? he asked abruptly.

Roar had to confess that he did. – Particularly now that it's work related.

– Viewing figures are bound to reach a million on Tuesday, said Dan-Levi. – Did you see what it said in *VG* yesterday about the last programme Berger's going to make?

Roar had hardly had time to open a newspaper the last few days.

– The headline was *Death in the studio*. The hype is insane. They all expect him to top everything else he's ever done before.

Roar wrinkled his nose. – Didn't think you Pentecostals sat around on your sofas entertaining yourself with blasphemy, pure and simple.

– That's precisely the point, Dan-Levi exclaimed. – If Berger had been a simple atheist, he'd be ignored. But the guy stands there and insists that he believes in a God.

– You mean Baal-something-or-other?

– Beelzebub. Atheism doesn't provoke anyone, but a celebrity who openly admits to worshipping the lord of the flies, the God of the Philistines, he'll get all the Christian condemnation he could wish for.

– Smart bastard, murmured Roar.

16

LISS LET HERSELF into the house in Lang Street. Imagined what Mailin did when she came home. Put her boots on the rack in the hallway, wandered into the kitchen, a glance at the washing-up piled and waiting in the sink. They took it in turn to keep the kitchen tidy, Viljam had told her. If it was Mailin's day, she'd get going straight away. She'd always be sure to get the dull stuff out of the way before it got out of control. Afterwards perhaps she'd sit down at the kitchen table. Did she listen for the sound of a door opening? Did she long to hear the sound of his voice from the hallway?

After doing the washing-up, Liss had a smoke out on the steps in the cold winter evening before snuggling up in a corner of the sofa with a blanket over her. She looked out; in the dark she could just about make out the patch of garden with the barbecue and tool shed. She'd put the notebook on the table; now she picked it up.

What I know about what happened to you:

10 December. 16.45: you leave the house. To the post office, then on to Morr Water. 20.09: text to Viljam.

11 December. Time?: leave the cabin. 15.48: text to Liss. 16.10: text to Viljam. 17.00: appointment with JH. 17.04: park the car in Welhavens Street. 17.30: text to Berger. 18.11: text to Viljam. 19.00: appointment with Berger. 19.03: call Berger, no answer. 19.05: text to Berger: you've been held up (according to Berger you never turned up). 20.30: due to be at Channel Six, you didn't show up.

12 December. 05.35: videos made of you. Imprisoned, naked. The eyes.

24 December. Package with your mobile phone arrives, posted the day before in Tofte.

She read through it all again. Without thinking, she wrote: *Ask him about death by water.*

She looked at the Post-it note she had taken from Mailin's noticeboard in the office.

Who were you going to ask, Mailin?

The Phoenician. Dead for fourteen days. Something about the crying of seagulls. And a whirlpool. I've killed too.

She sat there looking at that last sentence. Read it to herself, felt her lips move but didn't hear the words.

Something's going to happen, Liss. You can't control it.

She got up, crossed to the window, opened it and felt the cold grey air against her face. Everywhere the sounds of the city. *You're in the middle of the world, but no one knows who you are, or what you've done.* She pulled on her jacket, shut the front door behind her, pressed on down Lang Street. Had to buy some smokes. And get something down her. She'd decided on ice cream, but the first shop she came to was closed. It was a relief more than a frustration, because she needed to walk. Far. Then eat. A lot. Then puke. Then go to bed. Sleep, long.

She turned down into Sofienberg Park, didn't notice the figure that stopped on the corner of Gøteborg Street and stared after her for a few seconds before following between the trees. For the first time since Mailin's body had been found, an image of Zako appeared in her mind. Lying on the sofa. Was he sleeping? Could she hang on to that idea? That Zako had woken again in that flat in Bloemstraat, gone out to the bathroom, taken a shower and then headed into town. That he was with Rikke right now, that he didn't need Liss any more and could leave her in peace. When she heard footsteps in the snow behind her, she sensed they had something to do with her. The sensation became a thought: something will grab hold of me, tear me away from here, away from everything that stops me forgetting what I've done . . . There was a kind of hope in it, and the grip around her arm became a confirmation of the promise. She didn't resist, allowed herself to be dragged away from the path, into the shadow of a bare tree. He wasn't much taller than her, but his large fists pressed her up against the tree trunk, and she knew that if she went on standing there like that without resisting, it would happen again, the light pulling away and burning into everything around her. And if she didn't resist, she would disappear, and none of what happened in this park on this evening would be anything to do with her any more.

– Stop following me, he hissed. The mouth smelt of overripe bananas. In the dark, she saw the outlines of Zako's face, the high cheekbones and the pointed chin.

– I'll stop now, she murmured, and suddenly it dawned on her who it was. He'd grabbed her by the throat in that stairwell in Sinsen. He knew something about what had happened to Mailin. I am not afraid, she forced herself to think. No matter what he does to me, I'm not afraid any more.

– You were sneaking about in Mailin's office, she managed to say.

He bent even closer. – I didn't take anything.

She struggled to control her voice. – What were you doing there?

– I told you, he barked. – Had an appointment. Looked through a couple of drawers. Found nothing.

– You tore a page out of her appointments book.

The grip on her arm relaxed. – Mailin was OK, he said. – There's not many try to help. Enough that pretend to. I don't want to get mixed up in anything. What I don't like is you following me about.

– It's coincidence, she assured him. – Every time I've met you. But I have to find out what happened that day.

He released her. – What day are you talking about?

– That Thursday, the eleventh of December. Mailin went to her office to keep that appointment with you. She parked her car right outside. Then she disappeared. No one saw any sign of her.

He pulled away a step. – That can't be right.

– What . . . can't be right?

He glanced around. – She gave classes at the School of Sports Sciences. I got a lift with her into town a couple of times. I remember her car well.

He turned towards her again. – Other people besides me must have seen it that day.

He stared down into her face. It was still possible for anything to happen in that park. Liss saw Mailin's chalk-white face in front of her, the half-closed eyes filled with dried blood.

– Doesn't anyone understand anything? he muttered.

– Understand what? she was about to say. But abruptly he turned and walked away. She recovered, headed over towards the footpath to follow him.

– If you saw something . . . she called out. – You must say what it was.

He speeded up, began to run and disappeared into the darkness.

She turned off the light in the room, settled down into the sofa again. Could still taste the vanilla in her mouth. The traces of acid in her gullet and down her throat. Cold in her stomach, cold inside, shrivelled.

Sound of a door. Then Viljam's voice: – Are you home, Liss?

Home? She slept a few nights there, for want of anywhere else she could stand to be. It was his suggestion. He'd given her Mailin's spare key. Had it made Mailin happy when he came home and she heard that voice? Maybe there was something she wanted to tell him that would make him put his arms around her.

– Sitting here in the dark?

She sat up, picked up her lighter and lit the candle on the table.

– Mailin liked sitting like that too, he said as he sank down into a chair. – Candlelight in the room.

– I like it here.

– It's a nice house, he nodded. – Peaceful. Mailin and I . . . He stood up suddenly. – I meant what I said yesterday. If you want to stay here a few more days. You know she would have liked it.

A funny thing to say, but it was true, she realised. A lot of what he said was true. He grieved in the same way she did. That was why she could stand being there.

He disappeared up the steps, out to the kitchen. – Thanks for doing the washing-up.

– Of course, she said. – My turn, wasn't it?

She imagined him smiling at what she said; it almost made her smile too. For a moment it felt good to be sitting there. Viljam kept his distance. Not completely absent, but let her alone. Had enough stuff of his own to deal with. He and Mailin had been lovers for more than two years. He missed her, but not in the way she missed her. Mailin would become a memory for him, light with a great darkness around it. Then he'd get over it and find someone else. Liss would never get over it.

She went out to him in the kitchen. He was standing by the window, looking out on to the lit street.

– An old friend of yours was here earlier today, he said.

She looked quizzically at him.

– At least he said he was a friend. Looked pretty spaced out.

She had a thought. – Dark curly hair, scar on his forehead? Wearing a reefer jacket?

– Correct. First he asked for you, where you were and when you were coming back, then suddenly he wanted to know if Mailin lived here.

– He's no friend of mine.

She told him about Mailin's patient, how she'd come across him several times, how he'd followed her into the park.

– And only now are the police beginning to take an interest in this guy?

She didn't answer, was thinking of something else. – Mailin had a Post-it note hanging in her office. It had *death by water* written on it. Do you know where that comes from?

– *Death by water?* He seemed to be thinking about the question. Then he shook his head. – Sounds like a typical Mailin thing, whatever it is. It's the kind of stuff she was interested in.

17

LISS HAD ARRANGED a meeting with Jennifer Plåterud at the Pathology Institute at ten, but it was closer to 11.30 by the time she announced her arrival at the front desk. She'd taken three sleeping pills the evening before and woken to a hangover forty minutes earlier.

– Sorry, I overslept, she apologised when Jennifer Plåterud came to greet her.

She was smaller than Liss remembered from that morning she'd gone with Tage to do the identification. Couldn't be much above one metre fifty, because even with the high-heeled sandals she was wearing, she was still half a head shorter than Liss. She was heavily made up but obviously knew what she was doing. The blue eyes were made more prominent and the mouth seemed bigger than it was. Beneath her open doctor's coat she was wearing a cornflower-blue suit, and a string of what looked like real pearls around her neck.

– That's okay, she said. – I haven't been sitting in my office twiddling my thumbs.

Liss had forgotten that she spoke with an accent. It sounded American, as did her first name. Preferable to being Norwegian, anyway.

Her office was fairly large, with a window facing on to the square outside. On the desk was a photo of a man her own age. He stood there in oilskins holding an enormous fish up to the camera. Another photo showed two teenage boys on some steps, one sitting, the other standing.

– Yes, this is where I live, said Jennifer Plåterud. – You know what, I found an article about you on the net. It was originally in *Dagbladet*'s magazine. I didn't know you were about to start a career as a model.

She switched on the coffee machine in the corner. – Don't get me wrong, I haven't been checking up on you, a colleague mentioned it to me.

The reassurance was superfluous. There was something about this doctor's manner that didn't arouse Liss's suspicions.

– That article was just hype, she said dismissively. – I've done a few jobs, nothing big. Doubt it'll ever amount to anything more. Amsterdam isn't exactly the centre of the world when it comes to stuff like that.

– But there's no need to stay there, Jennifer exclaimed. – A young woman like you could be a big hit in Paris or Milan or New York. What the good photographers are looking for isn't just yet more glamour, but the unusual. I mean . . . She blushed beneath the make-up.

– Want to be my agent? Liss asked, and made the doctor laugh. Her laughter was surprisingly deep and ringing.

It was clear from the way she spoke that she was really interested in the fashion business, and from the collections and photographers she mentioned it was obvious she knew what she was talking about.

She interrupted herself: – But you didn't come here to swap tips about clothes and make-up, Liss. I'll call you Liss, and you can call me Jennifer.

The friendliness in the suggestion seemed genuinely spontaneous, and Liss felt there was no need for her to be on the alert. She was offered biscuits from a tin; she hadn't eaten since the day before and broke off a piece. It had a sweet coconut taste and a rather stodgy consistency.

– Home-made, Jennifer said as she ate one herself. – Can't buy these in Norway so I have to make them myself. Or actually, it's my husband that does.

– You're American?

– Absolutely not, she protested. – I'm from Canberra.

Liss thought about it; maybe it was somewhere in Canada. – So then you're from . . .

– That's right, Jennifer interrupted helpfully. – The capital city of Australia.

Liss took the proffered cup of coffee. – So how did you end up here? She noticed with a slight reluctance how she had been led into this rather too informal conversational tone.

– You know what, Liss, that's a question I ask myself too. Every single day when I get up and look out across the fields where we live. Jennifer, what the bloody hell are you doing here?

She dunked a wedge of biscuit into her coffee.

– Of course, in a few years' time the children'll be big enough to manage on their own. She glanced over at the photo of the two boys. – I've got plans to grow old under warmer skies than these.

– And your husband, is that what he wants too?

– Can't imagine that for a moment, Jennifer replied, surprisingly definite. – He's inherited a farm out in Sorum. That's where we live. Not that he's going to run it as a working farm, but he's put roots down there. Can't budge him an inch. But now tell me what it is you've found out.

Liss rummaged through her handbag. – I'm sure it's not really anything important . . .

She described the trip out to the cabin, unfolded the sheet of paper she had found inside the cushion cover, put it on the table. Jennifer picked it up. Her face changed, her pupils expanded, Liss noticed, and again she flushed from the neck upwards. When she'd finished reading, she stood up and crossed to her desk, opened a drawer, closed it again without taking anything from it.

– So it *is* important, Liss commented.

Jennifer blinked a few times, regained her composure.

– Not necessarily, she said. – But this was printed out on Wednesday the tenth of December. In other words, Mailin must have taken it out to the cabin with her. That in itself is significant.

She sat down again. – What was that about prints in the snow on New Year's Eve? Could they have been there before you arrived?

Liss dismissed the possibility. She'd seen no sign of tracks when she arrived. Moreover, it had snowed that evening.

– There's something else, too, she added.

Jennifer leaned forward. Her gaze didn't move for an instant as Liss described her encounter with the patient in Mailin's office, and what he'd said in the park the previous evening.

– I urge you in the strongest possible terms to talk to the police about this, Liss.

– You can pass it on to them.

– I am not a detective.

Liss pinched her lower lip. – I won't be going back there again. Won't be talking to either that idiot with the foreign name or that smarmy boss of his. I've never trusted the police. Never had any reason to.

Jennifer didn't protest. Didn't try to convince her she was wrong. Didn't try to get her to say things she didn't want to say.

– I don't think that guy sneaking about in her office could have done that to Mailin . . . killed her. But he knows something. I think he saw her just before she went missing. I'm going to find out who he is.

Jennifer sat up straight in her chair. – That is not your job, she said firmly.

– The police have had weeks now. What have they found out?

– That's exactly why you've got to help them, Liss. What's more, you might be putting yourself in danger if you get involved like that.

Liss got to her feet. – I'm not afraid, she said. – I'm never afraid any more.

18

THE SKY WAS like blue glass as Roar Horvath got off the plane at Flesland. The grass between the runways was glazed with rime, and the mountaintops on the horizon carried a sprinkling of white. He'd been in Bergen once before, a couple of spring days a few years earlier. On that occasion too there was the same bright, cloudless sky and sharp light. It was almost enough to start him doubting the city's reputation for rain.

In the arrivals hall he looked around for the sergeant who was supposed to be meeting him. Her name was Nina Jebsen and he had met her briefly the year before. She'd left the Violent Crimes section in Oslo just a couple of weeks after he started there himself. He seemed to remember her as dark and a bit chubby, and didn't spot her at first. The woman who came towards him, hand outstretched, was slim and blondeish, with highlights in her shoulder-length hair.

– Nice to see you again, she said, probably noticing his uncertainty. – No luggage?

Finally it dawned on Roar that the woman standing in front of him was Nina Jebsen.

– Well I don't need two suits when I'm not even going to be spending the night here.

– That depends on how vain you are. She glanced at his jeans jacket.

– This is a real hush-hush business, she continued once they were inside the car. Her Bergen accent seemed broader than Roar remembered. – My boss won't let me mention your visit to anyone else in the department. Is the National Security Service involved in this too?

He grinned at her little joke, liked the tone she was setting. – Pity for us you didn't want to stay in Oslo, he said, and heard how it sounded a bit more personal than he had intended.

She shrugged her shoulders. – Once a Bergener, always a Bergener.

He knew there was more to it than that. She had worked closely with Viken on the so-called bear murders case, and chosen to move on afterwards. According to the rumours Roar had heard, it was because she couldn't go on working with the detective chief inspector, who, for his part, had apparently been very keen to hang on to her. Roar dismissed these thoughts; he hadn't come to Bergen to poke around in old departmental rubbish.

– Were you working here when the Ylva Richter case broke? he asked.

She shook her head. – I'd just arrived in Oslo. And they were good at stopping any leaks. Even now, a lot of what was found is still not widely known about.

– Good work, Roar responded. – Especially bearing in mind the intense media interest.

– Maybe it'll have its rewards now. If it turns out there are connections to the case you're working on.

He said nothing. Viken seemed unconvinced that there was a connection. He was still furious with Jennifer for the way she'd gone behind his back. Roar had to concede that he was uneasy at the thought of his special connection with the pathology department being discovered, but it was worth it; he felt alive. He'd met a few women after his divorce. In the early days, a lot of pent-up excitement got released in town. A brief reminder of the life he had lived ten or fifteen years earlier. But his hunting instincts had become dulled. He'd read somewhere that men produced fewer hormones after they became fathers. Nature's way of ensuring they didn't disappear until the offspring had been provided with food and shelter. He smelled the perfume of the sergeant sitting beside him in the car, glanced over at her, quickly taking in the breasts, and the thighs beneath the smooth jeggings. If his instincts had become dulled, they were in the process of waking up again. That's a healthy sign, Roar, he told himself. Keep those interests healthy.

Nina Jebsen drove steadily, never exceeding two kilometres above the speed limit.

He leaned back in the seat. – From what I know about the Ylva Richter case so far, it's worth the price of the air fare at least. And it's so bloody lovely here.

With a glance up at the peaks surrounding the town he added: – And not a single drop of rain.

– Pretty soon the weather's going to be just as bad wherever we live, she answered. – In town here the architects have started designing buildings for a sea level two metres above what it is today.

To avoid people asking questions, Nina Jebsen didn't introduce him to anyone. Roar was led up to the third floor of the Bergen police headquarters and into a tiny office that was remarkably similar to his own.

Nina Jebsen closed the door behind them. – I'm working on three or four cases. No one knows that this isn't an interview in connection with one of those.

– Am I a witness or a suspect?

– Hard to say. She handed him a folder. – A summary of the Ylva Richter case. I suggest you read that first.

Three quarters of an hour later, he'd got the main outline. Ylva Richter, then nineteen years old, grew up in Fana, south of the city. Father a business lawyer, mother a textile artist. Two younger siblings. No reports of any problems in the family. Clean sheet for both parents, nothing except a number of convictions for speeding for the father. Ylva had finished at secondary school that year, marks were good; she'd started at business college but was still living at home. Active member of the swimming club, some success in the national championships at junior level. Apparently a popular girl, always surrounded by friends. Some boyfriends at secondary school but for the time being unattached. The circles she moved in could be described as constructive and healthy though inevitably with some use of recreational drugs. No one in her crowd with a criminal record. One boy treated for a psychological problem but not regarded as unstable.

On the evening of Friday 15 November 2003, Ylva Richter took the bus from the bus station in the centre of Bergen after spending an evening in town with some girlfriends. She had her own car but wasn't using it that evening as she knew she would be drinking alcohol. Last seen by the bus driver who dropped her off at the stop nearest her home. The time was then 00.30. Other passengers confirmed this. She did not arrive home and the police were contacted at two o'clock, after the father had gone down to the bus stop to look for his daughter. A patrol car was sent but the full-scale alarm not sounded till the following morning.

Five days later they found her in a wood about twenty kilometres north-east of where she lived, handcuffed, gagged and tied to a tree. She was naked. Her clothes were found later under a pile of heather some distance away. Marks from a heavy blunt object on the temple on one side of the head, a stone possibly, but the blows were not fatal. Probably done before she was dragged into a car. There followed an extensive account of the damage done to her eyes, which had been repeatedly penetrated with a pointed object, possibly a screw. She did not appear to have been sexually assaulted. The conclusion was that she had frozen to death.

The investigation had been extremely thorough. Over five hundred interviews with witnesses. Nina Jebsen had gathered together the most important ones. Parents, siblings, friends, bus driver, passengers. According to one girlfriend, Ylva described an odd experience she had on the way to the bar where they were to meet. Somebody had approached her in Torgalmenningen Square and offered her a tin opener or corkscrew. It was one of the many unexplained details in the case, and Roar was sufficiently struck by it to flip back to the description of the damage done to the eyes. All registered sex and violent offenders who were thought potentially interesting were interviewed, and a couple were given the formal status of suspects; in the case of one of them, an arrest was considered but then dropped. Naturally the case was not shelved, but the chances of solving it were considered minimal to non-existent.

While Roar read, Nina Jebsen had logged on to her computer and punched away rapidly at the keyboard. Once he was finished and laid the folder back on her desk, she wound things up, closed the document and turned towards him. Before she could ask him what he thought, he said:

– Let's talk to the parents first, then discuss things afterwards.

The Richter family house lay in an affluent suburb just south of the city. The man who opened the door and introduced himself as Richard Richter was of medium height with thin grey hair that was smoothed back with gel or hair cream. He smelled slightly of alcohol, Roar noted, as he and Nina Jebsen were admitted to the living room.

Anne Sofie Richter entered carrying a tray with a coffee pot and cups. She was slender and suntanned, with her hair dyed dark. She put the cups out for them, seemed alert, her movements quick.

Roar was well prepared. As they sat down, he said:
– Apologies if any old wounds are ripped open here. We would much prefer not to have to put you through this again.

Richard Richter remained standing at the foot of the table.
– Horvath, wasn't it? Let me tell you, Horvath, that the wounds have never healed, if that is what you are talking about. Just yesterday I found myself recalling the last conversation I had with her. I drove her into town that night. She turned and looked at me with that smile that was like no other smile; she said *see you, thanks a lot*, and that was the last I ever saw of my daughter.

He fell silent for a few moments.

– The rest is what happens in our imagination, he continued, struggling to control his voice. – We've got off the bus with her, walked from the crossroads where you turned off and up the hill. We've imagined the car there waiting, because we're certain about that, someone must have been waiting for her, and we have driven with her in the car out to the place in which she was found.

Roar glanced over at the wife. She sat there smiling like a doll, just as she had done ever since they arrived. Occasionally she nodded as her husband spoke for them both.

– I am not exaggerating when I tell you that this is something we go through every day. So your coming here and asking questions is not going to open anything at all, because nothing ever closed.

Again Richard Richter fell silent. Roar said:

– You will understand, of course, that I haven't made the trip from Oslo without good reason. But we need to avoid raising any false hopes of getting answers to the many questions you still have. There *may* be a connection to another case we're working on, and we want to know as much as possible about the very thorough groundwork our colleagues in Bergen have already done in investigating what happened to Ylva.

He hadn't intended to use her name, but now it was done, and neither parent seemed to react. There was no reaction either to his words of praise for the work done by the Bergen police.

– No stone must be left unturned. All of them, and not just once, but many times.

A cough from Richard Richter seemed to suggest that he had had enough of the speech-making.

– It's about the woman who was found, isn't it? In that factory.

Roar breathed out slowly. – I wish I could discuss things with you freely and openly, but in the interests of the investigation . . .

– Didn't she freeze too? Anne Sofie Richter wanted to know. Her voice was light and wondering, as though she'd stopped during a walk in the forest, curious to know what kind of a bird it was sitting in the tree and singing such an unusual song.

Nina Jebsen, who had been sitting listening in silence on the sofa, now said: – We're grateful that people like you exist who are willing to take the trouble to help us. As I said on the telephone, it's very important that you don't talk to anyone about this. Not even friends and neighbours. So far no journalist, neither newspaper nor TV nor magazine, knows that we are looking at this case again.

Richard Richter interrupted: – If that pack turns up at the door again, there's no telling what I might do.

He was still standing at the foot of the table, coffee cup in one hand, the other in his pocket. Roar could see how the fist opened and closed through the cloth of his suit trousers.

– You have been asked this before, Roar said, – but I would like you to think about it again. Did anything ever happen in Ylva's crowd that really took you by surprise?

He could hear that the question was much too wide ranging and tried again: – Could we ask you to make a list of the things she was involved in, let's say over the last two years before that fateful night?

Richard Richter let out a groan, but his wife said, still with that same doll-like smile hovering about her mouth: – That's perfectly possible. I've kept all her school diaries from secondary school. She always made a note of appointments and the things she did. The police already know a lot of this, but as far back as two years?

– Swimming outings, camping trips, school holiday trips, Roar nodded. – Also with the family. In other words, a pretty extensive job.

As they stood out in the hallway saying thanks for the coffee, Anne Sofie Richter turned and disappeared through a doorway. A few moments later, she was back again.

– I'm sure you've seen pictures of Ylva, she said, addressing Roar. – Including the kind taken after they found her.

He didn't reply.

– This is from the spring of that year, when she graduated from secondary school. I want you to see it, because this is what she was like, our daughter.

She handed him a framed photograph. He recognised her from other photos. The brown hair falling in waves from beneath the red student cap, regular features, brown eyes, full lips. Pretty girl, he was about to say, but managed not to. As he handed it back, he saw a vague resemblance to the mother, as though a last vestige of the young girl was still visible, stiffened, in the doll-like face.

– Thank you very much, he said as he shook her hand.

Out in the car, he had an idea. – Do you have time to drive to where the body was found?

Nina looked over at him. – Do *you* have time?

There were still four hours before his plane took off. He didn't know why he'd asked her.

– I'm guessing you're not expecting to find any tracks. After five years, I mean.

He gave a brief laugh. – You never know what's going to happen when the supersleuths from Oslo turn up.

She smiled too. – Pity for you I know that crowd so well that I'm not about to prostrate myself in admiration.

He liked the teasing tone. If his trip hadn't been a day return, he would have invited her out for a beer. He glanced at her hands on the steering wheel. Several rings, all with stones.

– Did you have problems with Viken? he risked asking her. – Was that why you left?

He could feel he was inviting the kind of intimacy there was no real grounds for after just the few hours in which they'd known each other, but she said: – It was something else. I know a lot of people find him difficult. It was never a problem for me. I would almost say I liked him.

Roar believed her. Among those who didn't avoid him like the plague, Viken was much admired. He realised that her reason for moving on had something to do with the bear murders, but chose not to press the matter.

She was following the GPS signal and turned off the main road as directed.

– Of course I don't know the exact spot. She drove on between the fields until they came to the forest at the end. – According to the report, it should be just about here somewhere.

As they parked, the sun slid down behind the mountains in the south-west. The sky took on a deep blue sheen, darker but still as clear as it had been earlier in the day. They found a track with footprints in the soft woodland earth. Roar went first. Abruptly he came to a halt. Behind some clumps of heather, next to a tree growing beside a rocky overhang, he saw a few objects. He hurried through the bracken. There was a lamp there with a thick white candle inside. It wasn't burning, but might have done so recently, because beside it was a bouquet of flowers, and, in a vase, five roses that were still fresh.

– Looks like we found it, Nina Jebsen remarked as she joined him. They remained there for a few moments, looking at the scene. Roar suddenly experienced a flash of memory of what it felt like to stand by the grave of someone missed. In that instant he was convinced there was a connection between the two murder cases. As though the place itself was telling him as much: the trees, the path winding on, but above all these flowers and this lamp. He knew there wasn't a shred of common sense in this kind of intuitive stuff, that it was distracting rather than useful. *Alert now, Roar*, he told himself. Full alert, level five steady. And by the time a couple of hours later he called Viken from the airport, he had assembled a handful of rational arguments that he felt ought to be enough to convince the detective chief inspector of the need to continue liaising with the Bergen force. The damage to the eyes and the fact that the girl had been hit on the head with a stone were just two of them.

But before he could voice even a single argument, Viken barked out: – I'm just about to send an email with some material to the police in Bergen. Have you got time to read it before you leave?

Roar told him where he was, and that the plane to Oslo was about to board.

Viken swore. – Then we might have to make another trip. We've got a new link to Ylva Richter.

He explained what Liss Bjerke had found inside the sofa cover at the family's cabin.

– When you get back, I'll tell you who she chose to give the information to, he rasped.

Roar had no intention of letting him know that he had already guessed who it was.

19

LISS PULLED OUT the Marlboro packet. Almost empty. She needed something else, too. Tampons. Something to drink.

She wandered into an open Bunnpris. Glanced at her phone. Message from Rikke. And one from the footballer, the one who was called, of all things, Jomar. She still had his jacket.

Rikke wrote: *Z's father asked about you at the funeral – gave him your address in Norway – forgot to tell you last time – hope that's okay.*

It's not okay, she fumed, maybe even said it out loud. It's not okay for Zako's father to have my address. What does he want it for? She chased the thought away. Imagined squeezing it out of herself; watched it fly away on a raven's wings into the cold Oslo night. The way she got rid of thoughts when she was a teenager. Didn't work quite as well now.

Jomar's message: *Call me. Must talk to you.*

Standing there at the freezer counter in Bunnpris, it felt good to know that he still wanted to meet her. Suddenly she called his number. He didn't sound surprised to hear her voice; seemed almost to take it for granted. It irritated her so much she nearly ended the call, but then controlled herself. Didn't want to seem childish or unpredictable. All the things she really was.

– What have you got to tell me that's so important? Did you win a football match? She was satisfied with her tone of voice. Just the right amount of sarcasm in it.

– Football? Don't try to talk shop with me. You'll find out what it is when we meet.

– Are we going to meet?

– Yes.

– Who said so?

– You did.

– Let's stick to the truth.

Afterwards she scolded herself for being so agreeable. She paid for the three things she had come in for and then went back out into the street.

Liss sat at the coffee table, directly opposite him.

– Sorry, she said, forgetting to maintain the sarcastic tone. She didn't really know what she was sorry about either. Maybe that she was twenty minutes late. Or that she'd run off with his jacket and not replied to any of his messages.

Jomar Vindheim gave her a teasing smile. – Quite okay. Doesn't matter what you're apologising for, Liss, it's quite okay by me whatever.

– Your jacket, she said, putting the plastic bag down beside his chair. – I didn't mean to nick it.

– I've reported you for theft, he said in a serious voice. – But I only had a very vague description, so it didn't help much. Now I've got the chance to get a clearer look at you.

She wasn't on his wavelength. He seemed to notice.

– Seriously, Liss, I'm the one who should be apologising. All this business with your sister . . .

– All this *business*? She'd found her way back to sarcasm again, but let it go. He was probably just trying to be considerate.

– I understand why you haven't answered any of my messages.

– Do you, she said.

– You've got other things to think about besides an old jacket, Liss.

It sounded as if he enjoyed repeatedly saying her name. Did he imagine that using it like that would bring them closer together?

– I actually did wear it, she told him. – Almost every day.

He grinned. – You could have stuck a pole inside that jacket and used it as a tent.

She looked at him. The slanting eyes were a surprisingly light blue colour. He wasn't handsome; there was something crude and disproportionate about his features, as though he was still passing through puberty and things hadn't found their rightful shape. A row of pimples arced across his forehead. Clearly all this was something not only teenage girls found attractive, but for example Therese too. Not to mention Catrine, but then she was always on the lookout for sex.

– Maybe you'd like to keep it?

She turned up her nose. – If I had a place to live, I could have hung it up on the wall, with your autograph on it.

This time he laughed and didn't bother with a comeback. He had an irritatingly white and regular set of teeth, and seemed sure of himself. He was a top-flight footballer and bound to be earning in excess of a million a year for playing around with a ball. And he certainly had other women besides Therese hanging around him. But from the moment he walked across to their table at the Café Mono, Liss was the one he had been concentrating on. And after she passed out at his place that night and then ran off with his jacket, he'd sent her four or five messages.

Just then she remembered something else from the evening they met.

– You know him, she exclaimed.

He looked at her in surprise.

– You know that guy who grabbed me by the throat. I saw

you talking to him just before. When he was standing in the doorway dealing dope.

He took a swig of Coke.

– Why didn't you say so before? she persisted.

The slanting eyes narrowed even more. – Did you ask me?

She hadn't. He could have no way of knowing why she was looking for the guy.

– I don't give a shit if he's your dealer, or whatever else you do. I just want to know who he is.

– Dealer? You think I'm into stuff like that? I know him from the sports academy.

– Oh yeah, right.

– It's true, Jomar assured her. – He was a student there a few years ago. Started at the same time as me.

– What's his name?

– Jim Harris. He had a real talent as a middle-distance runner. Great at the four hundred, even better at the eight hundred. Could have been a top athlete if only his head wasn't so screwed.

– Screwed what way?

– He can never finish anything. Makes a mess of everything. Ends up on the slide. To begin with he had people round him to help get him back on his feet, but they've all given up now.

– He was a patient of Mailin's.

– Was he?

She described the encounter in Mailin's office.

Jomar said: – If Jimbo found the office door open, then he probably went in there to see if there was any loose cash lying about in the drawers. He owes money to every dealer in town. That's why he's started dealing himself. I tried to help him for a while. Lent him money. Let him sleep it off at my place.

– I'm convinced he was after something else, said Liss.

– What makes you think that?

She told him what had happened the evening he came across her in the park.

– Ah, shit. Jomar's face took on a strange expression.

– Did you know about that?

He shook his head. – Of course not. But Jimbo rang me a few days ago. He said he'd seen you at that party in Sinsen and wanted to know if I knew you. I was stupid enough to tell him you were the sister of that . . . I don't think he had any intention of harming you. He's not like that.

– Didn't you realise it was him who grabbed me by the throat down in the stairwell?

Again Jomar swore. – I asked you to tell me what had happened.

She ignored him. – When he was holding me there in the park, something suddenly occurred to him. He ran off. Jim Harris, was that his name? Those were the initials in Mailin's appointments book. He must have seen Mailin that afternoon. Perhaps someone was with her. You understand what this means? This guy saw what happened . . . Where can I get hold of him?

– You don't want to be wandering about in the kinds of places where he hangs out, Jomar warned her.

She sat there looking down at the table. – I want you to help, she said suddenly.

In the days following the discovery of Mailin's body, she could face almost nothing. Thought as little as possible. Now she was seized by a need to do something, anything. In a rush she began telling him everything she had found out. Showed him the times from Mailin's call list. Told him about the videos.

– Mailin was filmed the morning after she went missing. Liss flipped through her notebook. – Those video clips were dated Friday the twelfth at 05.35.

It helped her to be speaking about all these details, as though for a brief moment they were no longer about Mailin but someone else altogether.

He listened without interrupting. She didn't know him. But he was outside it all, had never met Mailin, and for that reason it was possible to share it with him. Even what had happened at the cabin, the footprints in the snow, the printout she'd found in the sofa cushion.

Afterwards she looked across at him. Reluctantly she began to understand why Therese had been so angry with her. She liked his looks, but even more she liked how relaxed and almost modest he seemed. She hadn't intended to stay, just to hand the jacket back and offer some kind of apology. Now she'd been sitting there for almost an hour.

She stood up. – I must have a ciggy.

– I'll come out with you, he said.

She blew smoke out in the direction of the light above the doorway and studied the way the lead-blue formations gathered and then at once dissolved.

– When can I see you again? Jomar wanted to know.

She felt his look like prickling on her skin. Didn't mind at all that he never seemed to tire of looking at her. Just couldn't face all the explanations she would have to give. Why she couldn't meet him. Why she wasn't interested. Why she was who she was. Why she could never again face the thought of being with someone. Felt a sudden longing to be at the cabin. Sitting by the window looking down towards Morr Water in the dusk. The darkness gathering around her, thicker and thicker. The silence.

20

IT WAS CLOSE to one a.m. when she heard Viljam. He was moving about in the kitchen, then flushing the toilet and running the tap in the bathroom. This was how Mailin had lain at night. Hearing her boyfriend come home. Waiting for the footsteps on the staircase, for him to open the door, crawl in under the duvet, body close up to her. Didn't need to have her, or speak. Just lie there and sleep like that. Feel his arms around her in her sleep . . .

They're sitting in the boat. Mailin's rowing. She's wearing a large grey coat. Her hair is grey too and hangs down her back in long strings. The wind lifts them. Not the wind, because the wisps of hair move by themselves. Long white worms that cover her whole head and eat it. They've suctioned themselves to her head, and Liss can't seem to raise her hand to pull them away. But Mailin doesn't seem bothered in the least; she rows for land, in towards the tiny beach. They're going to pick something up there. But they don't get any closer to the man standing and waiting, because one oar is missing, and the boat goes round in circles. *Don't look behind you, Mailin, I mustn't see your face.* But Mailin doesn't hear and turns towards her.

Liss woke to a scream. She felt it inside herself, didn't know if it had come from her. *Feren, she.* She twisted round, picked up her phone. It was twenty to two. She opened her address list, found the name, pressed call.

– Dahlstrøm.

She could hear from his voice that he had been pulled up out of deep sleep. Imagined the bedroom he was lying in. Wife beside him in bed, awake too, half irritated, half anxious. Liss knew that Tormod Dahlstrøm had got married for a second time a few years earlier. His second wife was a writer and almost twenty years younger than him.

– Sorry for waking you, stupid of me.

– Is that you, Liss? He didn't sound surprised. Probably used to being called at night. Patients who were in trouble. Someone who needed to hear his voice just to make it through until the next morning.

– Sorry, she repeated.

– For what?

– It's the middle of the night.

He breathed in and out a few times. – Did you wake me up to say sorry for waking me up?

Even now he was able to joke with her.

– I had a dream, she said. – About Mailin.

He made a sound that might have been a half-quelled yawn.

– When I was at your place, on Christmas Eve . . . we talked about her research, into abuse. That psychologist she was so interested in. He was Hungarian, wasn't he?

– That's right. Ferenczi. He was a psychiatrist.

– Is that the way you say his name? she went on. – *Feren-she?*

– Roughly, yes.

– What are his other names?

– First name, you mean? Sándor. His name is Sándor Ferenczi.

Liss had got out of bed and was now standing naked on the cold floor. She walked over to the window, pulled open the curtain and looked out into the brown night sky above Rodeløkka. *Sand-oar Feren-she,* she murmured to herself, without even noticing that she had ended the call.

* * *

The time was approaching 2.30 as she punched in the code on the gate in Welhavens Street. She remembered that Jennifer Plåterud had said she could call her any time at all, even at night. Liss thought about it, but decided not to. She let herself in, didn't turn on the light in the stairwell. The smell of damp grew stronger with each floor she climbed, she noticed. In the room used as a waiting room the curtains were closed. It was pitch dark and she didn't know where the light switch was. She fumbled her way along to Mailin's office door, opened it. No longer Mailin's office. Someone else would be using it, as soon as her things were cleared out.

She closed the door behind her, turned on the light. Someone had been there, the police maybe, several of the folders lay on the desk. She started looking through the bookshelves, found the Sándor Ferenczi book she had seen the first time she was there, *Selected Writings* was the title. She pulled it out and began to leaf through it. Here and there Mailin had made underlinings in the text, along with small notes and comments in the margins. The corner of one page was turned over. Liss opened it to Chapter 33: 'Confusion of tongues between Adults and the Child. The language of Tenderness and of Passion.' There was something written in red at the foot of the page. Liss recognised Mailin's hand: 'Death by water – Jacket's language.'

At that same instant, the lights went out. She heard a sound out in the waiting room. A door opening. She jumped up. For a few seconds the neon light strip in the ceiling pulsed with a grey glimmer, then twice in quick succession, before going out completely. *You're not afraid, Liss Bjerke*, a voice shouted inside her. *You're never afraid any more.* She groped her way across the floor, put her ear to the door. Heard nothing. Or perhaps a faint scraping sound. She laid a hand on the doorknob. It moved. It took two seconds for her to realise that someone was entering from the other side. She jumped back, pressed herself against the wall. The door slid open. She could make out a figure in the darkness. A torch was switched on, the beam swept around the room and stopped on her face.

– Liss Bjerke . . . The name sounded from the darkness in front of her and at the same time inside her. As though it had left her and was now speaking to her from the doorway behind the torch beam. But the voice wasn't hers, it was light and slightly hoarse, and still had that American accent that was once so exciting but now seemed fake and showy.

– What are you doing here, she said.

She heard his low laughter.

– You've always been such a cheeky little minx, Liss. Breaking into people's property in the middle of the night and then asking them what *they* are doing there.

Pål Øvreby came a step closer. – Okay, I'll explain. Sometimes when I have an evening out and it gets late, instead of taking a taxi home I come here and get a few hours' sleep at the office. As you discovered a long time ago, I rent here. Five thousand two hundred and fifty every fucking month. So now I've answered your question, please tell me what *you* are doing here.

She couldn't see his face properly, but could smell him. Tobacco and beer, and clothes that hadn't been properly dried after washing. The smell forced its way into her and took the lid off containers with things she had hidden away. They were full of little animals. Now they began to crawl around inside her, from her head and all the way down her body.

– This is Mailin's office. No one can stop me from coming here. She tried to sound angry. If her voice sounded angry, she might manage to feel anger.

– You came to me before, Liss, you didn't suppose I'd forgotten? It wouldn't surprise me if you knew that I was sleeping in the office at the moment. My home life is shot to pieces.

He was standing right up close to her.

– And it's partly because of you, Liss Bjerke, he whispered. – It has a lot more to do with you than you realise.

He put his hand under her chin, lifted it, as if she was a child refusing to look him in the eye. – We had a good time together, Liss. You don't expect me to have forgotten that, do you?

He let his finger glide around her ear, the back of her neck, pulled her towards him.

She grabbed the torch from his hand, shone it into his face.

– Do you suppose, Pål Øvreby, that I'm afraid to kill? she hissed, and heard how her own voice sounded like a steel string. – If you touch me one more time, you will never feel safe again, not for one second. I'll kill you the instant you fall asleep.

He dropped his hand. She drove the torch into his stomach, slipped around him, out into the waiting room and down the steps. He didn't follow.

21

Jennifer Plåterud sat shivering with cold in the Bingfoss Hall. Over five years and she still hadn't quite understood what you could and couldn't do in handball, but it didn't matter that much. She celebrated when her younger son Sigurd's team scored, and agreed with the views of the parents who seemed to understand what was going on. She liked the sport, although not enough to bother to learn all the rules. It made the boys tough to go banging into each other and get knocked about. They were pushed to the ground and had to get up again without moaning. Very different from football, which Trym, her older boy, had played. There they learned to lie there writhing about as soon as anyone touched them. It looked as if getting knocked about a bit was all part of handball, and Sigurd was anyway a tougher lad than his big brother. The toughness was something he'd inherited from his mother, but in Trym, who was two years older, she recognised his father's laziness and evasiveness, and a bit more too.

During the break she went outside and took out her phone. For the second time in the course of the last twenty-four hours she called Detective Chief Inspector Viken, enjoying the suppressed irritation in his voice once she'd told him what the call was about.

– And you're still doing everything you can to persuade Liss Bjerke to come to us directly with her information, he said sourly.

– I'm not going to answer that, she replied. – It's not my fault if she has zero confidence in you.

How on earth did you manage to handle her so clumsily? she felt like adding, but didn't want to get into an open quarrel with the DCI.

– Isn't it better if she gets in touch with me rather than keeps what she knows to herself? she said instead.

In the final analysis Viken probably agreed that she had a point. – It sounds as though she might have managed to work out what her sister is saying in that video, he continued in a more composed tone. – Had you ever heard of this Ferenczi?

Jennifer couldn't suppress a little laugh. No specialist branch of medicine was more remote to her than psychiatry, which she associated with waffle, a lack of method, and absolutely no demand for results. But she'd googled Sándor Ferenczi in the morning after Liss's call and got over 112,000 hits.

– He's written a lot about children who have been abused, she informed him. – According to Liss, her sister was using his theories in her PhD studies. If I might be so bold as to make a suggestion, it would be to take a closer look at that thesis. Mailin Bjerke interviewed and apparently treated young men who had been the subject of abuse.

Midway through the second half of the game, Roar Horvath called. For some reason or other she knew it would be him even before she looked at the display.

– Just a moment, she said, and made her way out towards the exit.

– Need to talk to you, Jenny, he said, and standing out in the cold grey mist drifting up from the River Glomma, she felt herself blushing. – I was in Bergen yesterday. Was going to call you but it was past midnight by the time I got home.

If it was just about this trip to Bergen, he could have rung someone else.

– You don't need fancy excuses if you want to meet me, she said with a glance at her watch. She could be in Manglerud in a couple of hours, but then had a sudden thought that was immediately very hard to resist. Ivar was at an agricultural conference with his brother-in-law for the weekend, and she'd be able to farm the two boys out with friends for the night.

She sat, leaning back in the kitchen chair and drinking beer, watching as Roar whisked egg and milk, fried bacon, seasoned and chopped tomatoes and cucumber. She'd borrowed one of his shirts;it was the size of a maternity smock and she could pull her knees up under it.

– Have you heard anyone say your name in English? she said, interrupting his account of the trip to Bergen.

He moved the frying pan off the heat. – Sure, whenever I've been in England they've always got a big laugh out of calling me Shout.

– Rory's good, Jennifer said. – Maybe that's what I should call you. Or do you have a middle name?

He hesitated a moment. – Mihaly.

– Mihaly Horvath? That's about as un-Norwegian as you can get.

He poked his head into the fridge and took out a few packets of ready-chopped cured meat. – Mihaly was my old man's name. Roar was the best my mother could come up with. She didn't want me getting bullied at school because people thought I was a gypsy kid or something.

– So your middle name never got used?

He began spooning scrambled egg on to a dish. – My old man sometimes called me Miska.

– That's cute. I've been imaging this remote and very strict father. But he wasn't?

Roar gave a slight smile. – He came to Norway when he was

eighteen years old. His parents were vanished by the Stalinists. He didn't know anyone here, had to start from scratch. With nothing but his own two hands and a will of steel, as my mother used to say when she wanted to boast about him.

Jennifer emptied her beer glass. – My two boys have got middle names too. I actually wanted to name the elder after my father, but for once my husband put his foot down. No child should have to start at Sørum primary school with a handle like Trym Donald.

– The wise person gives way, Roar grinned as he set the plates on the kitchen table. She still hadn't been into his living room, and that was fine by her.

– What does Viken think? she wanted to know once he'd lit candles and seated himself opposite her.

– About you trying to take over the investigation?

She snorted.

– We should have picked up on the connection with the Ylva Richter case straight away, he conceded.

She drank more beer and tried to hide how much the admission pleased her, how pleasantly numb she felt, how good it was to sit here and have him serving an evening meal to her.

– Actually, I have a question for the pathologist.

– Don't worry about intruding on her free time, she encouraged him. – That's the way it is in this business. Always on the job.

– Could the damage done to Mailin Bjerke's eyes have been inflicted with a corkscrew?

He looked at her without the trace of a smile on his face, but still it took her a couple of seconds to realise he was being serious. And in that same moment she realised it was a clever idea.

– We've considered different types of screws and implements, she said, thinking aloud. – With a screw it would be hard to generate enough force . . . A corkscrew is a distinct possibility. What gave you that idea?

– Something that occurred to me when I was looking through the documents relating to the Ylva Richter case. One of a number of links . . . We've got to do absolutely everything we can to keep this whole association secret for the time being. Not just on account of the investigation, you can imagine the sort of hell that would break loose for her family if the connection leaked out.

Jennifer had no difficulty with that.

– I managed to persuade Liss that the printout she found has nothing to do with what happened to Mailin, she said. – I don't think she'll make the connection. And Ylva Richter's name wasn't actually mentioned in that particular article.

– Let's hope you're right, said Roar. He wrinkled his brow. – We've sent pictures of some of those involved in the case over to Bergen, he revealed. – One of the officers we're liaising with there has shown them to the parents.

– But no joy, I gather from your expression. Do you have anything at all that might point the finger at the man she was living with?

– Nothing so far. He's never lived in Bergen, but of course he might have gone there on the odd occasion.

– And still Viljam Vogt-Nielsen is number one on Viken's list?

Roar carried on chewing as he answered. – Viken is concerned that we don't overlook the psychology behind the murder of Mailin Bjerke. This business of the eyes being lacerated is a message we have to try to interpret. And the sheer rage behind those blows to the head. It points to someone in a close personal relationship to his victim.

He swallowed his food down with half a glass of beer. – And why was her mobile phone sent in the post?

– Maybe someone out there wants to play some kind of game with you, Jennifer hazarded.

Roar made a face that showed he was sceptical about her idea. – It can't be ruled out, but we're more inclined to think it shows a perverted sense of concern for his victim. He's killed her, but he doesn't want her to lie and rot there.

The furrows in his brow deepened and suddenly looked like three seagulls in flight, one with a large wingspan, flanked by two smaller ones.

– Whatever, we must keep concentrating on those closest to her. Her partner, of course, but also the stepfather. We're trying to get in touch with the biological father, too. Apparently he hasn't seen his family in over twenty years. He lives in Canada, but no one knows his whereabouts at the moment.

Jennifer had no difficulty in recognising Viken's thought processes in what Roar was saying. She'd heard the detective chief inspector talking often enough about signals and signatures and hidden messages in the way a crime had been committed. Her own view of psychological profiling was that it was an American fad. About as scientific as trying to follow a scent.

– The sense of smell is a pretty useful tool, she observed. – Especially for dogs. When Roar looked at her quizzically she added: – It isn't necessarily successful each time Mr Viken gets going on the human psyche.

Roar piled more scrambled egg on to his bread. He didn't answer.

– And talking about psychology, she went on, – what about Mailin Bjerke's patients? She presumably had a very *close* relationship to them as well. And you've hinted that one of them may have threatened her.

Roar looked thoughtful. She guessed he was wondering whether he'd already told her too much. She had to smile at the thought of what Viken would have said if he knew that she was sitting in the kitchen of one of his trusted associates with nothing on but a man's shirt. She remembered her panties were lying somewhere in the bedroom, or out in the hallway.

– One of the other members of the team is trying to find out about Mailin Bjerke's patients over the past few years, said Roar as he pushed his plate away. – Not easy, because only a few of them are registered with the social services. As regards those who were involved in her research, we may be able to get help from her supervisor, Tormod Dahlstrøm.

– Was Dahlstrøm her supervisor? Jennifer was impressed. Even she had followed his television series on the psychological element involved in cultural conflicts.

She chewed the remains of the cold meat, still ravenously hungry, she noticed. – What about this Jim Harris? Liss is convinced he saw something. Maybe he was the one who threatened Mailin that time so that she was afraid to carry on the treatment. He seems a distinctly dubious character.

– We're trying to get in touch with the guy, Roar told her. – Turns out it's not that easy. We might have to put something out via the media.

– It's got to be worth that at least. Mailin had an appointment with him at around the time she disappeared.

Roar shook his head. – We still can't say for certain that she was anywhere near her office that day.

– Even though the car was parked outside? You know roughly when she left the cabin, and you've got the time on the parking ticket.

– She might have been in several other places. We don't have either witness observations or an electronic trail.

Jennifer thought it over.

– What about the toll roads? she suggested. – Every vehicle that enters the city gets registered somewhere or other.

Roar grunted. – We've checked, of course. Mailin Bjerke paid by phone. The car was photographed on its way through the toll, but the company deletes the pictures after a couple of days.

Jennifer couldn't resist it. – So in other words, you were a little bit slow on the uptake. She added, jokingly: – For once.

The attempt to tease him seemed to have no effect, though the three seagulls on his forehead were almost gone now.

– There are limits to what you can manage to cover in the first few days in a missing persons case, was all he would say. – And the car had been found a long time before.

He gave her what was left of the scrambled egg.

– Do I look *that* hungry? she wanted to know.

– The evening is still young, it's not even eleven yet. He laid his hand over hers. – And I want you to be able to keep going all the way into the early hours of the morning.

With a sigh that was considerably less than a vociferous protest, she gave him to understand that she might be persuaded to spend the night in a bachelor apartment in Manglerud.

22

WHEN THE KNOCK came on the office door, Jennifer jumped to her feet and opened it. The woman standing out in the corridor was considerably taller than her. She might be in her fifties, the hair dark but the eyebrows not dyed, revealing that she had probably been a blonde.

– Ragnhild Bjerke, the other woman responded once Jennifer had introduced herself. – A pleasure.

The voice sounded stiff and flat, and the phrase hardly reflected what was going through the woman's mind as she stood there. Jennifer held the door open for her, but she stayed where she was.

– If you don't mind, I would rather see her at once.

Jennifer could well understand that Mailin Bjerke's mother didn't want to postpone what she had made up her mind to go through with. On the way down the corridor she said:

– It isn't unusual for relatives to be unsure whether or not they want to see the body.

She glanced over at her visitor. Ragnhild Bjerke's face was as stiff as her voice and showed no expression.

– I wasn't able to think about it before, she said. – Haven't been able to think at all, actually. Tage, my husband, suggested that he and Liss go that morning, Christmas morning. I didn't understand the significance of it. But now I must see her.

– Most people feel glad afterwards, Jennifer agreed.

The mortuary assistant was waiting by the chapel. His name was Leif, and Jennifer had asked him to handle the preparation of the body. He'd worked at the institute for twenty-five years and knew all the tricks of the trade when it came to making a body look as good as possible. After admitting them and folding back the sheet that covered the bier, he withdrew soundlessly. Hesitantly Ragnhild Bjerke approached. For almost ten minutes she stood looking down at her dead daughter, who lay there with hands folded across her chest and her ruined eyes shut. Then Jennifer broke the silence, moving a couple of steps closer. The click of the high heels on the floor startled Ragnhild Bjerke, as though bringing her out of a trance. She turned and wandered back out of the door again.

They sat at the small round table in Jennifer's office. Not a word had been said on the way back from the chapel. The visitor's face was as expressionless as when she had arrived.

– The ring, she murmured at last.

Jennifer recalled that Liss had noticed the same thing, the gold ring Mailin always wore. – It wasn't there when we found her, she confirmed.

– Someone's taken the ring, Ragnhild Bjerke said quietly, as though she were talking to herself.

Jennifer thought it curious that this was what Mailin's mother had noticed especially. – It must have been very special, she said.

It took a few moments for her visitor to respond.

– She never took it off. Mailin was named after my mother. When she was eighteen, she inherited her wedding ring.

– Then there must have been an inscription on it.

Ragnhild Bjerke nodded almost imperceptibly. – *Your Aage*, and the date of the wedding. No one could have done a thing like this just for a ring.

Jennifer didn't reply.

– I thought something would happen, Ragnhild Bjerke went

on. The voice was still a monotone, hollow. – I thought I would realise that she's gone. Her gaze was stiff too, but beneath lurked something that might have been panic. – I don't understand. I feel nothing.

Jennifer could have told her a lot about that. Told her of the conversations she had had with the bereaved down through the years. Now and then she had thought of herself as the ferryman who carried the dead person's relatives over the river, and then rowed them back again. She could have told her how common it was to be overwhelmed by feelings it was impossible to control. That it was normal, too, for a person to cocoon themselves and feel nothing but emptiness. But standing there she couldn't bring herself to say any of this. Something she hadn't felt the faintest breath of for a long time now surged through her, the strong desire for a daughter. A recognition of the fact that she would never have one was like the palest echo of the grief that hovered around the dead woman's mother.

– Liss trusts you, said Ragnhild Bjerke.

Jennifer felt that inevitable flush tinge her cheeks. – She's a fine girl.

Ragnhild Bjerke looked out across the car park. – She's withdrawn so far from me. In a way, I lost her first. Many years ago.

– Surely it's not too late to change things.

Without moving her gaze, Ragnhild Bjerke shook her head. – I've tried everything. She's never really felt any connection to me. Always been a daddy's girl.

– But she hasn't seen her father for years?

– Not since she was six. Ragnhild Bjerke swallowed a couple of times. – She blames me for his leaving. She thinks I was the one who drove him away.

– Isn't this something you could talk to her about now, now that she's grown up?

Jennifer could guess how like the mother the eldest daughter had been. Liss, on the other hand, she could find no trace of in Ragnhild Bjerke's face or body.

– Maybe it was wrong of me not to tell her the truth. Mailin was told, after all, but Liss . . . She's always been so fragile. I was probably afraid it would break her.

Jennifer struggled to divorce her own curiosity from her visitor's need to tell the story. – Did something happen between you and your husband? she asked cautiously.

– Happen? Something was happening all the time. He was a painter. All that mattered to him was success . . . That's a little unfair. He cared about the girls, in his way. Liss especially. As long as they didn't get in the way of his work. He had a studio in town, but often used a room down in the basement when he was at home. That was okay, because in those days there was a lot of travelling involved in my job.

Jennifer knew that Ragnhild Bjerke worked for one of the big publishing houses.

– I was away a lot promoting books, especially in the autumn. Often spent nights away.

– Why did he leave you?

Jennifer heard that her question was too private and was about to apologise when Ragnhild Bjerke said:

– He had a very high opinion of his own talent. Was convinced he was a great artist and that nothing must stand in his way. It meant he could allow himself to live any way he liked.

Jennifer didn't find the answer particularly illuminating but didn't pursue it.

– For years after he left, he wandered around without settling down anywhere. Suddenly we heard he had a big exhibition in Amsterdam. There were things about him on TV and in the newspapers. Everybody was talking about how this was the big breakthrough. Then it all went quiet again, and nothing came of it. It never did with him. Now he's in Montreal. He met a young woman who lives there. But he's been away travelling for several months. They can't get in touch with him. He still doesn't know that Mailin is . . .

Jennifer tried to imagine what it would be like to move so far away from one's children.

– Canada is quite a long way away, she said, encouraging her visitor to say more.

Ragnhild Bjerke continued to stare at a point far beyond the window. – That's not the reason he hasn't seen the girls for so many years. He didn't even get in touch when he was living in Copenhagen. He chose to live without them. But I think also there was a kind of compulsion involved.

She took out a handkerchief, held it to her nose as though about to sneeze, but took it away again without anything happening.

– He was a tormented man. Not when we first met, not when the children were very small. It started after a few years. Of course I knew his mother had a serious mental illness, and I got worried about him. Tried to get him to see a doctor, but he wouldn't hear of it. He began staying up all night. Wandering restlessly about the house. Or standing talking to himself by the window.

– Hallucinations?

– I don't think so. It was as though he was sleeping with his eyes open. Afterwards he couldn't remember me talking to him.

She took a little tube of lip salve from her handbag and ran it across her dry lips.

– And he had the most dreadful nightmares. Once I found him in Mailin's bedroom, standing by her bed and screaming. Finally I managed to get through to him. He was shaking, completely beside himself. 'I didn't kill them,' he was shouting. I got him out of there before he woke her up. 'You haven't killed anyone, Lasse,' I kept telling him. 'I dreamed it,' he sobbed, 'and I can't wake up.' 'What did you dream?' 'The girls,' he murmured, 'I dreamed I cut them up and ate their little bodies.'

She closed her eyes. Jennifer couldn't think of anything to say. The conversation had taken a direction she had no idea how to deal with. Roar had mentioned several times that the police were trying to get in touch with this father. What she was hearing now, in all confidence, was something that would interest the investigators. She ought to have interrupted and asked for permission to pass this information on.

– I called his doctor the next day, Ragnhild Bjerke continued before Jennifer could make up her mind. – But Lasse refused to go and see him. A couple of weeks later he moved out. He didn't say goodbye. Not to me. Not to Mailin. But Liss had some idea that he had been there and spoken to her.

She closed her handbag, sat with it on her lap.

– Can you understand why I never told this to Liss? She worshipped her father. Can you understand why it was better for her to blame me for his disappearance and to make me an object of hatred?

Jennifer didn't know how to respond to that.

– You said you were away a lot, she said instead. – Are you afraid he might have . . .

Ragnhild Bjerke opened her eyes wide. – He can't have done . . . I mean, it was just a nightmare. She shook her head for a long time, slowly. – I would have known. Mailin never hinted at anything of the kind . . . She tells me everything . . . always did . . .

Jennifer suddenly felt helpless and regretted having let things go so far. – Can I offer you something to drink? Coffee?

– A glass of water, perhaps.

With the glass on the table in front of her, Ragnhild Bjerke said: – I know why Liss came here. It's good to talk to you.

Again Jennifer felt herself flush. – Liss doesn't trust the police, she said.

– She never has done. Not since she kept getting arrested going on all those innocent demonstrations. And I don't know, I really don't, it isn't easy to sit through those interrogations. Being pressed about the slightest detail. As though they suspected you were the one who'd done something terrible to Mailin. Can you imagine what that's like, to feel yourself suspected of murdering your own daughter?

Jennifer heard something happening in the woman's voice and was waiting for it to surface again, but when Ragnhild Bjerke continued, it was still in that same toneless pitch.

– And Tage? He's the most trustworthy person in the world. He came to us and he was the father the girls had been missing and needed so much. He's never had any thanks for it. Even I haven't been good enough at telling him how grateful we ought to be. And then came all these questions about where was he when Mailin went missing, and when did he get back home. And I start thinking how I called him at the office several times that evening. He was supposed to be picking up Viljam, and I wanted to remind him to buy something to eat. He's always available on the telephone when he works late like that, but on that particular evening . . .

– You couldn't get hold of him.

– He said later there was some problem with the phone lines at the institute. But then you get all these questions, and suddenly this doubt is there, it worms its way inwards, and you can't face trying to think it all through.

– Did you tell the police about the telephone?

She didn't answer. Again Jennifer thought about asking for her permission to pass the information on, but when she looked into Ragnhild Bjerke's eyes, she dropped the idea. Certain stones should be left unturned, she decided. Later maybe, if it turned out to be important, but for the time being this woman should be left in peace.

Under the circumstances, even the pleasure of calling DCI Viken with several bits of information his own people hadn't got hold of was muted.

23

Wednesday 7 January, night

JIM HARRIS CAME running down from Fagerborg, crossed Suhms Street and carried on down Sorgenfri Street. No cars around, he had the whole road to himself. He could run faster a few years earlier, but he still wasn't far off. Had made up his mind now. No one believed in him any more, no one expected anything. He could hit back from below. Run his way out of it. Pay this debt, then back to the sports academy and set up some training sessions. Not a personal trainer, not yet, no one who mattered would have anything to do with him. But things would turn around. First pay off the thirty thousand. Karam had been asking about him. Repeated the threat to make a cripple of him. The only thing Jim was afraid of. End up in a wheelchair. He'd sent Karam a message. Before the week was over, he'd have his thirty thousand.

He turned into Bogstadveien. The asphalt was slippier there, but he accelerated as he headed on down the road. He'd show them, all those who'd turned their backs on him. Those who'd trodden him down into the shit. Mailin Bjerke was the only one who had never given up on him. But she made him so mad. She was actually pretty ruthless. Found the weak spot and then twisted. All the same, he'd gone there that Thursday. For the first time, she wasn't there when he arrived. Hadn't left a message or anything. The office windows dark. He was furious, kicking and kicking at the main gate. Walked a couple of times around the block. Her car was fucking well there, the Hyundai with the dent in the front bumper. Not hard to recognise. But it was only when he was about to turn the corner, and glanced round, that he saw what happened . . .

And now she was dead. He'd read about it in the papers a few days later. And yet he went back again. As though she would still be sitting there in her office promising to do all she could to help him. The door had been open, and he'd looked in. Opened a few drawers. Old habit. People left all sorts of stuff lying about. Her appointments diary was on the table; he looked up the day when he should have had his. There were his initials: *17.00 JH*. No one else due to see her that day. Below was written BERGER – Channel Six, Nydalen, 8 o'clock. And a message he didn't understand. Something about a jacket. He'd ripped out that page. Often wondered why he did things like that. Maybe to avoid getting dragged into anything.

So that girl who suddenly appeared was her sister. Not that you would have guessed. As unlike Mailin as you could get. A nervous, weird girl. Like something out a fairy tale. The Brothers Grimm, he recalled, that book he'd had lying under his bed all those years when he was a kid. This sister wanted something from him, kept showing up all the time. Obviously after him. That was why he stopped her in the park. She said something there that made him understand what he had seen in Welhavens Street that Thursday. At least understand enough to take a chance and lay out some bait. A stroke of luck. Because there was one person at least who had more reason to be nervous than him.

Jim had made up his mind not to ask for more than thirty thousand the first time. Then five or ten. Then raise it gradually. Could be a nice little earner on the side. He wasn't scared of Karam any more. He ran. Going to run his way out of it. Round the roundabout behind the National, down Munkedams

Way. Not slippy here. Good grip for the shoes. He was pleased with them. Grabbed them from a store in the Storo shopping mall. The alarm went off, but the security guard who could catch up with him hadn't been born yet. The shoes were as lightweight as the best he'd had from Nike, but the soles were better.

He didn't slow down until he reached the fjord. Could have kept on running the rest of the night. Getting close to his form from 2003, his best season, when he crushed the junior record for the four hundred flat, and the eight hundred. Eight hundred is the best. The others are done for by the time he starts his sprint, merciless, inhuman, impossible to respond to.

All the restaurants and shops on the fjord side had shut hours ago. Not a soul in sight along Aker Brygge. Should maybe have insisted on Egertorget. You got people there, even in the middle of the night. But the person he was going to meet insisted that no one should see them together. Jim knew that from now on he would be the one setting the conditions, so he'd gone along with the suggested meeting place on this occasion.

He stopped by the flaming torch that stood outermost on the quay. The Eternal Peace Flame. Peered down one of the alleyways. A couple of boats moored on the canal. Started walking along, keeping to the edge of the quay, towards the sculptures in the water. He checked his mobile phone: 1.35. The person he was supposed to meet should have been here by now.

Something rattled down on the boat deck on his left, metal on metal, a box or a weight or something falling. He turned and peered down into the half-darkness. In the same instant he realised that the sound had something to do with him, with the meeting he'd arranged, with what he'd seen that Thursday outside Mailin's office, with the thirty thousand he was going to get, but he didn't hear the footsteps behind him. Something hit him in the neck, boring its way inward from the side, and suddenly everything was clear around him and as bright as midday. He stood, frozen in this light, as his mouth was blasted open by what came gushing out of him.

24

On Wednesday morning, Liss was woken by a magpie screeching outside her window. She got up and closed it, but was too wide awake to sleep any more. She sat on the edge of her bed for a while, bare feet on the cold floor. Couldn't remember what she'd dreamed, but still something lingered, as if someone had been pecking and plucking away at her thoughts, helping themselves to the best bits and leaving small holes behind.

She pulled on trousers and a top, padded out into the corridor. Heard Viljam busy down below, and once she was finished on the loo went downstairs to join him. He was sitting at the kitchen table reading *Aftenposten* with a cup of coffee. Again the thought that he grieved in the same way she did, something silent, something he wanted to be alone with. She felt an urge to stroke his hair. It won't pass, Viljam. Just keep going anyway.

– Have you thought of how similar your name is to hers?

He looked up and gave her a quick smile. – Mailin noticed it, it hadn't occurred to me. It's almost hers backwards

Mailin must have noticed the other thing too, the similarity to their father. Not so much the individual features. Something in the eyes. A way of moving the hands. The timbre of the voice. The sorts of things Liss believed she remembered.

He folded up the newspaper and put it on the windowsill. – How long are you going to stay in Norway?

She didn't know if she'd be going back to Amsterdam. Mailin

had called her brave. Maybe it was the thought of Mailin being somewhere in the world that made her brave.

– I'll see after the funeral. She poured herself a mug of coffee. The mug was white with a large red M on it. – My mother still hasn't heard whether she can be cremated. That's what Mailin would have wanted. The police haven't decided yet whether they'll allow us to.

Mailin's dead body lying in the ground? Sudden thought: she mustn't get cold. We must wrap her in something warm. Blankets, or a duvet.

– Have you been in touch with any of your friends here? Viljam asked, obviously wanting to talk about something else.

– I had one night out. Just before Christmas.

She told him about the evening out with Catrine. The party she went to. Mentioned the footballer, although not the fact that she'd seen him again.

– What did you say his name was?

She had avoided using his name. He didn't belong in a conversation between them. She turned the coffee mug round and round. – Jomar something or other.

– Plays for Lyn? Jomar Vindheim?

– Something like that, she said, exaggerating her tone of indifference. – Have you met him?

– No, but anybody with the slightest interest in football knows his name. He's played for the national team. Even Mailin knew who he was.

– Mailin? She never had a clue about football.

Viljam shrugged. – There was a picture of him on the front page of the sports section. 'Isn't that Jomar Vindheim?' she said. Apparently she'd bumped into him somewhere or other.

To Liss it didn't add up. Twice she'd met Jomar. He hadn't said a word about knowing Mailin.

Viljam got up suddenly, went out into the corridor. She

heard him open a drawer in the chest. When he came back, he had a letter in his hand. *Not for me*, she prayed inwardly.

– Tage called in yesterday. Wanted to know how things were going. And deliver this.

He put it down in front of her. It had been sent to her mother's address in Lørenskog. The envelope was creamy yellow, the paper thick, the handwriting in ink, elegant and neat. There were Dutch stamps on it, and it was postmarked Amsterdam. On the back, the sender's name in printed capitals, *A. K. El Hachem*. She sat looking at it for some time, waiting for the reaction she knew would come. It took five seconds, maybe longer. In this brief interlude she had time to think, *Zako's surname*, and *damn you, Rikke* before her body took over. She excused herself, managed to get up the stairs and into the bathroom. Stuck her finger down her throat, but her stomach was empty. She stood stooped over, spitting down into the curve of the porcelain as the water formed a whirlpool around the outlet.

In her room she stood by the window, the letter in her hand. The magpie on the roof outside was at it again. *Throw it away without opening it*, it chattered. That'd make things even worse, she thought. Lie awake every night wondering what was in it. Wait for someone in uniform to come and pull the duvet off her and drag her out to a waiting car. A man wearing a grey overcoat sitting in the back seat. Wouters, that's his name, and she will never be able to forget it.

The writing paper was the same creamy yellow as the envelope, the heading a curling monogram formed with the initials AKH. *Dear Miss Liss Bjerke*. Zako had occasionally called her *Miss Lizzie*, she remembered, usually when he was about to say something sarcastic. A. K. El Hachem was not sarcastic. He was Zako's father. He hoped that it wasn't inconvenient of him to approach her in this way. He had heard that she had recently lost her sister, and expressed his deepest sympathies.

He realised that this was the reason she had been unable to attend Zako's funeral. She skimmed through these and several other extended formal courtesies, as convoluted as the monogram. She searched for a reason why she should now be standing here with this letter in her hand. Had to read more closely to find out. A few words about losing those closest to one, as had happened to them both. Zako was A. K. El Hachem's only son – Liss had always thought he had a younger brother; they had always been close, even if in recent years Zako had started leading a life his father could not approve of. Until the unthinkable happened, he had, however, entertained hopes that this son of his would return to the course laid out for him, become a partner in his father's firm, and later take over and carry on the hard work of four generations before him. For none among those who knew him could have any doubt that Zako was a young man of remarkable talents.

And now the father approached his reason for writing the letter. In conversations with his son over the past year, it had become apparent that something unusual had happened in his life. It concerned a woman. Zako had never had any trouble attracting women, it was a curse as well as a gift, but this young woman was, he had revealed to his father, not just one of many, but the only one. And the father had seen the change in his son. He had grown less hot headed, more thoughtful, more interested in planning for a secure future, more concerned for the well-being of his parents and sisters; in a word, the maturing of a self-centred young man that only a woman could effect, the thing his father had been waiting for with growing impatience as time went by, although never quite losing his faith that it would happen. There could be no doubt that this woman, that is, Miss Bjerke, had been sent to his son from a better world; the scales had fallen from Zako's eyes, and his life was about to take a turn in the direction his father, in the depth of his heart, had always longed to see it take.

A. K. El Hachem was writing to her to express his deepest gratitude that his son had known this time together with her, this reminder that life was good when one was open to what was good. In the darkest hours following his son's death, the knowledge that he had experienced something like this was an enormous comfort to him as a father, and to the whole of the family, and they had talked a lot about this Norwegian woman who had brought new light into their son's life. In conclusion, A. K. El Hachem expressed his deepest hope that at some point he would have the opportunity to meet her, whether in Nimes, where the family lived for most of the year, in Amsterdam, or in her own country up there in the far north.

25

THIS TIME IT was Berger himself who opened the door when Liss arrived. He took her jacket and hung it up for her.

– Did you give your butler the evening off? she said casually, and Berger confirmed that he had indeed done so.

– A couple of times a year he has a weekend off. He has his aged mother to visit, that kind of thing.

In the living room, music was coming from speakers she couldn't see. Indian drumming, it sounded like, with a kind of accordion and a man with a light, hoarse voice forcing curious sounds from his throat at a ferocious pace, up and down strange musical scales.

– Sufi music, Berger informed her. It meant absolutely nothing to her.

The smell in the room also had an Oriental origin. He picked up a smoking pipe from an ashtray and offered it to her. She declined. Hash made her distant and slow; her thoughts went off in directions she didn't like, became dense and nightmarish.

Berger slipped down on to the sofa, put his long legs on the table and puffed away.

– I hope you don't mind my taking my afternoon medicine, he said. – You who live in Amsterdam are probably used to this kind of thing.

– You asked me to come, she interrupted. No more than an hour had passed since she received his text as she was wandering around in the park at Tøyen trying to collect her thoughts.

– I did ask you to come, Liss, he nodded inside his cloud of cannabis smoke.

She waited.

– I liked Mailin, he said. – She was a fine girl. Preoccupied with her principles, but nevertheless fine.

– She had an appointment with you. That evening she disappeared.

– We talked about that last time.

– But now she's been found. If this has anything at all to do with you . . . She didn't know what to say, tried to calm down. – You don't seem in the slightest surprised. You seem cold and unaffected.

He shook his head firmly. – You're wrong, Liss. Death doesn't surprise me any longer, but I am not devoid of feelings. She deserved to live for somewhat longer.

She listened out for any kind of ambiguity in what he was saying.

– Death walks alongside us all the time, and you can choose to look another way. That will be the essence of my next show. Naturally it will be the last *Taboo* in the series. Beyond death, there isn't much more to talk about.

– Are you a junkie? she asked suddenly.

He half slumped in the sofa. Was wearing a sort of silky kimono. It wouldn't have surprised her if he was naked beneath it.

– You can't be in paradise all the time, Liss, that's what the junkies don't understand. You have to control it. You need a will of iron to balance on that particular razor's edge.

– And paradise, that's when you get a fix?

He showed his tiny white teeth. Lying slumped there like that, grinning, unshaven, his hair sticking up, he looked like a pirate chief out of some children's book.

– Try it, Liss. That is all I can say. You must try it. Or not. It's impossible to talk about it. It is how God reveals himself to us, giving us a ticket to a grandstand from where we can sneak a glance into the most complete perfection. Like wrapping a warm blanket around yourself, not around your body, but around your thoughts. Your soul, if you prefer. Within all is perfect peace. You desire nothing more than to be exactly where you are. No artist, no mystic has ever managed to describe the sensation. It is beyond words.

She tried to recall what it was she had thought of saying to him. He distracted her the whole time, and she couldn't seem to stop him.

– Can you live in such a way that death will be something to relish? he asked her. – Prepare yourself to turn it into your life's climax? Imagine you're having sex and achieve orgasm at the precise moment of your dying, disappearing in a movement that never ends. That is what my last programme will be about. But not in the way people might expect. You must never do what they expect, always be a nose in front.

He took a last drag from his pipe and put it back in the ashtray.

– How do you imagine you will die, Liss?

She couldn't bring herself to answer.

– Don't tell me you've never thought about it. I can see by looking at you that you're preoccupied with death.

Should she share her innermost thoughts with this semi-naked and wholly uninhibited priest? Tell him about the marsh by Morr Water. It would be like taking him out there, like having him there beside her when she lay down and looked up between the trees as the blanket of snow spread itself across her. She pulled herself together, but again he was there before her.

– There's something about you, Liss. You're from another place. You make me think of an angel of death. Do you know the effect you have on other people?

She sat up straighter. His eyes were growing distant now, as though he was looking deep inside himself.

– What did you talk to Mailin about?

Berger put his head back. The dressing gown slid to one side, and it occurred to Liss that he was about to expose himself to her.

– We spoke always of passion. She was interested in it. Passionately so.

– The passion of the adult, Liss corrected him. – In his encounter with the child.

– That too. Your sister was of the opinion that the recipe for a good life lies in in controlling the passions.

– While you believe they should be liberated.

He gave a hollow laugh. – Not liberated. Liberate yourself on them. Let them withdraw all the power from you. Would you really exchange fifty years of boredom for the intense pleasures of a year, or a minute?

– You sound like an evangelist.

– You're right, I'm more of a priest now than I ever was when I stood at the altar and delivered sermons from the Bible. I proselytise because I enjoy the staring and the contempt, but also the curiosity, the desire to allow oneself to be tempted. Where does that desire come from, Liss? Why have you come back here again?

– You asked me to come. I need to know what happened that evening Mailin went missing.

He picked up a remote control, turned off the music. – Did I tell you last time that I knew your father?

She sat there open mouthed.

– It was in the seventies, long before you were even thought of. We hung out with the same crowd. I was a lapsed priest; he was an artist with more ambition than talent.

He seemed to be thinking about something before he added: – I suspect that was Mailin's real reason for coming here. And why she said yes to the chance to appear on *Taboo*. She wanted to know what I could tell her about this father of yours who left you.

– I don't believe you.

Berger shrugged. – You can believe whatever you like.

– When . . . was the last time you saw him?

– Mailin asked me the same question, Berger sighed. – I met him in Amsterdam about ten or twelve years ago. It was when he had an exhibition there.

The pipe had gone out; he picked it up anyway and puffed away on it. It emitted a gurgling sound.

– I'm sure he thought he would make his name in the international art market. But he wasn't intended for great things. Deep down inside he knew that himself.

She sat stiffly on the edge of her chair, unable to take her eyes off him.

– But then he rang me not too long ago. He'd heard that Mailin was going to appear on *Taboo*. I think he's kept track of you two all along, from somewhere out there.

– You're making stories up to get me interested, she yelled at him. – That's what you did to Mailin, too. Enticed her here.

He sat up, leaned across the table towards her.

– You still believe that I am the one responsible for her death?

She couldn't say anything.

– You think I met her at the office, drugged her, carried her out to the car, locked her in the boot and drove her out to a disused factory. Undressed her and played with her until I got bored, killed her and then left.

– Stop it!

A spasm jerked across his face. – Why should I stop when this is what you came here to hear?

She stood up, suddenly unsteady. – I don't know why I came here.

He stood up too, rounded the table. Towering in front of her. She was forced to inhale the smell of his naked body, the male sweat, the unwashed hair, all kinds of bodily fluids, and the whiff of his guts from his mouth as he bent down towards her. Then something happened to his eyes, the gaze widened, and he began to shake. Suddenly he grabbed her by the shoulders, pulled her close to him, held her tightly.

– I know what happened, Liss, he muttered, his voice thick. – I liked her, I told you. She didn't deserve to die like that.

He squeezed harder. Liss feels the soft swell of the pot belly and the large sex hanging down below it. She knows what's going to happen next. The light is sucked away and burns itself into everything around her, opens up a room in which she can hide away. And just then the doorbell rang. The grip was relaxed, she pulled herself free, grabbed her jacket, ran out into the corridor, struggled with the lock.

There was no one outside. She slammed the door shut behind her, raced down the stairs and out into the street. Not until she reached Kirke Way did she stop running. She turned, but knew he would not follow her.

Her phone rang. She saw the name on the display. Still she took the call.

– What's the matter? asked Jomar Vindheim.

She muttered a few disjointed words, something about Berger.

– I'll pick you up, he insisted. – I'm in the neighbourhood.

She protested but was relieved when he ignored her.

26

– You need a cup of coffee, he said as she sat beside him in the car a few minutes later.

Coffee was the last thing she needed. She wanted to ask him to drive her to the flat in Lang Street so she could get into her room and be alone. – I can't face the thought of a coffee bar, she said.

– Then I've got a better suggestion, he claimed. – After all, you've been to my place before. You know you'll get out of there with your life and your honour intact. Even your senses.

– Senses? she exclaimed, not sure where he was going with this.

– What were you doing at Berger's? he said to change the subject as he accelerated through the junction at Majorstua. – Your sister?

She didn't answer. He passed through another junction, this time on amber, before saying: – You think Berger has something to do with it?

– I don't know, Jomar.

A weird name, she thought, it sounded strange when she said it. She decided to trust him, described what had happened at Berger's flat, but avoided mentioning anything about Berger's claiming to know her father.

– Did he threaten you? Christ, Liss, you should make a formal complaint.

She could still feel those fists squeezing her into that enormous, soft body . . . It never did any good reporting something like that. But what he said as he was holding her, that was something the police ought to know about. *I know what happened*. Ring Jennifer, she thought.

– I don't think he meant to make a threat. There was something or other he wanted to tell me. Weak of me to chicken out.

– Is it chickening out to get out of the way of a guy as unstable as that? Jomar smacked his lips. – Not such a brilliant idea to go there in the first place. Next time I'll come with you.

She tried to summon a smile. – Probably smart. Rumour has it that he's very partial to young lads, especially really good-looking ones . . .

She broke off, noticed that he was looking at her.

His flat seemed brighter than the last time she was there. And tidy, considering it belonged to a young man with a lot of time and money on his hands. Or maybe he had a housekeeper. A door in the hallway was ajar, and through it she caught a glimpse of a tall bedhead with wrought-iron ornamentation, and a punch ball hanging from the ceiling. The furniture in the living room certainly wasn't from IKEA. The sofa and the chairs looked like Jasper Morrison, but she avoided asking Jomar Vindheim if he was interested in interior design. Along one wall were shelves containing CDs and DVDs. She waited until he disappeared out into the kitchen to make coffee before looking at his collection. Rap mostly, and that was closer to the sort of impression she had of him. Action films and PlayStation games. *The Da Vinci Code* and a few other books. She took one of these down, *Atonement*, which she had read herself. Was standing with it in her hands when he came back in.

– You read this kind of thing? she blurted out, aware as she said it that it sounded decidedly patronising.

– Shocked? He handed her a cup of coffee.

– Didn't think most footballers could read, she said, trying to smooth things over with a more obvious irony.

He opened the curtains. The flat was on the ninth floor, and the Oslo sky hung outside the window like a crude grey canvas.

– A girl I met gave it to me, he confessed as he slipped down on to the sofa. – She insisted that I read it.

– I see, Liss responded, picturing a little football groupie who tried to attract his attention with the aid of someone else's talent. – And did you?

– Yep. Good stuff. Especially that you never really know if they survived the war or not. In the film, it was much too obvious.

She raised her eyebrows, exaggerating her own surprise. – So you like that kind of open ending?

– Worked well there anyway, he replied, ignoring her sarcastic tone. – The girl I got it from is actually a friend of yours.

It dawned on Liss that this friend had to be Therese, who had called her a bitch.

– Can I smoke, or do you want me to walk down the nine floors?

She could have managed to wait, asked mostly as a provocation, because suddenly she felt irritated. Not with him, if the truth be known, but he was there, he'd invited her back to his place, he kept popping up all over the place, sent her messages and didn't give up even though she had made it clear she wasn't interested.

– Sure, he said, got up and fetched a bowl. – Use this as an ashtray.

It was white with a drawing of a little Asian girl on it; her eyes were suggested by two lines, and she was holding up a poppy.

– Anyway, I have a balcony.

He opened the door and accompanied her out into the chilly afternoon, even went back and fetched a jacket for her. She recognised it and had to smile.

– What I liked best about that book, he said after he'd lit her cigarette for her, – is that it reminded me of my grandfather.

– Oh yeah. Was he falsely accused of rape and ended up a war hero? Suddenly she remembered something. – You met Mailin.

For a few seconds his face grew a shade darker. – That's right in a way. Briefly.

– Why didn't you mention it?

He shrugged. – Haven't really had the chance to have a proper talk with you. Not yet.

She ignored the invitation. – Where did you meet her?

– At the sports school. She ran a course there, about abuse in the world of athletics. It was a couple of years ago. I talked to her afterwards. I liked her.

His response did nothing to quell her irritation. She finished her cigarette and squashed it out against the head of the Chinese girl.

– Your sister was well liked by everybody. It's just too fucking awful. If there's anything I can do, Liss . . .

Stop talking about it, she thought, but didn't say it. Stop following me around, she thought, but she didn't say that either.

Back in the living room, she sank down into the sofa. It was so comfortable to sit in. She didn't want to leave yet, but she couldn't stay.

Jomar said: – I hope Jimbo's stopped bothering you.

She blew out her breath with a low whistling sound. – I'm not scared of him. If he was going to do anything to me, he would have done it in the park that night.

He didn't move his gaze when she looked over at him.

– I think you ought to learn how to look after yourself a bit better, Liss.

27

The time was 6.42 when Viken called. Roar Horvath picked up the remote and muted the sound on the TV.

– A body was found in the fjord by Aker Brygge this morning, said the detective chief inspector with no preamble.

– Saw that on the net, Roar replied. – Relevant for us?

– Jim Harris. Skewered through the throat with a sharp object. Probably a screwdriver. The carotid artery completely severed. Dead before he was dumped in the water.

Roar was on his feet, standing in the middle of the room. – When?

– Last night. Masses of blood on the quayside, right next to Tjuvholmen. Must have happened there.

– Witnesses?

– Four or five seagulls. None of them willing to say anything.

Roar glanced at the TV screen, a repeat of a La Liga match. – The guy had a drug debt.

– This isn't drug related, Viken asserted, and Roar too had immediately seen that it didn't fit the pattern.

The detective chief inspector's voice took on an unpleasant undertone as he continued: – Plåterud has been kind enough to let us have a résumé each time she's had a conversation with Liss Bjerke. It's time we resumed control of the interviewing of central witnesses. What's your opinion?

– Oh absolutely, Roar coughed. Jennifer had called him not more than half an hour ago, she was coming out to see him later that evening. – It isn't Plåterud's job to carry out interviews, he agreed, and cleared his throat again. – I'll get in touch with her.

– Get in touch with who?

– Liss Bjerke.

– I've done that ages ago. Have you checked her out against the PNC database?

– No, Roar had to confess. Liss Bjerke had been in Amsterdam when her sister went missing, and it was hard to see how she could be involved. All the same, he should have checked her against the list of offenders. It was a question of the reliability of an important witness.

– I thought not, Viken observed. – The girl has eight cases outstanding against her.

– Christ.

– Assaulting the police in the course of illegal demonstrations. Hauled in a number of times.

Roar thought about it and swallowed. – Then we've got a very good excuse for bringing her in.

Viken said: – We'll keep it in reserve in case we need it. It looks as though I'm going to be able to get her to come in more or less voluntarily. She demands to speak to a female investigator.

– Are we going to let ourselves be dictated to by a stroppy girl?

Viken snorted at the other end. – This is all about one thing.

– Of course, Roar noted. – Results.

He turned off the TV and made his way out into the hallway, took his shoes out of the box room.

– I've got your memo about Pål Øvreby here in front of me, Viken continued.

Roar had done a thorough job on it. The day after he had interviewed the psychologist who shared the waiting room with Mailin Bjerke, he had called back and asked a series of control questions. The guy insisted that he had not seen hide nor hair of Mailin on Thursday 11 December. On one point, however, he did change his statement. On thinking about it, he recalled that he had stopped as he passed her car parked on Welhavens Street. He bent down to see if Mailin was inside, apparently because there was something he wanted to ask her. What it was he had long since forgotten. Roar had wanted to know if there was a parking ticket in the window, but the psychologist was unable to help him there.

– Any new information? he asked now.

– I received a letter this afternoon, the detective chief inspector grunted. – I've put a copy on your desk. You'd better take a look at it next time you're down here.

– Is it about Øvreby?

– You might say that. A tip-off that the guy is involved big-time in a social security scam. Anonymous sender.

Roar got his other shoe on.

– Apparently something that's been going on a long time, Viken added. – The letter concludes as follows: *Mailin Bjerke knew what was taking place in the office next door.*

28

Thursday 8 January

ROAR SWUNG INTO the Oslo police station garage at 7.15. As he turned off the engine, his phone rang.

– Awake already? said Jennifer, obviously trying to sound surprised. – And here's me ringing to wake you up.

– Been up for hours, he shot back at her. – Showered, eaten, done some work. Even though I had female company until well past midnight. Just couldn't get her to leave.

– Oh that's too bad. And she probably forgot to pull the blanket over you before she left.

He could see her smiling, the face breaking up into tiny wrinkles.

– By the way, I've just been talking to Viken, she said. – I told him about a test finding that's come in that might interest you too.

She always sounded like a proud little girl when she had something important to relate.

– Are you calling to tease me, or are you actually going to tell me what it is?

She laughed. – I'm sure you'll hear it from the man himself, she said. – But then I felt like talking to you. Two birds with one stone. It's about the hairs we found on Mailin Bjerke. We sent them to a specialist lab in Austria.

Seconds ticked by in silence.

– Would you please get to the point, Jenny? I've got a ton of documents to get through before the morning briefing.

– The good news is that they've managed to get some DNA from them, even though the roots are missing.

– Not bad. You'll be sending us a profile?

– And then there's the bad news. All we've got is mitochondrial DNA.

– Meaning what?

– If we're lucky, we might find a DNA type that occurs in a relatively small minority of the population.

A female member of the team hurried past Roar's car and waved to him.

Jennifer said: – Anything new about Mailin Bjerke's father?

– You mean the stepfather?

– The biological father. The one neither of them has seen for the past twenty years.

– We're still trying to get hold of him in Canada, Roar confided. – For a number of reasons. Why do you ask?

– Ragnhild Bjerke came to my office yesterday.

– She did? Why didn't you tell us before?

Jennifer hesitated. – It was a sort of medical consultation. I'm not really sure how much I can reveal. There's something about this father, but . . .

There was a knock on the car window. Viken was standing outside. Roar jumped, broke the connection and tossed the phone on to the passenger seat. He wound down the window.

– Meeting's put back until ten, the detective chief inspector informed him, and then peered quizzically at him.

A few ancient images suddenly flashed through Roar's mind: his father bursting in through the bedroom door, shouting at him to get out of bed. Standing there naked, with Sara cowering under the duvet. Ordered straight into the shower, while she was sent home.

He didn't take in everything Viken said, something about him being on his way to Aker Brygge to take a look at the crime scene there with someone from the forensics unit.

– We've had some provisional results from those hair samples, Viken went on.

– So I heard.

The detective chief inspector's eyebrows wriggled into each other. – You heard already? From whom?

Roar could have beaten his head against the steering wheel. Or started the engine and driven off. He controlled himself and managed to reply. – Called Flatland. On a completely unrelated matter as it happens.

He picked up his mobile and shoulder bag and opened the car door. – At best we're talking about a fairly uncommon type of DNA.

He climbed out of the car, stood a good half a head taller than Viken.

– Have you seen *VG*? The detective chief inspector pulled a newspaper from his inside pocket, spread it open on the roof of the car.

Roar read: *Berger to reveal killer tonight on* Taboo? – Well I fucking never.

– My sentiments exactly, said Viken. – Since my interview with him yesterday evening, our friend has used his time well.

He pointed to something underlined with a pen: *Berger has been interviewed three times because he had an appointment with Mailin Bjerke on the evening she went missing. He is not especially impressed by the efforts of the police in the case. 'The gang of detectives they've got working on this case makes the police station look like a sheltered workplace. They're obsessed with trivialities and fail to pick up on the most obvious connections.' 'Are you saying that you have information that is important to the case?' Berger laughs heartily. 'If I did then naturally I wouldn't let VG have it. I've got my own audience to think about.' Berger refuses to say anything definite about his inside knowledge of the case, but he drops a heavy hint that he will be revealing what he knows in this evening's edition of* Taboo *on Channel Six. The subject of which is? Precisely – death.*

Roar shook his head. – Surely we can't sit around waiting for a TV show. He's playing with us.

Viken shoved the newspaper back into his coat pocket. – The guy is due on TV in a few hours' time. Doesn't he have an audience of seven hundred thousand? Nine hundred thousand? If we bring him in yet again without having anything new, what do you think that'll do to his viewing figures?

It wasn't necessary for Roar to answer. – What did you get out of the interview yesterday?

– Berger claims he walked from Welhavens Street up to the studio at Nydalen.

– In that case it should be easy to find witnesses. The man is not exactly invisible.

– He says he went by the footpath along Aker river and took plenty of time. Apparently he had received a piece of news earlier that day he needed to think about.

– And that was?

– Nothing that's any of our business, according to him.

29

About halfway through the therapy session, the door was slung wide open. Pål stood there glaring furiously at her. His eyes were red rimmed, his face grimy and unshaven. He looked as though he hadn't slept for several days.

– Need to talk to you.

Torunn smiled apologetically at the young girl sitting in the chair opposite her. To Pål she said: – I'll be finished in half an hour. Roughly. I'll come up to your office.

– I need to talk to you *now.*

She could hear that he was exerting himself not to shout. – So sorry, she said to the patient as she stood up. – I'll be right back.

Out in the waiting room, he grabbed her by the arm and pulled her along. She tried to free herself.

– Don't you touch me, she said as coolly as she could.

He let go of her and led the way into the common room. She closed the door behind them, knew she would have to counter his anger with an anger of her own that was even greater.

– What do you mean by barging in when I'm sitting there with a patient? I've had enough of this crap of yours.

He took a step towards her. – Are you trying to destroy me? he hissed.

– I couldn't be bothered to waste my time. You're doing fine by yourself.

– Have you snitched on me so that you'll get custody of Oda?

She'd been thinking about what to say when this came up. But his anger was unexpectedly strong.

– No idea what you're talking about, she said dismissively.
– What do you mean by *snitched*?

He looked her over, scowling. Somewhere in his eyes she saw a hint of doubt.

– Are you trying to say you don't know anything about it? he growled.

– Know anything about what? Would you please tell me what on earth you're talking about.

He straightened up, looked towards the door. – I've been talking to the police all morning.

– Interviewed?

She could hear how persuasive her surprise sounded.

– If you're lying to me . . . he began, but then had to start again. – If I find out it was you who went to the police . . .

She could see that he was serious. She had known him for eight years. They had lived together for four of them. She had long ago realised how weak he was, and let him know that she knew. But he was in a corner now. He was about to lose everything, and she saw a new side of him. She didn't doubt that he could turn dangerous if the pressure got any higher.

– Sit down, she said decisively. He slumped into a chair. – Just give me a couple of minutes to finish with this patient.

After getting rid of the young girl by saying something serious had happened, Torunn remained standing at the window. During every second that had passed since receiving the letter from Pål's solicitor, she had felt this intense hate towards him. He had made good his threat and started a process aimed at getting custody of Oda. She had understood that he was preparing to go the whole way, have her suitability as a parent evaluated by an expert, and use all Oda's small accidents against her. Dig up dirt that wasn't there. It was stupid of him. There was nothing she wouldn't do to win the war he had started. And she was tactically a great deal smarter than he was.

When she returned to the common room, he was still sitting there, motionless and staring at the table. She had considered rebuking him for having interrupted a session with a patient but saw now that it wasn't necessary. She sat down on the other side of the table and leaned towards him.

– If you want my help, first you have to tell me.

He glanced up at her. The look in his eyes was very different now. Reminded her of something that had been there during the early days, and for a second she felt pity for him. It surprised her, because the hatred was still there, boiling inside her.

– Someone has reported me for social security fraud, he said, and from the meekness in his voice she could tell he had already completely abandoned any notion that she was involved.

– I told you that this business with the social security statements is the stupidest thing you've ever done, she said to him, more comforting than accusing.

– I did it to give a few poor buggers a chance, you know that.

Did she know that? To begin with he had been helping some immigrants who had no money. She'd turned a blind eye to it, bought his argument that these people were on the very bottom rung of society's ladder and deserving of a few crumbs of the country's vast excess of wealth; that they didn't have the slightest hope of getting these crumbs in any other way. Helping them to a disability allowance that strictly speaking they weren't entitled to was, he argued, a sort of political act, a form of civil disobedience. But gradually he'd started receiving kickbacks, and before long he had more money than he'd ever dreamed of, and the economic advantages began to overshadow the political aspect completely. Time and again she had warned him, but it was as though he was addicted to the game and couldn't stop. It was only a question of time before the whole thing would be discovered. In the first instance by those closest, like Mailin.

– I can help you, Pål. You know I'm always there for you.

She got carried away by the compassion in her own voice and stroked his arm. Suddenly he lifted her hand and pressed it against his eyes, and his shoulders began to shake.

She stood up and walked round the table. – Now, Pål, she comforted him, – of course I'll help you. But we have to make peace with each other, you do understand?

It looked as though he might be nodding.

– And one other thing. You *must* tell me where you were on the evening Mailin went missing.

30

THE DOORBELL HAD rung three times. Liss sat on the sofa looking out on to the patch of garden with the stone-built barbecue and the tool shed sticking up out of the snow like a tombstone. She didn't intend to see who it was. No one knew she was living there, almost no one. She didn't feel the need to talk to any of Viljam's friends. Nor anyone else. But when it rang for a fourth time, she got to her feet and padded up the stairs and out into the hallway.

It was for her.

– You might as well open up now. I'm not the type to give up.

She had realised this. All the same, inadvertently, she had let slip where she was living at the moment. She should have been firmer with Jomar Vindheim, *the footballer*, as she continued to call him in her thoughts. No chance, she should have told him, neither in heaven nor in hell, of there being anything between us. Even in her thoughts *between us* sounded like a chord played on an out-of-tune piano. All the same, she had to admit that she liked how he wasn't easily put off.

She stood in the doorway and did nothing that might be taken as an invitation to him to step inside.

– Have you checked the net?

She hadn't. She'd slept in as long as possible. And then moved about the house as slowly as she could. Put off eating, even put off smoking.

– Not seen the newspapers or listened to the radio?

Something in his voice set alarm bells ringing.

– Best if I come in, he urged, and she could hardly stop him from slipping by her.

– If you've come here to tell me something, then say what it is.

– Jimbo's dead, he said. – Jim Harris.

They sat in the kitchen. She turned the cup round and round in her hands. It was empty; she'd forgotten to put the coffee on.

– Have you spoken to the police? Jomar asked. – Told them everything you told me?

– Last night. I was interviewed there. When did he die?

– Night before last. He was stabbed to death on Aker Brygge.

The policewoman who interviewed her had returned over and over again to this business with Jim Harris and his behaviour in the park. Several times she had asked Liss where she was the night before last, but never said a word about Harris being dead.

– Might it have been something else? she asked quietly. – Something that had nothing to do with Mailin?

Jomar rested his head in his hands. – Jim had drug debts. He owed money to people in the B-Gang. He told me so himself.

He rubbed himself so hard across the forehead that a broad red stripe appeared on the skin. – I tried to help him, but I should have done more. He came up to my place the other week and asked for a loan of thirty thousand. I could have managed it, but I'd already made it clear to him that I wasn't going to lend him any more money. It would only drag him deeper down into the dirt.

– Need a smoke, she said and got up.

Water was dripping from a crack in the guttering. She huddled back below the porch. Jomar stayed on the stairway, one step down. She sneaked a glance at his face. The slightly slanting eyes were coloured by the grey light, but there was something reassuring about them. That impression was reinforced by the mouth, though the lips were quite narrow. Suddenly a memory of that night at Zako's returned to her. Not of the lifeless body on the sofa, but something or other about the pictures on his mobile phone. She couldn't quite get what it was . . . The letter from Zako's father was still lying on the floor underneath her bed upstairs. If what he had written had been full of bitter recriminations, she might have been able to throw it away. But that gratitude of his was unendurable.

– Before Christmas something happened in Amsterdam, she suddenly blurted out. – Someone I knew died. I mean, more than just someone I knew.

He looked directly into her eyes. – Your boyfriend.

– In a way. I've been avoiding it. What happened to Mailin . . .

She filled her lungs with smoke, let it slowly ooze out again.

– Yesterday I got a letter from his father. And it brought it all back.

Jomar reached out for the Marlboro packet she'd balanced on the railings. – Can I take one?

– Not if it's going to ruin your career as a footballer.

She heard how silly her response was, and her need to talk was suddenly gone.

He lit up. – What were you going to say about the guy who died in Amsterdam?

– I'd prefer to hear about your grandfather, she said quickly.

– My grandfather?

She glanced over at him. – When I was at your place you mentioned him.

– You mean when we were talking about that novel?

She nodded. – I need to think about something else. What was it about *Atonement* that reminded you of your grandfather?

He inhaled deeply a couple of times. – The stuff about the two who were meant for each other. –

Liss half turned away. She had a response on the tip of her tongue but let it stay there.

– My grandfather was a fisherman, said Jomar. – He grew up in Florø. The day he turned twenty-two, he was delivering a catch to Bergen. He told me how he had a few hours free and spent the time wandering around Torgalmenningen. In one of the stalls a woman was selling clothes. This was during the war. He went over to her, and at that moment he knew she was going to be his wife.

– What about your grandmother? Liss said acidly. – Didn't she have a say in the matter?

– She gradually came to understand.

Liss had to admit she liked the story. She liked the way he told it, that he dared to do so without resorting to irony.

– And your parents, was that as romantic?

– That's another story altogether. Jomar fell silent.

– Are you never afraid of going insane? she asked out of nowhere.

He thought about it. – I don't think so. Very few footballers go insane, for some reason or other.

He flipped his cigarette down into the street, climbed up the last step and underneath the porch where she was standing. Don't do it, she thought as he lifted his hand and stroked her cold cheek.

Outside it had grown dark. Liss lay in bed listening to the magpie that never stopped hopping round on the roof and pecking at the tiles. She glided inward to a state between sleep and waking. The room changed, became a different room, one that she once lay in and slept in. She tries to wake up. Then Mailin is standing there, in her yellow pyjamas.

She forced herself to sit up, turned on the light, hit herself on the head with her palms.

– I'll call him, she muttered, fumbling for her mobile in her bag.

– Hi, Liss, said Tormod Dahlstrøm.

– I'm sorry, she said.

– For what?

She didn't know what to say.

– Waking you up in the middle of the night at the weekend.

He must have understood that she wasn't calling to apologise yet again but said nothing, gave her time. She started by explaining how she had realised that the words Mailin was saying on the video were the name of this Hungarian psychiatrist.

– Sándor Ferenczi? Dahlstrøm exclaimed. – Strange that she should be saying that. I assume you've contacted the police.

Liss described both her interviews. That she had walked out during the first one.

– Something's happening to me.

– Happening?

She took the plunge. – It used to happen a lot before. It's a kind of attack. I don't know whether I can describe it. The room around me suddenly becomes different, unreal. The light moves away, as though I'm not there, but at the same time everything is much more intense . . . Are you busy? Shall I call another time?

He reassured her that he had plenty of time.

– After I went to Amsterdam, it went away. No one there knew me. But then it began happening again. Just before Mailin went missing.

It was at the Café Alto, when Zako showed her the photograph. *Tell him about it, Liss. Everything that happened. He can tell you what you should do.*

At the last moment she changed her mind.

– Berger knew our father, she said quickly. – I think that's why Mailin kept going to meet him.

She told him what Berger had said about their father.

– Mailin once mentioned to me that she hadn't seen him

for many years, Dahlstrøm observed. – Do you remember him?

Liss took a deep breath. – I remember almost nothing from my childhood. Isn't that abnormal?

– There are great variations between how much we all remember.

– But to me it's as though it's been deleted, edited out. And then without warning something pops up.

Suddenly she began talking about the bedroom in Lørenskog. Mailin standing there in the dark, locking the door and creeping into bed beside her. The hammering on the door.

– Did she mention any of this to you?

– No, said Dahlstrøm. – We didn't discuss our own possible traumas. I gathered that Mailin, like most of us, carried some kind of burden, and I did recommend that she go into therapy herself. She hadn't got round to it, not yet.

He paused a moment before he said: – Tell me this about the bedroom again, in as much detail as you can.

Liss closed her eyes. Brought it back again. Mailin in the blue pyjamas, that could also be yellow, maybe several different episodes fused into one. Mailin with her arms around her. *I'll look after you, Liss. Nothing bad will ever, ever happen to you.*

– She said something else . . . Something about Mother.

Liss switched off the light, listened into the darkness. Somewhere out there Mailin's voice came back to her: *Don't tell anyone about this, Liss. Not even Mum. She won't be able to take it if she finds out.*

31

ODD LØKKEMO TURNED in to the petrol station at Kløfta. The gauge was only just down into the red, the reserve tank capacious, eight litres at least, and it was less than forty kilometres home. But the mere thought of running out along the E6 in the January dark was enough to make him shiver. Walking along an icy hard shoulder for several kilometres with an empty petrol can in his hand. The likelihood of it happening wasn't great, he argued, but then the consequences of it doing so were all the greater. He'd been turning these thoughts over in his mind ever since Minnesund.

He checked his mobile before getting out. No messages. He'd sent two to Elijah announcing that he was on his way. At the very least he deserved a reply. Though never explicitly stated, there was a tacit agreement that he keep out of the way until he received a message that it was okay to come home. It was always like that on days when Elijah was due at the studio in the evening. He had to have the whole house to himself. Couldn't stand the sight of anyone, especially not Odd. After the broadcast, things changed completely. Then he was like a complaining child who could never get enough attention and Odd was the most important thing in the world to him.

But it was probably not only on account of this evening's *Taboo* that Elijah wanted him out of the house that afternoon. Odd was certain he was expecting a visitor. The same visitor who had been there so often over the past few weeks. Once they had shared secrets like this, but now Elijah had become more and more cranky about them and wanted to keep them all to himself.

Odd pushed the button to pay at the counter. Didn't like using the credit card pumps. Often the receipt was missing, and that left him standing there not knowing how much had been withdrawn from his account. At last a vibration in his pocket. He almost hung the diesel pistol back in its cradle at once but overcame the impulse and continued to follow the rolling display, how many litres, how many kroner, the figures creeping slowly up towards a full tank, sixty litres, so slowly that the pump was clearly faulty; all the same, he forced himself to wait for the click inside the pistol, and even then he first washed the diesel smell off his hands in the shabby toilet, which had no paper towels, and toilet roll strewn across the floor all the way over to the washbasin, and picked up copies of *VG* and *Dagbladet* and a packet of salt pastilles, and paid the teenage girl, who didn't look at him once – overlooked, invisible; when did that happen, Odd, when did people stop even looking at you? Only then did he pull out the phone and read the message from Elijah. Sat there staring at it. *Don't come for another hour and a half.* He fought against a desire to call him. Rage at him that he had no right to stop him coming home whenever he wanted. It was just as much his home. It was his apartment . . . No, he would never sink to the depths of reminding Elijah who it was who owned the apartment. Last time he tried it, a few years back, Elijah moved out, and he had to beg him to come back again.

Odd switched on the coupé light, flipped through *Dagbladet*. He didn't want to sit there with the engine idling and it soon grew cold inside the car. He strolled over to the café and took a seat at the window. Looked at *VG*, which he had already read. He'd been out and bought a copy that morning along with some croissants, and burst in on Elijah with it, sat on the edge of his bed and woken him up by shouting the headlines at him: *Berger to reveal killer tonight on* Taboo?

Odd was used to the way Elijah attracted publicity. The *Taboo* series was the most successful thing he had ever done. Not artistically, of course, but in commercial terms. Elijah had always been prepared to do anything at all to create publicity around his name. But using Mailin Bjerke as bait for an audience hungry for sensation, surely that was going too far, even for him? Elijah wouldn't hear a word of it. *This is not bait. This is the real thing. Even you, Odd, who think you know everything that's going on, even you'll get a shock.*

He refused to say any more.

The time was 7.20 when Odd turned down Løvenskiolds Street. Cruising round the block in search of a parking space, he passed Elijah's car in Odins Street and noted that Elijah hadn't used it this evening either. Must have been at least a week since he'd last driven it, a relief bearing in mind the state he was in these days. They'd discussed selling the BMW. Make do with Odd's Peugeot. It means something when two people have one car, thought Odd. Especially at a time like this.

He let himself in. Peered into the hallway. The smell of fresh bread made him feel happy. He'd prepared the dough this morning before going out, leaving Elijah to put it in the oven. The fact that he'd remembered to do it even on a day like this was heartening. In the bathroom, water was trickling from one of the bath taps. He went in and turned it, not that it made any difference. Stood there a moment, listening. It was not often this quiet in the apartment. In some ways it was good to come home to silence. It showed a kind of respect, like the way Elijah had warned him and asked him to stay out of the way. So he didn't surprise him with one of his young lovers. *A necessity of life* was Elijah's usual excuse. *What about me?* Odd had asked not long ago. *Your job isn't to keep me alive, Odd, but to make sure I die with at least a minimum of dignity.* Then he'd laughed, the way he always did when things threatened to get serious.

Odd opened the door into the living room. Elijah was sitting in his office chair in the flickering light of the screen saver from his computer, his head thrown backwards. The rest of the room was in darkness. The thin Japanese silk dressing gown had slid open, revealing his chest and his naked lower half. Odd sighed as he thought how he would have to call the studio and inform them that there wouldn't be any show this evening after all. Felt relief at the realisation that this time Elijah had gone too far, raising expectations he couldn't meet. It was going to be embarrassing and humiliating.

He crossed the floor and bent to stroke Elijah on the cheek. Only then did he notice the wide-open eyes, the gaze fixed not on him but on infinite emptiness.

32

It had started to rain by the time Roar Horvath parked his car further up Odins Street, and when he turned the corner, it struck him like a whip. He turned up the fur collar of his leather jacket.

The area in front of the entrance was cordoned off. A crowd of people thronged around the warning tape. A couple of TV cameras were present, journalists, but most of them were just curiosity-seekers who had heard the news of Berger's death. It had been broadcast at 21.30, as his show was about to start. As Roar stepped over the tape, someone shouted: could he say anything about the cause of death? It wasn't part of his job to talk to the press. and he carried on towards the door without turning round.

Five or six forensic specialists were at work up in the apartment. He was handed a pair of plastic shoe covers and shown the narrow channel in the corridor he could use to walk along. There were people working in every room he passed.

He looked into the living room. Berger was seated in the same office chair as he had been in when Roar had arrived to interview him nine days earlier. The chair had been pulled out into the room and turned round. On the desktop computer a screen saver displayed movement inside a stellar cluster that ended in an explosion before the whole thing started all over again. In front of the computer, just out of Berger's reach, a tourniquet and a hypodermic syringe lay in a silver bowl.

Inside the syringe was the residue of a milky white liquid and something that looked like blood. Berger was wearing a kimono. It was open – the belt lay next to the chair – and he was naked beneath it, his body collapsed like a sack containing some doughy substance, his organ hanging over the lip of the chair. It occurred to Roar that maybe it would be Jennifer who had to bend over this corpse and open it.

In the kitchen, he found Viken talking to the man who had let Roar in when he was there before. His name was Odd Løkkemo, Berger's live-in partner and the owner of the flat. Roar nodded, indicating that he remembered him, but Løkkemo didn't notice him.

– Let me just check I've got all this, said Viken. – You had been to Hamar to visit your sister and you got here a few minutes before seven thirty.

He turned his head, interrupting himself: – Horvath, can you get someone from the patrol to go and locate Berger's car. It's a BMW X3. Metallic black. It's parked somewhere around the block here. He handed Roar a piece of paper with the registration number on. – Tell them to cordon off the area round the car. Forensics will fetch it as soon as one of them is free.

Roar went out into the corridor and left the apartment, following the channel shown to him. He hadn't spoken to Viken since the encounter in the garage that morning. He'd had to think quickly to explain where he'd got his information from. Something in the detective chief inspector's tone in the kitchen suggested to him that he had been exposed. – Alert, please, Roar, he muttered to himself. Level seven.

He passed the message about the car on to a constable who was standing by the outside door. Just then Jennifer appeared, stepping over the tape. She was wearing white overalls that looked a couple of sizes too big. He held the door for her.

– What have you got for me today? she said in a formal way and walked on by without waiting for an answer.

Once the street door had closed behind them Roar replied:
– TV celebrity dead in his own home.

– Anyone watching TV tonight knows that.

Roar added: – Found an hour and a half ago with a used syringe next to him. Looks like heroin.

He followed her up the stairs. She was wearing the same perfume as usual, but had obviously given herself a double dose. He had never liked it, he realised.

Up in the kitchen, Viken had finished with Løkkemo. Jennifer put her head in, briefly greeted the detective chief superintendent before turning to Roar. He was looking the other way.

– I've checked with Hamar, said Viken, who seemed rather abrupt. – It looks as if it checks out, he did spend the day there. We'll talk to him again tomorrow. I asked him to book in at a hotel for the night. He won't get much peace here.

– He won't get much out there either, Roar observed with a nod in the direction of the outer door. – The crocodiles are waiting to be fed.

Viken made a face. – Bon appétit.

Løkkemo's skinny, bent figure slipped by them out into the corridor; they heard the click of the front door.

– Accident or suicide, Roar offered provisionally.

– Or someone was here and lent him a helping hand, Viken interrupted. – According to Løkkemo, Berger had someone here all afternoon. He showed me a text that appears to confirm that. Received a couple of hours before he arrived back.

In the car on the way over, Roar had managed to call Nydalen. – Berger sent his producer an email half an hour before he was found, he offered. – He asked to have a statement read out on TV.

He fished out his notebook and read the quote: – *I have left*

and do not expect to return. Regret is futile, forgiveness meaning-
less. The end is the end. Afterwards – nothing.

– Is that all? Viken didn't seem as interested as Roar had
hoped.

– The same message was mailed to *Dagbladet*, *VG*, *Aftenposten*
and NRK. It might be read as a sort of confession. I mean, he
was planning to make this revelation live on TV.

– And you think this mail is what he was referring to? Viken
growled. – The man lived and breathed publicity, and then he
goes and kills himself and ends these *Taboo* shows with a tame
fart of an email read out by someone else? He shook his head.
– The people in charge of the programme tonight must have
known what it was going to contain.

– Not a lot of joy there, Roar answered. – A couple of guests
had been invited, but Berger was going to be running the show.
He liked to improvise, didn't want others deciding too much
in advance. But the producer maintains that the guy was going
to talk about his own death.

Viken stood up. – Anyone trying to persuade me that what
we have here is the suicide of a repentant killer is going to
have a pretty tough time of it, he said firmly. – You'd better
go and talk to the neighbours, here and in the houses on either
side. If Berger did have a visitor, one of them might have seen
someone arriving or leaving.

He was on his way out when he seemed to change his mind
and pulled the door closed. – One other thing, he said, looking
directly at Roar. – It's none of my business what you get up to
when you're not at work.

Roar glanced across at him, held his gaze.

– Who you shag is your own private business. But as long
as we're working as a team, we need to be able to trust each
other. I'm sure you understand.

Roar could have pretended not to have any idea what Viken
was talking about. But suddenly he felt an anger he hadn't felt

for a long time. And if he opened his mouth, there was a chance it would explode right in the detective chief inspector's face. He decided to say nothing.

– When you say something to me about who you've been talking to, where you got your information from and so on, it has to fit with the facts. If that isn't something I can take for granted, then it's no use.

Viken left, closing the door behind him and leaving Roar to wonder just what it was that would be no use.

The neighbours weren't much help. The elderly woman on the floor above had let her cat out and thought she might have heard a door slam. That would have been about 7.30, which fitted with when Odd Løkkemo said he came back home. Not surprisingly, most of those living in the same house on Løvenskiolds Street had plenty to say on the subject of Berger. Enough opinions there to enthuse the editor of the letters column in *Aftenposten*, but nothing of any value to the investigation.

By about 10.30, Roar was finished. He avoided going back to Berger's apartment again, didn't want to meet Jennifer, who would almost certainly still be working there. On his way to the car he came across a couple of forensic staff working on a black BMW that he knew had to be Berger's.

He crossed the road. – Started already?

– A preliminary look. We'll be taking it in for a thorough examination.

– Any titbits for a hungry investigator?

A slight grin. – What do you expect? A loaded gun? A bloodstained knife?

Roar grinned back, standing there in the rain, the memory of Viken's outburst still fresh in his memory.

The forensics guy opened the boot. – We did find something. Don't know how interesting it is.

He pulled away the felt mat covering the floor. There was a small object next to the seat back. Roar took out his torch and switched it on. Saw that it was a ring.

The forensics guy offered him a pair of plastic gloves. Once he'd got them on, Roar bent inside and picked it up, holding it in the light. It was a gold wedding ring, with an inscription.

– *30-5-51,* he read. – *Your Aage.*

33

JENNIFER PLÅTERUD HAD lost count of the number of autopsies she'd carried out over the years. For several reasons she was certain that the one she was on her way to now would be one she would remember. She had finished her external examination of the body the evening before and taken the necessary blood samples, collected hairs from the head and body, sperm residue, saliva, and matter beneath the fingernails. She had called Leif and agreed on where the opening incisions should be made. Her assistant was a trusty old workhorse who always did what was asked of him, and when Jennifer switched on the light in the autopsy room at 7.14, she noted that the body cavities had been opened. The precise cut of a bonesaw had removed the skull cap, leaving the brain exposed.

She spent the first few minutes making a plan of work. Then she fetched pus bowls, test tubes and extra probes. The trainee arrived at 8.10. She was a single mother who needed a job with no exhausting night shifts, and her interest in forensic science was hardly passionate. Fortunately she was good with her hands and had a talent for finer surgery, which went some way towards making up for her lack of enthusiasm. But she also had a tendency to chatter, and with a poorly concealed pleasure at once remarked how dreadful it was that the enormous yellowing body that filled the steel table in front of them belonged to the man she had seen so many times on television that autumn.

– Does this body *belong* to anyone now? Jennifer responded with a touch of contempt. She couldn't endure small talk while opening a body. The trainee took the hint and kept as quiet as she could.

Over the next few hours the two women worked in intense and deep concentration on the dissection of Elijah Berger's body. The brain was detached from the medulla oblongata and removed and the surface closely examined without anything of note being found. As expected after the external examination there were no signs of trauma, no abnormalities in the blood vessels. Jennifer decided that it should be preserved in formaldehyde for further tests.

At about ten, Korn popped in. He had just got back from a long journey that same morning, and even though he had the weekend off, he'd driven directly from the airport to the institute after he'd heard the morning news bulletin.

Jennifer briefed him: no obvious signs of damage to the inner organs, findings thus far consistent with the cause of death that had been her first assumption: an overdose of heroin.

– I'll be here for the rest of the day, Korn assured her. – The front desk is getting so many calls from the media, someone has to deal with them.

Jennifer was more than happy to have him around. Not that she had anything against talking to journalists. The problem was that she couldn't say anything about what she knew, or what she thought. She bent down once more over the swollen belly and followed the blood vessels leading into the liver – it was as distended and fatty as one would expect in someone who cultivated an image as a substance abuser – to the place on the underside of it where she would make her cut to detach it. Just at the point where she put the tip of the scalpel, she discovered a swelling. It was as large as a golf ball, with a lumpy surface.

She took a break at a couple of minutes past eleven. Tried to get in touch with Viken to let him have a preliminary report. He had switched to voicemail. At the same moment her own phone rang. The number was unrecognised, and she didn't have time to take the call but did so anyway.

– This is Ragnhild Bjerke . . . Mailin's mother.

Jennifer was surprised she thought it necessary to add that information just a few days after her hour-long visit to the office.

– Of course, she said.

– I've seen the news. Ragnhild Bjerke was silent for a moment. – Is it true what they're saying? That he might have killed her?

Jennifer breathed out heavily. – Well of course that's something the investigators will have to . . .

– Do *you* believe it was him?

Ragnhild Bjerke's voice was as toneless as before, but the fear lying just beneath it was even more noticeable over the phone.

– I wish I could give you an answer, but I have no grounds for making any assumptions about that. Jennifer felt the same helplessness as when they had spoken together last time. – I am sorry, she added.

– It was a relief to see you on Tuesday, Ragnhild Bjerke continued.

– You're welcome to come back, Jennifer said. – Any time, if you think it'll help.

– I've been thinking over what you asked me about.

Jennifer did a quick scan of their conversation. – Oh? she said, but with no idea what Ragnhild Bjerke was talking about.

– I lay awake thinking about it all that night. Of course I was worried at the time, when I had to spend nights away from home. Lasse drank. Later on I realised he must have been on drugs as well. He was more unstable than I gave you the impression of. He had these really huge mood swings. But he was so fond of the girls, I could never bring myself to believe that . . .

Jennifer looked at her watch. She still had a lot of work left to do, but she couldn't end the call.

– Mailin never mentioned anything. But then I never asked straight out. And when I think back, perhaps she did say something after all. Once she wanted me to put a safety lock on their doors. One like she'd seen in a film on TV. Why didn't I react to that and get her to tell me what she meant? And every time I had to spend the night away, she would behave in a funny way, despairing, but she never said anything, never cried, never protested. Thinking back on it now, I don't understand how I could have left them alone like that. Trusted Lasse like I did. He'd been having those nightmares for a long time.

She fell silent.

– I don't think you should blame yourself, said Jennifer. – You're suffering enough as it is.

– Did I tell you that he knew Berger?

Jennifer didn't know anything about that.

– They were hanging around with the same crowd at the time I met Lasse. Those were wild parties. But then that kind of thing is exciting when you're a teenager and you've met an artist with a boundless faith in his own talent.

After the call, Jennifer tried Viken again, but still no luck. She decided to call Roar. It would give him the chance to invite her round on her way home that evening.

– Stuck in traffic, he groaned, sounding annoyed. – First off I sleep in big-time, then I get caught up in an accident at the Teisen junction. Should have been at a team meeting five minutes ago.

– Then you'll probably get a ticking-off from Dad, she teased, though she had gathered that he was in no mood for jokes.

– It's wild, he complained. – Reminds me of the Orderud case.

– We've been getting it here too, she consoled him. – If we didn't have security guards, they would probably have broken into the autopsy room.

For an instant she imagined a horde of bellowing journalists pushing her up against the wall, and photographers sticking their cameras down into the belly of the half-autopsied corpse.

She sighed and suddenly felt a powerful need to talk about something else to him. Nevertheless she said: – Want to hear something from the autopsy? Berger had pancreatic cancer.

She heard an expulsion of breath at the other end. – Well that wasn't what killed him.

– Of course not. The first results from the blood tests confirm the theory of a heroin overdose.

– But you're saying he had a fatal condition?

– Exactly. I contacted Ullevål Hospital, spoke to the consultant who was treating him. The tumour was discovered more than six months ago. The hospital gave him three months, and in any event no more than six.

– Did Berger know this? Roar grunted.

– They were completely open about it with him. He'd accepted it, according to the doctor I spoke to.

– So he was waiting to die all the time he made those programmes? Wasn't he receiving treatment?

– Only painkillers. And he was also treating himself, as you know. He actually expressed a preference for heroin over morphine.

As she ended the call, there was a knock on the office door. A young woman she recognised as a technician at the trace analysis unit put her head round.

– Something here we'd like you to look at, she said, waving a document.

Jennifer took it, unfolded it and sat studying it. After a while she raised her head to the technician, who was still standing there, and peered thoughtfully at her. She had asked about something or other, but Jennifer didn't hear what it was. She took the receiver off the cradle, and the young woman, realising she wasn't going to get an answer, disappeared, closing the door behind her.

34

FIVE MINUTES HAD passed since Roar hung up when Jennifer called again. There was still no movement in the queue of traffic, a few hundred metres from Teisen.

– Wish there was some way I could help you, she chirruped.

– Then send a helicopter.

She laughed, sounded as if she were in a good mood.

– I just got a test result delivered to my desk.

He had tried to explain to her that she mustn't use him as a channel of information; it had already caused him enough trouble as things were. Before he could repeat his warning, she said: – The hairs we found on Mailin Bjerke turn out to be a quite rare form of mitochondrial DNA. It belongs to just one in ten of the population of Norway.

– Berger?

– He has the same variant.

Roar pressed his horn as a motorcyclist threading his way through the queue bumped into a side mirror with his elbow. When he'd finished swearing, he announced in an exasperated tone: – Jenny, you need to tell this to the head of the investigative team, not me.

– I've called Viken three times, he's in a meeting and not answering.

The meeting I should've been at, Roar groaned to himself. It occurred to him he ought to hang up and make sure he heard the rest of what Jennifer had to say from Viken. But he couldn't resist: – Of course that doesn't make it anything like definite that the hairs come from Berger.

Jennifer confirmed this. – And one other thing, she went on.

The traffic seemed to be freeing up a little. Roar slid forward thirty metres before again coming to a halt.

– Another thing? He could hear how irritable he sounded. – Sorry, Jenny, I'm a bit stressed out here.

– That's no wonder. You're for the big stick when you eventually get there, Mihaly Horvath.

He didn't like her using that name. – Let's hear it.

– Liss Bjerke called last night.

– Again?

– She still insists she'll only talk to me.

– Even though we got a female officer to carry out the interview, exactly as she wanted?

The inside lane began to creep forward and Roar swung over into it.

– Berger and her father were old drinking buddies, Jennifer told him.

– They were?

– Liss was at Berger's on Wednesday. – He tried to put his arms around her and then muttered something about knowing what had happened to Mailin.

– And what was it that he knew?

– She didn't find out. He was so stoned that she preferred to get out of the place.

Roar moved back into the outer lane. Jennifer had more news. This time about Mailin Bjerke's mother. Something about how this poor harassed woman was most bothered about the missing wedding ring. And that they should check whether the phone lines were down in parts of Blindern on the evening Mailin went missing.

– Jenny, we don't know that it was the evening of the eleventh she went missing, because we don't have any witnesses who saw her that day.

Suddenly he gave a start. – What was that about the ring?

At one of the team's first morning briefing sessions in December they had heard about a ring that had been removed from Mailin Bjerke's finger. One of the others was supposed to have checked it out, but Roar had heard no more about it.

– If Mailin Bjerke wore a wedding ring, he said once Jenny had finished explaining, – there was presumably an engraving on it?

Just asking the question felt like casting a line into a lake in which there were hardly any fish at all. When he got the bite, he jumped:

– *Your Aage*, said Jennifer, and then gave him the date of the wedding.

He was through the junction at Teisen and the end of the queue was in sight when his phone rang yet again. He picked it up and read the display before tapping the answer button: – I'm stuck in a traffic jam, I slept in and haven't eaten yet, I'm eighteen minutes late for an important meeting, I've got complications left, right and centre, so if this is bad news, please leave a message on my voicemail. Or preferably someone else's voicemail.

– Nice to talk to you too, Dan-Levi replied. – You who always wanted to be where it was happening. Anybody that's heard the news over the last twenty-four hours knows that you are in clover right now.

Finally the queue of cars started breaking up.

– I've given some thought to what you were asking me about at Klimt, his friend went on.

– Did I ask about something?

– About *if thy eye offend thee, und so weiter*. I've unearthed quite a bit of stuff about Berger. Baalzebub, for example. According to the Old Testament, it was the prophet Elijah who exposed that lord of the flies as an impotent god. Our Elijah, alias Berger, urges us in an interview to start worshipping these false gods again. Allow me to quote: *I am not godless, but I must worship a god whom I can leave behind here, one I don't run the risk of meeting on the other side.*

– Does this story have a point, Roar groaned. Finally he was able to accelerate past the damaged car that stood pressed up against the crash barrier, its front smashed in.

– Be patient, Roar Horvath, and thou shalt see. Berger was obsessed by the idea of being a prophet. Not to preach the coming of the Messiah, but to rid us all of any belief in salvation. That is, an anti-prophet, in contrast to the Elijah he was named after. I've been looking at some of the lyrics he wrote when he was lead singer with his group Baalzebub. Interested?

– Cough it up.

– In the song 'Revenge', Berger tells a story from the Bible in which Elijah, God's prophet, assembled the prophets of the false god Baal on Mount Carmel. Elijah challenged them to show that their god could make fire. When they couldn't do it, he got God to perform the miracle. So people saw the difference between the true and the fraudulent, and Elijah took Baal's prophets to a river and had them killed there, four hundred of them, in God's name. According to Berger's lyrics, Baal's prophets return from hell and tear out Elijah's eyes.

Roar gave a weary grunt, but Dan-Levi had no intention of stopping yet.

– In another song, 'The Hell of the New Age', he describes how he journeys to hell and releases billions of criminals, killers, child abusers and blasphemers and instead fills up the place with priests, lawyers, teachers and psychologists, all those who

spread lies about the world we live in. And that is just the lyric
we actually hear. Remember, the songs could be filled with
hidden messages, sung so fast that we only pick them up
subconsciously.

Roar thought this over. – Strong stuff, Dan-Levi, but I
doubt whether the Old Testament and a few punk rock lyrics
from the 1980s would stand up as evidence in the Oslo district
courthouse.

He let Dan-Levi carry on for a while on the subject of biblical
motives for murder. It seemed to lower his stress levels a bit.
His friend was a good storyteller, and in Roar's opinion he
would have gone a lot further in life as a preacher or a court-
room lawyer than as a journalist.

– Say hello to Sara, he said before he finally ended the call.
He felt a quick jolt of surprise afterwards; it was a long time
since he had sent a greeting to his teenage love.

The meeting room was full when Roar let himself in some
forty minutes late. He had to stand with his back against the
wall next to the door. In addition to Viken, the five other main
investigators were there, and several people from the forensics
department. Even section leader Sigge Helgarsson had decided
to attend. Roar consoled himself with the thought that he had
hardly ever been late for a meeting before and so could expect
to be cut some slack. As his father used to say: 'Once is nothing,
twice is a habit.'

Viken was holding forth on the subject of psychological
profiling. Apparently these theories stemmed from a period
he had spent working in England, and on several occasions he
had given Roar examples of how knowledge of a perpetrator's
psychology could prove decisive in solving complex murder
cases. Not many others in the department shared his interest,
Roar had realised. Viken was in frequent touch with some

retired psychologist in Manchester, supposedly a leading expert in the field, though neither his bosses nor his colleagues seemed particularly impressed by the fact.

– The psychological profile of Mailin Bjerke's killer is strikingly similar to that in the Ylva Richter case, the detective chief inspector was saying.

He stood up, picked up a felt marker pen and made some notes on the board. – It appears that Ylva Richter was killed by someone who already knew her. Someone of about her own age, with a roughly similar background. He probably didn't plan the murder but approached her in the first instance for some other reason, perhaps hoping for sexual contact. Things got out of control, possibly because he was rejected.

– What about the eyes?

– Punishment. Sadistic aggression. There may also be a symbolic element involved.

He glanced around the room, ignoring the new arrival. – The perpetrator will have undergone certain changes after the murder. If he was local, then he probably moved away, at least for a while. New surroundings, job, school. As for his background, it is not unlikely that he has himself been the victim of serious violence or sexual assault.

– And therein lies the motive? asked Sigge Helgarsson.

The section leader was just a few years older than Roar, a pale, thin Icelander who looked as if he suffered from chronic lack of sleep. According to Viken, he was having trouble combining the duties of leadership with family life.

The detective chief inspector nodded slowly a couple of times as though he had been waiting for the question and was glad someone had finally asked it. – The motive behind a murder such as this is always complex. Let's recapitulate: Mailin Bjerke hides away a printout concerning the Ylva Richter case. Immediately afterwards, she is murdered. Jim Harris might have seen something that had to do with the abduction or the murder. Berger goes public in *VG* and implies that he knows what happened to Mailin. Before he can reveal what this is, he too has gone to the great beyond. Naturally we can't rule out the possibility that these events are unconnected, but there is a much greater possibility that what we're dealing with here is a person who has killed four times, possibly even more than that.

Roar struggled to control an impulse to interrupt. He had long wanted to be in a position like this, be the one who came up with the decisive bit of information, the kind of thing that could turn a case around and lead to a breakthrough. *I've spoken to Jennifer Plåterud* . . . He could imagine Viken's reaction when he gave the source of his information, and for once it was enough to quell his ambition to be the smartest kid in the class. But he couldn't resist the temptation to at least say *something*.

– We do know that Mailin Bjerke had certain information about Berger, that she'd talked about revealing this live on *Taboo*.

Everyone turned to look at him. Viken said: – Before you arrived, we managed to discuss the possibility that Berger took his own life, or that he took an accidental overdose. We've also looked at the possibility that he felt threatened by something Mailin Bjerke knew about him. In other words, that a man who made a living out of having a bad reputation might suddenly get cold feet because one more corpse was added to the pile. But if you have something interesting to add to the point, Horvath, then we're dying to hear it.

If not, then please shut up, Roar concluded in his thoughts, regretting profoundly that he hadn't put a sock in it. He'd had less than four hours' sleep and knew that his critical faculties were suffering. But with the eyes of the whole gathering on him he decided to go ahead anyway and say something.

– Elijah Frelsøi, aka Berger, was named after the prophet Elijah, he began, and realised immediately that he had started down a ski jump that was way too steep. – The guy was completely obsessed by prophesies . . . and he apparently believed we should worship false gods, like Baalzebub for example, also known as the lord of the flies.

Roar felt like a ski-jumper who had made his effort too early and got caught in a crosswind and what's more had forgotten to fasten his boots on. Attempting to land feet first, he reeled off something about the prophet Elijah killing the four hundred false prophets, and how these four hundred, in Berger's version of the story, came back and tore out the prophet's eyes. He also made a quick reference to the gospel of Matthew, or was it Mark: *if thy eye offend thee, tear it out*. Dan-Levi's exegesis might possibly have had a speck of interest in it, but in Roar's version that speck was impossible to find. He stood there knowing where the ring found in Berger's car came from, about the DNA match and Berger's possible attempt to tell the dead woman's sister that he knew what had happened. Very shortly the whole gathering would know this too, but not from him. He held three aces, or at least two aces and a jack, and all he could show was a two of clubs, and no one, least of all himself, had any idea what they could do with it.

– Thank you, Horvath, Viken said, interrupting. – All that's missing here is that the descendants of Jesus Christ turn up in Oslo pursued by a six-foot-six albino contract killer. As it happens, not unlike Berger.

The laughter that ensued was the best thing Roar could have hoped for. The kind of laughter that dissolved the tension when things got a bit too fraught in a difficult case. And Viken seemed more than happy to have had just such an opportunity handed to him on a platter. Even Flatland's stony face cracked up. A couple of minutes later, when the meeting ended, the bony, angular technician gave Roar a nudge in the ribs on the way out.

– From now on I'm going to call you da Vinci, he announced, turning away, no doubt so that he could savour his grin alone.

35

ROAR PARKED JUST beyond the church. There was still another half-hour before the funeral was due to start, but already the crowds were packed outside the church door. Women in muted colours, men in shades of dark grey and black. He had used the occasion as an opportunity to buy himself a new suit. It was charcoal grey, with a thin white stripe. He walked down between the graves and stopped at the edge of the crowd of people.

A few minutes later, Viken showed up. He caught sight of Roar, standing there fiddling with his phone, looking as if he was texting.

– Well there you see, he said measuredly as Roar walked across to him, and it wasn't immediately clear what he meant. It was the first time the two of them had been alone together since the conversation in Berger's kitchen. It had occurred several times to Roar to visit the detective chief inspector in his office and explain why he had lied about his source that morning in the garage, but the mere thought of talking to Viken about Jennifer Plåterud was enough to put him off the idea. Anyway, the feeling that he had anything to confess was in itself ridiculous He pulled himself together, called for a full alert and reminded himself that he was thirty-four years old, not sixteen.

Just then she arrived. He made a face and looked the other

way, heard the sound of her stilettos on the asphalt. He ought to have known Jennifer would turn up. For some reason or other she'd got close to both Liss Bjerke and her mother. When he turned, she was standing there, a quick blink of the eyes that was possibly intended to express surprise at the sight of him wearing a suit. Roar was familiar with her views on the lack of style of Norwegian men. As for Viken, well, he was probably an exception; he would have been voted best-dressed detective chief inspector on the force if any such competition existed.

– Working lunch? Jennifer said quietly.

– For us, not for you, the detective chief inspector responded.

Roar looked at her with a gaze that revealed absolutely nothing. Had he known he would end up trapped between Jennifer and Viken, he would have found some excuse to give the funeral a miss. The evening before, she had called and hinted that she might be able to pop round and see him. He told her that Emily was staying with him, that he had to get up long before the sun to get his daughter off to kindergarten in the morning, and that he was on his way to bed already. Jennifer took the hint.

Roar had been to Lørenskog church a number of times before, most recently when his nephew was christened there a couple of years previously. The church was from the twelfth century, a simple lime-washed building with south-facing windows and glass that filtered the light, coloured it and dropped it at an angle down into the nave, which was now packed with mourners.

They managed to squeeze in on the second row from the back. Crowds of people stood at the rear by the door and out in the porch, some unable to get in at all. The nave was decorated with more floral tributes then Roar Horvath could ever remember having seen at a funeral before. The white coffin was covered, as were the altar and the whole of the aisle.

He felt the pressure from Jennifer's thigh. She was sitting between him and Viken. The detective chief inspector's gaze swept around the nave. Not for one moment had he thought the case was solved. Roar had expected that finding the ring would make him change direction, but when they went through the latest information on Friday afternoon, Viken had declined to be impressed. He pointed out that Berger received a steady stream of visitors, and that the TV celebrity had been almost continually stoned over the past few weeks. That someone might have planted Mailin Bjerke's ring in his car was not only conceivable, it was downright probable according to him. That this same person could have got hold of a tuft of hair from Berger's flat and placed it at the scene of the crime was equally likely.

– A touch far-fetched perhaps, section head Helgarsson had objected at the afternoon briefing.

– Far-fetched? Viken expostulated. – That someone might wish to divert suspicion, or for some reason be looking for a way to take revenge on the man? He wasn't exactly loved by one and all.

Helgarsson had attended the meeting with a view to finding out how many officers he could transfer from the Mailin case to other duties. At the press conference immediately prior to the meeting, he had been careless enough to express the view that they now had *evidence that undoubtedly implicated the late Berger with the murder of Mailin Bjerke*. This was of course self-evident; no one could seriously doubt that Berger had something or other to do with the crime. For the newspapers, however, what Helgarsson said was more or less the same as announcing that the case had been solved. And if that later turned out not to be so, then no desk editor was going to lose any sleep over it. Helgarsson's statement was more than enough reason for them to use the whole front page to announce that Berger was presumed to be the killer.

It didn't worry Viken, it would give them peace to work in for a while, but within the department he argued fiercely against the talk-show host being the man they had been looking for. He used the same arguments as he had on the Friday, before the latest information became available, and it might have been the case that he appeared more certain in his views than he really was as a way of preventing resources being taken off the case. Whichever it was, Helgarsson didn't gamble on opposing him, but he did make it clear that they had only a limited amount of time at their disposal before he would be looking at the question again.

Roar leaned a little to one side in order to study those sitting on the front pew. Some of them he was able to recognise from behind. The stepfather closest to the aisle. After Jennifer had called him when he was stuck in traffic near Teisen, Roar had contacted Oslo University. No one there knew anything about problems with the telephone lines on 11 December.

Next to the stepfather was a woman with a thick neck and stooped shoulders. Mailin's mother, Roar guessed. Next to her again he noted Liss's long reddish hair, and then Viljam Vogt-Nielsen, sitting motionless with head bowed. He appeared to have done all he could to assist in the inquiry without being overly enthusiastic about it. To Roar he seemed genuinely crushed by the loss of the woman he'd lived with, and he had alibis for most of the relevant times they were interested in. But it was obvious that Viken was by no means finished with him.

Judging by his speech, the priest had known Mailin for a good many years. He described her as the personification of goodness: warm, considerate of others, not least those who wandered the darkest roads. One of those wanderers had threatened her, thought Roar. Perhaps more than one. The work of making a list of her patients hadn't got far. Mailin's

supervisor had been able to help them sort out which of the
young men had ended up participating in her study. One had
died of an overdose; another had been admitted to the spinal
unit at Sunnaas Hospital after a traffic accident a year earlier.
The other five had got in touch with the police on the advice
of the supervisor, and it didn't look as though any of them
could be connected to the murder. But the social security office
had records for only a few of her remaining patients. Mailin's
computer, with all her journal notes, had never materialised,
and no backup had been located either. With the permission
of the chief county medical officer, they had eventually gained
access to the filing cabinet she shared with her colleagues in
Welhavens Street. It contained a few drafts for her doctoral
thesis, but no journals.

As it happened, Mailin's two psychologist colleagues were
sitting a couple of rows in front of Roar, over by the wall. He'd
noticed them on the way into the church, hand in hand. Initially
Torunn Gabrielsen had lied in order to give her partner an
alibi for the evening of 11 December. Facing accusations of an
extensive benefits fraud, Pål Øvreby had finally changed his
story, though the prostitute he claimed to have spent several
hours with had still not been traced. He had given them a first
name, a hotel room in Skipper Street and, for some unknown
reason, the girl's age. She was apparently at least seventeen.

The coffin was raised and carried down the central aisle. At
the front was Viljam, with Mailin's stepfather on the other side.
Behind them three young men, almost certainly relatives, held
the other handles. They had still not heard from the biological
father, despite making extensive efforts to get in touch with
him.

Roar recognised the last of the pallbearers as Mailin's supervisor, because Tormod Dahlstrøm was one of those media
psychiatrists who had an opinion on everything from marital
breakdowns to the catastrophe in Darfur. Behind the coffin

Liss and her mother walked side by side, Liss almost a head taller. She was looking at the floor in front of her. Then others gradually joined the procession. Elderly people, children, adults. Roar recognised a couple of faces from Lillestrøm and, well back in the escort, a very promising top-flight footballer. It struck him that Mailin Bjerke was the type who brought all kinds of people together, and though he had never met her, he could feel the grief in the church streaming through him.

Outside, the sun was making tiny fractures in the cloud cover. The coffin was placed in the back of the hearse. Several hundred people were gathered in silence around it. Closest was the stepfather, standing with his arms around Mailin's mother, Liss a metre away from them with Viljam. In a tree nearby, a bird that Roar identified as a great tit began to sing. It was pretending spring had already come.

As the hearse started to move away, the mother pulled herself free and ran after it. Roar heard her shout something that must have been her daughter's name. She caught up with the hearse and it stopped. She tried to open the rear door. The stepfather and a couple of others arrived and took her by the arm, but she held on tight to the handle. Her shouted cry had turned into a long-drawn-out wordless scream. It reminded Roar of Emily, waking up alone in the dark.

They stood there with their arms round Ragnhild Bjerke for a long time before she released her hold on the car, and it continued on its slow journey out through the gates and down the old main road.

I'M STILL SITTING *in the room you just left. The dust has settled back-down on the living-room floor, but outside the wind is rising. All the things I would have told you if you hadn't run out of here. But you had no reason to stay. Maybe you were afraid of me too, of what I might do to you. You owe me nothing. But I must finish writing this, not because I need to confess, but because this story needs to be told.*

After I stopped Jo that evening he was about to walk out into the waves, I took him away from the beach with me. His parents were drunk all the time and completely irresponsible. He had no one to care for him. I took him back to my apartment. He was freezing and I made him take a shower. Aren't you going to shower too? he asked. He was twelve years old, Liss, and I know he bore no responsibility for what happened.

Afterwards I got him to tell his story. There had been an incident with this girl, the one called Ylva, and something to do with a cat. He was mad about this Ylva, and furious because she'd gone off with another boy. I spoke to him about it for a long time. I promised to help him. Sooner or later, Ylva would be his, I had to swear it. When he left my apartment later that night, I felt certain that he wouldn't make another attempt to drown himself. And that became a turning point for me. That he should survive. Not just that particular holiday trip, but afterwards too. So I had to see him again, I knew it that morning when I saw him boarding the bus for the return flight to Oslo . . .

Naturally that wasn't the only reason. I wandered through this waste land, still felt parched. It was thirst that drove me to see him again. It was forbidden. But it saved me. A few drops of water are all I need, I said to myself, and Jo needed it as much. He was happy when we were together. But he never forgot what I had said to him about the girl he met in Crete. He was always reminding me of my promise, that I would show him how to get her, teach him what he needed to know. Ylva was the princess and Jo the prince who would steal her heart away. Even though he was about fourteen years old by now, the game went on. In the same way as the pact was a game. It's the kind of thing you can say to a child: rather die than tell someone else the secrets we share. We sealed this secret and holy pact with blood from small cuts made on the palms of our hands. And his childish enthusiasm made me feel once again a touch of forgotten joy; it was these drops that reminded me there is water out there somewhere in that waste land through which I wandered.

Did I fail to understand how damaged he was? Not even when he told me how he could turn into someone else, a person who stood in a dark cellar hitting out wildly with a sledgehammer. Did I not understand that these games with which we amused ourselves were, for him, something very much more than games? That they became the stories around which his life revolved, that they kept everything in motion? Did I not even understand years later, when I saw the reports of a young woman found dead outside Bergen? Did I not react when I saw her name?

PART IV

1

VILJAM GOT BACK at about two. Liss sat in the living room looking out the window, the notebook in her lap. She heard him tidying up in the fridge, squashing empty plastic bags in under the sink. Then his footsteps across the floor and down the stairs.

– I'm making a stew. Are you eating here today?

She shrugged. – The footballer has asked me out.

– Isn't it about time you started using his name? Viljam asked with a little smile, it caused her to look for the sort of feeling Mailin must have felt when she saw him smile like that. Something intense, joy or sadness.

He put a piece of paper on the table beside her. – Maybe he'll just give up if you carry on pretending you don't give a shit about him.

She picked up the paper, a notification that a parcel had arrived for her from Amsterdam. Don't go and collect it, she heard herself think. Since the funeral, she had almost managed to keep what had happened that night in Bloemstraat out of her thoughts. But it didn't take more than a package in the post for it all to come back to her. She had thrown away the letter from Zako's father, though she could still remember word for word some of the things written in it. *You've got to tidy things up, Liss.* That's what Mailin would have said. *Tidy up and move on.* Had Mailin been there, she could have told her where to move on to.

– Is it the post office up on Carl Berners Place? she asked.

– Correct. I can pick it up for you if you like. Have to get some exercise before I go off to work.

He stood leaning against the banisters, maybe expecting her to say something more.

– Viljam, I've been sleeping here almost every night since Christmas. It wasn't the plan.

He straightened up, looked at her. – It helps having you here. Would have been even more awful without you.

She almost gave in to an urge to get up and hug him. Get as close to Mailin as she could.

He popped back in again half an hour later and handed her an A4-size package. She left it lying on the kitchen worktop, drifted out on to the steps and lit a cigarette. Consumed it slowly as she watched the darkness settle over the rooftops. Wondered whether to throw the package away unopened. I'll never go back there again, she thought. Must send Rikke a message, tell her to stop forwarding mail. Ask her to give my clothes away to the Salvation Army. The DVDs and the armchair she can keep.

The package contained two letters from the school, a late payment reminder and a couple of other bills. And a reply from a modelling agency. Wim had promised to try to get something organised with them. For once he might not have been bluffing. She tore the letter to pieces without reading it and dug down to a package at the bottom of the pile. On the outside of it her name had been written with a blue magic marker. She recognised Mailin's small, sloping handwriting. The padded envelope was postmarked 10 December, the day before she went missing. Liss struggled to open it, her hand was shaking and she couldn't get her fingers under the flap, had to fetch a knife from the drawer.

There was a CD case inside. A small note was attached to it: *I said on the phone that everything was all right, but it isn't.*

Look after this CD carefully for me. Will explain later. Trust you, Liss. Big hug. Mailin.

By the time she got up from the kitchen table, it was dark. She hurried up the stairs and into Viljam and Mailin's room. She switched on the computer on the table by the window, stood there pinching her lower lip hard as she waited for it to boot up.

There were two documents on the CD: Liss opened the first, entitled *Patient Example 8: Jo and Jacket*. It ran to several pages and was in the form of an interview.

Therapist: *Last time you were talking about a holiday trip to Crete. You were twelve years old. Something happened there, something that made an impression on you.*

Patient: *It was that girl. Her and her family were in the apartment next door. She liked me. Wanted us to get together. She wanted me to do all sorts of things.*

T: *What things?*
(Long pause)

P: *For example that about the cat. Wanted me to torture a cat. It only had one eye, and I felt sorry for it, but Ylva wanted us to catch it and torture it.*

T: *She made you do things you didn't really want to do?*

P: *(nods) And when I said stop, we mustn't do this, she got the others to gang up on me.*

T: *What about the grown-ups, didn't they notice what was going on?*

P: *They were only interested in themselves. Apart from one.*

T: *The one you mentioned last time, the one you called Jacket?*

P: *He was the one who wanted me to call him Jacket. That's what they called him when he was my age. His father ran a clothes shop. Gents' outfitters was what he called it. He didn't want me to call him anything else. Later on, of course, I found out what his real name was. Maybe I already knew it that first time. I mean, I'd seen his picture in the papers.*

T: *He was well known?*

(Pause)

P: *Jacket read something to me. A poem in English. Which he translated. About a Phoenician lying drowned at the bottom of the sea. Handsome young man, strong and muscular. Now all that was left was a few bones. 'Death by Water' it was called. Later on we read it together.*

T: *You had many conversations with him?*

P: *He kept showing up. Seemed to be there when I needed him. Don't you believe me? Think I'm making this up?*

T: *I believe you.*

P: *I was very low. Had made up my mind to disappear. Walked out on to the beach in the dark. Took off my clothes and was on my way out to the water. Was going to swim far out until I couldn't swim any more . . . Then he appeared out of the shadows. Been sitting in a chair, looking out. It was as if he'd been waiting for me. 'Hey, Joe,' he said, like in that Jimi Hendrix record, that was what he used to say when he saw me. Without me having told anyone, he knew what I was going to do. He made me think about other things. Took me up to his room. We sat there talking most of the night.*

(Pause)

T: *Did anything else happen?*

P: *Such as?*

T: *Last time you hinted that something had happened between you and this man, something . . .*

P (angry): *It's not like you think. Jacket saved me. I wouldn't be sitting in this chair now if it hadn't been for him. You're trying to get me to say that he abused me.*

T: *I want you to say what happened in your own words, not mine.*
   (Pause)

P: *It was cold. He let me shower in his room. Afterwards he towelled me dry. Put me in the bed . . . Lay beside me. Kept me warm.*

T: *You felt that he was looking after you.*

P: *More than that. When I got back to Norway . . .*
   (Pause)

T: *You met him again in Norway.*

P: *He showed up one day, that same autumn. Outside school. We went for a long drive. Stopped and walked along the beach. He liked me. Everything I said and did was okay.*

T: *And after that?*

P: *I met him again. Went to his house, spent a whole weekend there. Several times, as it happens.*

T: *And your parents, did they know about this?*

P: *This was between Jacket and me. We made a pact. It was holy. What we did together was nobody's business but ours. He helped me in all sorts of ways.*

T: *What did he help you with?*
   (Pause)

P: *For example he showed me what to do with Ylva next time I met her.*

T: *Ylva? The girl you met in Crete?*

P: *I don't want to talk about that any more.*

Liss read the rest of what was presumably the transcript from a therapy session. It was so detailed it might have been recorded on tape and then transcribed. She opened the second document. It was called *En route* and consisted of commentaries on a whole series of conversations. She scrolled down through it. Beneath a heading *Patient Example 8* Mailin had added:

Therapy concluded after fourth session. Obviously cannot be used in the study. Delete interview or keep it anyway?

Her phone rang. Liss saw that it was Jomar. She'd promised to get in touch before six, she recalled, and now it was half past.

– I've booked a table, he said secretively, – and I'm not telling you where.

She was still deep in Mailin's world of thought. Reading through the document, she had heard her sister's voice asking the patient questions. Mailin cared about him and wanted to help, but she hadn't pressured him.

– We have to be there by eight.

– Okay, Liss answered, pulling herself together. – Do I have to wear an evening gown?

She heard him laugh at the other end. – Well they do have one star in the Michelin catalogue, but they're not that fussy about attire. He added: – As you know, I have a jacket you can borrow. It's so big you don't need to have anything on underneath it.

Liss ejected the CD from the computer, put it back in its case, and opened her notebook.

The name of the eighth patient is Jo.

She thought for a few moments before continuing:

Dahlstrøm said you ended up with seven patients in your study, but in the draft outline I found in the office you wrote that there were eight young men. Didn't Dahlstrøm say something about patients who had themselves become abusers were not to be part of it?

Mailin could have kept the CD in a safe place if she was afraid the information might end up in the wrong hands.

Why did you send it to me? What do you want me to do, Mailin?

Again she read the note taped to the CD case: *Trust you, Liss.*

You were due to meet Berger before Taboo *was broadcast. You heard that he had committed offences. Does that have anything to do with the CD? Is Berger the person known as Jacket?*

Did you talk to him about Father?

She had to show the CD to someone. Did Jennifer have a duty of confidentiality, or did she have to tell the police everything she found out? Liss visualised her handing the CD over to the detective chief inspector she had met that day at the police station . . . *Trust you, Liss.* Mailin trusted her. And why should the police be told about her patients now the investigation was over?

She put the CD back inside the envelope, took it up into the room she was borrowing, wedged it under the mattress. Made up her mind to talk to Dahlstrøm about it all. Visit him at his home again, maybe even do it tomorrow. He would know what she ought to do with this CD, if it was the right thing to hand it over to the police. And she had another reason for wanting to see him. Was already walking around discussing it with him in her thoughts.

She wandered back into Mailin's room, opened the wardrobe in search of something to wear. Found a lacy blouse she would never have chosen herself in a shop. Lace suited Mailin, but not her. But tonight this was exactly the blouse she wanted to wear. And underwear Mailin had maybe been saving for a special occasion, because the price tag hadn't even been removed. It was black and smooth and transparent. She put it on and looked at herself in the mirror beside the bed. The fasteners for the bra were at the front for easy opening, but of course it was too large, and she unfastened it and let it slip to the floor.

It was a long time since she had felt the thrill of seeing herself in a mirror wearing nothing but a string. Knowing that someone else would be seeing her standing like that in a few hours' time . . . Berger's voice: *I know what happened, Liss.* The words came tumbling through her and she had to sit down. The day after the funeral, Jennifer had rung. Liss asked her if it was true what the papers were saying, that Berger had killed Mailin. And not only her, but Jim Harris, who had seen something that day. Jennifer couldn't tell her what they had found, but Liss gathered that the police now had evidence.

She couldn't rid herself of the thought of that last visit to Berger, the smell of him as he squeezed himself against her. In the notebook she wrote: *I will find your grave. Every night I will go there and push the stone over and trample down everything that grows there.*

2

Liss was dressed, had put on her makeup and was on her way out when she received a text message. She froze halfway down the steps. The name of the sender was like an ill omen, and she didn't breathe normally again until she had read it through.

Judith van Ravens sent her condolences. She had been reading the papers and thinking a lot about Liss and how she must be feeling, she wrote, though Liss didn't find that particularly credible. A relief that the crime had now been solved, she went on. She was about to travel back to the Netherlands and wanted to get rid of the pictures she had kept. She was sending them now to Liss, so that she could decide whether to delete them or use them in some way. If necessary, Judith van Ravens was still prepared to make a statement to the police, she claimed, even though what she had to say had no bearing on the case.

Liss had her finger on the delete button, but changed her mind. Maybe these were the last pictures to be taken of Mailin. And even though they would perhaps remind her of the person who had asked to have them taken, she felt she had to keep them.

She opened the file, stood in front of the mirror in the hallway as the pictures were downloaded, slowly combing out her still-wet hair. It was the first time for several days, and each time the brush stuck, she had to tug so hard it sent shock waves across her scalp.

The figure of Mailin appeared on the screen as she exited

the main entrance on Welhavens Street. Liss scrolled down to one of the close-ups, taken at a tram stop. Her sister was standing gazing upwards somewhere over the rooftops, as if she was looking for the source of the light. Liss had seen these pictures once before, on Zako's mobile. She had a thought. Not so much a thought, more like a rush through the head. She scrolled back to the picture of Mailin in the gateway. On the next picture a figure appeared behind her; on the one after, he was standing beside her on the pavement. Liss's arm sank down. In the mirror she saw her own eyes, the pupils so huge she could have disappeared into them.

Sometime later, he rang again. She was still sitting on the floor of the hallway. The ringing sound woke her from her trance.

– Has something happened?

– Yes, she said.

– When are you coming? I've been waiting three quarters of an hour.

– I'm not coming.

She didn't feel the slightest trace of disappointment. He had said he had met Mailin only briefly. He had lied to her. People told lies almost all the time. Herself too, when necessary. Jomar Vindheim was no worse and no better than anyone else.

– You were at Mailin's office. Two weeks or so before she went missing.

He didn't answer.

– You've been there several times. You knew her.

If he'd spoken now, she could have ended the call and switched off her phone. But his silence provoked her. She could feel how the anger took possession of her, alarming because she didn't know where it came from. She started calling him things she had no reason to. Accused him of being wicked, calculating, and stupid enough to think he could fool her. The whole thing took off and she lost control completely.

Everything that had been bottled up, that she hadn't realised she had suppressed. Somewhere deep in her thoughts, remote from the rage that swept over her in ever larger waves, was a hope that he would hang up so that he wouldn't have to stand there and have all this shit pouring over him. But he didn't hang up.

It petered out, like cramp after a physical effort. Presently she was able to compartmentalise her anger, divide it up into portions small enough to be choked back. Finally she sat there, trembling on some kind of brink, the first feeling to come to her would overwhelm her totally, whether it was the anger flaring up again, or the grief that would take hold of her. Only this time it would never let go again.

– I'm sorry, said Jomar.

The first thing that came to her was laughter. Started in her stomach and throat, then took possession of her whole body. There was no mirth in it. Just another expression of what raged inside her. She saw herself lying there in the hallway, skirt in a twist around her waist, her crotch showing behind some flimsy material, the make-up that must be running across the vacant gaze.

– It was stupid of me, he said, trying again, having heard the result of his previous effort. – I can explain.

And that was a quote too. Maybe it wasn't possible to say anything that wasn't a quote, she thought as she lay there.

– You don't need to explain.

He ignored her. – I didn't mean to lie to you, but you never asked, and I couldn't bring myself to talk about it. Maybe it was embarrassing. And once I hadn't said anything the first time, it became impossible to talk about it later.

He sounded genuinely sorry. Enough for her to let him finish what he was saying.

– I had a few appointments with her a couple of years ago, when she gave those lectures at the sports academy. Things weren't too good for me. Some family stuff. I saw her about four or five times. She helped me, I . . .

– Get to the point, if there is one.

– When we finished that time, we agreed that I could get in touch later if I needed to. And a couple of months ago I found I needed someone to talk to. I went there twice. Was due to go a third time but then all this happened.

– I've got to hang up, she said.

– Are you coming here?

– No.

– Then we can go to my place instead, I'll fix us something to eat.

The suggestion prodded at her smouldering anger. – It won't work, she said as calmly as she could.

– What won't work?

– You and me.

He was silent. Then he said:

– I want you to know what happened to me after I met you. Can we meet to talk about that?

She got up from the floor. – I have to go away for a few days. Get out of town.

– Tonight? The cabin you mentioned?

She didn't answer.

– Can we meet when you get back?

She hung up.

3

HEAVY, WET SNOW had been falling all day. The motorway was slippery and Liss had to force herself to keep her speed down even though there was very little traffic. Driving slowly made her restless, and she clipped a headset on, connected her iPod and clicked forward to some electronica she used to like. After a couple of minutes the music got on her nerves and she tossed the player on to the passenger seat.

She had created an image of Jomar Vindheim. Fooled herself into thinking he was someone who spoke his mind and kept his word. Someone who was always straight with her. Who didn't lie. Who wasn't like her.

She turned off the E6. The road up into the forest was even more treacherous; she had to choose second gear on the hills, but she didn't mind driving slowly now. The calm of the cabin at Morr Water was already reaching out to her. Fields and copses slid by in the dark, snow-clad, still . . . The fact that Jomar had known Mailin and been her patient changed how she thought of him. She could have found out more about what he was hiding, got things under control. Or she could have said even worse things to him on the phone, made sure that he couldn't stand the thought of ever seeing her again. She could have told him she had killed someone.

The snowploughs had cleared the forest track from the parking place at Bysetermosan up to Vangen. But when she came to the turn-off for the summer path, she had to get out her snowshoes. The snow that had fallen during the day was drier and lighter than down in town, and beneath it was a layer of crusty snow. She began making her way into the forest. Stopped and listened. Mailin would have a grave where Liss could light candles and leave roses in a jar. But here was where she would come to feel close to her sister.

She had to use a snowshoe to brush the snow away from the outhouse door. Got out a spade, dug a path to the veranda and cleared the cabin door. It was good to feel the sweat running down her back. Good to do the things that had to be done whenever she was at the cabin. Get the stove and the open fire going, tread a path down to the water, drop the bucket into the channel in the ice below the rock. Once she'd returned with the water, she undressed and ran outside again naked, rubbed herself with snow, lay down on the ice-cold blanket, rolled around a few times, lay there on her back until she felt numb and the pain of the cold was beginning to spread from her legs and up into her back.

Afterwards she rubbed herself hard with a terry towel until patches of red appeared on her pale skin, spent a few minutes jumping and dancing around on the living-room floor before sinking down into the chair in front of the open fire. Sat there for some time, looking into the flames.

You were the one who taught me that, Mailin, how to make warmth inside your own body. Not wait for someone else to come along and make it for you.

There were a few blank pages still left in the notebook.

Everything I've written here is addressed to you.

Again she had the strange thought that somehow or other her sister was able to read it. As though the little notebook were the threshold to the place where Mailin was. In minute detail she began to describe the night in Bloemstraat. Everything that had happened. Everything she'd done.

When she was finished, she fetched the bottle of red wine she'd shoved into her rucksack and took two wine glasses from the cupboard. It was only after she'd looked through the kitchen drawer that she realised the corkscrew was missing. She'd noticed it was gone that evening before Christmas, but had forgotten to bring along a new one.

It wasn't like Mailin to remove things from the cabin. At the foot of the second-last page of the book she wrote:

Remember, corkscrew is missing.

She carried the paraffin lamp over to the bookshelf to find a book. Choose one she'd already read, one she could fall asleep to before reaching page five. The row of books bulged slightly in the middle, Mailin was usually careful to adjust the spines so that they stood in a straight line. She had a way of going round the cabin and making minor adjustments to things. Getting Liss to tidy away things she'd just thrown aside, arranging the little glass figurines on the mantelpiece in a symmetrical pattern. Mailin liked to create order but didn't let herself get irritated by other people's chaos.

Liss pulled out a crime novel she had yawned her way through at some point in the past, tossed it on to the sofa and put both hands against the spines of the books to push them into line. They didn't move. Determined to carry out this small correction in Mailin's own spirit, she removed the six or seven books that were sticking out. Something lay at the back, blocking them. One of the books had obviously fallen down. It was unbound and not very thick. Liss took hold of the cover and fished it out, held it up in the light of the paraffin lamp from the table.

Sándor Ferenczi, she read. *The Clinical Diary of Sándor Ferenczi.*

4

ROAR HORVATH PUT his foot down in the overtaking lane. Between the lanes, a ridge left by a snowplough threatened to pull the car sideways. He dropped his speed and regained control of the wheel.

The news was over and he switched to the CD player. There was an old Pink Floyd album on the desk and he turned it up full volume. It was Friday evening and he had been at the office since early that morning. The last few nights he had slept very badly. At work he had been going through every single interview with witnesses in the Mailin case for a second time. He felt like a marathon runner who crosses the line and is then ordered to run it all over again. He had counted on following up the work done in Bergen and getting in touch with Mailin Bjerke's closest relatives again. That he had instead been put to the task of reading documents seemed like a demotion rather than anything else. He was tempted to ask Viken straight out if there was any connection with the little deception he'd been guilty of that morning in the garage.

His mobile rang. Roar turned off the music and fumbled for his hands-free, then remembered he'd left it lying on his office desk. He clamped the phone against his ear with his shoulder.

– Hello, this is Anne Sofie.

He quickly scanned the list of women he was on first-name terms with but found no Anne Sofie. Ylva Richter's mother wasn't on that list, but he was quickly able to identify who he was talking to from the polished Bergen accent.

He said that it was nice to hear her voice again, something it hadn't seemed natural to say to her husband when he had spoken to him earlier in the week. He had been checking to see if there was a possible connection with Berger, asked if their daughter had ever spoken of the celebrity or been especially interested in his music.

– Thank you, likewise, Anne Sofie Richter replied, and the dolly-sweet voice conjured up an image of her face in his mind. As though covered in wax; that was the impression he'd had when he visited them.

– My husband and I have talked a lot about what you called him about last Monday. We can't remember that Ylva was ever interested in that television person.

Roar adjusted the mobile, which had slipped out of position.
– Did she own any of his records?

– Not that we know of.

Anne Sofie Richter was silent for a few moments before continuing. – I did send you that list of the activities Ylva was involved in at school and in her spare time.

– We're very grateful for that, Roar assured her. – We've certainly found it useful, in some ways.

– But did you find anything there?

He was negotiating a narrow bend in the Store Ringvei; the road was slippery and a Nor-Cargo trailer laid itself up tight against his side. Had he been with the traffic police, he would probably have stopped the guy and given him a hefty fine. On the other hand, he wasn't driving strictly by the book himself either, not with his back hunched and holding a mobile phone between his ear and his shoulder.

– I'm afraid I can't comment on that at the moment.

– There's one other thing I remembered.

He was entering the tunnel at Bryn and didn't hear so well.

– I don't think it's of any importance . . . he made out before he had to drop his speed to get daylight between himself and the trailer.

– Importance?

She carried on talking. The sound from the Nor-Cargo monster echoing along the tunnel walls was like a brass band from hell.

– Everything is important, he yelled to Anne Sofie Richter. – Just one moment. He dropped the phone and took the turn-off directly after the tunnel, pulled into a layby and switched on his warning light.

– Everything is important, he repeated. – I'd like to hear what you have to say.

It took a couple of seconds for her voice to return at the other end.

– Something happened once. It was so long ago I didn't write it down on the list I sent you.

– How long ago?

– In the late summer of 1996. Or early autumn. We were on a week's holiday in Greece.

Roar grabbed a pen and an envelope from the glove compartment.

– How do you spell that? So that's *Ma-kri-gialos*. On Crete. What happened?

– One evening when we went back to our apartment after a meal out, we found a kitten. Someone had hung it on a rope that was tied to our door. One side of its head was completely crushed. And then the eyes . . . It was unpleasant, the boys were small. We didn't sleep very well after that. My husband reported it, but you know, the police down there weren't exactly . . .

Dead cat, Roar had noted. Hanging from the door.

– Of course I realise this can't have any connection with what happened later, but you did mention holidays and so on and unpleasant experiences.

– What did you say about the eyes?

– It was my husband who saw it, I couldn't bear to look at the poor creature. But apparently both eyes were cut to pieces.

Roar started tapping his pen against the envelope. – Now tell me everything you remember about that episode. Absolutely everything.

– I've just told you all there was.

– What about Ylva?

– She was furious. We had a cat of our own in those days. And then she said something . . .

When Anne Sofie Richter didn't say any more, Roar urged her to continue: – Then she said something?

– It was something about one of the boys there. Someone her own age. She thought he was odd and did all she could to avoid him. I don't know what it was about, but as soon as she heard about that cat, Ylva said she knew who had done it. We asked her about it, and that's when she said this about that boy. But it was just something she believed, she hadn't seen or heard anything. He was in the apartment next to ours. A terrible family that got drunk and made scenes and left the kids to fend for themselves. I've never seen anything worse, not anywhere . . .

– Can you remember the boy's name?

– It was something short, like Roy or Bo.

– And the family, can you remember anything more about them?

She couldn't, and he assured her that it wasn't surprising after more than twelve years.

– But I spoke to my husband and he thought he might remember. You know how it is, when people stand out from the crowd in that sort of way, some kind of nasty association attaches itself to the family name. We tend to remember them better than other people.

There was no more room on the envelope. Roar found a parking ticket in the door pocket and scribbled down suggestions for the surname Ylva Richter's father had offered. For almost half a minute after the end of the conversation he sat staring at one of them in particular. Then he picked up his mobile again and began a directory search.

5

A WIND HAD got up. Liss had been sitting for a long time staring into the fire. An hour, maybe more. The fire had gone out, but it was so warm in the little room that she didn't feel the need to put on more logs.

The embers changed all the time, a brilliant orange that gave way to black, then glowed up again. A picture appeared, she didn't know if it was a memory. They're sitting like this in front of the fire, Mailin and her, one on each knee. *There's a little man standing between the logs.* It was her father's voice. A gnome? *Yes, a tiny little humpy-backed one. He keeps puffing and blowing on the embers, because once they go out, he'll be gone for ever.*

She picked up the wine bottle again, tried to force the cork down into the neck. Gave up and went out into the kitchen, climbed up on a chair and found a couple of miniatures at the back of the top cupboard. One was vodka, the other egg liqueur, half full. She had never liked vodka but transferred the tiny amount into a glass. The taste was nauseating, but it felt good as it etched its way down her throat and into her stomach. Afterwards she dug her bag of food out of the rucksack. A packet of crispbread, an apple; she couldn't stand anything on the crispbread. Leaned against the kitchen surface and ate, washed it down with the rest of the vodka. Listened to the sound of the rye as it broke and was crushed between her teeth, and the wind that periodically tried to make its way down the chimney.

Suddenly she began to doubt what it was she had actually found in the book hidden at the back of the shelf. She fetched it and settled down once again in the chair in front of the fireplace. On the back cover were a few lines about the author. Sándor Ferenczi had struggled against professional hypocrisy. Then something about him being sensitive and self-critical. Liss flipped through it for the fourth or fifth time. No underlining or notes in the margin. It looked almost as if the book was a recent purchase. Mailin had brought it with her to read here.

She came to that page somewhere near the middle in which a few letters had been written in the space below the print. She lifted the lamp and again studied the sloped handwriting: *Ylva and Jo*. The letters were smudged, probably written with charcoal from the fire. Suddenly she had an image of her sister's dead body in the Chapel of Rest at the Riks Hospital. The pale, waxy skin, the wrinkled hands, the thumb and index finger of the right hand blackened with soot. That was what had happened: Mailin had been sitting in this same seat that day, just before she was murdered. She'd picked up a piece of charcoal from the fireplace . . . Liss turned the page. There was the rest of what her sister had scrawled: *Ylva Richter and Johannes Viljam Vogt-N.*

With a sharp blow she smashed the neck of the wine bottle against the rim of the sink. Sacrificing one of her T-shirts, she stretched it over the jug and filtered the wine through it, the tiny splinters of glass catching in the burgundy stain. She drained the first glass in one. Took the second back to the fireside with her, picked up the notebook.

Is Viljam's full name Johannes Viljam?
Ylva and Jo.

She recalled that the name Ylva was mentioned in the interview with the eighth patient.

Is Viljam the person you call Jo in the CD?

Then Viljam must have been your patient. Why has he never said anything about that?

Ylva Richter.

The name seemed familiar to her, but she couldn't think why. Was it something she'd read? Or someone Mailin knew?

Why did you write her name in the book you brought with you? Why did you have to write it in charcoal and hide it on the bookcase? Why was the name of the author of this book the last thing you said as you lay there in that factory? Why did you have to leave in such a rush you didn't have time to clear out the fireplace? Why did you go to meet Berger, Mailin? You must have known it was dangerous. You're not like me, you're always careful about where you go.

She sat for a while, staring at the gnome fighting to stay alive in the embers.

Was Viljam your patient before you became a couple?

Searches for help. Is met with passion. But you were going to marry him.

Ask Viljam about that.

Was he the eighth patient? Was that what you were going to reveal on Taboo *that evening? Jo and Jacket?*

If Jacket was Berger and Viljam was Jo . . . Viljam looks for tenderness and protection. Exploited by a bastard. Damn that Berger. He's with the Devil now.

Abruptly she stood up, so angry she couldn't sit still any more.

Who is Ylva Richter? Is she someone Viljam's been seeing?

She took out her mobile. For once she wished she could pick up a signal there. Not to call the police, that could wait. This was something she had to ask Viljam about. Get some answers about what was going on here. Mailin had helped Viljam. Because she couldn't have just used him. Mailin was goodness itself. Liss drained the rest of the wine glass. The thought of that goodness awoke something in her too, something similar. She made up her mind: she would speak to Viljam at once, this evening. Find out if this was true about him and Mailin. Walk up Kringlesåsen and pick up a signal there and call him. Stand up there in the dark and tell him what she'd found out. That she knew how much pain he had suffered.

She shrugged on a jacket and pulled down the snowshoes from the shelf above the door. She had killed a human being. But she felt Mailin's goodness in her. Stronger than all the bad things Liss had done.

6

Roar put the bowl with the remainder of yesterday's tomato soup into the microwave. He found two hard-boiled eggs in the fridge. He peeled one and ate it. For a second he thought of ringing Viken immediately but dropped the idea for the time being. If the phone call he was waiting for gave him the answer he expected, then he would have an ace up his sleeve, and one that he had come by on his own. The embarrassment of the briefing the previous week was still fresh in his mind. This time he would make sure he played his cards right.

The microwave pinged; he took out the bowl, cut up the other egg and dropped the pieces into it. For some reason, the sight of the white boats bobbing in the grainy orange soup made him think of something that had been bothering him for several weeks now. He had promised his mother he would call in and drive her out to the cemetery, help her get rid of the burnt-out remains of the Christmas Eve memorial candles and generally tidy up around the grave. She was more than fit enough to do it by herself, but it was obviously important to her that they do the job together.

His phone rang. He swallowed down a half-chewed slice of egg before answering.

– This is Arne Vogt-Nielsen here. I've checked that thing you asked me to.

– Great, said Roar encouragingly as he picked up his pen and notebook and pushed the piping-hot soup to one side.

– You asked about a holiday in Greece. Autumn of 1996.
That's correct, I did take the family to Crete that year. Usually
we went to Cyprus, a couple of times Turkey. The kids enjoyed
it best there, in Alanya, and a hell of a good hotel.

Roar wasn't interested in Turkish seaside resorts. – Whereabouts in Crete?

– Place called Makrigialos. Not too bad, but a hell of a
drive in from the airport, you know how it is, fifty degrees
inside the bus, all those winding roads, with the kids all
whining and the mums all grumpy from being up since the
crack of dawn . . .

He made a smacking noise with his lips at the other end.

– And this was in September 1996?

– Check, departure on the seventh, back on the fourteenth
according to the receipt from my following year's tax return.

Roar resisted the temptation to ask why this trip had shown
up on the man's income tax form.

– Can you remember if anything special happened on that
holiday? He was in a hurry now and added: – Something
about a cat?

– Christ, yeah. You don't forget something like that. We
head off a few thousand kilometres for a nice family week
away from home and end up with the world's most difficult
neighbours.

In vain Roar tried to interrupt the tirade that followed
on the subject of people from Bergen who thought they owned
the place wherever they happened to be.

– The bloke being a lawyer didn't make matters any better.
I had to take him down three or four pegs. He came bursting
in on us demanding to know if it was Jo who had killed that
cat and hung it on their door. I kicked him out. The next day
I asked Jo about it, and he said he thought it was that idiot's
daughter who had done it and was trying to pin the blame
on him.

Again he made a sound with his lips as though he were sucking on a boiled sweet.

– But now tell me what it is you're really after. Because obviously you're not ringing about a cat that got killed in Crete. You're with the Oslo police, isn't that what you said? Or did I get that wrong? Did you say you were with the RSPCA?

Suddenly Roar wondered whether he had misunderstood. – You said Jo? We are talking about your son Viljam, aren't we?

– That's right. We've always called him Jo. He's named Johannes Viljam after me. My name's Arne Johannes.

– But now he calls himself Viljam.

A few strangled cries came from the other end, which Roar did not immediately identify as the sound of Vogt-Nielsen laughing.

– That lad's always been a one-off. When he became a teenager he decided he was going to call me Arne. He got this idea that I wasn't his real father. Some kids play the most fantastic games. Of course, he didn't really mean it. But when he left home after finishing secondary school, he insisted on being addressed as Viljam. Claimed he wouldn't even answer people who still called him Jo.

– So he left home early?

– That's right. Autumn 2003. After he left school, he messed about round here for quite a while before he settled down. I mean, he couldn't spend the rest of his life lying in bed, so I took him in hand, got him moving, made sure he got his driving licence and helped him get himself a car. Then I sent him off to look for places to study. He's always been a bright lad, and his school-leaving certificate was bloody brilliant, give him his due.

– He travelled about, you say . . . Was he in Bergen?

– He might have been. He wanted to study somewhere far away from home. It was best for everybody, it seemed to us.

Finally he ended up in Oslo studying law. But now you tell me what this is all about, otherwise this conversation is over.

Viken got into the passenger seat. – The emergency response unit will be ready in five minutes. We'll follow them.

– Armed? Roar asked.

– We're talking about someone who's killed three or possibly four times.

Roar drove out through the gates of Oslo police station and drew up alongside the pavement.

– You doubted the partner's explanation from the very start, he said, not averse to confirming that Viken had got it right all along.

The detective chief inspector accepted the veiled praise without visible response. – Can we be sure the father won't call him? he wanted to know.

– I repeated it to him three times, Roar replied as he turned off the engine. – I'm certain he understood. What's more, he hasn't had any contact with Viljam for a long time.

– In other words, not exactly the best of father–son relationships.

– Probably not. It seems that for a number of years before leaving home, Viljam denied that Vogt-Nielsen was his real father.

Viken glanced across at Roar. – When did he move out?

– Just before Christmas 2003. The family lives in Tønsberg. Viljam was going to study in Oslo.

– Ergo he left directly after Ylva Richter was murdered.

Sleet began falling again. The wind wafted the wet flakes against the windscreen and Roar turned on the wipers. Viken repeated what the psychological profiling had said about Ylva Richter's killer: someone her own age from a similar sort of background, a person who made changes in his life after committing the act.

– I questioned the father closely about the time when Ylva was murdered, said Roar. – He remembered that Viljam got his driving licence that autumn. He was given money towards a car and spent a lot of time driving round in it.

– To among other places Bergen, Viken observed with a glance at his watch. – We've got five men with us. This is not some holed-up shooter we're going to arrest. But if the man gets cornered, then anything might happen.

– He might have a weapon.

– I'm guessing he doesn't. But that's enough guessing.

As two cars came flying through the gates, Roar started his engine. Passing through Grønland he said: – You're right about making changes. Not only did he leave home and want nothing more to do with his family, he changed his name too.

Viken turned towards him. – But it is still Vogt-Nielsen?

Roar explained how Viljam had refused to answer to the name of Jo after he moved away.

– Exactly, Viken exclaimed, as if this was what he had been expecting to hear. – He changes his name too immediately after killing Ylva. Anything else on the family?

Roar repeated what Anne Sofie Richter had told him about them.

– The father seemed very keen to let me know that Viljam has two younger siblings who still live at home and who are doing very well indeed. It sounds as though the mother is in a nursing home.

– Really? She can't be all that old.

– I didn't have time to get any more detail.

– Of course not. You've used the time well, Roar. A solid day's work. Top marks.

He grinned at his own irony, but Roar noticed how pleased he was. He wrenched the wheel down hard as a cyclist came skidding down off the slippery pavement.

– Bloody hell, he shouted. – If people really want to kill themselves, then leave me out of it.

– Berger's part in all this is very unclear, said Viken, sounding as though he hadn't even noticed the near-accident.

Roar accelerated and went through a red light to keep pace with the two squad cars.

– Maybe his own version is the correct one, he suggested. – Could be Mailin wanted to talk to him about some of the practical details of the programme.

– And the connection between Berger and Viljam Vogt-Nielsen?

– Viljam wanted it to look as though Berger was the killer. He goes to see him, takes away a few strands of hair and plants the wedding ring in his car.

– To do all that, he must have known him pretty well.

– Either that or he began the relationship with Berger after he'd killed Mailin.

Roar thought his own arguments were convincing. – Once Berger realised what was going on, he didn't have enough to go to the police with, so he decided to reveal the killer's name live on air.

Viken looked to be weighing this up. – If there's anything else there, we're going to need Viljam Vogt-Nielsen's help in digging it up.

The two squad cars parked one on each side of the house. Roar pulled up on to the kerb a little further up the narrow road. They could just make out the shapes of officers splitting up as they surrounded the building. The clock on the dashboard said 11.16. A minute later, Roar heard Viken receive a message on his headset.

– They're going in, he said in a low voice.

Two of the uniformed figures were on their way up the steps. They disappeared into the house.

– The door was unlocked, Viken observed.

That means arrest, thought Roar. It wasn't too unlikely that the inspector would want him present at the interrogation. Viken was known to be particularly good at getting confessions.

At 11.32, the door was thrown open wide.

– We're on, said Viken as he stepped out into the driving snow.

– Have they got him? Roar asked when he caught up with him.

Viken put a hand over his headset, listened. – No one home. Call the father again. Get him to tell you whether he warned his son after all.

As Roar entered the hallway, Viken was coming down the stairs. – The lights are on all over the house. The computer, and the coffee machine. And as you heard, the door was unlocked. What did the father say?

– He swore he hasn't been in touch with Viljam.

Viken carried on down into the living room, checked the French windows. – Locked from the inside. If we can believe the father, it looks as though Vogt-Nielsen has just popped out on an errand. There's not much chance anyone else could have warned him.

He stood there looking out at the patch of garden.

– We'll check that tool shed straight away.

– He's hardly likely to have hidden anything in there, Roar objected. – The guy's not stupid.

Viken dropped his head very slightly. – I want to see what tools we *don't* find in the shed. If there's anything the owner of the house can tell us is missing. A sledgehammer, for example.

7

THE LAST OF the embers in the fireplace had gone out. The little gnome is gone forever, thought Liss. Maybe she said it as well, quietly, to herself. She checked the empty jug she had filtered the red wine into. The vodka too was gone. Even the half-bottle of egg liqueur. She needed more to drink. Needed to disappear into something, because she was still not tired . . . Could see nothing through the window of the room, but the wind had gained in strength – she could hear it in the chimney, it had started howling down to her – and she could feel that it was still snowing. Again the thought that it wouldn't stop snowing, that the whole cabin would get snowed up. That she wouldn't be found until they dug a way in. Or come spring, when it all melted. She would still be sitting in this same chair in front of the fire, in the same position. Her heart frozen, all the currents flowing through her body stilled, her thoughts stopped in mid-motion.

She picked up the notebook again. *Viljam needed you, Mailin. You wanted to make everything right again. That's why you were with him. You crossed a boundary. You shouldn't have done that. But you did it to help him.*

Viljam had seemed relieved when she rang.

He's glad that I know what happened with Jacket. Viljam had you, Mailin. Johannes Viljam. Now he has no one. But how can I ever help anyone? I've killed a person. That's who I am.

Suddenly she got up, took down the album of old photographs, turned to the portrait of her grandmother. Elisabeth, that was her name. The eyes in the black-and-white picture were more intense than her own. She might have been anything between forty and fifty when it was taken. Had travelled twice as far as Liss into this impossible life.

Elisabeth got stuck. Tried to pull herself free. Never managed it. Elisabeth became Liss. Someone has to carry the darkness on, Mailin. You've always shed light all around you. I spread darkness. Everything I touch freezes.

She had to pee, tottered out unsteadily in her boots, pulled a jacket over her shoulders. Didn't bother taking the torch. Could find her way around here blindfolded. The wind buffeted her as she rounded the corner. Tiny grains of ice that jabbed at her eyes and forced her to keep them closed. They melted against her skin and ran down her cheeks. She heard something, listened out. As though the wind had gone off with her steps and now threw the sounds of them back at her. She carried on, high-stepping through the deep snow, unhooked the latch on the outside toilet, fumbled her way to the closet, lifted the lid and sat down on the cold surface. The wet blast raced through the toilet, penetrating deep inside her.

Afterwards she stood still again for a long time, listening. The wind and that sound that wasn't wind, approaching from somewhere close by. Not my footsteps in the snow, she thought. These footsteps are coming from behind. Two arms locked around her. It was as though she had been expecting it. She jerked in an attempt to free herself. One of the arms let go. At that instant, pain flaring down her throat. Like being bitten by a snake. It burnt, and the warmth spread out into her shoulder and chest.

– Stand still, he whispered in her ear. – Stand still and it'll be all right.

She lay slumped on her back on the sofa. Imagined how the snow had forced its way into the room. She wasn't cold. The blanket of snow wrapped around her was warm.

He was standing in the centre of the room, his back turned; must have put more wood on the fire because it was burning again. Without moving her leaden head, she followed his outline with her eyes. From the waist and up to the hair that hung dark and wet on the shoulders.

She managed to open her mouth, tried to find out what she had to do for her lips to shape sounds, things that could turn into words.

– What . . . have you done to me.

The echo of her words came rolling back at her. He didn't turn round.

– A shot. It'll do you good. You'll feel good.

Viljam, she tried to say, *Johannes Viljam, Jo. We'll have a good time. Together.*

She opened her eyes as far as she was able. Cold now. Dark in the room. Just a few glowing embers left in the fireplace. Couldn't see him but knew he was there. Heard the sound of his breathing.

Her hands held fast in some way. Fastened together. She was lying in a corner of the sofa, naked. Her mouth felt swollen.

– Viljam.

She heard a noise from over by the table. That was where he was sitting. Still wearing his outdoor jacket, she could make out, the hood pulled down over the head now.

– I'm cold, she managed to say.

– It's better to be cold. Things don't hurt as much then. The cold is an anaesthetic.

The tone of his voice was different. Not different, but something that had been faintly present in it before was stronger now.

– Why did you give me that shot?

He turned towards her. – I like being together best this way. Calm and easy.

He tossed something on to the mantelpiece.

– I see from your call list that you haven't rung anybody but me this evening. We've got plenty of time.

– Can you take off these handcuffs?

He made a clucking sound with his tongue. – This is the way it is now, he said, and sounded saddened. – You'd best get used to it. The way Mailin had to.

She closed her eyes. Still she managed to keep the thought at bay. The thought that it wasn't Berger who had killed Mailin.

– You called me that morning. After she went missing. I could hear how upset you were.

He stood up, crossed the floor and stopped in front of her. She could just make out the lines of his jaw, the shadowed eye sockets.

– She shouldn't have gone prying into that business with Ylva.

Liss twisted round. – Ylva? Is that someone you're having a relationship with?

He shrugged his shoulders. – Used to have.

– Did Mailin find out?

– Yes, she did.

He stepped towards the fireplace, turned an almost unburnt log over and made it flare up again.

– There was an article about an unsolved murder in one of the magazines she subscribed to. It was only when she read about it that she began to see the connection. Before she was due to come out here that day, she sat searching on the net. Logged off when she heard me come home. Deleted the history. But I was able to restore it while she was in the bathroom. A load of old stuff about Ylva. She was reading it behind my back.

Liss struggled to compose her slowly drifting thoughts, couldn't relate them to what Viljam was standing there and saying.

– It had been more than two years since I'd said anything about Ylva. That was during the first sessions in the office in Welhavens Street. And she still had her notes from those days on the CD, even though she'd promised to delete them. Delete everything that was said about Jacket.

Finally Liss got it: the printout she had found inside the sofa cover. The girl in Bergen was Ylva. There was something about her in the newspapers years ago. She'd been murdered.

– You were at work the day Mailin went missing, she whispered, because it still seemed possible that these thoughts did not belong together. – And then at home with my mother and Tage.

He came closer again.

– That's what you think. What everyone thinks. But when she was supposed to be coming out here, the day before, she went to the post office to deposit some money. I followed. Waited for her in the car. She could have run off when she saw me there, but she got in. She had a whole pile of printouts about Ylva and what happened that time in Bergen in her bag. I'd interrupted her when I came home, and now she'd been to the post office and continued searching on the net. That's why I came out here with her. I was with her when she was in pain.

– Was it here? Liss managed to say.

– Was what here?

– That you stabbed her in the eyes with a syringe.

– Not a syringe. The corkscrew. I had to screw it in.

He bent over her, his eyes just about visible. Liss's body felt too heavy for her to move.

– Is that what you're going to do to me?

He didn't answer.

– Don't you want me to see you?

– Shut up, he said, startling her. That new tone in his voice was darker now, pushing the familiar one away. She tried to put together something to say. Something that could stop what was about to happen, make it change direction.

– But Mailin left here again. She didn't go missing until the next evening.

He laughed briefly. She didn't see it, but she could hear the muted clucking sounds.

– Think it over while I make a quick trip to the shed. It wouldn't surprise me if you worked it out. You know, you're not all that slow. Just a shame you never learned how to use it.

She heard him open the outside door.

Is that when you wrote it in the book, Mailin, while he was out in the shed? You managed to get over to the fireplace and pick up a piece of charcoal. Maybe you couldn't even see.

The stuff he'd injected her with came surging back, retreated, surged inwards again. Each time she became more and more sleepy. Let yourself flow on these waves, don't want anything any more. *I'll look after you.* An image appears in the darkness, Mailin naked and bound. She's bleeding from the eyes. *It mustn't happen to you, Liss.*

She rocked over on her side, got to her feet. The chair was still next to the kitchen cupboard. With one foot she managed to push it over towards the work surface, climbed up on to it. Wriggled upright back first. Turned so that the window latch caught under the handcuffs and then gave a jerk. The latch snapped off. She couldn't reach as high as the upper latch with her hands. She stretched up, bit round it and snapped like a fish taking bait. Pulled it halfway open. Another bite and it was loose and she flipped it free with her tongue.

The window was frozen. She pressed her full weight against it, but it didn't move. She leaned back and butted as hard as she could and it flew open.

She didn't feel the coldness of the snow on her bare feet. *Not the outhouse, Liss! You've got to take the other direction, away from the cabin.* She ran from the veranda, part of the way down towards the lake, hid behind a tree, climbed again, up in the direction of the cliff, the wind blew the fresh snow away there, the hill would be firmer underfoot, if she could get up there, she could run. She dragged herself over a snowdrift, fell and couldn't break her fall. Something ran down into her eyes; she rubbed her face in the snow, darkening it where she rubbed. Sank down and crawled on. Maybe what she was hearing were footsteps in the snow. She lay still without moving, listening into the wind. Then she crawled on, another metre up the slope, then another, rolled up over the edge and on to the top of the cliff.

He stood leaning against the pine trunk in front of her. Tutted in mock sadness when she tried to get to her feet.

– Oh Liss. I did try to tell you.

He bent down to her. An axe in his hand. – You're not going anywhere without me, he whispered. – Not until I say so.

8

SHE WAS SWEPT into the warm doze as though by a tidal wave. That was where she heard the voice. It was no longer Mailin's. It was her father who had made his way through the snowdrift to tell her something.

This place is yours, Liss. Yours and Mailin's.

But it's *you* who owns the cabin.

He stands by the window looking out.

From now on, you two are the owners. I have to go away.

Odd way to say it. Not like when he's going to Berlin or Amsterdam. Be gone a few weeks and come back home with presents for her.

He sits on the edge of the bed. Strokes her hair. He doesn't usually do that. Usually stares at her for a long time with a strange smile. But he never touches her.

Why do you have to go away?

He says nothing for a long time. Finally shakes his head slowly.

You're the one I'll miss, Liss. We're the same, you and I. Nothing anyone can do about it.

Viljam had lit the paraffin lamp. He had put the axe down on the edge of the fireplace and was standing there reading her notebook. Everything she'd written to Mailin. She couldn't bear to think about what he had done to her. Only that he had let her grow cold. Liss was cold too, huddled up in a corner of the sofa. She wasn't angry with him. He'd given her another shot. The good pain was tightly packed around her.

– Jacket stopped you when you were going to swim out and die, she tried to say. Could feel her voice full of thick sauce. – He saved you.

Viljam didn't look up from the notebook, turned over a few pages, seemed engrossed in what she had written.

– You needed someone to hold you. But he used you.

Abruptly he tossed the book aside and loomed over her. – Where do you get that from?

She couldn't lift her hands to defend herself.

– Did she send you anything else? Have you got more CDs? If you've hidden anything, then . . .

It took a few seconds for her to understand what he was talking about.

– There was only one. The one I told you about when I called.

He straightened up again.

– Why didn't you want anyone to know about Jacket? she groaned. – He was the one who did things to you. You were innocent.

– You understand fuck-all, so don't talk about it.

He laughed. As suddenly, he was serious again.

– He took a helluva chance letting me come to him. He could have lost everything, ended up in jail, been stoned, ostracised, strung up. Do you understand? He took that chance so that I could be with him. How many are there who care so much that they'll risk everything just to be with some fucking kid?

– I understand that, she murmured.

He picked up the notebook again, sat in the chair by the fireplace and carried on reading.

She pulled herself up from the sofa, struggled across the floor and into the light from the paraffin lamp. Stood naked in front of him, hands cuffed behind her back so tightly that the pain flashed from her wrists down into her fingertips.

– You killed someone, he said without looking up.

First time she'd heard someone else say those words. But as things stood, it meant nothing at all.

– Everything written there is true, she heard herself reply.

– And now you're going to offer to keep your mouth shut if I let you walk out of here.

The thought hadn't occurred to her.

– I can't let you go, he said. – I came out last time you were here. Had to find out if you knew anything. I could let you go then, but not now. I won't fool you into believing that. I'll be honest with you. You'll never leave here again.

He tossed the notebook into the fire. – Do you realise that?

Liss saw the way a tiny flame began to wrap itself around the red plush cover.

– It wasn't because of that business with Ylva that I couldn't let Mailin live, he said tonelessly. – Jo and Jacket swore an oath. Death before anyone else knew about them.

Alongside the burning notebook Liss saw the remains of a book cover. *Sándor Ferenczi,* she read. The inside was a roll of flaking ash.

– Mailin found out about it, she murmured.

– She never gave up, Viljam interjected. – Kept asking and asking who Jacket was.

Liss tried to hold on to some of the thoughts that were seeping away into the distance, somewhere far from the room she was in, far from the smoke from the fireplace, from the dust and the cold wooden walls, all the smells that would remain behind after her and Mailin, after her father, who once stood by her bed and said he was going away, after his mother, who had sought refuge here before the world came and brought her in.

– Mailin realised that Jacket was Berger.

Viljam looked at her for a few moments. – That's what happened, he answered.

– He was going to expose you on *Taboo*. He was going to break the pact.

Viljam shook his head. – I was at Berger's house every day after Mailin . . . went missing. Finally he realised what had happened to her. He even wanted to talk about *that* in front of the camera. He was certain he had me where he wanted me. I got him to believe that I would appear on his programme and confess. We sat and planned it together. Shock TV. He looked forward to it like a kid. Pity to have to deprive him of that enjoyment.

The high she was on was utterly unlike anything Liss had ever experienced before. – You're fucked up, Viljam, she snuffled. – You're a fucked-up piece of shit.

Distantly she realised that this was what he had been waiting for, that she would make him angry. He leapt up, forced her down on to the chair by her hair. At the corner of the fireplace was a coil of rope, he twisted it around her waist, tightened it across her breasts and knotted it behind the back of the chair. He made a noose out of the loose end and put it over her head.

– You're no different from any of them, he growled. – Won't be missing you.

She started to cough. – Mailin did everything she could to help you, she managed to say. – Mailin looked after you.

He snorted. – She tricked me into talking. And while I was talking, she sat there stroking me. Stripped me naked. Had me in her office.

– You're lying. Mailin would never have done that.

He tightened the rope around her neck. – Maybe your sister wasn't quite the saint you think she was.

– But she lived with you, Liss choked. – You were going to get married.

His eyes widened and darkened. *Keep Midsummer's Day free*, she heard somewhere inside herself. It was him, Viljam, who had sent that message from Mailin's phone.

She forced herself to say the one thing she knew she mustn't say:

– She was going to leave you.

He gave a jerk on the rope, it cut into the skin of her neck. Then she felt her head growing, the room filling with a reddish smoke.

– She was supposed to love everything about me, he hissed, – no matter what I'd done. No matter what they'd done to me. But she lied. I have never been able to stand people lying to me. Do you understand? When someone starts to lie, it's over.

Suddenly he took the tension off the rope. The air etched its way down into her chest. – Have you understood now? Have you seen enough?

Patches of red pulsating inside fog. Then they grew paler, and things cleared again. She could see he was holding something in his hand, a needle for a hypodermic syringe. He pulled it out of its sheath. She felt him place the needle against her cheek, make a careful scratch, draw it up in the direction of her right eye.

– Have you seen enough? he asked again.

She tried to turn her head to one side. He tightened the noose. The red-flecked fog came whirling back.

She opened her mouth. – Viljam . . . *Jo*.

It sounded like a prayer, but it didn't come from her. The voice was dark and hoarse.

– Now it's Jo, he howled. – Sweet Jo and all the rest of it.

He lowered the needle and drove it into her nipple. The pain was even sharper; it travelled on through the breast and released something in her back like the tendrils of a jellyfish spreading and burning through her whole body.

– *You're a nice boy, Jo. You're so nice, so nice*. There's nothing you can't do to me. Not one fucking thing. Because that's the way you think, you too. You think I don't know you, Liss Bjerke? You think Mailin didn't tell me everything worth knowing about you? The rest being rubbish.

He drew out the needle, moved his hand to her forehead and placed a finger on her eyelid, pulled it up. She was totally awake now, straining as hard as she could to move her head. He grabbed hold of her hair and held her in an iron grip. She felt the cold tip touch against the eyeball. Like an insect landing there with its great sting ready. A couple of pricks, and then a membrane breached. A different pain, this one. It tore her open, and there was nowhere for her to hide. Her eye ran over, the light from the lamp changed colour, things turned black, and from this blackness an arc of rainbow colours spun.

– I'll show you the place, she shrieked.

He bent down close to her face. – What place?

– Down by the lake.

He pulled the needle out again; fluid ran down her cheek.

– Not the other, she pleaded. – Not yet. Not until I've shown you the place.

– The one you wrote about in the notebook? Where you're going to lie down in the snow and look up through the trees and freeze to death?

She tried to nod. – It isn't far away.

He placed the needle against her eyelid. Then he withdrew it, untied the rope, pulled her up by the hair and shoved her across the floor.

– Show me, he hissed, grabbing the axe from the fireplace. – Show me the place where you want to die.

She walked in front of him, barefoot and naked. The wind was blowing straight off Morr Water, stinging against her breasts and thighs. His footsteps in the snow a few metres behind her. *You're afraid, Liss.* Mailin's voice is gone now; it's her father talking to her. *At last you're afraid.* I am afraid. *You don't want to die.* I don't want to die. She put her head back. Through her one eye she could just make out a strip of something grey in the darkness between the trees. That strip is all that's left. And the sound of the wind. That was what I wanted that time you left, to lie down in the snow, feel the cold wrap itself around me and dissolve me. *You're the one I'll miss, Liss. We're the same, you and I.*

She turned to face the tall, slender figure. The face came out of the grey, pressed right up against hers.

– Can I sit on that rock up there for a moment? Look out across the water. Just a few minutes.

He grunted. She could no longer feel her feet. The cold had eaten its way up her legs, as far as the knees. She slipped on the icy rock.

– Help me, she pleaded.

He climbed up beside her, squatted down, took hold under her arms and lifted her up. For a moment they were standing close to each other. She looked up into his face. The eyes weren't angry any more. They were filled with something else.

– Poor Liss, he whispered.

She dived forward suddenly, butted him with all the strength that was left in her frozen body. He wavered, standing on the edge and flapping with his arms, dropped the axe and tried to hold on to her smooth shoulder. One second, two seconds. Then he tumbled backwards. She heard something hitting the jutting rock, and a splash as he slithered down into the open channel in the ice.

She slid down the track on her backside, got to her feet. Thought she heard him calling, didn't turn round. *It's the wind calling.* She began scrambling through the deep snow. *Not to the cabin. He'll find you there.* She ran past the shed. *You will not die, Liss.* She crawled along the slope until she found the place where it wasn't so steep. Snaked her way upwards. The snow kept pulling her down, but she didn't want to disappear into it any more. It was tougher up on the top. She tried to run, between the trees. Stopped behind a thick spruce. Then she heard footsteps, squatted down below the lowest branch. That whisper in her ear: *Liss, you're not going anywhere without me.* She slumped against the trunk, pressing her cheek to the rough bark.

A little later, a minute maybe, or perhaps ten: she stood up again. Peered out from under the branches. She knew these trees. They showed her the way to go. It was her forest, not his.

She stumbled over the snowdrift and down on to the road. Wanted to put her feet down beneath her, but they weren't hers any more. She tried crawling along on her stomach, hands still locked behind her back. She managed a few metres before her whole body shrivelled. She curled into a ball, drew her legs up under her.

In the distance, the sound of an engine. She turned her head, enough to see the light dancing between the trees. *They've come to fetch you, Liss. This is where you were going.*

EPILOGUE

Tuesday 20 January

JENNIFER PLÅTERUD SWITCHED off the computer, hung her
white coat in the cupboard, let herself out into the corridor
and locked the door behind her. She had just decided she was
going to treat herself to a new pair of boots. She'd seen them
on the net at Hatty and Moo. They were made of antelope
leather too, but with a bronze buckle that gave them a touch
of roughness that suited the mood she was in these days.

The time was 4.15 The tenth class parent–teacher evening
was due to begin at seven, and in Ivar's opinion it was time
she took a turn for once. She had also promised to have dinner
ready before that, because both boys had sports practice to go
to. Thinking about it, it was actually Ivar's turn to go to the
meeting, and she was annoyed with herself for letting herself
be persuaded. She took another glance at her watch and decided
to stick to what she had already decided to do. In spite of all
her domestic obligations, she headed up towards the main wing
of the Riks Hospital and into the large hallway that always
reminded her of an aeroplane hangar.

As she headed up the steps towards the gallery, she thought
of Roar Horvath. Earlier that day, she had called him and
hinted that she might possibly find herself in the Manglerud
area one day soon. But he had other things on his mind and for
the third time that week she got a vague response. Why couldn't
he tell it like it was? Did he think she wouldn't be able to take

it? It annoyed her, not having had the chance to show him how little it bothered her. She'd made a mistake about him. The first time she met him, at the Christmas party, she had got the impression of a man of sanguine disposition. But then who isn't sanguine at a Christmas party? Now he seemed to her more and more a combination of the phlegmatic and the melancholic, not all that different from Ivar and Norwegian men generally. It wasn't the first time she had got something so badly wrong, but any re-evaluation of the Hippocratic system was completely out of the question.

As she walked along the third-floor gallery, faces streamed towards her. Some she recognised, nodded to in passing; most of them were strangers. She would miss him for a few days, she had decided, and then it would be over. That was the usual way of it when things were allowed to rest in peace. She had even got over Sean. At least, it had become possible not to think about him. And this fling with Roar Horvath hadn't really amounted to anything more than a bit of therapy. For a while it had muted the fear of withering away completely, and now she didn't need it any longer.

Following instructions from the reception desk, she knocked on the next-to-last door in the corridor. It was dark inside, and it took a couple of seconds for her to realise that someone was sitting in a chair by the window.

– Hi, Liss.

The young woman turned. One eye was hidden behind a large bandage.

– Hi, she answered tonelessly.

Jennifer closed the door behind her. – I heard you were still here. Just called in to see how you are.

Liss switched on a lamp, she looked even thinner than the last time Jennifer had seen her, at her sister's funeral. She had a Melolin compress around her neck, fastened with tape.

– Got all I need. They're looking after me.

She nodded towards the table, where there was a jug of orange juice and a packet of Marie biscuits. On a plate beside them lay a slice of bread and cheese, untouched.

– They're discharging you tomorrow?

– Think so.

– How's the eye?

Liss gave a slight shrug. – They're going to take another look at it before they let me go. They don't know yet.

Jennifer sat down on the edge of the bed. – Have you spoken to anyone . . . about what happened?

Liss made a face. – Some bloke doing a psychiatric survey was here. A complete nerd. I turned him down as politely as I could, and that seemed to make him happy.

Jennifer had to smile. – Anyone else? Your mother, or your stepfather?

– They do the best they can. My mother needs help more than I do.

In the pale light of the lamp Liss's face was a faded grey oval beneath the bandage. Jennifer felt like stroking a hand across her hair.

– The detective chief inspector came by. The one named Viken. He wanted answers to a few questions.

– They'll probably have to interview you, Jennifer nodded. – Even if your doctors say as much rest as possible.

– It took them almost ten hours to find him.

– I heard that.

Jennifer had carried out the autopsy on Viljam Vogt-Nielsen after he was brought up from under the ice, but she didn't want to say anything about that.

– Do you think he suffered?

– No, Jennifer said firmly, adding: – He lost consciousness before he hit the water. He must have hit his head on a rock when he fell.

Liss sat a while staring out of the window.

– I pushed him. I heard his head crack against the outcrop.
But I ran away. It sounded as if she was rebuking herself.

– That's why you're sitting here today, Jennifer protested.

Liss began twisting a lock of hair around her index finger.
– And because the detective chief inspector decided they should
come out to the cabin. He realised Viljam might be there.

It didn't surprise Jennifer to hear that Viken had made it
obvious who Liss could thank for having been found.

– I've killed someone.

Jennifer got up and stood beside the chair. – Dear Liss, she
said as she touched her shoulder. – I'm not a psychologist, but
it's normal to feel that way after going through such an awful
experience. Survivor's guilt, it's called. I recommend that you
talk to someone about this. Not all shrinks are nerds, after all.

After Jennifer Plåterud had gone, Liss lay thinking for a while
about what she had said. Did she need to talk to a psychologist?
When Chief Inspector Viken had been there, she had kept it
together as much as she could so that she could tell him what
had happened down by Morr Water. It had helped her. The
chief inspector too claimed that the primary motive for his visit
was to see how she was getting along. But he didn't protest at
all when she started telling him what she knew.

– He followed Mailin to the post office. He waited for her
in the car outside and went with her to the cabin. How he
managed to make it look as if he was in Oslo the whole time
I have no idea.

– I can help you there, said Viken. – He came home in the
evening to work, and then returned to the cabin afterwards.
He must have held her captive there that night and then driven
her to the factory early on the morning of the eleventh.

– Was that when he filmed her? The date on the video
was the twelfth. She thought about it. – It isn't difficult to change
the date on a mobile.

Viken gave a wry smile. – Your deductions are good. I don't think there's much wrong with your head, even if it was frozen for a while.

She liked his tone, straightforward and no fake sympathy.

– He must have sent the message to Berger from her telephone, she said. – And probably several others. *Keep Midsummer's Day free next year.* – Did he kill Jim Harris too?

– We have reason to believe he did, Viken confirmed. – Harris saw something he shouldn't have seen.

– He was at Mailin's office that afternoon . . . The car. He saw Viljam parking her car.

– Exactly. It was only later that he realised what it meant. I'm guessing he tried to make a little money from what he'd found out. Everyone has to live off something.

– But Viljam was at lectures the whole of Thursday, and then on the Justice Bus.

Viken pushed the upright chair back and stretched his fairly short legs. – We've been through the security camera pictures from the Ibsen car park and seen Mailin's car on its way in in the morning. When Viljam had a break from the Justice Bus, he had time both to shop at Deli de Luca and move the car up to Welhavens Street. It's not difficult, he wouldn't have needed much time.

Liss realised she was sitting there twisting and twisting at a lock of hair. She let her hand fall to the armrest.

– I found something out, she said. – Viljam was sexually abused. He met Berger on a holiday in Greece when he was twelve years old.

Viken raised his eyebrows.

She told him about the CD Mailin had sent her, repeated what she could recall of the document's contents. The inspector listened without interrupting her. Sitting there in the chair by the window of the hospital room, he seemed less insistent. Less threatening.

– Jacket was the nickname Viljam used for Berger.

– If you're right about this, Viken exclaimed, – that fills in quite a lot of important blanks for us. If Viljam was twelve years old, it might have been 1996. He didn't say the name of the place?

– I think in Mailin's document it said Crete.

Viken seemed energised now; he took out a piece of paper and made a note. – Is it possible that there are other CDs? he wanted to know.

– Viljam destroyed the one Mailin sent me. He destroyed everything Mailin wrote. He and Jacket swore an oath together. They swore to die before they would tell the world about the two of them. Mailin couldn't be allowed to live because she found out who Jacket was.

– And yet Berger's plan was to name Viljam as the killer, live on television? That was what he implied in that story in *VG*.

Liss recalled what Viljam had said about that.

– He got Berger to believe that he was going to confess to the murder on *Taboo*.

Viken rubbed two fingers over his clean-shaven chin as she finished her story.

– Berger must have lost the few powers of judgement he still had left, he observed. – This business of some kind of pact is still not clear to me, but if what you say is true, it would explain why he admitted Viljam to his apartment. We can only guess exactly what happened. But we found traces of . . . well, the two of them engaged in sexual activity in that apartment just before Berger died of an overdose of heroin.

Liss didn't feel the need to hear any more about that.

– That girl in Bergen, she said instead. – Ylva Richter. Why did Viljam seek her out more than seven years after the holiday in Crete? Had he been in touch with her in the meantime?

Viken spread his hands. – We'll have to wait for the rest of the investigation to see if we find an answer to that. And anyway, certain things we just have to live with without understanding them.

There are a lot of things we have to live with, Liss thought once Viken stood up to leave. Waking up that day in hospital, it occurred to her that she had paid her debt. She had come face to face with death but been spared. In the days that followed, sitting and looking out of the window with her one good eye, that feeling had gradually diminished. Because what sort of calculation was that? Was it supposed to mean something for Zako, or his family, that she herself had very nearly been killed?

For a moment, as Viken stood with his hand on the doorknob, she was on the point of blurting out everything that had happened in Bloemstraat. She opened her mouth, but in that same second changed her mind. Don't tell anyone. Carry it alone. Live alone.

One of the nurses came in. She knocked as she was closing the door behind her.

– Got everything you need, Liss?

She said her name as though they were old friends meeting again. Actually she was an auxiliary nurse. A bit chubby and sharp eyed, but friendly enough in her professional way.

Liss wasn't hungry, and she didn't need a stranger's hand to hold. But there was something she did need.

A few moments later the nurse was back, and placed a pen and a little notebook on the bedside table.

She sits high above the ground, head almost in the clouds. She's holding his long hair, like reins, but she's not in charge of what happens, and suddenly she's thrown down and comes sailing through the air towards the ground at a terrific pace. Just before she's smashed to pieces, she is caught in an enormous pair of hands. They lift her up on to the shoulders again. She shrieks and pleads with him to stop, but again she is thrown down, flies through the air, is caught. It happens over and over again, until the point comes where all she wants is for it to go on for ever.

I should have written that in the book you gave me, Mailin. And not a word about what happened that night in Amsterdam. Because that isn't where it began. All stories begin somewhere else. By Morr Water, maybe, or in a house in Lørenskog, long before I was born. This is the way to carry it with me: write about it without saying a word. What happened, and what could have happened, what brought something else in its wake, shadows within shadows, rings around rings. A finger dipped in the water moves round. Somewhere down in the cold darkness I am born.

The telephone on the wall rang. She recognised the nurse's voice.

– I've got your boyfriend on the line, shall I put him through?

Liss screwed up her one good eye, then had to laugh. – I don't have a boyfriend.

– Well that's what he said when I asked.

The nurse didn't seem to understand, but without pursuing the matter further she put the call through. Liss was not surprised to hear Jomar's voice at the other end.

– Is this what you call the gift of cheek? she grunted. – When did you become my boyfriend?

She heard him grin. – It was the nurse's idea. I just let her get on with it. Let people believe what they want. That usually works.

– And what makes you think I might want to talk to you?

– I have to know how you are.

She was sitting there in a worn tracksuit Tage had brought her from the house. The legs were too short and the colour was something she liked when she was about sixteen. She was unwashed, wearing no make-up, and wrapped in a bandage that covered half her face.

– Well at least don't even think about coming here, she said, exasperated. – I'm sitting here like a one-eyed troll.

– Okay, I'll leave it till tomorrow.

– I'm being discharged tomorrow.

– I can come and fetch you. Drive you home.

Where might that be? She realised she didn't have anywhere to go.

– You do remember, don't you, everything I said to you on the phone that night?

– Every single word, he assured her.

– That is how I am, Jomar Vindheim. I like you, but there can never, ever be anything more between you and me.

– You already said that eleven times. Can you hear me yawning? The noise he made into the receiver sounded more like snoring.

– I didn't bring anything here with me, she interrupted. – So I don't need to be picked up.

After hanging up, she wrote in her notebook:

But there is one person who could take hearing about what happened in Bloemstraat. Someone who can tell me what to do. Maybe he's the one person in the world you trusted most, Mailin.

Wednesday 21 January

THE DOOR TO Dahlstrøm's office was locked. Liss knocked, waited; nothing happened. She walked round the corner, past the garage, up to the stairs to the main entrance. The doorbell was in the form of a miniature relief depicting a landscape. The button itself was between a pair of peaks stretching up into a dark sky. She heard two deep notes sound inside the building. At the same moment the door opened. The girl standing there couldn't have been more than six or seven years old. Her hair hung down her back in two thick dark braids.

– Your name is Liss, she said.

Liss had to admit she was right about that.

– Did you lose your eye? the little girl wanted to know. She was wearing a pink padded jacket and a pair of boots and looked as if she was on her way out.

– Not completely, Liss replied as she walked in. – And I see *you* have lost a front tooth.

– Yeah, but what does that matter, a new one'll come. The girl opened her mouth and pointed to a white outline that was just about visible through the gums. – I've lost eight teeth, she explained, guiding Liss around her mouth as she went through them.

– But you lost your sister, she asserted once she was finished.

Liss realised that Dahlstrøm had told his daughter about her.

– I don't know what *your* name is.

– Elisabeth, the girl replied. It was strange to hear that frail little voice pronounce the name.

– That was my grandmother's name too, said Liss. – That's funny.

– Is it *so* funny? the little girl said, rolling her eyes. – I know this girl in 2b who's called that. Plus a teacher. Plus Mum's aunt.

Tormod Dahlstrøm appeared in the hallway.

– Liss, he said, not surprised, because he knew of course that she was coming, but it seemed to her that he was pleased to see her. She didn't like it when people she hardly knew hugged her, but if he had done so she would have let him.

He turned to the little girl.

– Remember to look both ways before you cross the road, Betty. With a worried look he stroked her hair.

His daughter sighed. – Daddy, you've told me that a hundred times!

Liss couldn't help smiling.

– Yes, I probably have, Dahlstrøm conceded, gathering the two braids in his hand. The bands that fastened them at the ends were decorated with ladybirds, one yellow and one red. – Don't forget to wear a hat. There's a terrible wind blowing.

Once the little girl had run off down the driveway, he took Liss's leather jacket and hung it behind a curtain next to the mirror in the spacious hallway.

– I've got the house to myself for a couple of hours. Let's go up into the living room.

Liss was glad they wouldn't be sitting in his office; it made her feel more like a guest and less like a patient.

He let her go up the stairs ahead of him. There was an open fire at the far end of the room.

– Do you want anything to eat with it? he asked when he arrived with the coffee. – Not even a piece of Belgian chocolate?

He said it in a teasing way, she thought, and for a moment she wondered if he was testing her, noting the way she declined, coming to his own conclusions about her attitude towards food. She felt as if she was revealing herself the whole time. Astonishingly enough, it didn't make her irritable.

– What did the doctor say about your eye? He peered at the bandage.

– They don't know yet. They think I'll keep my sight. But it'll never be as good as it was before.

He nodded, didn't try to comfort her. – What about all the other things that happened?

The other things? Did he mean the rope that was tightened around her neck? Viljam's face as he was strangling her?

– I want to talk to you about something else, she said. – Viljam was destroyed on the inside. He came to Mailin for help. She seduced him.

Dahlstrøm sat there looking at her. The eyes widened slightly, but even now he still didn't seem surprised.

– You knew that, she exclaimed.

He settled into the high-backed chair. The eyes were deep-set beneath the forehead. The gaze from within them made her feel calm. Was there nothing that made him uneasy? She knew there was. She had heard the slight fear in his voice as he said goodbye to his daughter. Her name was Elisabeth, and there was a road full of cars she had to cross.

– During several of our counselling meetings a couple of years back, Mailin talked about a patient she was particularly worried about, he said. – It was clear that he was very badly damaged.

– Viljam was abused by Berger from the age of twelve. Mailin sent me a CD with a record of the conversations she had with him that time he came to see her.

– A CD? This is something you should talk to the police about, Liss.

– I've already told them. But when I called Viljam, he got me to tell him where it was. He destroyed it. He seemed obsessed by the idea that no one should know about him and Jacket – that was the name he called Berger.

– But Mailin might have made other copies.

Liss picked up a chocolate from the little rose-patterned plate. – I'm certain Viljam destroyed them all. Or else the police would have found them.

Dahlstrøm crossed one leg over the other, rubbed the hollow in the bridge of his nose with a finger. – He can't have seen Mailin more than three or four times before she suddenly decided to end the treatment. I asked if he'd threatened her. Her reply was evasive. And then I realised what was happening.

Suddenly Liss felt a terrible anger. – Exactly what she wrote about. That people get abused. Children who need tenderness and care, who open themselves and are met with desire and abused. He went to see Mailin because he felt so fucking bad. She was supposed to help and ended up sleeping with him instead. Fucking hell!

She tore the paper off the chocolate and bit it in half, squeezed the soft centre between her tongue and her palate.

– Mailin ended the treatment immediately, she said once she had calmed down. – It would have been considered a crime if she hadn't gone on seeing him. And the moment she broke up with him, he could have reported her and had her convicted. Maybe she would have been barred from practising for life. You read about shits like that in the papers. How could she have done such a thing?

Dahlstrøm looked to be thinking long and hard about what she said, yet he never seemed to lose touch with her.

– You know, even the best of us are capable of mistakes, he said at last. – Serious ones sometimes. We'll never know what went on in her office. I think the best thing is to just drop it.

– I don't think I can.

Dahlstrøm stood up, looked out of the window. The day had begun to turn grey. He stroked the thin wisps of hair back over his head, went out into the kitchen, returned with the coffee jug and refilled their cups.

– Mailin was skilled. She helped a lot of people. She meant well. A thoroughly good person. But she's something more than that to you, Liss. Something far more than a human being.

Liss looked down. Regretted what she had said.

– She's an image of everything that's good in life. You needed that image. It might be that you've reached a point now where you're going to have to live without your guardian angel. And maybe that'll be better for you.

What he said was quite right. Every single word. And yet she shook her head, suddenly frozen.

– I've killed someone.

Dahlstrøm leaned towards her. – You had no choice, Liss, if you were to survive yourself.

– I'm not talking about Viljam. I killed someone else.

She closed her eyes. For an instant she was sitting high above the ground; she let go the reins, was tossed up into the air and came hurtling downwards . . . She didn't dare to look at him. Finally she noticed that he had leaned back in his chair.

– Is this something you want me to know, Liss?

She couldn't answer, but realised that he was giving her a choice. It might remain unspoken, unsaid.

– His name was Zako. He lived in Amsterdam. We were a couple, in a way.

She spoke with lightning rapidity, as though it was a matter of urgency to close off that road ahead on which she could walk alone.

Tormod Dahlstrøm said nothing. He sipped some coffee, put the cup back into the saucer so softly that the chink of porcelain was almost inaudible.

How long she sat there telling her story she didn't know. She felt as though she were anaesthetised. Her body was numb, time stopped, the only thing in the room was her voice. First she told him the most important facts. Then she started again, in more detail. Not once did she look up. If she met his eyes now, her story would recoil on her, it would turn inside and explode everything it encountered.

When she fell silent, he once again crossed his legs. She could see his foot dipping up and down once or twice, then still, then dipping again.

– It sounds as though I'm the first person you've told all this to.

She felt herself nodding. He was the only one who knew. If there was a single person she dared give so much power to, it had to be Dahlstrøm. Only now did she fully understand why she had come to him. His reaction would decide what she must do once she left that room.

– I don't think you want advice from me, he said. – It's enough that I know about it.

She tried to work out if that was right. His mobile started to vibrate. It was on the desk behind him.

He stood up and looked at it. – I have to take this.

She stood up too.

– You mustn't go now, Liss.

– No, she said, I mustn't.

He disappeared out into the kitchen, closed the door behind him. She could hear his voice through the wall, not the words, but a low note that made her feel calmer again. Suddenly overcome with gratitude that a man like him existed. Mailin must have felt the same sense of calm when she talked to him. Mailin too needed someone to help her carry her load.

She strolled over to the window, looked out. The grey was denser now, but it was moving, and the light behind it was sharp. The snow in the garden was wet and covered in twigs and autumn leaves. The property ran up towards the forest, where it was framed by trees that swayed mightily in the wind. One window was open slightly and through it she could hear the sound, the way they moaned.

The sideboard was covered in family photographs. She recognised the daughter she had met in the doorway, wearing a white frock with bows on it and a satchel on her back. Another was of Dahlstrøm, taken a few years earlier, the hair thicker, the face firmer. But with that same calm gaze. Constitution Day, 17 May. He was wearing a suit and tie, and a boy that looked like him was sitting on his shoulders waving a flag. The next picture was of a dark woman with wavy hair. There was something Greta Garbo-like about her face. It was a black-and-white picture, and Liss guessed this was Dahlstrøm's mother. Another photo showed the same woman wearing a long, waisted frock. A man with dark, slicked-back hair had his arm around her. He too had deep-set eyes and a chin that jutted even more than Dahlstrøm's. Liss picked up the photo and held it to the light. It struck her that she was surprised that Dahlstrøm had parents, as though she had been thinking of him as belonging to a completely different species.

At that moment he came back in. She was startled, didn't have time to put the photo back. It didn't seem to bother him in the slightest.

– Are you interested in family histories?

She gave it a moment. – It's interesting to see who we get what from.

– Who do you resemble most? he asked.

– My father, she answered without hesitation. – I get it almost all from him. And his mother, my grandmother. If I showed you pictures of her, you wouldn't be able to tell the difference between us.

– Are you like her in other ways too?

She found a lock of hair and began twisting it. – My grand-mother on that side was strange. No one understood her. I'm sure she felt she didn't belong in this world. She died in the mental hospital, Gaustad. Liss avoided saying her name.

– You say that as though there was a sort of forewarning in it. There was a question somewhere inside his observation.

– Maybe . . . She wriggled away from it. – Isn't your life also determined by who your parents and grandparents were?

– To a certain extent, he answered. – My father wanted me to be somebody, preferably a doctor. He had no views on psychiatry, there's not much prestige in it. He ran a gents' outfitters, as people used to call them in those days. He spent more than sixty years dealing with clothes, and in his eyes I had taken a big step forward. At the deepest level, that was what life was about for my father, to help the next generation take another step up the ladder.

Something struck her. She didn't know where it came from. She was still standing there with the photograph of his parents in her hand. She lifted it up and stared at the well-dressed man with his arm round this woman who was looking not into the camera but beyond it, smiling, if that was what she was doing.

Mailin's document on the CD, she thought. There was some-thing about Jacket's father there.

– I read everything I could find on the net about Elijah Berger . . . His father didn't sell clothes. He was a pastor in the Pentecostal church.

Thoughts that had been lying jumbled up and separate from each other suddenly whirled together. She turned towards Dahlstrøm and heard herself whisper: – Jacket.

She glanced up at his face. It stiffened, the eyes narrowing in the depths beneath the forehead. And then she knew it. – They called you Jacket where you grew up.

– That is correct.

She felt she didn't have enough air. Viljam never said that

Berger was Jacket, *she* was the one who had come to that conclusion. Viljam said he would rather die than reveal Jacket's true identity . . .

Dahlstrøm's gaze didn't waver. To avoid it, she closed her eyes. The shame surged through her. Apologise to him, she thought. Dahlstrøm is a good person. Apologise to him, Liss, for what you're thinking. Was there any way she could get out of here without looking up, just turn and run for the door without having to meet his gaze again? *What will be left of me, Mailin?*

– You told me a story from Amsterdam, Liss. You made a mistake and the consequences were terrible. I listened to you until you had finished. Now I want you to listen to me.

– How long was he lying in the water before he died? she murmured.

She was still standing with the picture of his parents in her hands. Didn't dare to put it down.

– Spring thirteen years ago, he began, and from the corner of her eye she could see that he had collapsed a little, placed one arm on the sideboard and rested his head in his hand. She didn't want to hear, but couldn't tear herself away.

– I stopped him when he was going to drown himself. I saved him. And he saved me . . .

Reciprocal help, she thought in disbelief. Is that what you call it?

– You had sex with him, she managed to say.

The shame continued to stream through her, hitting in bursts.

– Only the once. Or just a few times. Carefully. On his conditions. He was proud of it. I did everything I could to help him, Liss. Please understand that. He couldn't keep on coming to me, but he wouldn't let go.

She noticed a current deep down in his voice. She could let herself be carried along by it, wherever he wanted. She could throw herself at him and let him do what he wanted. Or hit him with a stone. Until he lay on the floor bleeding from the eyes, unable to rise any more.

– Ylva Richter, she said. – You knew that he had killed her.

He shook his head slowly. – You must believe me, Liss. I no longer had any contact with Viljam. Eight years went by without my seeing him. One day he showed up in my office. He stood in the doorway, wouldn't sit down. He was standing on the brink of a precipice, staring down. I couldn't begin treating him, but I knew someone who was unusually talented.

She was struggling to comprehend what he was saying. – It was you who referred him to Mailin.

Only now did she raise her eyes. His face looked grey, and the lines on his forehead sunken, squeezing it.

– Mailin found out. She realised that you were Jacket.

– My dear Liss. If you only knew . . .

His voice grew thicker. Still that need was there: lean into him, let him put his arms around her, carry her away. But it was vanishing. The other thing was overtaking now. If she let it loose, it could fill the whole room, crushing everything that stood in its way.

– Had you not destroyed Viljam, he would never have killed Mailin. She said it without raising her voice, and the fact that she did so made her anger manageable and she was able to control it. – You killed Mailin.

Then he said: – There is a limit to how much guilt you can ask one person to assume, Liss. Once that is reached, you have to stop pouring, or the person goes under. If I manage to stay afloat, I can help many people. If I don't, they'll find that they're alone again.

She felt his hand on her shoulder.

– You told me of your fatal mistake, Liss. I've told you mine. It's possible for us to say that we're quits. That we have something that binds us together. That there are two of us to share the burden as we walk down the road.

She looked at him. Saw no sign of grief in his eyes, or regret. And there was no passion in what he was offering her either. It was a partnership. Start a firm, with themselves as joint owners, for the transporting of corpses.

She moved her gaze to the window. The wind swirled up a rain of dead leaves and then laid them down again, making a pattern.

Without saying anything more, she turned away from him, crossed the living room and found her own way out.

As I sit here in the living room looking out on the winter afternoon, I continue our conversation in my thoughts. How could you who knows everything about a child's needs allow yourself to do something like that? you ask. And again I try to tell you about that spring thirteen years ago, before the trip to Makrigialos. I had patients, I had TV programmes, I had regular columns in newspapers and magazines. Everyone had a piece of me. And I had something for everyone. Then came that day in early April. When I let myself into the living room, Elsa, the woman I was married to, was sitting in that chair you have just vacated. She asked me to sit down on the sofa. Then she said: 'I'm moving out, Tormod.' I didn't believe her. Ours was a good marriage. Our children were happy. We did things together, she and I, even still had a sex life after almost twenty years. 'It's not true,' I said. But three days later, she was gone. I walked into a storm. It was everywhere, around me and inside me. I didn't know if I could survive it. Then suddenly it was gone.

That was when things became difficult. Getting up in the morning. Washing, getting dressed. Not to speak of going to the shops. Or taking the kids to after-school activities. I had been tossed aside, washed up in another landscape. Complete stillness. Utterly dead. No trees, no colours, nothing but that huge black sun up there, sucking all the light into itself. All I heard was the sound of my own footsteps as I trod through the ashes. A friend and colleague, well intentioned, perceptive, came to talk to me, friendly and cautious at first but then tough and decisive. One day early that autumn, he tossed a few clothes into a suitcase and drove me out to Gardermoen in his car. He'd booked me on a holiday. He was actually supposed to come with me, but something happened at home, illness, and he had to cancel at the last moment.

You can't make me believe the relationship between you and Viljam was reciprocal, you say, that you were equals.

We were, Liss. In the beginning. But Jo, as I still think of him, bonded with me. He clung to me as if it was a matter of life and death. He worshipped me. And wouldn't let me be anything else for him but the god that he needed.

And Ylva, you ask, how could you fail to know who had killed her?

I saw no connection. I want you to believe me, Liss. A girl in Bergen named Ylva. A front-page picture in the newspapers. Maybe she resembled someone I'd seen at a holiday resort many years previously. Maybe not . . . Of course I would have seen the connection if I could have faced looking for it. Because we often talked about her. I had to build up a picture of her in his imagination. Teach him how to approach her. She was a symbol of womanhood. I guided his desire in that direction, towards her, towards a girl his own age. Not Ylva in a literal sense, but Ylva as an image.

Do you understand me, Liss? Tell me you understand me.

You aren't here any more. All that remains in the room is the sound of your footsteps crossing the floor. The sound of the door closing. The sound of the last words you said to me: You killed Mailin.

Maybe you know that whatever happens now is entirely up to you. Wander like a blind person. The unending drought. Or chance upon a few drops of water. A peace that passeth all understanding.

She reached Frognerseter Way and carried on down through the smell of cold exhaust. It started snowing again, but the wind had dropped by now. She passed the metro station, continued along the banks left by the snowplough. Her feet were still painful from the chilblains after being frozen at Morr Water. A steady stream of cars came towards her, splashing dirty snow over them.

She turned off when she reached the Riks Hospital and stamped her way along the road that twisted by Gaustad. The country's first insane asylum, she knew that. Had stood there for more than a hundred and fifty years. Her father's mother had been locked up in there for a few months before she died. Had she done it to herself? Had she twisted bed linen and clothes together into a rope and fastened it to the light fitting in the ceiling, looped it around her neck and kicked away the chair? No one talked about it; what happened had been deleted from history by silence. What was left of her? A few black-and-white photos of a beautiful woman, strange and distant.

On the path leading towards the lake at Sognsvann, the snow lay deep. Liss kept on walking. Heard the sound of her own footsteps. At one point she stopped and turned round, studied her tracks through the dense, driving snow. Soon they'll be gone, she thought, and the thought latched on to another: He caught me just before I smashed to pieces. He threw me down, but never dropped me once.

By the time she reached the lake, she had made up her mind. She didn't carry on up into the woods but took a right turn and headed across the car park. She stopped outside the entrance to the sports academy and sent a text message.

It took three minutes for Jomar Vindheim to come running down the steps.

– Sorry if I interrupted your lectures.

He stood there open mouthed, staring at her.

– Thought you ought to see the one-eyed troll after all, she said. – Because I'm sure you like going to freak shows and stuff like that.

He stepped closer. For the second time he laid a hand on her cheek. This time she didn't take it away.

– There are two things I want to ask of you, Jomar.

– All right, he said.

– The first is that you take me home to your flat. Treat me the way you were going to that night we were supposed to be going out.

He stood there looking down into her good eye. Maybe he was searching for a code there, something that might explain what was happening.

– Liss . . . he said finally.

– I'll tell you the other thing later, she interrupted. – My only condition is that you don't talk about your grandfather. Not a single word.

He was thinly dressed, wearing only a T-shirt, but he put his arms around her as though she were the one who needed warming.

She stood naked by the living-room window on the ninth floor, trying to make things out through the driving snow. On a clear day I bet you can see a long way from here, she thought. The whole city and out over the fjord, down to Drøbak, maybe further . . .

Mailin hadn't said anything to their mother about those nights at the house in Lørenskog. She'd wanted to protect her. Now there's no one who knows what happened, thought Liss. No one but the person who went away and never came back. And me, who cannot bring it to the surface . . . That was where she must live from now on, in the place between what she could not remember, and what she would never be able to forget.

She heard Jomar getting out of the bed. He came into the room, crossing the floor. Hands around her from behind. They smelled of something that reminded her of sap, not too sweet, not too strong. It would be possible to learn to like these hands.

– The nurse at the hospital said you should be my girl-friend.

The way children talked to each other. She had to laugh at him.

– She probably meant for a while, she answered.

He pulled away and looked at her through the grey light.

– There are a lot of things I don't understand about you, Liss. But it doesn't matter, because I've got a long time to find out about them.

She looked down. – There were two things I was going to ask of you, she said. – Now I'll tell you what the second one is.

It took almost three hours to drive into the city centre. Several times he pulled over to the side of the road, into a bus bay, or up on to the kerb, and turned off the engine. Sat looking out of the front window as she told her story. By the time he stopped at the barrier outside Oslo police station, it had become evening.

– I'll come with you.

She shook her head.

– Then I'll wait here, he insisted, pointing to an empty space on the other side of the little cul-de-sac.

– Jomar Vindheim, haven't you understood a single thing?

– I'll wait.

* * *

The girl behind the counter was about her own age. She was dark, with Asiatic features. There was a photo of her on the ID that was pinned to her uniform shirt.

– Yes, how can I help? she said in a voice pitched midway between friendly and dismissive.

– I want to talk to a detective chief inspector named Viken.

She'd thought about it. It had to be him.

– Viken from Violent Crimes? I can't just . . .

– It's about a murder.

The girl behind the counter blinked several time before she managed to say:

– Are you certain? Then we need to talk to the crime response unit.

Liss supported herself with both hands against the counter.

– It happened a long time ago, more than a month. And it wasn't here, it was in Amsterdam.

The girl picked up the phone. When she put it down again, she said:

– He'll come and fetch you in about two minutes.

Liss waited by the column in the middle of the great hall. Through the windows at the top, up on the eighth floor, she saw that it had stopped snowing. She let her gaze drift down the galleries, towards the main exit. Two minutes, she thought. It'll take him two minutes to finish what he's doing, walk down that red corridor, take the lift and get down here. For the next two minutes it's still possible to leave by that door with neither Viken nor anyone else here ever knowing why I came.

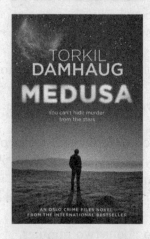
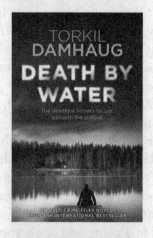
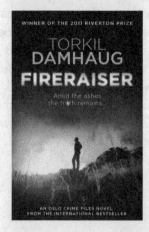